DANGEROUS VISIONS

KIMBERLY MCKAY

DANGEROUS
VISIONS

KIMBERLY MCKAY

OTHER BOOKS

Other books
by

Kimberly McKay

The Books in the 'Forgiveness Series'
Finding Kylie
Facing Redemption
Coming Home
Saving Grace
The Books in the 'Forgiveness Series'
Endless Possibilities
Dangerous Visions

Stand-alone books
Second Chances

DANGEROUS VISIONS

All rights reserved. No part of this book may be reproduced or transmitted in any means, electronic or mechanical, including photocopying, recording or by information storage and retrieval system without written permission from the publisher or author, except for the inclusion of brief quotation in a review.
This book is a work of fiction. Names, characters, places, and incidents are either the product of the author's imagination or are used fictitiously, and any resemblance to places, events, or persons living or deceased is purely coincidental.

ISBN-13: 978-1721780228

Printed in the United States of America

❦ Created with Vellum

COPYRIGHT © 2019 KIMBERLY MCKAY
ALL RIGHTS RESERVED.

To my Okifam, Each of you inspire me daily. May we always be forever young and forever family.

ACKNOWLEDGMENTS

To my wonderful team of beta-readers. Thank you for not pulling any punches when needed and lifting me up when I'm on target.

Thank you for Marcia Feisal – you're not only my favorite professor, but the best editor, and a true friend for life.

And this book wouldn't be complete without former agent Rick Raines who gave me valuable feedback.

1

In less than twelve hours, Savannah Miles' somewhat quiet life had been turned on its ear, chasing her from a successful business to becoming a hunted woman. As she scanned the bus for a seat in the back, she peered over her shoulder for the umpteenth time before drawing the hood of her sweatshirt around her face.

Once seated, she drew in a shaky breath and mentally recounted everything she had just walked away from. Her friends, business, and her devoted four-legged baby would all have to survive without her, but would she without them? And for how long? Her frantic mind spun with countless unknowns.

One step at a time.

First, she had to safely make it out of town so she could regroup and form a plan of action.

Cries from a newborn alerted her of a young woman's presence as the two settled into the seat next to Savannah. She almost lifted the corners of her lips in response to the new mother's gracious smile, yet found she couldn't exert the energy. Instead, Savannah stared past her with a glazed look. She fiddled with the drawstrings of her hoodie and blinked, unsure any of this was real.

It was at that moment that Savannah wondered when or if she'd make it back home. She blinked back tears, unwilling to draw more attention to herself.

If only she could call her assistant or best friend to let them know what happened, but an explanation could put them in danger. Against her better judgment, she sent them both a short text, letting them know she was leaving town seconds before smashing her cell and tossing it in the nearest trash can.

With a heavy heart, she slipped her bus ticket into her backpack and leaned against the window, staring into the dark abyss that threatened to swallow her whole.

At least I'm not totally alone.

At the thought of her cousin, Danny, she breathed a sigh of relief. The second Danny found out she was in trouble, he arranged for her travel to his family home...all in efforts to keep her safe from the recent danger that darkened her doorstep.

Savannah furrowed her brow and laid a hand on her belly. The thought of the man who'd put a price on her head made her stomach burn as if tormented by fire.

Benny, who she'd come to find, was nicknamed 'The Bone-breaker,' was someone she wouldn't have normally crossed paths with, but sometimes her work took her to some unusual places. Although, this was the first time it had taken her to the outskirts of Nashville where she'd run into Benny at a small strip club.

If only I hadn't overheard. Savannah dropped her head into her hands.

No matter how many alternative solutions she imagined, the fact of the matter was - she had overheard. Her impeccably bad timing had put her in the wrong place at the wrong time.

"Breathe," she whispered.

At a questioning glance from the young mother, Savannah offered a weak smile before peering into the night. She could do this. She would survive. Besides, she had Danny's help. Although her cousin was on assignment, he promised to send someone to protect her once she arrived at the bus terminal.

As the bus started and she moved further from her life and the Nashville city lights, Savannah assumed the tension between her shoulder blades would dissipate. However, the pit at the bottom of her stomach became increasingly more bothersome, especially when she noticed a heavy-set man, who seemed to be watching her more closely than he should.

Savannah shifted in her seat so that another passenger became a barrier between them, much like she used to do in school when she avoided a teacher's adamant stare.

She winced. *Please, be looking somewhere else.*

Ever so slowly, she peered around the back of the passenger's head. Surely, the man, she immediately nicknamed 'The Beast,' would have lost interest by now.

She inhaled, eyes wide when the Beast's eyes gleamed with anticipation and not the kind that signaled fun. Savannah's face pulled tight with worry. Soon, she found it difficult to swallow, and when she tried, it was as if a handful of gravel slid to the pit of her stomach.

It was then that years of instructions flooded back as her mind raced with scenarios of how to escape. Her father, God rest his soul, had taught her a few fundamentals in life.

Sit with your back to the wall, so you can survey your

surroundings, looking for an exit strategy if needed. Be aware of things like someone who watches you more than they should.

Savannah sunk into her seat and away from the Beast's glare, thankful to be on the last row. Without the threat of passengers behind, she could rest a bit easier knowing there wasn't someone behind her in cahoots with the stranger.

From the corner of her eye, she noticed the young woman next to her nodding off. Once the hum of the engine lulled them both mother and child into a deep sleep, Savannah eyed the woman's diaper bag.

She gave her one last glance before rifling through her bag as expertly as she could without disturbing her sleep. When she found a cell phone, she secured it into the pocket of her hoodie, zipped the bag closed, and exhaled a sigh of relief.

Again, her father's teachings flooded her memory. As a military brat, she'd been trained to blend in and immerse into a crowd. The key to staying under the radar was not to draw attention to yourself.

It's a little too late for that. Savannah grimaced. But when in need – use what you can to defend yourself.

Savannah forced her attention back up the aisle to find the Beast's hardened face still blazing at her from his seat. She could almost read his thoughts. His eyes told her a story with an ending that didn't look pretty.

As the bus slowed to exit, the only option was to put as much distance between them as possible. She may not have known who he was, but it was clear that he was aware of her. And, he had plans to finish what Benny's men had started the night before.

The Beast readied himself in his seat, looking as if he was going to pounce once the bus came to a stop. Her one saving grace was an elderly man sitting in the aisle seat, blocking her would-be captor from stepping out to do her harm.

If she could stretch around the woman and her child – she could bolt down the aisle and get to the nearest exit without incident.

"Please let this work," she whispered, scanning the bus for anything she could use to defend herself. The only thing that came to mind was the elderly man's cane, which would be the last resort.

How do you even know he's after you? The analytical side of her brain antagonized her. She shook her head. She was paranoid, but she'd rather be paranoid than dead.

When the bus stopped outside a well-lit diner, Savannah eased by the mother and child. She held her breath as the elderly gentleman rose from his seat and fumbled for his bag and his cane.

Savannah spirited down the aisle with a prayer of thanks. The old man gave her just enough time to keep a safe distance between her and a dangerous demise.

As she fled the steps of the bus, she stole a glance over her shoulder, and what she saw in the Beast's eyes sent her fleeing for the diner. It would be a matter of seconds before he would catch up to her.

Once she flung open the door and tore inside the diner, she scanned the room - hoping for options to escape. She eyed the women's bathroom door. Unless it had a window she could squeeze through, it would be a death trap. She briefly considered an exit to her left, but it was a gamble. If she didn't time it right, Benny's henchman could easily spot her as he came through the front door. In a split decision, she rushed through the swinging doors toward the kitchen only to collide with a line cook who stumbled backward.

"Hey! You can't come back here." He steadied them both to keep her from falling.

Savannah stepped from his reach, and asked, "Is there a back way out of here? Someone's after me."

When she turned her warm amber eyes on him, the rough edges around his face softened.

"Hold on." He placed his hands on her shoulders. "Shouldn't you call the police?"

She shook her head. "There's no time."

He searched her panicked face and jutted his chin down the short hall.

"That way. It leads to two doors. Push the blue one open... the white one is the freezer."

"Thank you!" She started for the hall.

"Wait!" On a whim, he called after her. "There's an alley that leads to the main street. Go toward the fields and keep running. You'll find a farmhouse. It's a safe place."

"How do I know I can trust you?" Her voice faltered. At that moment, a bell sounded alerting them to more foot traffic entering the diner. Her eyes went wide with terror.

The line cook yanked a chain from his neck. "Take this. The barn is safe. It's my family's property."

Savannah took the cross from his hands without much thought and shoved it into her pocket before starting for the doors and disappearing into the night.

2

As a few horses stirred below, Savannah tucked her head in the crook of her arm and sighed with relief. Morning light filtered through the small slats, signaling that she'd made it through the night.

She propped up on an elbow to scan the galley through the boards beneath her. In the last eight hours, every sound gave her pause and kept her from resting for more than a few minutes at a time. Even the shifts in the wind as they whipped around the barn sent waves of powerlessness over her. Each strong gust had her believing it was her last moment on earth.

Savannah couldn't evade sleep any longer. Just as she rested her eyes, a loud groan permeated the barn. Savannah shrunk behind a large bale of hay and held her breath. She peered through a hole beneath her, unsure of who was entering below.

"It's just me." A soft voice beckoned.

When Savannah noticed the man who helped her escape, she slumped to the loft floor with relief before peeking her head over the railing.

"You can come down. You're safe." He pulled the door behind him shut and waved her down.

She nodded in silence and searched for the ladder that she'd pulled up to the loft the night before. It was her fail-safe to keep anyone from sneaking up to her hiding place.

Once she hitched the wooden step ladder back in place - she took two rungs at a time until she found firm footing below. Slowly, she turned to raise a hand in greeting.

"Thanks. For last night." She cocked her head. "I don't know many people who would help a stranger like that."

"No problem. I'm Jordan." He offered her a brown paper bag.

When she didn't immediately step forward to claim it, he placed it on a table next to the stalls and sat on a bench near the exit.

"I thought you might be hungry."

Savannah blinked, unsure if she could trust him. Although he had aided in her escape, she knew not to let her guard down.

As if he could read her thoughts, he stood to leave.

"I won't hurt you, miss. I just thought you might want breakfast. It's not much, but it's all the missus had in her fridge this morning."

"Your wife?"

"Yes, ma'am." Jordan paused. "Do you need me to call anyone?" He took off his ball cap and wrung it in his hands. "It's obvious you're in over your head. I saw the guy you were running from, and he looked like a man driven by demons."

Savannah's heart squeezed with panic. She had dodged a bullet by a thin margin but wasn't out of the woods yet. Whoever he was - he was just one of many that Benny could have sent after her.

She breathed in through her nose and out her mouth, trying to steady her heart rate.

"Did he say anything?" Her voice came out in a whisper.

"He had your picture and asked everyone inside where you went."

"Did anyone see me?"

"No, ma'am." Jordan slowly shook his head. His warm eyes beckoned. "And I covered for you. I told him you slipped out through the side entrance near the bathrooms and headed for the rest stop."

When Savannah blinked in awe, Jordan's dimples flashed from across the barn.

He tipped his head toward the door. "You know – where ladies of the night troll for truck drivers or a ride."

"Yeah, I figured." She grinned. "But thanks for the visual."

"Anyway, he took off like a bear being chased by a hornet's nest – and a clumsy one at that."

"You think he's still in town?" Sweat trickled down her back.

"Probably turning over every stone." His voice dropped. "Just what kind of trouble have you gotten yourself into? I don't need no trouble, but I couldn't very well let you get killed last night."

"I'm sorry, Jordan. You're right. Thank you for your kindness. If you hadn't helped me last night..." She shivered at the thought. Savannah slipped the stolen cell phone from her pocket.

"I made a call last night once I was hidden away in your loft. Someone should be on their way to get me soon."

For a split second, a vision of the Beast flashed before her. She blinked, trying to erase his eerie stare from her memory and continued, "I've never seen that man before, but I know who sent him. And I don't want to lead that kind of danger to your door. I promise I'll be gone soon."

Jordan's cautious eyes searched hers.

"Ma'am. I'm all for helping a damsel in distress, but…" His face twisted with a look of worry.

She held up her hand to stop him.

"No, I understand. You have a family here."

He raised an eyebrow and nodded.

Just as she was about to elaborate, her stomach growled. Neither fear nor stress could override the fact that she'd not eaten in nearly twenty-four hours. Finally, she moved toward the brown sack and unrolled the top to discover a couple of homemade sticky buns.

"My favorite." Her mouth watered as she reached inside the bag. With one bite, she moaned a sigh of relief and sent Jordan a look of thanks.

Savannah almost choked as his cheeks burned with a slight shade of pink. She licked her fingers and rolled up the bag. Just when she was about to apologize for swooning over the sweet treats, his name was called from afar.

Jordan cleared his throat. "That'd be the missus. I told her I let a friend stay the night in our barn, but I didn't tell her it was a young woman, let alone a pretty one."

"The fewer people who know about me, the better." She cocked her head.

Jordan nodded in agreement. "She'll be off to work in a few. Could you stay in the loft until then?"

"My ride should be here in a couple of hours." She pulled two fingers across her mouth as though zipping it shut. "Mum's the word 'til then."

He raised a hand and sent her a nervous grin.

"Jordan?"

"Yes, ma'am?" He paused at the door.

It was then that she remembered that she hadn't told him her name. The fewer people that knew that, the better, too.

"Thank you." She laid his cross necklace on the table where the brown paper sack had been.

He lifted a hand. "Keep it. It seems you might need it worse than I do."

She sent him a look of thanks before slipping the chain around her neck and slowly climbed the rungs to the loft.

"Godspeed," he called after her. "Oh, and there's a bathroom out back if you need to freshen up or anything." He nodded in retreat and closed the door behind him.

Once she was alone in the quiet alcove, Savannah fell to her knees and bent her head. He may have been an unwilling guardian angel, but he was one just the same.

"Thank you, Lord." Her soft voice carried through the empty barn as she laid her head down too tired to retrieve the ladder.

She looked at her watch and groaned. She had an hour before the extraction. She wasn't sure who her cousin was sending, or how he would find her, but she prayed she'd be safe until then.

3

Anderson Evans had been aimlessly riding for weeks to stop only long enough for fuel, food, and sleep. His journey had taken him from his home in West Texas to a small town just outside of Oklahoma City.

He planned to continue riding northwest and camp under the stars until he figured out his next stop, but that was before his partner, Danny Stone, called in a favor. No matter what ghosts he was running from across state lines – Danny's call took priority.

Retrieving a girl from a barn and hiding her away would be like riding a bike. His career with the agency had been just that – a lifetime of extractions with witness protection included. On his last case, Anderson was in a car accident that left him in a coma for three weeks.

Although he recovered physically – mentally and emotionally was another issue altogether. Unbeknown as to how - his head injury left him with flashes or images of things to come. Now, he rode his motorcycle to clear his mind of things that couldn't be explained away.

His first experience occurred once he awakened in the hospital. The brush of a nurse's scrubs against his arm gave him a vision of her sitting alone in the cafeteria crying.

Anderson shrugged it off as a side effect of his pain medications until the same nurse came into his room an hour later. Her puffy eyes were far different than the ones he'd seen earlier. The tell-tale tissues stuck in the pockets of her mascara stained scrubs had him doing a double-take.

From there, vivid visions flooded daily life so much that when he kissed his girlfriend, a flash of her in bed with a co-worker sent him into sensory overload. From his neighbors to his partner, he saw things about their personal lives that he didn't have the right or desire to see.

Ending a casual relationship was one thing. There would always be another girl. But when visions interfered with his ability to do his job, he knew he needed some time off. How could he focus on keeping people safe when images he couldn't interpret kept him from staying sharp?

A month after the accident, he took leave from his job and headed home to Purity, where the visions subsided. He attributed the short reprieve to the presence of his loved ones and lack of stress from his job, but on the night of his sister's wedding, another blinding vision took him to his knees.

Ever since, Anderson had been on his Harley traipsing from town to town. And no matter how far he drove, the same image of a young woman's hands grasping at the grass as she was dragged away screaming kept plaguing him.

He shook his head and slowed his motorcycle toward a four-way stop. Danny's timing couldn't have been worse, but he couldn't turn him down. His partner had saved his life more than once, and Anderson owed him.

As the barn came into view, Anderson scanned the

perimeter for any activity. When he was sure that all was quiet on the home front, he drove around to the back of the barn, parked his bike, and quietly entered.

Savannah struggled to keep her eyes open, but after staying vigilant most of the night, sleep finally came. Thoughts of the last few weeks turned to dreams, giving way to the day she met Jade.

Her business as a maid-of-honor for hire and wedding planner took her many places, including other states, to meet with potential brides. Her clientele consisted of brides-to-be who may have had friends, but they had no one they could rely on for the heavy-lifting.

Savannah's services were a much-needed solution. She provided a mixture of planning when it came to a bridal shower or bachelorette party. No duty or detail was too big or small. She made sure the big day went off without a hitch for all her brides.

Eventually, her business grew enough that she hired a capable assistant and a small staff. Within two years, she claimed the top spot on the 'Top Forty Under Forty' list, and she graced the cover of Nashville Entrepreneurs.

It was then that she knew she'd finally made it. Savannah had more than enough business to handle, leaving her with the luxury of being able to pick and choose her clients, which were the sole reason she should have turned down her latest prospect the instant Jade sashayed into her office.

To say Jade made an impression would have been an understatement. The potential bride strolled across the room in her metallic bustier, her flesh bubbling over the top, and extended a firm handshake. When Jade slid a few rolls of one dollar bills from her designer purse, Savannah should have had more sense.

Shoulda Coulda Woulda...

The words rolled through her dream-like state, bouncing like dice against a brick wall. Jade's attire and one-dollar bills wadded and wound by rubber bands screamed stripper, yet her tearstained, false eyelashes batting with the explanation that she had no one to stand up for her had Savannah surrendering against her better judgment.

Soon, her new client took her from aspiring empress of the Nashville elite to working with an underground side of her town that she never imagined, let alone experienced. When Jade confirmed she was an exotic dancer, Savannah wasn't surprised. It would have shocked her if Jade had said otherwise.

Even though Savannah second-guessed herself daily, Jade's enthusiasm for her wedding day pulled at Savannah's heartstrings. Her compassion for helping a girl out won over logic. Every bride should have the right to celebrate her big day with a supportive maid of honor by her side.

As days turned into weeks, Savannah found herself enjoying Jade's company. Her new client's passion for life was contagious. And, as with every upcoming bride, Savannah befriended Jade as if they'd known each other for years.

In the final stages of planning the bachelorette party, Jade requested a meeting at her club, needing to go over a few last-minute changes. Although Savannah was quick to object, Jade reassured her it was safe.

"We have security and everything. I promise that no one will bother you, and when we're done, I'll have one of the guys escort you to your car."

Savannah would never forget the day she stepped into the dimly lit club. The music vibrated so loudly, it pulsated within her chest as well as everywhere else throughout her body.

A bright purple haze illuminated the stage as a young girl who couldn't have been more than seventeen, slid to her knees to give the front row a show. When Savannah saw her, her mouth dropped.

"See something you like?" She heard a raspy voice from behind.

Although he intended to sneak up on her, the stench of stale beer and cigars gave him away. Savannah spun to face him, thinking he must have been at least seven feet tall. His square jaw and crooked nose gave him the appearance of an extreme fighter.

"No. I'm here for Jade." Savannah cleared her throat.

When he said nothing in reply, Savannah pursed her lips and waited. His gaze slid down her body as if he were memorizing every detail.

Her first instinct was to flee to her car for safety, but she stood her ground, refusing to let him intimidate her.

Finally, he nodded toward a dark hallway to the left. "Back there. Third door on the right. Don't enter the one on the left. It's off-limits."

Savannah nodded and backed away, eager to put as much distance between them as possible. As she turned toward the back of the club, he grabbed her by the arm and spun her around.

He raised an eyebrow. "You sure you're just here for Jade? I could teach you a few things."

Savannah yanked her arm away. "I'm sure."

"If you change your mind – I'll be here!" He yelled at her back as she fled toward the dressing room.

She glanced over her shoulder with a frown. Savannah wove through a few tables and entered the hall.

"Third door on the right... Third door on the right," she chanted.

As organized as she was — anyone in her life could testify that she was as directionally challenged as they come. If someone dropped her in the middle of the forest with a compass, she'd still end up going in the wrong direction.

She paused outside the dressing room and looked over her left shoulder at the door parallel to it. As a few murmurs sounded behind it, she wondered what shady dealings were going on inside.

With one last glance down the hall at the man she'd just encountered, she wrinkled her nose with disgust as he raised an eyebrow at her and pointed in the direction of the door on the right. Savannah pushed it open and escaped inside with a sigh of relief.

Once in the brightly lit room, she surveyed a handful of girls as they donned their attire, or lack of, until she saw her client and bride-to-be in the corner, applying her makeup.

Once Jade noticed Savannah in the mirror, she spun around and opened her arms for a quick hug.

"You're here!" she shrieked.

"I told you I would be. Although some mutant at the front almost had me running for cover. He tried to convince me to str—." Savannah stopped short of saying it. Although she could never imagine herself onstage like Jade, she didn't want to sound judgmental.

"Don't mind Benny. He's harmless unless you threaten one of us." Jade wobbled her head back and forth and started to count on her fingers. "Or steal from him. Or rat him out."

"For what?" Savannah's stomach clenched as she remembered the murmurs behind the closed door across the hall.

Jade shrugged her shoulders. "I don't ask or tell, but honey, with your cheekbones and eyes… and your obvious assets." Jade swiveled to face her and took her by the hands before extending Savannah's arms and giving her a once-over. "You would bring in a mint. You have that exotic, but sweet girl-next-door look."

Savannah withdrew her arms and covered whatever assets Jade referred to stammering, "Yeah, well - never gonna happen."

Jade's mouth flattened. "Of course, not. You have a thriving business, but for some of us, there is no choice."

Savannah slid from the counter to a vacant chair next to Jade and noticed a few other women, who sent condescending glances in her direction.

"No, I'm sorry. I didn't mean anything." She sent a wan smile to a few girls in the room before turning back to her friend. "I have a big mouth, and sometimes I trip over my tongue." She winced.

When Jade responded, it was with a genuine lift to the corners of her mouth. Savannah sent her an apologetic shrug as Jade's phone dinged. It was then that Savannah wondered what had brought the bride-to-be to this place in life. Although the two had discussed plenty of details surrounding Jade's upcoming nuptials, Savannah still knew nothing about her life.

"So, what's your story?"

"Nothing to it." She pushed her phone into her bag and dabbed some glitter on her cleavage. "Girl meets boy, falls in love, has a child, and then the boy leaves them both with no means to take care of themselves."

"You have a kid? How come you never told me?" Her heart swelled with emotion.

Jade's face lit up with pride as she retrieved her phone and scrolled through her photos.

"I don't know. I'm pretty protective." She pushed the phone toward Savannah. "That's my Samson. He's my first love. Everything I do is for him."

Jade swiped the screen. As another photo appeared, she smiled at the face of a handsome man, who looked to be a bit rough around the edges but had kind eyes.

"And Zach, my fiancé, is going to be a good father to him. Then maybe, just maybe, I can quit this dump. That's the plan anyway." Her voice fell.

Savannah was about to ask when she would get to meet Zach when Benny walked in. He glared in their direction and pointed at Jade. "You're up in five."

"We didn't have time to go over my notes." Savannah frowned.

Jade glared at her boss. "Send Gigi out. I'm busy."

He slid a toothpick from between his lips. "You want to sass me? You don't need a job? Some special clients are here tonight. They're on a limited schedule and want you."

Jade scrunched her nose. "Fine."

She then looked at Savannah and said, "My set takes about twenty minutes. Can you wait?"

"Sure." Savannah sighed.

Savannah studied Jade as she stepped toward the stage door, taking a deep breath in preparation. Once Jade's name was announced, she put on a bright smile and raised her chin with confidence before sailing toward the entrance of the stage.

Savannah had to give her credit. It took guts to strut your stuff for strangers. It wasn't something she was ever willing to do, and after hearing Jade's story, she was glad she never had to.

As if Benny could read her thoughts, he leaned down so that they were nose to nose. Alcohol permeated her senses, and Savannah struggled not to gag.

Benny's eyes narrowed in response. "You think you're too good for this?"

When he grabbed her by the arm, she shook her head and winced, knowing it would leave a bruise.

"Take your hands off me." She lifted her chin and glared, hoping the rest of the girls provided her with a buffer of safety.

"Wake up, little girl." Benny's cold eyes penetrated hers like a deadly spear. "All it takes is one stumble, and you'll be at my doorstep, begging for a job."

SAVANNAH REMEMBERED it like it were yesterday, and yet, so much had happened to her since then that it seemed like a lifetime ago.

In her dream, she could still hear Benny telling her to wake up. Only this time, his voice was much gentler as if it were someone else, though Savannah wasn't willing to take that chance.

While dreaming, she formed a fist and swung forward. When her right hook connected with something other than a ghostly image, she woke up howling. It was then that she realized that she wasn't the only one in pain.

"I said wake up... not clock me!" Anderson yelled as he doubled over and cupped his eye. "What do you think you're doing?"

Savannah pushed the cobwebs of the dream from her mind and crawled toward the back of the loft.

"What do you think you're doing?!" she shrieked.

Anderson didn't have to open his eyes to know her voice. It impacted him like a tsunami wave on dry land, knocking him forward until he was bent like a baby on the ground, holding his head. The intonations of it were identical to the pitch that had flooded his mind for weeks. It shook him so hard that he found it hard to breathe.

Savannah almost forgot to be scared as he fell forward in a fetal position.

"Hey, buddy. You alright?" She nudged him with her foot.

"Ugh." He took a deep breath. "In and out," he instructed himself as he exhaled.

Savannah rolled her eyes and groaned.

"Did Danny send you?" She raised an eyebrow, wondering how safe she would be with someone who crumpled after one hit from a girl?

"Will you give me a minute?!" He held up a finger with one hand while clutching his head with the other.

Savannah frowned and looked him over. He was long and lean, but by no means too thin. She could tell he took good care of himself by the way his muscles defined themselves with every movement he made. His blond curls were unkempt, yet not long enough to harbor a shaggy look. However, without seeing his face, it was hard to tell.

When he finally looked up, her breath hitched. His eyes were the most crystal blue she'd ever seen. The only thing she could compare it to was the ocean off the coast of Okinawa, where she'd lived as a teen. Well, to be fair, she could only attest to one eye as he was still covering the other one.

Savannah gulped. If gazing into one eye had her heart skipping a beat like this – she knew she'd be in trouble when he was able to look at her with both.

"You're...Danny's cousin?" He forced out each word as if he were struggling to breathe.

She nodded in haste. "And you are?"

"Anderson Evans. His partner."

Savannah raised her eyebrow. She'd heard about Anderson and his heroics, but he didn't seem to live up to the tales that Danny told.

"I'm supposed to trust you? With my life? After you folded with one punch from a girl?"

Anderson sneered in her direction but immediately cursed when his face pulled taut, sending excruciating pain around his eye. Who knew it took so many muscles in and around his face to send her one look?

Savannah shook her head. "Don't be such a baby."

"I'm not." He paused, gritting his teeth. "You know what?" His mouth flattened. "Never mind. Danny didn't tell me I was going to be babysitting a brat."

She curled her fingers into a fist. "I can give you a matching set, you know."

He took note of the fire that blazed from within her light-infused eyes as they darkened with anger. If he weren't so irritated by her, he might think of her as beautiful.

Savannah's mouth flattened as Anderson appraised her from head to toe. If it were another time, his full lips and luminous eyes might have had her knees going weak, but as soon as he opened his mouth, all appreciation went out the window.

"The quicker I get you to safety, the faster you're out of my way." He reached for the plastic bag he'd brought with him and tossed it to her. "Is there a place where we can get you taken care of?"

She sent him a blank stare.

"Like a bathroom?" He shrugged and sent her a look.

"You need to go?" She smirked.

"No. You do." He motioned toward the large bag. "And don't come out until you're finished."

Her brow furrowed as she rifled through the bag and pulled out some scissors, a hairdryer, and a couple of boxes of hair dye.

"Nuh-uh. No way!" She shook her head before tossing the bag toward him.

"You're a walking target. Stop being so stubborn and let me do what I do best."

Finally, he uncovered his swollen eye to stare her down the best he could.

"Wow. That looks like it hurts." She winced and reached for his face, but he backed away from her touch.

"You feel bad?" He smirked.

"Sort of." She crossed her arms. "But I'd have to like you to feel bad about it."

"Well, I don't like you either, and you're wasting my time." He pointed at the bag. "I bought three colors. Pick one and rinse your hair in the sink once you're done. Make sure to take off some length."

The two stared one another down for what seemed like

an eternity before Savannah begrudgingly snatched the plastic sack at her feet and headed down the ladder.

Once outside, Anderson mounted his bike and watched her enter the washroom. As she stepped inside the door frame, he hollered, "When you're done, wash out the sink and put your hair clippings and trash in the plastic bag. Bring me the trash when you're done."

She spun to face him with a defiant look. "Why?"

He groaned and looked up at the sky. "Just do it."

As she disappeared into the tiny room, he shook his head and texted Danny.

You so owe me – big time.

It was then he remembered how her voice affected him. He struggled to block out the images of her struggle for survival. If she was the one, he'd had visions of - danger would follow no matter how good he was at his job.

4

"Hand me your backpack." Anderson extended his hand and waited.

Savannah adamantly crossed her arms and shook her head no. He'd already made her chop off and dye her brown hair to a color reminiscent of a midnight night sky.

As she eyed her reflection in the window outside the bathroom, she felt like screaming but held it at bay. The last thing she wanted to do was give Anderson reason to comment on anything.

She imagined him ordering her to put her big girl panties on and get on his bike. Now, suddenly, he was ordering her to hand over her backpack, which held the last of her earthly belongings.

"Just hand it over." He paused and glanced behind her. "Wait! Where's the hair you cut off?" When he knitted his brows, another sharp pain emanated from his swollen eye.

"Dang it!" He turned his head to the side and took a breath.

"What?"

"Nothing." He counted to ten, ignoring the pain around his eye.

"Where did you put the trash?"

"In there." She gestured to the door behind her. "In the garbage can."

"Please go get it." He slowly strung the words together. Before she could turn on her heel, he reminded her. "Leave your backpack."

Savannah grunted something inaudible before tossing her bag to him and spinning back toward the restroom.

Anderson held his tongue. Although she was the innocent victim in this scenario, if she wasn't careful, he might end up taking her out himself. What was it about her that brought the worst out in him?

It took her a few minutes to gather the empty box, plastic gloves, and all her discarded hair and shove them into the plastic bag he'd given her earlier. She reached for the hairdryer but decided to leave it.

Before returning to Anderson, she glanced once more to the mirror and let out a deep breath. The only feature still recognizable was her amber almond eyes and heart-shaped lips.

"You know that you're being too hard," she said, pointing a finger at her reflection. "It's not his fault you're in this predicament."

She ran her fingers through her hair, trying to make it presentable. "But this..." She puffed some air out of the side of her mouth toward her bangs. "This is his fault."

She wrinkled her nose at her reflection and pushed her dark bangs from her long eyelashes, before raising an eyebrow.

"Well, it's not too bad." She shrugged, thinking her new cut and color gave her an Ashley Judd vibe.

Savannah tied off the plastic bag and stepped outside with a renewed outlook. The right thing to do was to cut Anderson a break.

The second she rounded the corner; however, a truce was the last thing she had in mind. Anderson tossed her backpack into a barrel, before squeezing some lighter fluid over it, and lighting a match.

As her backpack went up in flames, she tossed the plastic bag to the ground and rushed Anderson from behind.

"What the?" He grunted as she barreled her shoulder into his side like a defensive lineman would on the field.

As he tumbled to the ground, he wrapped his arms around her - bringing her down with him.

"What did you do?!" She pounded on his chest.

Even if he wanted to answer her, he couldn't. Another vision flashed before him, ripping him from the present toward something unknown in the future.

Struggling to regain composure, he finally pushed the images away to find her Aurelian eyes staring down at him as if he were the enemy. Within them, he noticed smoldering flecks of brown. He blinked and shook his head.

"Let me go," she huffed as she fought to get free.

"You're the one who tackled me." He gritted his teeth and threw his hands up as she pushed off him with a glare.

Savannah's pouty lips had been tempting before, but with this dark, broody look she was now sporting - they were nearly too much to bear. He dragged his attention away from her mouth and inhaled, counting to ten.

"If we're going to make this work." He exhaled. "You have to stop attacking me, or I might decide to leave you behind, no matter how much I owe Danny."

Savannah lowered her lashes as a single tear escaped.

"You ruined my bag." Her voice quivered as she stared into the flames that burned brightly before them.

The look on her face reminded him of his kid sister when she discovered Santa wasn't real. He sighed, unsure if she'd hit him again if he tried to comfort her.

Against his better judgment, he scooted closer and wiped a tear from her cheek, finding the need to comfort her insurmountable regardless of her on-again-off-again personality.

"Hey," he whispered. "It's going to be okay. You have a lot on your plate...and you're worried about a backpack?"

He stole a look over his shoulder, where the contents of her backpack lay after he dumped them to the ground. He hoped she wouldn't have another fit when she saw he'd gone through it.

"It's not just a bag." She let out with a soft breath. "It was my mom's, and it was her favorite color...sky blue. And, now...it's – gone, like my hair!" She ran a hand through her bangs before wiping her face dry.

Anderson tilted his chin to the sky and shook his head with regret. Danny hadn't told him that her parents were dead.

"Savannah," he moaned.

Something about her, visions aside, had his insides churning. Anyone that had experienced what she had in the last few days would be scared out of their wits, and yet, she seemed to fight fear with fire. A backpack? One single sentimental item made her come undone? It quickly dawned on him how sensitive she was and how hard she fought to hide it.

"I'm sorry." He stood and extended a hand to her while retrieving the plastic trash bag from the ground. "I really am."

When Savannah slipped her hand into his, tingles spread through her arm like wildfire. She immediately pulled away only to see Anderson's face lit up with curiosity.

Savannah took a step back and stammered, "It...it's...not your fault. You were just trying to help." She eyed the barrel one last time. "But, you didn't have to kill my backpack."

"Yes, I did. For two reasons...first, the guy chasing you last night probably recognized enough about you to remember what you're wearing and the color of your bag. And secondly, your bag is too long for my bike."

She gave him a curious stare.

"It's not like I'm driving a roadster." He pointed at the short seat. "You'll fit behind me, and that's about it."

"You could have warned me..."

He touched her arm. "You understand that your mom's memory is still intact even if the backpack isn't, right?"

She nodded, holding back more tears.

"Okay, then." He tossed the plastic sack into the fire. "We have to go into town. Danny didn't know your size, and you need new clothes."

"I don't need new clothes." Her heart skipped a beat. The last thing she wanted to do was head into town.

"You've got to ditch your old ones. And I'm sure you could use a little something to eat?" He searched her face.

When a look of worry claimed her features, against his better judgment, he ran his hand down her back to comfort her and nodded toward his bike.

"Don't worry. I'll keep you safe."

At his touch, Savannah wrapped her arms around herself as chills permeated her skin. She shook her head and blamed the sensation on the fear of the unknown, but knew it was partly due to the inexplicable draw that this man had.

Anderson swept her belongings from the ground into a smaller drawstring bag. He mounted his bike and slid his shoulder bag between his legs before handing her a helmet.

"Here." His face filled with regret. "Put this on and pull down the visor. It'll keep anyone from seeing your face. I have a quick stop to make at the general store. We can get some food once we're on the road, and then we'll head for one of our safe houses."

"Wait. You guys have more than one?"

"We have a few options at our disposal." Anderson raised his brows with a look of mischief before wincing.

"Your eye hurting again?" A look of guilt crossed her face. "I'm so sorry." She reached to touch the outer edge of it.

It was an intimate and gentle gesture that had Anderson pulling away as his breath caught. He had one rule: Never get involved with an assignment. Although he was on leave, that rule still applied, especially since he wasn't sure how his visions tied in or how either of them played a part in them.

"Forget about it." He brought her hand down and helped her into a sitting position behind him. "Just hold tight."

Savannah did as she was told and wrapped her arms around his midsection, laying her cheek on his back as they pulled off the dirt road toward civilization. As they drove toward the sleepy town, she hoped they weren't driving toward danger.

5

During the three weeks that Savannah had been at the safe house, she'd done everything she could to stay occupied. Without a cell phone, which was once a lifeline to her business and social life, she was at a loss.

She scanned the horizon for Anderson, who was on yet another perimeter check. When his three-wheeler came into view from across the open field, she sighed and dipped a sponge back into some sudsy water before tossing it onto the hood of a farm truck.

If anyone had told her a month ago that Jade's wedding would result in dropping everything and hiding out at an abandoned farm in the middle of nowhere, Savannah would have never believed them. That was before she rescued Jade from Benny by hitting him over the head with a small statue in the dimly lit hallway of the strip club.

Once she and Jade tied up Benny and called the authorities, Savannah assumed she was in the clear. After all, it was an attempted kidnapping, and Benny was behind bars. However, it went deeper than that.

The authorities not only hauled off a scowling Benny, but they unknowingly uncovered a human trafficking ring that he'd been running from his office. With Jade's testimony, the local authorities reeled in a few bigger fish than they expected.

Afterward, when Savannah and Jade had officers assigned to them for round-the-clock protection, Savannah was reminded how true the old saying, *Let no good deed go unpunished*. She was a fool to think she could continue her life as if nothing had happened.

"Benny happened. That's what happened," she mumbled as she scrubbed down the dusty work truck in the middle of the deserted homestead.

What started with Benny resulted in fifteen more arrests before it was all said and done. And, the minute Benny made bail and skipped town, he put a target on Jade's back and her own.

All this transpired as she was wrapping up Jade's wedding. The feds were kind enough to allow Jade and her fiancé to marry as planned, but put them under protection and ushered Jade and her family to an undisclosed location. Savannah refused the program, unaware that a killer was on the loose looking to even a score.

"Stupid girl," Savannah grumbled as she slapped a sponge onto the hood. "I'm always trying to help and look where it got me."

Round-the-clock police protection gave her some comfort in the beginning, until the moment when her golden retriever let out a deep growl in the middle of the night.

As her dog lurched toward the back door, baring her teeth, sounds of shattering glass triggered her house alarm and immediately sent Savannah sprawling on the floor, searching for the gun under her bed.

Even though the officers were seconds from entering, Savannah couldn't take the chance that someone sinister wouldn't barge into her bedroom. Without pause, she shot off two rounds through her ceiling and waited with her gun trained on the door.

Once the police thoroughly inspected her home, they found a jagged brick that had been tossed through the window. It had a note tied to it that read: *You're not as safe as you think. I'll be watching.*

Police protection or not, that was all it took for Savannah to scroll through her contacts for Danny's phone number.

Once her parents passed, it was Danny who took her to the shooting range and continued her firearm training like her dad would have. She had no plans to enter the military, but her dad thought every female, especially the ones in his life, should know how to handle a gun. He and Danny were of the same mind.

He was the big brother she never had. And when Danny discovered she was in danger, he read her the riot act for not calling him the second she found herself in trouble. Now, here she was in some sort of safe house with Anderson.

Anderson. Savannah tossed the soapy sponge into the bucket. She kicked the pail of dirty water over before leaning against the side of the truck with a grimace. He had been a thorn in her side from day one.

She glanced up as he dismounted the three-wheeler and pushed it into the shed behind the home. As he locked the shed doors in place and turned toward her, she huffed and rolled her eyes. He made her crazy; yet, she knew he was doing his best to keep her safe. She couldn't fault him for that, even if he put her in a foul mood.

Savannah paused, listening for road noise only to hear the rustle of the leaves as the breeze danced around them. It made her wonder just how far away they were from civilization. The long drive to the rustic home had been smattered with tall trees, giving her the sense that she was hidden under their cover.

She lifted her face toward the sun rays as they filtered through the leaves. She took a deep breath with a single thought occupied her mind. Although pleasant for the time being, too much solitude could easily bring her to her knees.

The rumble of a plane interrupted her thoughts as it flew overhead. She averted her attention to the sky, wondering where the nearest airport was and sighed. If she stood still and tuned the world out, she could imagine herself on a military base as fighter jets flew overhead for training. Although the biplane sounded nothing like an F-18, the sound of any aircraft was home no matter where she stayed.

As she dried off her hands and made her way to the porch, a short ring sounded from a cell phone on the steps. She didn't have to look to see who it was since Danny was the only one with access to her new burner phone. Much to her dismay, she couldn't call anyone — not even her best friend, Ava. It didn't matter that she had a business to run, Anderson didn't care about those sorts of details.

He didn't care when news broke about Ava's recording contract or when her friend's songs played on the local radio stations. Savannah should have been celebrating by her best friend's side, but he wouldn't allow even one call to congratulate Ava. The man was infuriating!

"You. I have a bone to pick with you," Savannah blurted out before Danny could get in a word.

"Hey Smiles," he said, calling her by her pet name.

"Don't 'Smiles' me." She let out a growl. "When can I check in with work? I have a wedding coming up! My poor assistant is probably going crazy. And, when can I call Ava? She and my Brody are probably worried sick," she said, referring to her dog.

Danny's soothing voice came through the line.

"Nan is a very capable assistant. I called her and told her that there was a family emergency. Although she has big shoes to fill, she's handling it. And Ava was worried, but I gave her the same story. And as for your dog ..." Danny grunted.

"You lied to them?"

"I think this classifies as a family emergency. Don't you?"

"Ava would know better. I'm surprised she didn't press you for more details."

"She did, but the fewer people who know, the better."

"Ugh." Savannah stomped down the length of the wrap-around porch. "I'm dying of boredom here, cuz! I have work to do, and your former partner – that's another story altogether. He watches over me like a hawk."

Savannah shot Anderson an evil eye from a distance before turning her back on him.

"When will this be over? I just washed a freakin' truck for goodness sake. When have you known me to wash my car, let alone a farm truck?" She threw her hand in the air, gesturing toward the broken down vehicle. When Danny's chuckle sounded through the phone, she about lost it.

"Seriously?!" Her voice rose an octave. "You're laughing?"

Suddenly, the tone of the conversation took a turn. Danny paused and let out a breath.

"Your daddy would want me to protect his most prized possession," he said.

Those words packed a punch. She couldn't count the times her dad told her to take care of herself because she was *his most prized possession*. Even after all these years, his words were enough to take her back to her teen years.

"I miss him." She sniffled through the phone. "I miss them both."

"I know you do." Danny paused. "We all do. Your momma was as kind as they come. And your dad? Well, he was the reason I chose to serve my country."

Savannah's eyes watered at the thought of her father, who was a career Marine. His duty stations had taken her and her mom everywhere from D.C. to overseas, where she graduated from high school on a tiny island in the Pacific. She had a love-hate relationship with Okinawa. Although it offered some of the best memories of her life, it was also the place her parents died in a freak accident.

Afterward, the military packed their belongings, shipped her and everything her family owned back stateside, and assigned someone to help her navigate through the final steps of saying goodbye to her parents.

There were times she resented moving every couple of years. She'd finally feel like she belonged when her father would come home with that look that meant he received new orders. And within weeks – sometimes months they'd be packed up and gone. Before she could process how to say goodbye, she had to say hello to a new group of kids.

Looking back, it was a benefit more than a detriment. Moving helped Savannah adapt to anything that came her way. She may have been the new girl wherever she went, but she could turn obstacles into opportunities like no one else.

She looked around, wondering if anything could have prepared her for this.

Danny interrupted her thoughts.

"Look, kid. My only care is to keep you safe." His loving tone dropped an octave.

"I know," she groaned and slumped to the bench outside the front door.

He cleared his throat. "That's why I'm calling. I've been keeping tabs on the situation for you. Benny's disappeared – probably across the border by now. There's still a hefty price on your head, and until we find him – it's not going away."

Savannah stood up with a look. She scrunched her brow and threw her free hand in the air.

"What the heck, Danny? How are we supposed to find him if he's untraceable?"

"No one is untraceable." His voice lowered.

Her heart lurched. "Including me? You think they'll find me here?"

She searched the empty horizon for signs of trouble as she imagined a variety of scenarios in which Benny or his men would come after her.

"It's going to be okay. You have Anderson at your side."

She let out a sound. "That's not much reassurance. He seems a little off to me. Not to mention that I knocked him to his knees when he came to rescue me. I accidentally clocked him, and he crumbled like a cookie." She scoffed.

"And in the meantime, I'm trapped out here in the middle of nowhere. I've not seen one car since Anderson brought me here. I've not seen one person!" She threw up her hand. "How do people live like this anyway?!"

Danny laughed and said, "Lots of people pay good money for that kind of solitude. As far as Anderson — he can be trusted. He knows what he's doing. And if you got the drop on him – it was a fluke. At least it would have been before he —" Danny paused. "Well, before he went on leave."

"That doesn't sound good. What? He couldn't hack it?"

"Nothing like that, Sav. He got injured, so don't mention it."

"Great." She rolled her eyes. "If anything goes south, I'll be protecting him."

"Anderson is more than capable. He's the best partner I've ever had." Danny paused. "Truly. He is. I wouldn't trust your life with anyone else. Besides, not every man lives up to your dad. Give the guy a break, Sav."

Savannah clamped her lips, unsure of what to say. Staying silent was never her strong suit, so when neither spoke, she finally relented.

"Fine," she sighed. "But, I don't have to like it, and he needs to stay out of my way. I don't need him sticking so close that I can't even go pee without him checking the room first."

Danny's belly-laugh belted through the line.

"I'm sure it's not that bad."

When she grunted on the other end, he added, "I'll talk to him."

"See that you do," she said, running a hand through her newly cropped hair.

Savannah took a collective breath and closed her eyes. When she opened them, she cocked her head, noticing the sun as it slipped below the horizon.

Bold streaks of purple, pink, and orange sprouted across the sky as far as she could see. Sunsets like these were the only things she could say were a plus as far as she was concerned. Her face softened. It was as if God pulled out his paintbrush and painted across the sky just for her.

Just when it seemed as if things were somewhat right in her world, a loud pop sounded in the background of their conversation. It reminded her of the backfire of a car.

"Tomorrow, Smiles. I gotta run," Danny said.

Muffled noises came through the line as if he was on the move – and in a hurry.

"Danny, are you okay?"

"You know it, Cuz," he said with a cheery tone.

She could tell he was trying to put her mind at ease, but the more commotion that sounded through the phone, the higher her stress level shot through the roof. A succession of pops resonated in the background.

"What was that a gun?" she asked.

""Nah. Don't worry. It's nothing I can't handle." When he replied, it sounded as if he were running, trying to catch his breath. "Tell Anderson I'll be in touch."

Once the line went dead, Savannah panicked. Her first instinct was to find Anderson. Surely, he'd be the voice of reason.

She whipped around to find him standing only a few feet away, staring at the phone in his hand. When his eyes met hers, they mirrored her dread.

6

After last night's vision, it shouldn't have been a surprise that they were about to grab their gear and run. When Anderson's arm brushed against Savannah's after dinner, an image of them escaping in a dark SUV flashed before him.

While he was getting used to these images of what was to come, the physical aspect of them still took their toll. Anderson gripped the back of his chair for support. As Savannah peered at him with distrust, he fumbled to regain composure - thankful she said nothing.

The sight of them in a government-issued vehicle was nothing short of unexpected, but he pushed it to the back of his brain and forged through the next day. He had too much to do, like keeping Savannah safe.

As he approached the porch, her tense posture gave him pause. While her tone and gestures signaled irritation, he found it somewhat endearing. She had spirit or *chutzpah,* as his grandmother would say.

His heart lifted along with the corners of his mouth as he approached the edge of the wrap-around porch. Just as he was about to ask how Danny was doing, Anderson noticed an incoming text.

When he read the words on his home screen, his mind went into a tailspin.

You're compromised. Get Sav & your family to safety. You know the place – D

Suddenly, memories of last night's vision haunted him as he glanced at Savannah, who'd whipped around to face him, eyes wide.

"I heard a gunshot!" She held up her phone and searched his face for something – anything to assure her that everything was okay.

Anderson took a step forward but offered nothing of the kind. Instead, he ran his hand through his thick, blond locks before sitting on a nearby bench. He needed to think.

"Anderson?" Her voice shook.

He raised his index finger toward her before scrolling through his contacts to search for his father's number. On the third ring, he found himself holding his breath, praying his family was safe.

Savannah peered down at him, hoping to get a read on him, but he avoided her stare.

"Are you calling Danny?"

When he didn't respond, She clamped her lips, unable to push back the fear that something terrible had happened to her cousin. Finally, she wrapped her arms around her midsection and bent toward him.

"Please," she whispered. "I just tried calling Danny back, and he didn't pick up."

By the tone in her voice, Anderson knew she was on the brink but couldn't help her right now. He put his finger to his lips and returned his attention to his call.

When his dad finally answered on the fifth ring, Anderson dropped his head with relief and exhaled.

"Dad, it's time. Gather everyone. You know the place?"

Savannah watched as Anderson nodded at whatever his dad was saying.

Time for what? She was dying to ask, but it was clear she had no choice but to wait.

"Yeah. I'm okay." Anderson frowned. "I don't care if Alexis hasn't told Tyler about the emergency protocol. Make it happen. I have no details yet...just that it's not safe."

As images of what might have happened to Danny flooded Savannah's imagination, she leaned against the banister and focused on a spider that crawled across the porch.

He has to be okay. Savannah exhaled as anxiety began its ascent up her spine.

Once Anderson was certain his father everything under control, he glanced at Savannah. As would be expected, her tense frame and blank stare signaled stress, but he needed to focus on what came next. And for that to happen, she would have to be able to move quickly.

Anderson crossed the porch with the phone in hand. When she finally met his gaze, her golden eyes gave him pause...they were filled with uncertainty. He hoped she could handle what came next.

Anderson slipped his arm behind Savannah, resting his palm on the banister. He wrapped up the conversation, all the while gazing into her eyes, hoping to convey the assurance she needed.

"And, Dad?" He paused. "Yeah, I'm safe, but listen. Don't trust anyone. Don't stop for anyone."

Once he ended the call, he searched Savannah's face, unsure where to begin. Her eyes swirled with dismay. Just as he was about to explain, a few tears escaped and tumbled down her cheek.

He'd seen women cry before. It was a hazard of his job, but this time, it was different. Seeing how vulnerable she'd become tore at his heart. He brushed her tears away and softened his gaze.

"Are you okay?" His voice barely a whisper sent shivers down her spine.

"You're scaring me," she whispered in return before taking a step back. "Danny's call ended with a noise. It sounded like he was in trouble. And now you..." Her voice fell.

He would have loved to reassure her, but without knowing all the details, he had no idea how to address what would come next or if they'd be safe.

"Have you kept your things together like I asked? All in one place?"

Her eyes widened as she searched the land around them, unsure if they were safe any longer.

"Hey, I've got you." He rubbed his hands on her arms as the air crackled around them. Her cheeks flushed at his touch.

She was close enough to pull in for a kiss, but he kept his distance. Getting attached emotionally wasn't forbidden in his line of work, but it wasn't smart either.

He pulled away and said, "Grab your bag and be back in five minutes."

As she started for the door, he dropped his phone to the ground and smashed it to bits with his heel. Savannah sucked in a breath. After having done the same thing to her phone in the not too distant past, she knew it wasn't a good sign of what was to come.

Anderson shook his head. At the moment, soft and slow

would not get them very far. If he'd learned anything about Savannah in the last couple of weeks, he knew he'd have to get under her skin so she'd push past her fear.

"Don't just stand there! Get going!" He frowned and pointed toward the front door.

His gruff tone would have irritated her any other time, but instead of smarting back, she spun on her heel to retrieve her things, praying once more for their safety.

THEY STOPPED ONLY a few times for gas and necessities during their trek across a couple of state lines. Just as she was about to ask the proverbial, *are we there yet*, Anderson turned down a back alley toward what seemed like a deserted warehouse.

Savannah eyed the desolate buildings and shivered. It was stark in comparison to the farmland they'd fled. Wherever they were, she hoped it wasn't their end destination.

As if he could read her mind, he sent her a reassuring look before pulling a remote from his jacket. He pointed it toward a brick building and clicked a button before glancing over his shoulder.

Her look of confusion was to be expected. It was clear that clicking a remote at a solid brick wall would be a pointless task. However, when a portion of the wall receded, slid into a hidden panel, and revealed a looming metal door, her jaw dropped.

Anderson raised his eyebrow and pushed yet another

button. This time, the thick metal door raised and allowed them inside access.

"What is this place?" She eyed the opening as they approached.

From her seat on the back of his bike, she peeked around him and squinted at the dark interior.

Anderson exhaled. She'd been a trooper over the last fourteen hours, never once asking where they were going. At first, her silence was a nice change of pace from her fiery retorts, but it soon dawned on him that the lull was just a sign that she had met her emotional limit.

Anderson could relate. He was still navigating the overwhelming emotions that came with his newly found curse as scenes randomly played before him. He'd even had one while on the road. Thankfully, it was when they'd pulled over for a pit stop.

He shook his head at the memory. Although this new vision was unsettling, one particular detail gave him hope. The previous premonition, in which she was fighting to survive, was no longer. It seemed as if this new vision had replaced it. That fact alone sent a surge of relief through his worn spirit.

Even so, this new epiphany provided another set of problems. He envisioned her being held captive in an abandoned room at an unknown location. The only comfort it held was that she was not alone. He had also witnessed himself handcuffed to a headboard only feet from where she was bound in a chair.

A small part of him thought this was a victory. Something he had done changed Savannah's future. Could what he considered to be a curse actually be a gift?

"Are you going to answer me?" Her voice echoed

through the arrant interior, breaking him free of his thoughts.

"This is one of my..." He paused to slip off his helmet. "I guess you could call this one of my stashes or my cache."

Savannah eyed the dimly lit room that revealed itself as they entered.

"What do you keep in here? A jet?" Her face glowed with intrigue.

"Not at this one." He winked.

"Shut up!" She punched him in the arm as she swung her long leg from the back of the bike.

Savannah shook her head free from the helmet as her dark hair framed her oval face in such a way that had him temporarily mesmerized. Whether he liked it or not, she captivated him.

"I may or may not have one somewhere else. I could tell you, but..."

"Whatever." Her dimples deepened as she sent him a look.

"Listen." His eyes darkened.

Savannah waited, sensing the shift in his mood.

"Entering this building means I'm technically back on the job. I have a leave of absence, but only for a short time."

She blinked. "Danny told me about that."

"Just what did he say?" A shadow of distrust fell across his face.

"Just that you got injured and needed some time."

"Yeah." He sighed. "Well, there may be more to it than that." As he watched her face light up with intrigue, he added, "But that's for another time. Please, don't say a word once inside, and be ready to leave when I signal you."

He parked his bike near a wall and extended a hand to her.

"Stay close. It's about to get dark."

She cut her eyes at him as her laughter echoed through the room. "Is this your way of hitting on me, Evans?"

He raised an eyebrow and sent her an inviting grin. "If I ever decide to make a move on you, you'll know it."

Savannah blinked, unable to drag her eyes away or provide a witty response. Every time she thought she had a handle on whatever it was between them, he threw her off guard. She licked her lips and finally averted her eyes, mentally berating herself.

Anderson dipped his head to hide his amusement, but took a breath, quickly getting back to the task at hand.

"You will need to stay close, though," he said. "And remember, once we're through the next door – stay near the entrance and keep quiet."

As she slipped her hand in his, the friction between them had her second-guessing herself. If he were to bring her in for a kiss at that moment, she wasn't sure she could turn him away.

Shake it off, Savannah. She angled her head from his and followed him toward an interior door. Anderson, ever the gentlemen, pretended not to notice. He squeezed her hand and dropped it.

Anderson pushed the front of the hand-held remote up to reveal another layer, where a digital screen was displayed. A green light glowed on the screen until he placed his thumb on it, transitioning the screen to bright blue. Next, the thick overhead door they'd just passed through closed behind them.

Once the door shut, massive steel beams bolstered into concrete walls, securing it into place. They stood in pitch-black darkness, leaving Savannah without a clue how to navigate. She clung to Anderson's arm and buried her nose into his jacket.

She inhaled, thinking he smelled like fresh air mingled with the familiar scent of leather. His masculine essence had her reeling. She could have stood there forever and was almost sorry when she heard him say, "Lights."

Within seconds, fluorescents pinged above one after the other to reveal they were in a concrete bunker. Anderson winked at her before approaching the interior door, where a security panel was installed to the right.

He glanced over his shoulder and sent her a smile. "Don't peek."

Savannah raised a brow as he entered a code and waited. Soon, the panel door lowered to reveal a small compartment. From inside, a white tube protruded.

It reminded Savannah of the straws filled with sugar she ate as a young girl, but this one was more flexible. Anderson leaned forward to blow into it. Instantly, a computerized voice sounded.

"Welcome, Agent Evans."

He responded to the computer in kind. "Thank you, Eve."

"Your DNA has been confirmed, Agent Evans. You may enter." The voice announced as the door unlocked, giving them access.

Savannah looked at Anderson in disbelief as he winked in her direction.

She blinked as a row of lights turned on one by one to illuminate the interior. She grabbed the back of Anderson's jacket, hiding behind him as if walking into a haunted house.

"It's okay," he whispered.

Just as she opened her mouth to speak, he put a finger to

her lips. He ushered her inside and pointed to a spot near a dark corner.

Savannah wondered why he needed to keep her presence a secret when no one else was with them but reminded herself of the danger that Danny and Anderson faced in their careers.

If he thought it was best for her to sit idly by, she would, but she'd want answers very soon. She peered at him as he threw open a few cabinet doors searching for something.

Anderson reached for a handful of passports and a stash of currency, as a flat-screen monitor lit up with a woman's face he didn't recognize. He squinted, taking in the firm lines around her sharp eyes as she stared him down with a look he couldn't interpret..

Whoever she was - she now sat in a chair that was typically reserved for the Director of Odyessy. There could only be one reason Director Sanger no longer occupied his chair. This new and malevolent face staring back at him meant something terrible had happened while Anderson was away.

Mentally, he did the math. Between Danny's cryptic text and this snide stranger on-screen, internal alarms began to sound. They were in worse trouble than he had bargained.

After reading Danny's text, he assumed the danger was from a foreign threat. If there was anything he'd learned in his career, it was that nothing should ever be taken at face value. Anderson's gut twisted with dread when he realized the threat was from within his agency.

"Welcome back, Anderson." The woman's raw voice filled the speakers.

"Thank you. I'd say hello, but I don't know who I'm saying hello to."

"I'm the new Director."

"What happened to Sanger?" His throat went dry as he awaited her response.

The Director stroked the leather upholstery with a gleam in her eye. It was nothing short of predatory.

"Director Sanger had an unfortunate accident. It's a sad loss for us all." She faked a look of pity, before continuing, "I see that you've entered your cache, so I take it that you're back and ready to go? Otherwise, you know you don't have the authorization to access anything."

At the sound of her voice, goosebumps trailed his arms. His jaw clenched as a sense of foreboding pulled at his chest as if someone were tightening a corset around him. It was a struggle to breathe.

Anderson pinched the bridge of his nose, knowing what was coming next, and instantly a flash of the new Director barraged him. She was in the Director's dark office, smiling deceptively into the monitor at Anderson while texting his whereabouts to another team of operatives with clear instructions to kill.

The vision lasted long enough that he knew he had seconds to come up with a plan. He released a deep breath to calm his senses as his mind spun with questions.

How did the sound of her voice send him into a vision-like state? Was she so evil that her essence infiltrated the monitor? Was that even possible? Or had his abilities evolved to the point to where he could see what was to come outside the sense of touch?

To date, his acute intuition was usually limited to something physical. Other than the dreams or visions of Savannah before he met her, it took a personal encounter. While his insight disrupted his life, there was comfort in the fact that he had some control and knew their origin. Yet, this time, whatever source spurred his vision was not about being close.

Anderson shook his head. No matter how it happened this time, he was grateful as it gave him critical insight. Once more, he was coming to realize that his visions, although first thought of as a burden, were a blessing as they hopefully helped him stay one step ahead of danger.

"Are you alright?" Her faux look of concern filled the monitor.

He blinked and gave her the most reassuring smile he could muster.

"Yes, ma'am. It's just a sinus headache." He released his nose and sent her his most charming grin. "And, I'm ready to get back in the game."

Anderson paused, hoping his poker face would hold under pressure. Now that he knew there was a team of operatives on their way, he needed to play along and get Savannah to safety.

"Perfect. Glad to hear you're back. I look forward to what's coming next." She leaned forward with a smile so wide it almost overtook the span of her face. Anderson narrowed his gaze. He wanted to tell her what she could do with her fake sentiment but held his tongue. He needed to continue without raising suspicion.

"In fact - why don't you stay there, and I'll have a team bring you in safely? You and Miss Miles?"

Anderson froze. How did she know about her when Savannah was safely hidden from view? There was no way the new Director could have seen her unless they'd installed more cameras while he was away. He briefly dropped his head. He should have been more careful.

Anderson cocked his head toward the monitor, he lowered a hand below his waist and gave Savannah a small wave. He eyed Savannah from the corner of his eye and motioned for her to stay quiet.

"Nope. Sorry to disappoint, but it's just me. Director?"

The sound of the Director's chuckle sent chills down his spine.

"That's Director Brennen, and Anderson, as the new head of this department, the first thing I did was upgrade some of the areas that were lacking in security, like each operative's arsenals."

"That's mighty big brother of you, Director Brennen. Whatever happened to trusting your team in the field?"

"That died with your former boss."

A look of satisfaction crossed Director Brennen's face that spoke volumes evoking a sense of dread that spread like wildfire through Anderson's body. As she narrowed her eyes, malevolence seeped from every pore.

Anderson found that it wasn't just her eyes that covered him in darkness. It was as if her essence infiltrated the screen and surrounded him where he stood. For a minute, he thought it was just his intuitive nature that was tuned into her spirit until something happened that had him blinking in awe.

When a green fog poured from the monitor, Anderson thought his mind was playing tricks on him. A shivering sensation slivered around him as the dense smoke coiled its way around his body like a snake. Anderson sucked in a breath and tried to act as naturally as possible under the circumstances.

He shook his head. His visions had always been internal...until now. Although a hallucination – the fog was so dense that he wondered if Savannah saw it too. When he glanced over his shoulder, her benign face told him otherwise.

Once the green mist was at his neck, a putrid stench that reminded him of sulfur filled his nostrils. It took everything he had to stand his ground as he fought the gag reflex that accompanied it.

If Savannah hadn't been watching closely, she might have missed it. After weeks at his side, she knew him well enough to see that something wasn't right. The tremor in his hand, paired with the look on his face, had her wondering about the cause.

Anyone else would have easily overlooked it, but this wasn't the first time she'd seen him react in such a manner. It was as if something were plaguing him.

Anderson licked his lips, nodding as if listening with anticipation. When the Director's laugh filtered through the speakers, he had to fight the urge to vomit. He winced and swallowed, hoping his poker face would stay put.

"Evans, I've read your file and know pretty much everything there is to know about you. Even if we hadn't given your arms cache an upgrade in security, you're too much of a protector to leave someone stranded for even a minute."

Savannah rolled her eyes – didn't she know it. Yet, in this instance, she was grateful for his overprotective nature, especially since the Director's voice made the hair on the back of her neck stand at attention.

Anderson gave a curt not. "Okay, ma'am. We'll wait for you to pick us up. And I look forward to meeting you."

He powered down the monitor and slammed his hand on the counter before spinning to face Savannah.

Savannah rushed to his side and wrapped her arms around his waist to hold him up. As she searched his wild eyes, she wondered if he was panicked or on the verge of getting sick.

"Are you going to be okay?" She urged him to the stool and motioned for him to sit.

"I'm fine." He scanned the room for additional cameras that he may not have been aware of, noticing a small button at the counter, opposite of his monitor. At first glance, he missed it as it looked like part of the cabinetry. Now, he knew otherwise.

"Hop up here while we wait for them." He motioned to a spot on the countertop, next to the computer. While he wanted to tell her to hurry, he couldn't alert anyone at the Odyssey in case they were listening.

Savannah squinted in his direction, giving him a look that needed no interpretation.

He dropped his voice to a whisper. "There's not much time. Sit up here and act natural."

"Okay." As she slid in place and blocked the only other camera that he knew of, Anderson furiously went to work.

This time, when the monitor lit up - code streamed across the screen as Anderson's fingers flew across the keyboard.

Savannah watched him with a curious wonder for a matter of minutes before he finally took a deep breath.

"Got it." His shoulders sagged with relief.

"Got what?" she asked.

"The new Director locked me out of any of my toys inside. They're coming, so we have to work fast."

Anderson jogged to a small alcove and punched in a code. A door to their left opened, revealing a secondary garage.

A multitude of lights powered on and illuminated the room, revealing a large armored SUV with tinted windows. Savannah eyed the scene with wonder. Just what kind of people did he work for?

"Get inside - now!" he ordered. "I've locked them out of the security system for now, but it won't hold for long. I'm sure they have a team working on it as we speak."

"Didn't you say we were going to wait for them?" She frowned as he shoved her bag into her arms and nudged her forward.

When he didn't answer, she opened the passenger door as Anderson loaded the back of the SUV with enough supplies to host an army. She blinked at the speed in which he accomplished his task.

Once he slid onto the driver's seat, he ripped open the panel beneath the steering wheel and pulled out a small black box. Anderson tossed it out the window toward the concrete wall with enough force that she was sure it would smash to pieces.

"What was that?" She frowned.

"Something they could use to track us." His eyes narrowed.

"Why would they do that?"

Savannah didn't know what was more frightening – the silence that filled the vehicle or an answer that was looming.

He looked her over, unsure if she was ready for the truth, and decided against giving her any details for now. Her eyes flickered with anxiety as he sat without an explanation. He shook his head and reached to retrieve another smartphone from the glove box.

"Let me guess. A backup?" she asked.

He raised his brows and slipped his 9mm Luger from his holster before using the butt of the handle to smash the phone to smithereens and dump the debris outside his door. He then glanced at her backpack.

"Still have your burner?" He held his palm out and waited.

Savannah dug through her bag in haste before handing the last line she had to her cousin. As Anderson destroyed it, a sense of dread overcame her.

"How will Danny reach me?" After her last phone call with her cousin, all she could think about was his safety.

"He's a big boy."

Anderson started the engine and slowly drove from the building. As the vehicle crept into the alley, he looked both ways to search for any signs of trouble before retrieving a handful of caltrops from his duffle bag in the back seat.

"What are those for?" She eyed what looked like a cross between a Chinese throwing star and a pyramid with nails.

"They'll take out the tires of anyone who comes after we're gone." He peered down the dark alley.

They still could be lying in wait.

He thought of his family as he applied gentle pressure to the gas to ease from the garage opening. He hoped they'd make it to the safe house unharmed and untraced. Although he'd prepped them for years in case something like this happened, they weren't trained operatives.

"What if Danny comes here looking for us?" She frowned as he switched off the interior lights of the car and stepped outside to strategically place a few caltrops across one of the alley's entrances.

"He won't," he said as he returned to the vehicle.

"How do you know?"

"Because we have a protocol for this sort of thing."

He put the SUV in drive and pulled in the opposite direction. With the caltrops behind them, any cars approaching from behind would be sidelined.

Savannah's soft voice broke his train of thought.

"Protocol for what sort of thing? What's happening, Anderson?"

Instead of answering, he said, "Hold on tight."

His eyes brightened for the first time in hours as he steered them down the dark alley with the headlights off.

"Stay low, in case," he commanded.

Savannah held her breath and prayed as she sunk deeper into her seat. Her heart raced with the fear of the unknown.

As Anderson sped off into the night, he realized what came next could get tricky, but he had a few things to accomplish before joining his family.

7

Anderson was never more thankful for Danny than he was at this moment. As the senior agent in their partnership, Danny was the one who drilled the possibility and importance of an exit plan.

Both knew that entering an off-the-books agency could someday put them in danger for any number of reasons, especially if the wrong person was at the helm. He prayed Danny's foresight would never come to fruition, but today proved that his partner's paranoia came in handy.

As Anderson started his exit strategy, he said a prayer for Danny, hoping he made it to the safe house they'd secured for a situation such as this. Whatever this was...

The drive to the mall was a quiet one. Anderson glanced at Savannah, who had curled her legs into the passenger seat and leaned her head against the window, chewing on her thumbnail.

Anderson sighed. Since he met her, they'd experienced quite a bit. Although she could bring out the worst in him, he admired her strength. Not many people could handle an ounce of what she'd been given. And while she'd had a smart mouth, he recognized it as her way of coping.

Once the light turned green, he turned right and pulled into a mall parking lot.

"When we enter the parking garage, keep your head down," he said while slowing at a crosswalk.

Savannah raised her chin in defiance. "That depends. Are you going to tell me what's going on?"

He cocked his head in her direction. "I knew it was too good to last."

She narrowed her eyes. "What was?"

"Nothing." He shook his head. "I promise, but first, can we get out of town?"

She pursed her lips and raised a brow in defiance.

He groaned. "It's a long story, and we don't have much time. I promise I will. Just work with me."

"Fine," she mumbled as she dipped her chin to her chest.

Once in the parking garage, he scanned the multitude of cars, hoping to find one that was out of camera range and the right age. He released a disparaging breath when the only vehicles in sight were more recent models.

"This won't do." He shook his head, still searching the endless rows of cars.

"Can I look up now?" she asked as he turned down the next aisle.

Just when he thought he'd run out of options, he spotted an older VW Van and a beat-up station wagon parked on the last row. Both were manufactured prior to vehicle tracking systems.

"Bingo." He loosened his grip on the steering when he noticed both were parked in a blind spot. "You can look up now."

Anderson parked out of camera range at the end of the row and slipped from the vehicle with a flat metal tool in hand.

Savannah watched in awe as he glided the tool inside the window of the van and popped the lock. As soon as he opened the door, he motioned for her to join him.

"What are you doing?" She stepped in next to him.

Ignoring her question, Anderson ushered her into the driver's seat.

"Do you expect me to drive a stolen car?" Her jaw dropped. "Are you leaving me?!"

Anderson propped an arm on the roof of the vehicle and leaned toward her with a lazy smile.

"No, I'm not leaving you. Look. We don't have much time. See those?"

Anderson motioned to a nearby security camera pointed in the opposite direction.

"No one can see us right now. What I've done here won't be on camera and can't be accessed by mall security or anyone else that could tap into their feed. But...we entered together in a known government vehicle, and they'll be looking for us."

He scanned the parking lot. "If they haven't already tailed us here. They can tap into any security feed throughout the city." When he turned his crystal blue eyes on her, they filled with urgency. "Sav, we have to outsmart them if we're going to make it out of here."

"Who are you talking about, Anderson? And why are we running? I mean...there's Benny and his grunts, but what's changed?"

"Just trust me. We have to move – now."

Savannah blew out a breath and grabbed the steering

wheel. She bobbed her head back and forth and said to no one in particular, "Trust me, he says. Trust me."

She pointed her finger at him. "The last time I listened to someone who said that - it landed me in a borrowed car. Only what my high school boyfriend really meant to say was that he'd stolen it. Then, he wrecked it and shoved me onto a city bus back to school... all before landing himself in jail. This doesn't seem to be too far off from what you're suggesting we do now!" Her voice rose an octave. "I don't want to get arrested!"

"Look!" He paused to lower his voice. "Danny trusted me to protect you for a reason. If you don't listen – going to jail will be the last thing you have to worry about. We need to leave in separate cars to distract them."

"They'll expect us to switch cars and leave together. That means they'll check every camera feed for two people in one vehicle. Leaving separately might be enough to throw them off and give us a head start."

He pulled a ball cap from his backpack and tapped the brim, giving her a once over. "Use this to block your face from view and avoid turning toward any cameras. They're positioned at the corners and above the turns on the way out of here. Make sure you follow me out of town, okay?"

Instead of answering, Savannah clamped her lips and breathed in through her nose. When were things going to stop spinning out of control? She stared past Anderson toward the sky and prayed for God to go before them to prepare the way.

"Okay?" he repeated as she searched the skies for something unseen.

While they needed to exit the parking garage as fast as possible, he took his time to kneel next to her. The second it hit the ground, a flash of him kneeling before her in another surrounding washed over him, but he shook it from the edges of his mind.

The moment he angled her chin to make eye contact and his fingers brushed against her cheek, a current shot up his arm. He pulled back, blinking. He took a breath and tried again, unable to dissect anything between them at the moment other than how to earn her trust.

"Savannah, you can do this. Just follow me and flash your lights if you see anyone or anything in your rearview mirror that concerns you. I promise to take care of you."

She nodded, slipping her seatbelt in place when she realized she had no idea how to start the engine. Just when she was about to ask, Anderson slid his hands between her knees for the panel beneath the steering wheel.

The instant his arms brushed across her thighs to cross a few wires beneath the dash, Savanna held her breath. When the engine finally sputtered to life, she exhaled and patted the dash. *I know how you feel, old girl.*

Unaware of his effect, Anderson leaned in to check the fuel gauge. "It should be enough to get us where we're going."

He turned to find they were eye to eye. He dropped his gaze to her pink and perfect heart-shaped lips.

Savannah inhaled and dragged her focus from his full lips to his crystal-clear eyes wishing they'd met under different circumstances.

"Um, thanks," she murmured as he cleared his throat and backed away.

"Yeah, sure." He ran his hand through his hair. "I'm, uh, going to start that van across the row and load it with our supplies from the SUV, okay?" He raised his eyebrows. "And you're going to follow me."

She nodded and closed her door. After loading the van,

Anderson hotwired his vehicle and pulled from his parking spot. As Savannah put her car in reverse, she clamped her lips and breathed in through her nose, wondering what in the world would happen next.

***

THEY DROVE for what seemed like an eternity, yet when Savannah glanced at her watch, she was surprised to discover they'd only been on the road for a few hours. She glanced in her rearview mirror and said a prayer of thanks that no headlights were shining behind them. As she followed Anderson with blind faith down the dark two-lane road, she was never more grateful to see city lights on the horizon.

"Finally," she said.

Within twenty minutes, they both found parking spots at a playground. Unsure of how to kill the engine, Savannah slid the gear into park and left it running. She rested her head against the steering wheel and allowing every muscle in her body to relax. For the first time in hours, it seemed like she could breathe.

"You did well," Anderson said as he opened her door.

She sent him a weak smile as he leaned inside to cut the engine. Once it came to a stop, soft sounds of cicadas and a few gentle laughs carried through the breeze. It was then that Anderson spotted some teens skating just inside the park.

"Look." He raised his eyebrows and pointed. "That right there...is opportunity."

Savannah looked at him from under full lashes and shook her head.

"For what? Are you going to steal their skateboards, so we can escape on foot?"

He threw his head back and laughed before taking her hands into his and pulling her close. As his laughter subsided, he shook his head and asked, "Is that what you think?"

The instant his hands ran over her smooth skin, Savannah's breath hitched, and she lost her train of thought. She blinked and glanced back to the teens, trying to cover her reaction.

"Well, you've already stolen two cars. And your van is loaded with weapons, so..." Her voice dropped.

"Well, I would like to brush up on a few lipslides." His eyes sparkled as he referenced a skateboarding technique while glancing at her mouth.

Savannah narrowed her eyes at the double entendre and shook her head. She may have feigned dislike, but her sparkling eyes told him differently.

He slid one of his hands through his thick hair and grinned. "It's good to see your sense of humor is still intact."

"You could say that. I think I'm more in shock than anything." She paused and lowered her voice. "I have no idea what's going on."

Her soft voice pulled at his heart.

"I know. Let's get some food and new burner phones. And then - I'll tell you everything."

"If we're supposed to be in hiding, how will we do that?"

"Like I said..." His dimples flashed. "Opportunity is knocking."

Savannah slid to the hood of her car as he called the teens over before meeting them halfway. She couldn't hear what they were discussing, but when both kids eagerly nodded, she made a face.

Anderson could convince an angry mob to hold hands and sing Kumbayah. He had a plan even on the fly. Savannah cocked her head. His resilience amazed her.

After Anderson handed the teens a wad of cash and they skated into the dark, he jogged toward Savannah with a knowing grin. She had a hard time not returning it. After all, he was incorrigible.

"So, you gave them money, and they left? If I were them, I'd skate off and never come back." She blinked toward the dark horizon. The night seemed to have swallowed the skaters whole. "You know they're gone."

He settled on the hood next to her and sighed. "Oh, ye, of little faith."

"I've got faith, but it's directed elsewhere." She pointed toward the night sky while reaching for the cross around her neck.

He raised an eyebrow and said, "Good to know." He searched the horizon and continued, "But, what I meant was those skaters are on their way to the local drug store. They'll be back with a couple of cell phones and some food."

"Who is to say that they won't ditch you?"

"Says me. I gave them some incentive to return."

"I don't think threatening them within an inch of their life will do the trick, double-oh-seven." She smirked.

At her reference to James Bond, he dipped his head and looked at her from beneath his lashes. As his dimples made an appearance, Savannah fought the sudden urge to trace them with her fingertips. She balled her hands into fists to make sure they behaved and stared into the night to avoid his gaze.

"They'll come back." He sent her a questioning look. For a second, he swore he saw a flash of desire in her amber eyes but quickly dismissed it after she focused on something in the park.

"Anyways, they're teenage boys. There are only a few things that motivate them." Anderson sent her a sideways grin. "And money is one of them. With the amount of cash that I just offered them, they'd be fools not to return."

"Or they'd be wise to take it and run." She snickered.

"Just trust me."

She squinted and wiggled a finger in his direction. "There are those words again."

When it came to men, she didn't trust easily. Since no one compared to her father and the few semi-serious relationships she'd experienced had ended in disaster, trust wasn't something on her agenda. Even if Anderson reminded her of her father, she didn't plan on falling for his charm - at least not entirely.

"People have to earn that." She pursed her lips.

Anderson was about to ask about her past when the sound of an approaching vehicle overrode his curiosity. His heart pounded when a dark SUV rounded a curve in the road near the park.

Anderson put an arm around Savannah's waist in haste and pulled her in for a kiss. As he leaned her back, he expected to be met with resistance, yet was pleasantly surprised when her soft lips opened and matched him kiss for kiss.

What transpired out of necessity transformed into something profound. The underlying chemistry both sensed but ignored exploded between them.

Anderson's mind spun as he found himself in uncharted waters. When he kissed her, it changed him. It was as if she branded his heart. There were never any kisses before hers, nor could he fathom any after. There were just hers, and at the moment, he could drown in them. Once the air stilled and any hint of an engine had long since passed by, Anderson pulled away. He peeked through partially open lids and stared at her with wonder.

Savannah touched her lips and opened her eyes, unsure of the emotions that still surged through her. She sat up, putting some distance between them as her heart pound wildly from her chest.

"What was that?" She frowned at the sense of loss her lips experienced when he pulled back. She focused on the hood of the car, fully aware that his eyes were trained on her.

"I told you – you'd know if I made a move on you."

Although he downplayed it – initiating their kiss was much more than a move, and they both knew it. It was more like earth-moving, soul-shattering, or mind-blowing. Anderson's lips chilled as the warmth from her skin fell absent. It was as if a part of him died without her lips breathing life into him.

Savannah stilled, hoping he couldn't tell how much their connection had shaken her to the core. Determined, not to fall under his spell, she relied on a tried and true defense mechanism – sarcasm.

"So, you call that a move? I've had better." She shrugged.

Anderson cleared his throat and shook his head in response.

"There was a..." He pointed into the distance, wondering which direction the SUV went.

Would she even believe him if he told her his motive?

Regardless, he'd do it again in a heartbeat to take her into his arms. *No, you can't let that happen again.*

When he noticed Savannah's comical grin, he narrowed his eyes and sent her a sideways glance.

As Savannah watched his wheels turning, she basked, knowing her feminine powers ruled over him just as much as his kiss wielded her into a pile of putty. As if he could sense her delight, his face suddenly hardened. Savannah searched it, wondering what deep thoughts brewed behind his ice-blue eyes and finally decided to let him off the hook.

"Don't worry. I saw the car. Think it was the same people who are after us?"

"Not sure." He shrugged, scanning the dark road where the vehicle disappeared. "But, I figure it was better to be safe rather than sorry."

"Oh? Kissing me was a safe choice?" She raised an eyebrow with a challenging stare.

Anderson wanted to say yes, but after tasting her soft lips, he knew better. He'd have to keep his distance - if there was such a thing. The fact that she was under his protection meant they'd be joined at the hip for an undisclosed period.

Savannah glanced at her watch and exhaled. "I think your new friends took your money and ran. They've had plenty of time to get back by now. Don't you think?"

Anderson cocked his head and looked at a spot over her shoulder with an air of confidence.

"You were saying?"

She glanced over her shoulder as both skaters came into view.

"Do you always have to be right?" Her face scrunched with disdain as the boys finally came to a halt near their cars.

"Hey, man." Anderson slipped off the hood and shook

the hand of the tallest of the two skaters while taking a plastic sack from him.

"It's Kip." When Kip narrowed his almond eyes, it looked as if he were asleep. He then gave a short nod and said, "You said you'd pay us more?"

Kip turned his attention to Savannah and openly gawked.

"Hello, beautiful." Kip gave her a slow once-over.

"In your dreams." She rolled her eyes and then grabbed the sack from Anderson while keeping her focus on Kip. "You don't get another dime unless you brought us what we need. Is it all here?"

As she dug through the sack for the phones, Kip nudged his friend, Jimmy, who handed her a white paper bag and a soda.

"Here." Jimmy shrugged. "The burgers should still be hot."

Savannah's face softened once she eyed the greasy burgers.

"You're both my new favorite people." She shot the kids a flirtatious grin and sighed with a roll of her eyes. The smell of warm food had her stomach grumbling with desire.

She dropped the sack with the burner phones at Anderson's feet and eagerly took possession of the paper bag. She sniffed the contents with a look of wonder. Whatever was inside smelled like a slice of heaven.

After unwrapping a burger, Savannah moaned with pleasure as she sunk her teeth into a greasy patty with cheese.

"I could kiss you right now," she mumbled through her food, eyeing Kip, who grinned and stood a little taller.

"Easy there, kid." Anderson chuckled and dug a handful

of hundred dollar bills from his pocket. "This is all the reward you're getting tonight."

Kip's face lit up as he eyed the cash. "Thanks, dude."

Jimmy, the shorter of the two skaters, eyed the money with concern and asked, "Shouldn't we count it?"

Savannah chuckled and waved them off. "Just trust him. It's all there."

The corners of Anderson's mouth twitched before he gave her a satisfied once over.

Kip and Jimmy didn't waste any time. They each shoved a couple of hundreds in their pockets and pushed away on their boards.

"Later!" Kip yelled over his shoulder and waved.

Anderson cupped his hands. "Remember, you never saw us!"

The boys waved in dismissal as Anderson turned his attention back to Savannah, who was mid-bite in her burger with the most satisfied look on her face. As another sigh of delight escaped her lips, Anderson raised his brow.

Over the last three weeks, they'd been eating a variety of microwave dinners and canned vegetables. It was nothing to write home about, but nothing to dismiss either. If he'd known her love for burgers was this intense – he may have broken protocol and gone into town.

"If all it took was a burger to win you over, I'd have bought you one a long time ago."

She paused mid-bite and shot him a look. "You really know how to kill a mood."

His belly laughs echoed through the night. "I've been told differently, but okay. I'll give you that."

"You haven't been the easiest to put up with. You know that?" Savannah glared in his direction.

His lips flattened. He knew the last few hours – heck,

days, had been hard on her. He sighed, contemplating how much to tell her. He motioned for her to sit with him on the curb.

Anderson had planned to fill her in with as few details as possible. Keeping her in the dark wasn't an option, but telling her too much could put her in more danger than either of them could handle.

He laid a hand on her arm and opened his mouth to speak when a current wrapped around him and wound up his neck. Flashes of light exploded behind his eyes while a dense fog visible only to him appeared. When another vision bombarded his senses, he grabbed his head and bit his lips to keep from yelling out in pain.

The vision of them bound in a sparse room replayed as if on repeat, yet this time, something had changed. Anderson could sense everything as though it were in real-time, instead of a mere thought or image of what was to come.

As Anderson stumbled to his knees, Savannah leaped from the curb to catch him. She searched his eyes, but it was useless. He was somewhere else, but where?

"Hey! Are you okay?!" she yelled in vain.

Anderson was overcome with the image of Savannah, who was bound to a chair near his bedside. Caught between two worlds, he was aware enough to force his way back to Savannah in the present but chose to stay anchored in the future. He needed to know what they were up against.

Through the fog, he noticed Savannah's arms were tied behind her back, and she was kicking his leg, trying to alert him of something or someone. Whatever it was, the two of them were in danger, and Savannah seemed to be the only one alert enough to make a difference.

While Anderson was walking through their future,

Savannah was yelling in their present. As hard as she tried to snap him out of it, Anderson found he could only focus on what the future was showing him.

Just then, everything changed. Anderson scanned the room to observe that time stilled, which caused everything in the future to move in slow motion.

Once the pain faded from behind his eyes, he squinted, taking in every detail around him. His gaze again landed on Savannah. Whatever she was so desperately trying to tell him was slurred. He blinked, frowning at the image of his body lying on the bed. He appeared to be asleep.

Anderson shook his head and decided to worry about his future condition later. Finally, he scanned the room for any clues about where they were being held, as Savannah's words broke through the thick haze that bound them.

"Snap out of it!" He heard her yell from the chair.

He stepped between her chair and the bed, where the future version of himself lay and looked from her anxious face to his limp body below, wondering what their captors had done to him. It had to have been drastic to immobilize him to the point where she couldn't get his attention. Had they drugged him? Or was he dead? He studied his chest. Thankfully, it slowly rose and fell.

Just then, the vision faded, and he sensed Savannah's strong arms as she tightened them around his chest. It was like she was pulling him from the depths of an ocean, and the dark of night wrapped around them like a thick sweater on a hot summer's night.

"Anderson!" she yelled for the third time, unsure of what to do.

Savannah glanced at the burner phones at her feet. If they had been charged, she could have called for help, but since they were still in their packaging – it wasn't an option.

A sense of helplessness engulfed her as she scanned the area aware that they were alone without a soul in sight.

She slowly rocked Anderson in her arms and raised her face to the sky as a moan escaped from her throat.

"God, please let him be okay." She exhaled.

She began to pray – her words just above a whisper. "The Lord is my shepherd ..."

As she wiped the sweat from Anderson's brow, her soothing words filled his spirit with strength. Just as she finished, his eyelids fluttered open, and he searched her face.

"Hi." His voice barely escaped his lips. Anderson finally raised from his bent position and tried to stand. He stumbled to his knees, taking Savannah with him. He drew in a shaky breath.

"I'm okay." He lifted his gaze to meet her concerned eyes.

His faint voice was unconvincing, but Savannah finally withdrew her arms and brought her forehead to rest against his.

"I'm sorry," he murmured.

"Don't," she whispered.

She took his face in her hands and peered into his eyes. His crystal blue hue morphed into the shade of an evening sky. She frowned, wondering if it was normal or if something else was going on.

Savannah shook her head, as the barriers she'd kept drawn around her came crumbling down. After her parent's death, she became an expert at keeping people at arm's length. Yet with Anderson, it seemed she forgot how.

Worrying about another human being was to be expected, but to care this much about him was not. She was inexplicably drawn toward this man, yet he singlehandedly drove her crazy.

"You're so pale." She touched his brow with the back of her hand.

"Am I?" He clamped his lips and withdrew from her touch. If she didn't stop stroking his skin, he wasn't sure he'd recover.

"When are you going to tell me what is going on?"

"It's nothing. It was just a headache." He shrugged it off.

"You're lying. I've seen you do this before. Like when we first met – and then when you acted a bit off inside your bat cave or whatever you call it. And a few other times, too. Only with each instance, it gets more intense."

He eyed her with a look of surrender and sighed, saying nothing in return.

"You're scaring me," she whispered.

"Don't be scared. It's nothing." He dropped his gaze.

"Come on, Anderson. I make a habit of studying people. It comes with my job."

"Oh, yeah? Tell me more." His eyes twinkled.

She pursed her lips, fully aware of his intentions to change the subject.

"You can't charm your way out of this one. Although I don't know what's going on with you, I know you're not experiencing simple headaches. It's something bigger." She put a finger to her lip and paused as a thought struck her.

She kneeled in front of him and searched his face. Her brow furrowed.

"Does this have to do with your injury? Are you having seizures? You were in a coma, right? It could be a brain tumor."

When Anderson dropped his head into his hands, Savannah assumed it was the onset of another episode. She laid a hand on his arm for whatever came next. When he started shaking with uncontrollable laughter, she shoved him and sent him sprawling onto his back.

"You're laughing at me?" She jumped up. "You! Just when I think you're a nice guy, you go and do something like this! I swear!"

Savannah dusted off the back of her jeans and headed for the van. It didn't matter that she didn't know how to hotwire a car. She was going to try. Then, she could leave him and his sense of humor on his behind, where she pushed him.

"Wait!" His voice, still bubbling with laughter, faded as he scrambled to his feet. "Just wait." His approach was softer this time... more desperate. He paused before reaching for her arms.

Although his demeanor changed, she wasn't willing to let go of her pride. Savannah stepped away, with arms folded and turned from him unable to reign in the anger and mistrust that burned in her chest.

"I wasn't making fun of you." He touched the back of her arm, hoping she'd face him.

Instead, she took another step away.

"Right now, laughter is the only thing keeping me sane."

When she continued to give him the cold shoulder, he sighed and stepped closer, hoping she'd listen.

"Savannah, if you only knew."

Finally, she spun to face him. The daggers that flew from her eyes told him it was time.

He rubbed a hand across his five o'clock shadow and sighed. He wanted to draw Savannah near but kept his distance. Unsure of her reaction to what would come next and fighting the urge to hold her, he did the next best and most intimate thing he could.

He told her the truth.

8

"What do you mean you lost them?" Director Brennen fought to keep her composure as she sat across the desk from one of her senior operatives.

Instead of yelling, she sent him a look that left him shaking in his boots. "You and your team are the best of the best, Franks. How could you lose them? He's coming back from medical leave with a civilian in tow."

Franks cleared his throat and paused, thinking every word through before responding. What happened next could determine his fate. He answered as if his life depended on it because more than likely - it did.

"Ma'am. Anderson is a highly-trained operative. When we arrived at the unit, his vehicle was missing, and any tracking device we could have used was destroyed."

Director Brennan pulled up a city grid and thoroughly studied it. Anderson could be anywhere, but with their network, they would find him. It was just a matter of time.

"Director?" Franks interrupted her thoughts.

"Calculate the time and the distance he could travel toward all towns in this area." She drew a circle around the point of origin. She tapped the computer and sent him a look. "Cover all the bases with this one, Franks. Don't leave any stone unturned. You understand?"

"Yes, ma'am."

"You better find him and his partner. And, don't come back in until you have confirmation."

"Confirmation?"

"Yes."

Franks swallowed.

Being at the end of one of her steely glares wasn't something he ever wanted to experience again. It was as if she was mentally taking him out with one look.

Brennen soon turned her attention to her monitor, where headshots of both Danny Stone and Anderson Evans, as well as a few other ops officers, were displayed. The only two that still evaded and taunted her were Stone and Evans, as the rest had already been successfully executed.

When she accepted the position at Odyssey, the plan was clear. Ops officers who agreed to her terms were retained to serve in a new capacity, but the handful shown her screen, like Anderson and his partner, were wired differently. Their code of ethics kept them from conforming to anything outside of honorable intentions.

Men like them simply weren't candidates for her vision, which meant there wasn't room for them on her team – especially if they were the moles she suspected had infiltrated the group and turned Sanger on to them.

Director Brennan narrowed her eyes. She'd taken this position after months of careful planning on her and a handful of key operatives' parts. These last couple of rogue agents could undo months of preparation, and there was a lot of money on the line if Danny and Anderson weren't taken care of.

Director Brennen drummed her fingers on the desk in time with her pulse and lowered her voice.

"And Franks?" She swiveled in her chair to face him.

"Yes, ma'am." He stood.

"Failure is not an option."

Understanding the implications fully, he gave her a short nod and exited her office. As he shut the door behind him, he let out a breath and closed his eyes before one of his men approached.

"I see you're still breathing." Underwood, a fellow operative who served under him, smirked.

"Not for long if we don't find the last two on our list. Tell me you've made progress. We don't have room for errors like this last one."

"The teams we sent to surrounding towns came up empty, but we have traffic monitors running in every city. And, we got a hit on their vehicle."

"Where?" he asked as they passed through a set of double doors.

They entered a room lined with monitors and the best technology known to mankind. If Anderson or his partner were out there, this team would find them.

"Anderson and the girl entered a mall parking lot about seventeen miles from the storage unit."

Franks scanned the room, which was filled with a handful of analysts who were busy at work. He turned to Underwood as another team member joined and sent them a knowing look.

"Find them. It's your asses on the line."

As Agent Franks stalked away, his eyes gleamed with determination at the thought of hunting down two of his former co-workers. He was a man driven to succeed no matter how far into the darkness it led him.

9

"So, wait a minute!" Her eyes bulged. "You mean you can see the future?"

Anderson sighed.

Well, at least she didn't think he was insane. There was some consolation in that.

As he drove to a nearby gas station and parked across the street, he shook his head. "No, it doesn't work that way."

He scanned the perimeter of the parking lot and lifted his chin in her direction.

"Help me watch for an older model car or truck. We've got to switch out." He tapped the dash. "We're almost on empty."

After he told her about his abilities at the park, she sat, unable to process what she heard. Instead of discussing it further, he figured he'd give her time. When she was ready, he knew she'd be more than willing to share her thoughts on the subject, but until then, he scratched the VINs off both vehicles. Then, they left the van behind and drove toward town in the station wagon.

Of the many ways, Odyssey could find them, checking

security feeds was one of them. Stopping for gas meant dodging video cameras. For now, the only choice was to find another vehicle.

They parked in the cover of night and watched as an older model truck pulled into the gas station across the street. It stopped at one of the pumps. Once the driver topped off his gas tank and drove away, Anderson tailed him into a run-down neighborhood.

Although he kept his distance, by his third turn in the neighborhood, he fell back to stay under the radar. Finally, the driver parked the truck in front of a home and jogged inside.

Anderson passed it by and made a U-turn at the end of the street. He parked nearby where he had a vantage point of the truck and the house in which the young man entered.

"Now what?" Savannah sighed.

Anderson glanced at his watch. It was nearly midnight. Chances were whoever owned the truck was in for the night.

"Anderson. We can't steal his truck," she whispered through the dark.

"We're practically on empty, and that pickup has enough room in the truck bed to carry all my gear. Plus, it's got a cover on it to keep it secure." He gave her hand a squeeze. "We don't have too many options right now."

She bit her lip, unsure, before finally giving a short nod.

Once the lights in the home turned out for the night, Anderson breathed a sigh of relief.

"We're going to wait an hour... to make sure whoever is inside is asleep. Then, I'm going to hotwire the truck, and you're going to follow me to the outskirts of town. That's when we'll switch everything out and move on."

Savannah clamped her lips and closed her eyes. Stealing went against everything she'd been taught. When they took the cars from the mall, she was in so much shock she didn't have time to think, but this brought a whole new awareness of the situation.

She'd seen the man who would be without a truck. It was too personal and clearly too hard to ignore the fact they were stealing.

"This is still wrong!" She frowned. "Can't you leave him some money or something?" She glanced at the duffle bag in the back seat.

Anderson's sideways grin did nothing to ease her guilt. She knew him well enough to recognize that he was about to try to appease her or say something irritating. True to form, he did both.

"We're escaping for our lives, and you want to give some guy a bit of money when his insurance probably takes care of it?"

"If he has insurance." She raised her voice above a whisper.

"Okay." Anderson eyed the man's front porch "I'll slip something into the slot in his door. Once I come back, I'm going to put the truck in neutral and roll it down the hill to the end of the street. You'll need to follow me out at that point."

When she narrowed her eyes, he sighed, knowing another demand would follow.

"How much money will you leave him?" she asked.

He shook his head. "Enough. Okay? He'll have enough."

She drew in a shaky breath. "Okay."

Anderson started the van once more and reached for the duffle bag. Once he stuffed a couple of rolls of cash in his pocket and quietly exited the van, he whispered, "Get ready to go."

After they dumped the van outside the city limits, they drove a few more hours on back roads to avoid traffic cameras toward the state line of his home state.

When Anderson crossed into west Texas, he released a ragged breath while fighting the urge to relax. Though the vast skies and open plains symbolized the comforts of home, he still had to keep up his guard. Finally, they pulled into the parking lot of a no-name motel.

As he parked the truck, Savannah sent him a sideways look. *This place could be the lead story on the five-o'clock news.*

She glanced at the exterior, wondering what kind of nefarious activity could have taken place and scanned the parking lot for anyone or anything to confirm her suspicions.

"We're not really staying here. Are we?" She grimaced.

"The less security, the better. And, I bet the manager can be paid off to keep our stay private." He flashed a few fifty dollar bills before exiting the car and jogging toward the entrance.

Savannah eyed the grungy exterior. If it looked this dingy on the outside, just how much worse would it be on the inside?

Anderson exited the building when a scantily clad woman rested her hip against the side of the truck and blocked his access to open the driver's door. Although Savannah couldn't hear the exchange between the two, it was clear he'd just been propositioned. Instead of turning her away, he pulled a fifty dollar bill from his pocket.

After Anderson slid into the driver's seat, Savannah sent him a curious stare.

"You gave her money?"

"Yeah, so?" He put the truck in reverse and pulled around the back of the motel.

"Not that she probably doesn't need it..." Savannah was always for helping those in need, but this was a new side to Anderson. "But why?"

"I hate to see someone that desperate." His features softened. "I gave her some cash and asked her to go home for the night."

"That was nice," she said with a look of appreciation.

"It's a dangerous world out there."

"Speaking of..." Savannah eyed the rusted hotel door as Anderson killed the engine.

He slipped from his seat to unload some of their supplies and looked at her from across the hood.

"Would you rather sleep out in the Texas desert with the scorpions and the heat?"

She shrugged, unsure of which was worse.

Once inside, she looked around the room and wrinkled her nose, making a face. "I've seen reports on these places. They never wash the linens or clean the bathrooms."

Anderson tossed a couple of sleeping bags in her direction. "Spread these out on top of your mattress."

"Both?" She laid one on the bed with a look. "You mean your future-telling ability didn't show you that you'd be sleeping on the ground? We're not sleeping in the same bed, cowboy." She tossed his sleeping bag at his feet with a smirk.

Anderson chuckled. "I wasn't suggesting anything. I just thought we both could get a good night's sleep. I've been camping out for most of the summer until Danny called me to rescue you."

She sent him a stink-eye, which Anderson ignored. "Ever since - I've been on high alert. Not to mention recovering from a black eye." He wiggled his eyebrows, and for the first time, the muscles across his face didn't scream in protest.

Savannah rolled her eyes and let out a sound that nearly resembled a chuckle. She studied his face with curiosity, noticing that his bruise had faded over time. She let out a sigh, thinking she missed the dangerous look it had given him.

"What are you thinking?" His dimples deepened.

She spun on her heels to avoid the thoughts that his dimples evoked. "Are you saying you can't read my mind?"

"Look! It's not..."

When he reached for her arm, he spun her around so fast that she stumbled back and fell into his chest. Immediately, he lost his train of thought as her shining eyes sparked with desire.

Her breath hitched, and suddenly, it was as if all the air had evaporated from the room.

"It's not like that." He swallowed, his voice barely a whisper.

Savannah focused on the vein in Anderson's neck that pulsed with the beat of his heart. If she tipped her chin even a fraction – she'd be unable to keep from rising to her toes and starting something she couldn't finish. She closed her eyes and took a step back. Kissing him would only confuse the issue - which was to stay alive.

It took everything Anderson had not to pull her back within his grasp and claim her tempting lips. When she stepped away, he rubbed a hand across his jaw and mentally counted to ten to clear his mind of how her gentle curves pressed against his body.

"I'm sorry," she apologized and sat at the end of the bed.

"No, I'm sorry." He started but realized they might not have been apologizing for the same thing.

"For what?" She sent him a look of confusion.

Unwilling to make it any more awkward than it already was, he said, "You first."

"I just meant that...I know it was hard trusting me with everything you've been through. The fact that you did means a lot. I was not trying to belittle what you're going through because I, for one, would be going out of my mind."

Anderson sat on the bed next to her.

"At the beginning, it seemed like I was, but lately, being near you has broken open some sort of dam. Visions are coming faster than ever before. Before you – they were cryptic and confusing."

Savannah melted just a little. "And after?"

"When you hit me, it wasn't your punch that took me down...it was the vision that accompanied it and the sound of your voice."

He looked at her lips once more. As the tip of her pink tongue darted to the corner of her mouth, he quickly drew his attention elsewhere.

"So, I do hit like a girl?" She chuckled.

He turned back to her with a grin. "You pack a punch. It gave me quite a bruise. Don't underestimate your strength."

He let out a half-laugh and touched the area around the eye that had almost healed.

"But having you near me, Sav. It's opened something up inside me. My visions are taking shape. I get these – they're almost like signals." He dragged in a breath. "The dreams I had of you before we met have changed."

She leaned in, batting her eyelashes. "You dreamt of me before we met?"

He dropped his gaze, unsure if revealing anything more was wise.

"No. Yes - maybe."

She poked him in the leg. "You did."

"I'm not sure if I need to say anything else." He shook his head. Anything more might be too much for her to handle, but then, she leaned in with those luminous eyes, and he lost his senses.

He visualized her as a child and knew her father was likely never be able to deny her anything. He also knew as long as she was looking at him that way – neither could he.

He drew in a deep breath. "Okay, brace yourself."

A slight frown claimed her brow before her determined stare gave him the assurance and permission he needed.

"I had a vision of someone dragging you away." Anderson searched her eyes. "Your screams permeated my mind as I saw your hands grabbing for anything you could find for security."

Savannah's eyes widened. The sober look that crossed her face pulled at Anderson's conscience. He slipped from the end of the bed to kneel at her feet.

He tucked a few stray locks of her hair behind her ear and searched her eyes. "But that vision went away." He stroked her jaw with his thumb. "It's not going to happen."

She bit her lips from the inside and lowered her lids, wanting with every touch to lean into him and enjoy how his caress sent her insides reeling, yet his words overrode her senses. More than anything, she was terrified to ask what came next.

"I don't..." She let out a ragged breath and opened her eyes. "How do you know?"

Savannah stood to put some distance between the two of them. She crossed the room and came to a stop at the window as she stared out to the almost deserted parking lot. Anderson lifted from his knees and debated about what to do next.

When she finally turned, she asked, "You still need to fill me in on who we are running from. How do we know they won't take me? Or Benny's men won't catch up with me?"

"That image is gone. Something we did altered your – our course. What I used to think was a curse because of how your screams haunted me at night is now becoming quite the asset."

"What have you seen that's changed?"

Anderson shook his head. The new vision was enough to keep him up at night, wondering what it meant. How could he explain it to her?

"Let's start with what we're up against first," he said.

She eyed him with distrust. "Somebody does get to me – don't they?"

"They get to us. I'm always with you. In my vision, we're both alive." He crossed the room and took her hands in his. "I promise I won't let anything happen to you."

At that moment, she realized how much he reminded her of her father. Anderson had his warmth and tough-as-nails attitude while being quick on his feet. And, as much as she hated to admit it – he was just as trustworthy.

If Anderson told her nothing would happen to her, she could believe him.

"I can see that."

"You're having visions now, too?" A slow grin swept across his face.

His playful demeanor was enough to rid her of her nerves. With one wink from Anderson, a warmth that spread through her chest bringing her center.

"Yeah, something like that." She dropped her gaze to

stare at their joined hands. How could something as simple as his touch send her heart rate through the roof? Savannah withdrew her hand and swallowed.

"You said these visions are becoming an asset? Did you ever think of them as a gift?" She stared at the ground, avoiding his gaze.

"If they are – then, they're the gift that keeps on giving." He chuckled and blew out a frustrated breath.

"No, seriously." She finally made eye contact. "Are you familiar with the prophets in the Bible who had the gift of dreams or visions? Daniel had many dreams of the future."

"I highly doubt God considers me important enough to transform into a prophet." Anderson shrugged.

"I'm not saying you're a prophet." She frowned. "Not everyone that is given the gift of waking dreams or visions is a prophet. I know that those of us who are faithful are all blessed with gifts. Some are more prevalent than others, like yours."

His eyes narrowed at the concept. "So, my accident was a gift?"

Savannah drew her knees to her chest and wrapped her arms around them with a sigh. "Well, maybe it was needed to bring on your visions. You said they were becoming an asset, right? Who is to say your visions aren't from God? I think He's trying to help you sort out what to do next."

"Listen, Savannah. That's a great theory, but I'm more concerned with how to manage them than find out where they came from." He stood to peek out the curtains, before turning back to her.

"These people who are after me – and you, by association, put Benny and his people to shame. I took this job to protect you from a low-life criminal, and because of me, you're in over your head with an organization that has no rules or boundaries. There are no limits to their power."

Savannah winced. Spiritual gifts or not, Anderson was right. They seemed to be in a heap of trouble.

"Just who are they?" she asked.

"I know who they used to be." He sighed and pinched the bridge of his nose. "Danny and I were brought in undercover to an off-the-books organization called Odyssey."

"I thought you were CIA, right?"

"Technically, we're still with the CIA. Without knowing what we're up against..." He paused. "I need to regroup with Danny. We need to know who's after us before I know who to trust."

Anderson stood and paced. "Telling you any of this could put your life in danger, but since they're after me – you're already there. I might as well prepare you for what could be ahead."

She lifted a hand. "Let me get this straight. You both were undercover in an undisclosed group? I'm confused. Did you work for good guys ratting out bad guys or ..."

Anderson gave a short nod. "It was an off-the-books group that started about five years back as an extension of the CIA. Only an elite set of recruits were chosen based on their test scores."

"Academic ones?"

He cocked his head and squinted. "Sort of, yes. What they were really looking for was something more. Like, our capacity for certain skills – like shooting, recovery, hunting the opposition, computer skills, and psychological tests - those sorts of things." He tried to keep it as simple as possible and waited for his words to sink in before he continued.

"Danny and I scored well in all categories, yet our ethics

and personality scores didn't align with a certain division within Odyssey. We were assigned to what was called the Retractors. We were a rescue team, highly trained to retrieve people from areas our government wasn't authorized to be in or in areas that no one dared enter."

She crossed her arms and waited.

"There was a secondary compartment to Odyssey – the Redactors."

"And what did they do?"

"When you see a report on the news and words have been blacked out or redacted?"

Savannah stood and nodded, resting her hip against the dresser. When he didn't answer right away, she motioned with her hands for him to continue.

"Well, Danny and I saved people. The other side of the organization - didn't."

"Mercenaries?"

He shrugged. "Yeah, but not at first. They were primarily snipers assigned to take care of persons of interest who were considered a threat to our country. It didn't take long before their scope of what was considered a threat changed. Our boss at the CIA suspected the Director at Odyssey had let the power go to his head."

"The lady on the monitor."

"No, Director Sanger. Initially, they thought he took bribes and sent tactical teams to eliminate whoever had the highest price on their head. What started as a team of operatives trained to take out dangerous targets became a sniper-for-hire program within our government."

Anderson noticed her wide eyes and nodded. "Yeah. Exactly. Danny and I were instructed to find the evidence against Director Sanger and shut it down."

His chest heaved with a sigh as he contemplated what

could have been. "The targets were supposedly acquired based on the government's need to shut down certain factions within foreign groups, like in Iran."

"Like ISIS."

"Yes, but two years into the program, something changed. Although there were enough justifiable hits to keep the department from coming under fire, we observed a break in protocol."

"Like what?"

"Well, every team has a signature – something that you recognize if you look closely. When analyzing data, we realized a signature was noticeable within what were supposed to be accidental deaths of private citizens – people who were not a threat, here and abroad."

"Why would they need to be taken out?"

"Some had ties to certain political parties or organizations. Some were on the fast track to be in power in other areas of the world. If you looked from a big-picture view, people were targeted depending on the groups they aligned with."

"So, someone at Odyssey wanted to control certain factions and eliminated people to make sure the world stayed within their window of opportunity?"

"Yeah, basically, but it wasn't as obvious as it sounds. Our boss at the agency saw a pattern and sent us in to find out who at Odyssey had been corrupted, thinking it was Sanger."

"And was it?" Her eyes widened.

"We thought so based on the data, but we couldn't trace the source. We thought we found the smoking gun, coded emails sent to Sanger from an anonymous server. But we couldn't break the code to know if the messages meant anything."

"Since you were injured and on leave, how did Danny's role in this play out? Did he find the missing piece? Is that why you're running? Did Director Sanger find out?"

"See. That's just it. Other than a few emails which didn't really point to anything sinister, there wasn't proof that Sanger was dirty. In fact, Danny believed that Sanger was clean. He has these gut instincts..."

"Oh, I know about those. He knows things that make you shake your head. Sometimes, I wonder if he has an inside track to people's minds."

"Exactly!" Anderson's face lit up. "Anyways, he thought Sanger was truly trying to improve the world by saving one person at a time, by taking out a real threat to better the world. The evidence could have pointed to him, but with Danny's gut screaming at him the way it was – we thought Sanger was being set up to take the fall. We couldn't prove it just yet, but we were getting close."

Anderson rubbed his chin with a far off look. "On my last assignment-"

"When you were injured?" Savannah asked.

Anderson nodded. "It was a simple grab in a non-conflict area. It was easy. Too easy."

He stopped mid-pace and cut his eyes.

"It was too easy..." His voice fell.

Savannah's brow furrowed as he worked through whatever he had to come to terms with. When he finally spoke, he was no longer speaking to her, but himself.

"Danny and I were supposed to transport the target together." He shook a finger. "At the last minute, he got food poisoning, and I told him to stay behind to cover our tracks. No one else knew that, though. As I shuttled our target to an undisclosed area, my SUV was broadsided by another vehicle. The next thing I remember is waking up in the hospital."

Anderson frowned. He stared into the distance as if sorting out memories.

"What is it?" Savannah interrupted his thoughts.

"Maybe we were getting too close and now this," Anderson said, waving his hands toward the interior of the room. "Plus, Director Sanger's mysterious exit."

He shook his head while he scanned the room. "The night before my accident, Danny convinced me he could approach Sanger. He hoped Sanger would help us dig deeper into some of the redactor team files. We could only go so far without inside help, and knowing what we did about Sanger, Danny hoped he'd be our Hail Mary. I just hoped Danny wasn't wrong."

"Only..." Anderson took a deep breath. "It looks like we might have got him killed. And, now, for some reason, they're coming after us."

"But you don't know who the bad guy is."

"Bad guy?" He chuckled at her expense.

"Okay, Agent Evans. I don't know what to call it. I work with bridezillas, not guerillas or spies. Although, some of my brides could have given that creepy lady on your monitor a run for her money. Don't mess with a debutante and her dress, or there will be a price to pay."

"Hey." He put his hands up and grinned. "I believe you."

"So, if whoever is responsible for Sanger's death is coming after you – that says something."

"Oh yeah?" His eyes twinkled, thinking how much he liked bantering with the likes of Savannah Miles. She wasn't just a beautiful face. Goodness knows, he had already figured that out.

"Yeah." She shifted the side of her mouth to make a face. "But what *does* it say?"

Anderson's face sobered. "It means they believe their identities have been compromised. The only way they would think that is if Sanger uncovered something before he was taken out."

He hoped his gut wasn't leading him down the wrong path. If he were to betting man, and he usually was, he'd believe it was an accurate assumption.

Savannah watched his solemn face transform into one filled with energy. It was as if a switch had flipped. Although exciting to watch his mind at work – the prospect of what it meant for them was daunting.

"Who, though?" She grabbed a bottled water from the ice chest and tossed one to Anderson before opening her own.

"That's what Danny and I still have to figure out, but this new Director is caught up in it. I'm sure of it."

She lifted a hand and made a face. "If we find Danny! If these people haven't found him yet."

Anderson shook his head. "There's always a backup plan if we get separated. Just like we are, he should be on route to a safe house that's off the radar from any organization."

"What?!" She jumped to the bed and bounced a few times before hopping down and punching him in the shoulder multiple times. "Why wouldn't you tell me? Where? How?"

When Savannah gave him a light shove, he held up his hands.

"Easy, woman!" He took a step back. "It's one we purchased as a safety net a few years back when we entered Odyssey. I really won't know until he gets there, but he's a big boy. He should make it okay."

Savannah's brow furrowed. She wrapped her arms around her midsection and exhaled.

"What if he doesn't make it?" she whispered.

"One step at a time, okay?"

When she closed her eyes, he wanted nothing more than to pull her into his chest for reassurance and hold her until the tension drained from her shoulders. Instead, he nudged her with a shoulder and sent her a lazy grin.

"Besides, who do you think you're dealing with here? Danny's a rock star. Who do you think trained me?"

Savannah rolled her eyes with feigned sarcasm. "The guy who went down with one punch. That's reassuring."

DANNY STONE UNDERSTOOD it was a risk to stop for a night's sleep, but he also needed to recharge. Lucky for him, he had a knack of always staying one step ahead of trouble. Living the life of an operative was natural as breathing. He had his instincts to thank for helping him stay alive for all these years. He wasn't about to doubt them now.

Although this time he'd barely escaped being shot up like Swiss cheese, he still thanked his lucky stars for his good fortune. Odyssey had tracked him to the motel on the east side of Texas and might have trapped him if Danny hadn't paid for three rooms instead of one.

Just minutes before a loud commotion sounded down the hall, the tell-tale sign of his palms burning had him on high alert. He was overcome with a sense of urgency as though he were covered in a blanket of fire, spurring him into action.

When a crash sounded nearby, he looped his arms through his backpack and reached to secure his gun. Danny glanced over his shoulder at the entrance to his room. It was barricaded by whatever wasn't bolted down.

Within minutes, the sounds of wood splintering into pieces came from a few doors down the hall. He shoved on his ball cap and crossed the floor for his balcony.

It was a gamble, not knowing which room they'd check first. Heck, depending on how many teams were out there, they might split up to check multiple places simultaneously. If Danny were heading the team, he would have, but he had a backup plan for any outcome. Thankfully, no one had captured him – yet.

Sounds of feet pounding down the hall had his heart beating in double time. He checked over his shoulder and tugged on the bedsheet he'd tied to the steel bars of the balcony last night. Once he was sure it was secure, Danny scaled down the side of the building.

A loud crack sounded from above, followed by yells. The cheap desk and chair Danny used to block his doorway were serving their purpose, stalling Odyssey and barely giving him enough time to escape.

Danny ran around a corner and flattened his back against an exterior wall out of sight. With seconds to spare, a man's voice sounded from his balcony.

"No, ma'am. He's not here." Danny frowned at the sound of the man's voice.

Ma'am? Since when did anyone from his team answer to anyone other Director Sanger?

Danny tapped the camera function on his phone and flipped it to selfie mode. He slid his phone unnoticed around the corner to get a glimpse of who was coming after him.

After he snapped a couple of shots and zoomed in on their faces, he let out a slow breath. He recognized the pair of agents that stood on his balcony. Underwood and Blaire were two of the fiercest agents on the team.

"Yes, ma'am." Blaire touched the comms in his ear. "He escaped down the balcony before we got to his room. We've got teams in place, and all exits in town are being watched. We'll find him."

Danny leaned his head against the wall with a sigh. He glanced at the parking lot where he parked the car he'd stolen last night. It wouldn't do him any good to drive it out of town now.

It was then that he saw a truck stop across the street. His eyes gleamed as he ran toward a large semi that had just rumbled to life.

SAVANNAH FOUGHT the dread that continued to creep up the base of her spine. The thought of anything happening to her cousin sent her mind into a tailspin.

It wasn't just worrying about his well-being that plagued her. If anything happened to Danny, she would truly be alone. Savannah's chest constricted as panic clawed its way through the depths of her soul.

Anderson sensed her mood shift. He could tell as she fidgeted with a cross pendant that hung around her neck that she was struggling to keep it together. He placed his hands on either side of her face, forcing her to look at him.

"Breathe."

She squeezed her eyelids shut and inhaled.

"Deep breath out. Come on. You can do it," he coaxed.

Between Anderson's soothing voice and a few calming breaths, Savannah finally exhaled with ease. She looked at her hands, which were still shaking. He must have noticed it too because he slid his palms from her neck and down her arms to cover her fingers. Savannah shivered in response.

"You okay?" he asked, looking at her through his thick lashes.

She nodded yes, yet with the way he was looking at her, she was anything but.

"Good. Besides, Danny is not the one you have to worry about, Smiles."

In a flash, she forgot her anxiety and sent him a look that would send most men running for the hills.

"I'm gonna kill him for telling you."

"It's a cute nickname." He grinned.

"He's dead to me."

"See? That's the spirit." He grinned. "Besides, the only person you really have to worry about is my niece, Lani."

Savannah wrinkled her brow and cut her eyes at him.

"I didn't tell you?"

"You seem to have a habit of that." She crossed her arms.

When Anderson grinned, Savannah caught her breath. He was nothing short of cover-worthy. It was then that she realized he was still talking. She snapped back to reality, focusing on his every word.

"My family will be there too. So, you'll have the honor of meeting my mom and dad. Also, there's my kid sister, Alexis, and her new husband, Tyler. And, my niece, Lani, who swears she talks to our dearly departed grandmother."

Savannah cocked her head and laughed.

"Of course. Of course, she does. Spiritual gifts obviously run in the family." She nudged him with her shoulder. "You're becoming a really good distraction. Has anyone ever told you that?"

Her words lit his heart with a warmth that was quickly becoming a habit. It took everything he had to restrain from kissing her soft lips.

As his gaze fell from her mouth to the bed, he imagined a bath full of ice water and visualized submerging into it. He dragged in a breath and reached for his sleeping bag. "Time to turn in. We have a long drive ahead of us tomorrow."

Savannah was sure if she should be disappointed or relieved that the moment passed. She exhaled as she grabbed her backpack and said, "I'm just gonna clean up."

In the five minutes it took to brush her teeth and change into a t-shirt, she exited the bathroom to find Anderson shirtless and asleep at the foot of the bed. He'd already unrolled her sleeping bag and spread it the width of the bed.

A mixture of gratitude and desire swirled through her as she tiptoed around him and settled on the bed. His even timber filled the room as he slept. She turned on her side with a sigh, knowing she wouldn't sleep a wink.

10

At first light, Savannah heard him rise from the floor and close the bathroom door behind him. She opened her eyes at the sound of the water as it barely trickled from the rusted showerhead.

She must have dozed for a few more minutes because before she realized it - she awakened to the sound of an electric razor buzzing from the other side of the thin bathroom door.

She shielded her view of the morning light as it streamed through the curtains and searched the room for a clock. She noticed one on the dresser across the room, but it was either broken, or Anderson had unplugged it. Either way, it wasn't like she had a schedule to keep.

She rolled to her side and sat up, careful not to touch the comforter beneath the sleeping bag.

"Great," she mumbled as she stood. "They'd better have a coffee maker that works around here somewhere."

As she searched the room, Anderson stepped from the bathroom, wearing nothing but a towel. If that wasn't enough to send her hormones racing, then his new appearance was. He looked like he was fresh from boot camp.

Savannah lifted to her toes and ran her hand along the thin stubble that covered his head.

"You shaved your head." She marveled at how much he now looked like a younger version of Clint Eastwood.

"Yeah." Anderson barely got out. Standing this close had them both in dangerous territory, but he stayed as though glued in place, his eyes transfixed on hers.

"I like it." Her pupils dilated, eclipsing her honey-colored eyes.

Savannah should have taken a step back, but the energy in the room was so thick that she couldn't.

When the phone rang, they jumped apart. Savannah bit her lip and internally berated herself for allowing her hormones to run wild.

Anderson reached for the phone. He eyed her with concern as he listened, only muttering a few 'uh-huh's' and a 'thanks' before he hung up and rushed to the bathroom to slip on some jeans. When he came out, he was placing a gun into his waistband with a determined look that sent shivers down her spine.

"Who called?" She pulled on her jeans in preparation. She knew that look. It meant they were about to be on the move.

He pulled a gray t-shirt over his broad chest as he started for the front door.

"The girl from last night," he said in a rush.

"The prostitute?" she asked, confused.

He nodded. "Stay here and get everything ready to go once I'm back."

"You can't leave me here. What's going on?"

"She said a couple of guys were here a few minutes ago,

flashing our pictures and she sent them down the road saying we were here...but had already left."

"How does she know? I thought you sent her home."

His mouth flattened. "I guess this *is* her home. She was on her way out the door when they approached her. She was grateful for what I did for her last night and covered for us."

"How could they know where we are?" Her mouth parted. "You've been so careful..." She peeked through a crack in the curtain.

"They have ways...even as careful as we've been. Stay here."

He pulled the curtains tight and sent her a look, much like a father would a disobedient child.

She raised a brow, muttering, "Not like I have much choice."

After he slipped outside, she shoved her belongings into her pack. She reached for her toothbrush to brush her teeth when she spotted the sleeping bags and wrinkled her nose. Surely, Anderson didn't expect her to pack them. After they'd been on the germ-infested linens and grimy carpet – she hoped not.

Savannah dropped to a chair with a sigh. Solace was in short supply these days as worry clouded her mind wherever they went.

As she was a praying girl, she did the only thing she knew to do. She retrieved her Bible from her backpack and opened it. The pages fell open to the book of Philippians.

She looked at the moldy ceiling. "Philippians 4:13. I can do all things..." She smiled. "You know exactly what to say to me, don't you, God?"

At that moment, Anderson rushed in eyes afire with an

energy that she now recognized as a passion for his work. Even in the midst of danger, he was raring to go.

"I got a look at their vehicle when they left the parking lot. It was Odyssey, alright." He grabbed a few bags and tossed them into the truck bed. Once everything was stowed, he offered her his hand.

"You ready? They could be back any minute. Luckily, for us, there are no security cameras here. We can get a jump start if we hurry."

Savannah slipped her Bible and toothbrush into her cinch pack and wrinkled her nose. "I suppose we won't be stopping for coffee."

Anderson motioned toward the top of the truck, where a cup of steaming coffee sat on the roof. Savannah retrieved it and inhaled. The pleasant aroma instantly struck a chord.

"I could cry." She smirked at him from under her lashes. "My hero."

"I try, but we'll have to share. There wasn't time to grab two cups, and it's straight-up black. No sugar or cream, princess." He winked.

Savannah ignored his attempts to get under her skin.

"As long as it's caffeinated, I'm good." She inhaled once more before taking a sip.

He took one last glance at the room, making sure nothing was left behind. When he noticed the sleeping bags, he sent her a look.

"They're gross." She drew in her shoulders as if chilled.

"Okay. I'll get us new ones if needed."

"Maybe we could stop somewhere tonight with at least a one-star rating?" she asked.

Anderson took the coffee from Savannah before slipping in the driver's seat. He took a sip and placed it in the cup holder before hot-wiring the truck once more.

"Tonight, we're crashing at a friend's."

As they passed the signs for I-40, she asked, "Are they close by?"

"They're about three hundred miles southeast of here."

She sent him a look, asking, "Which way is that?"

"Southeast?"

"Yeah."

He shook his head and put his foot on the gas, spurring the old truck forward.

"It's this way." He pointed out of his window and grinned at her. "You just sit back and get some rest, okay?"

"I'm just going to enjoy my coffee and let you do the heavy lifting, Agent Evans." She took a sip, letting the warm liquid roll down her throat with a moan of pleasure.

Anderson glanced at her from the corner of his eye and shook his head. She was something else alright. Now, he just had to get them safely to Tawni's place without incident.

DIRECTOR BRENNEN WALKED into the control room as her analysts worked overtime, studying maps and coordinates.

"Anything?" She frowned at Franks as he stepped in beside her.

"There was a string of stolen cars reported from east Arizona and Kansas." He pointed to a monitor that pinpointed various incidents. "When connecting the dots from both Danny's and Anderson's last known locations, we could determine what direction they're heading."

"If the thefts are related to our targets," she said.

"We ruled out the reports that had arrests accompanying them... or the vehicles found within the same city of origin. It left us a trail of breadcrumbs that pinpointed to our agents, ma'am. Looks like both are heading to Texas."

"Give me an update on Agent Stone!" Brennen hollered across the room to a senior analyst.

"We tracked him to a hotel, but his trail went cold."

She turned her impenetrable eyes on Franks.

"Failure will not be tolerated." Her thin lips flattened.

Franks looked to his team of IT geeks who were typing furiously at their work stations. It was just a matter of time.

"Look." He waved his hand. "Based on their calculations – data input, ideal locations where one would lay low, minimal security zones where they would stay off-camera, routes, hotels–"

"Franks, I want results, not excuses." Director Brennen crossed her arms.

"And you'll get them, ma'am."

"We got a lead on Agent Evans at a hotel!" Someone from his team yelled.

Suddenly, a flurry of activity followed. A group of analysts collectively yelled in their headsets to the teams in the field as they continued to search the camera feeds.

Director Brennon sneered across the room as a few others hollered in celebration at the news.

"Find them!" she yelled over those who were barking orders in their headsets. "And Franks?"

"Yes, ma'am."

"Report back to me as soon as you know something." She spun for her office.

"My pleasure, ma'am," Franks said at her back.

Dangerous Visions 107

THE SMELL of stale beer and smoke rolled from the Brass & Buckle Alehouse. Savannah studied the dingy exterior, wondering when the last time the business had a remodel or if the owner cared.

The bronzed lettering on the sign looking to have once been a beacon, but those days were long gone. Now, only a dime bulb shone at the edge while a few others flickered during the afternoon sun.

"We're staying here?" Her mouth twisted with distaste. "I'm not a prima donna or anything, but please tell me this is just a bathroom break." She clamped her lips and sent Anderson a look of hope.

His dimples deepened. "Nope. This is it. Grab your bag."

He tossed it to her from across the hood and locked up the truck.

"Once we're inside, I'll find Tawni and get a key to her garage in back. She keeps it cleared out for me – just in case."

Savannah shook her head. He had friends on call at a moment's notice in case he had to hide? Who lived like that? Anderson and Danny did apparently.

"Okay, but I actually have to use the ladies' room. If there is such a thing in there."

His chuckle did nothing to improve her mood. "For someone who's not a prima donna, you're sure sounding high maintenance."

"No, I'm not. But everyone has their limit." Savannah

rolled her eyes, thinking of the roach-infested motel they'd left behind.

"Don't judge a book by its cover. It's a respectable place." He rounded the front of the truck to join her near the front door of the building. "You'll see."

Savannah grumbled as she slipped her arms into her small bag, before trailing him toward the entryway. He ushered her inside and nodded toward the back corner.

Inside wasn't much better than the exterior. The dark, dingy vibe screamed dive bar, but much to her surprise, the diverse crowd was anything but expected. She narrowed her eyes as they adjusted to the light.

It was then she noticed the crowd was a lot less intimidating than she'd first assumed. They spanned the gamut from bikers to corporate types and interacted as though they'd known each other for years.

"The bathrooms are at the back of the building by the stage." Anderson nudged her forward. "I'll be at the bar. Come find me when you're done."

As she slipped through the crowd, Anderson observed a few men trailing her with their eyes. He scanned the room just to be safe. Even though he assumed the patrons here weren't a threat, he waited until she was near the women's restroom before searching the bar for his friend.

He waved down the nearest cocktail waitress and asked, "Where's Tawni?"

The waitress motioned toward the stage and continued on her way, just as Tawni's smooth voice filled the sound system.

"Hey, ya'll. Welcome to open mic at the Brass & Buckle."

A few claps erupted around him as she continued.

"We've got a great line-up, but don't let that stop you if

you want your shot at the cash prize. We always welcome newcomers."

A collective murmur and a few cheers escaped the crowd as she beamed in return.

Anderson slid onto a barstool and beamed, waiting for his friend and a former assignment to notice him. A few years back, he'd rescued her from an underground extreme fighting organization in Thailand.

When on stage – no matter the reason - Tawni was in her element. Although she'd always been a fighter, she'd come a long way from the first time he laid eyes on her.

When Anderson finally caught her eye, her face lit up. She gave a small wave in his direction before wrapping up her speech.

"First up, we have Brandon and his old guitar singing an original song." She waved someone to the stage. "Give him some love, people. Take it away, Brandon."

Tawni whispered something to a co-worker after stepping from the stage. She checked her phone and sent what looked to be a text message before ushering her employee to a table by the stage. She gave him some quick instruction before making her way through the crowd with open arms. As soon as she was within reach, Anderson wrapped her into a bear hug.

That's how Savannah found them, holding each other with familiarity. The jealousy that coiled its way into the depths of her belly not only startled her, but it left her with more dislike of this place than when she entered.

She eyed Tawni, whose long black curls lay perfectly against her generous curves. Her features were nothing short of captivating.

Savannah slid next to Anderson and cleared her throat. Anderson dropped his arms from around Tawni and was about to introduce Savannah when Tawni let out a string of curse words.

"What?" Anderson asked with a look of confusion.

Savannah narrowed her eyes with distrust.

As Tawni's dark chocolate eyes filled with regret, Savannah narrowed hers. If Savannah hadn't already taken an immediate dislike for this woman for the fact that she'd wrapped herself around Anderson and seemed flawless – Tawni's response to her would have been enough.

"I'd say nice to meet you, but usually people don't swear when they meet me." Savannah's features hardened.

"No, it's not that," Tawni said, pulling out her phone. "If I'd known you were with Anderson."

"What? You wouldn't have thrown yourself at him?" Savannah blurted.

"You think I was throwing myself at him?" Tawni put a hand on her hip. "Oh, honey. You're so far off the mark."

Tawni's attitude subsided when she thought about the actions she just put in place. When a shadow crossed Tawni's face, Anderson narrowed his gaze at her with laser-like precision.

"What's going on, Tawni?" He crossed his arms and waited.

"Well." She paused. "See for yourself." Tawni offered her cell phone over and winced.

"What have you got yourself into now?" he asked as he turned the phone over to read what was on the screen.

Tawni shrank back as the color drained from Anderson's face.

"Tell me you haven't done anything with this." His ragged voice dropped an octave.

When Tawni said nothing in return, Savannah reached for the phone.

"What is it?" When Savannah scrolled through the app on Tawni's phone, she brought her hand to her throat with a gasp. "Why is there a photo of me on your phone?"

Tawni sent Anderson a look of apology. "It's an app used on the dark web for people who are looking to move information or people. When someone is looking for a person, they post it here. It's kind of like the Most Wanted posters you see in government buildings. Only..." She shrugged.

"These posts are used to find innocent people." Savannah glared at Tawni, whose face filled with regret.

"Well, they're not all innocent." Tawni fumbled to retrieve her phone as Savannah held it behind her back.

Savannah spun on her heel and continued scrolling through Tawni's cell phone. She froze in her tracks when she found some of herself.

There were a variety of photos from her Nashville magazine photoshoot to her profile photos from social media. There were even some sketches of what she might look like if she altered her appearance. One, in particular, seemed dangerously close to how she appeared today. "Dang it!" Savannah exclaimed before glancing at the instructions below her photos. She looked at Tawni in horror. "The instructions say to add a location if seen."

"Tell me you didn't." Anderson grabbed the phone and opened the location file on her app to discover they'd been compromised.

"Tawni!" Anderson glared at his friend.

"What?!" She held up her hands. "I didn't see you two come in together! How was I supposed to know you were even coming today, let alone bringing someone?"

Tawni walked behind the bar, grabbed a beer, and twisted the lid off before taking a drink. She set it down with a thud as she dropped her head in shame.

"I'm sorry, Anderson." Her face filled with regret.

Savannah lowered to the barstool across from Tawni and cradled her head in her hands.

"Great. This is just great." She raised her head and groaned. "It's got to be Benny's guys, which means we've gotta get out of here."

"Do you know where they're traveling from?" He broke eye contact with Savannah and redirected it across the bar at Tawni.

Tawni shrugged. "Usually, when one of these goes out, the response time has varied. Normally, I would get a message asking me for more details, but not today."

"That doesn't sound good." A sense of dread overcame him.

"Maybe they didn't get it. That's good, right?" Savannah sat up a bit straighter.

Anderson laid a hand on Savannah's shoulder.

"We should still get going. I don't like the feel of this." He scanned the room before pulling Savannah to her feet to leave.

Tawni sighed and stepped from behind the bar.

"I'm sorry. I had no idea."

Anderson stared at the ground. When he looked up to meet Tawni's eyes, what she saw in them had her taking a step back.

"Anderson-" Tawni started.

"No. I didn't pull you out of a bad situation so that you could get involved with something like this." He pointed at her phone. "Delete that app and cut your ties before you get mixed up with something you can't handle."

"It's good money." She rested her hand on Anderson's bicep.

"At what price?" Savannah narrowed her eyes at Tawni's

touch. "You could have gotten me killed tonight! I'm just lucky I have this guy to watch my back."

Savannah took a step closer to lay her hand on Anderson's other arm and sent Tawni a challenging stare.

Anderson looked to Savannah and hid a grin. If he didn't know any better, he would think she was laying claim to him.

Tawni blinked at the challenge in Savannah's eyes but didn't have time to respond because a handful of men, looking as if they were on a mission, entered her bar.

"Ugh. Don't turn around," Tawni muttered. "I said, don't look." She scolded Savannah, who almost glanced over her shoulder. "There's trouble walking in."

Savannah closed her eyes. Fear clawed at her spine inch by inch until it seemed she would suffocate. She swallowed, hoping to keep it at bay. Fear would do nothing but cloud her judgment.

Anderson's gaze immediately swung toward the entrance, where five large men wearing jackets paused and scanned the room as if on a mission.

"I take it they're not friends of yours?" He spun back to face Tawni.

"No." She shook her head. "And with the way they're peering through the crowd, I'd say they're searching for your girl."

Anderson ducked, pulling Savannah to his side, blocking her from view.

"We need to create a distraction. As far as I can tell - the post on your phone said nothing about Savannah traveling with anyone."

She shook her head in response. "He's right." She turned to Savannah. "The post on my app only spoke of finding you."

Savannah's mind spun with the options as Anderson thought out loud.

"We need to split up. Tawni, can you keep Savannah safe in a back office or something so I can work the room and take these guys out quietly one by one?"

Tawni reached for Savannah's hand. "Come on. I've got a place for you in back."

Savannah shot her a look as if she were speaking a foreign language and yanked her hand from reach.

"Are you crazy? You just alerted the devil to pick me off, and you think I'll go with you? No way." She crossed her arms and stood her ground.

Anderson licked his lips and took one more look over his shoulder.

"Smiles, don't be stubborn."

"I said, don't call me that." Savannah gritted her teeth.

"We don't have time for this. I trust Tawni with my life, and if she says she'll hide you away, she will."

"No, there has to be another way." Savannah stared daggers at Tawni, who replied in kind.

Just then, a few bars of music sounded through the speakers and soared to a crescendo. Savannah's eyes gleamed with recognition before her mouth thinned with determination.

Anderson sent her a sideways glance as his stomach twisted. He knew that look. A plan was hatching in that beautiful mind of hers, and whatever it was could land them in more trouble.

Suddenly, Savannah started for the stage and said, "Follow my lead."

"Follow your what?" He stared at her back as she dodged through the crowd.

Once Savannah made her way to the back of the room

and took the steps toward the stage, Tawni's full lips twitched with appreciation.

"Well, color me surprised. Your girlfriend has guts."

Anderson's face hardened. "She's not my girlfriend."

Tawni gave him a look that said she thought otherwise. "Then, what is she?"

"She's a piece of work, that's what she is," he added.

What is she doing? He glanced from the men in the room to her slim figure as she took the last of the steps. *She just alerted everyone in the bar to her presence.* He groaned.

"Well, whatever she is to you..." Tawni paused. "You never looked at me like that when you were protecting me."

"You were never a pain in the butt like she is."

Her look of admiration wasn't lost on Anderson. He knew Tawni had feelings for him. Most women he rescued from dangerous situations developed them. It was a hazard of the job, but most emotions fell by the wayside once the adrenaline rush ended. Reality quickly set in once he left for another assignment.

Tawni was a realist. Even though she still carried a torch for Anderson, she knew they had very different paths in life.

He averted his gaze from her to find Savannah talking to a tightfisted musician on stage. Whoever she was, she didn't look too happy that Savannah was about to interrupt her. Anderson's whole body went on alert.

Tawni chuckled and pulled at him from behind. "You've got it bad. What are you going to do? Protect her from the guitar that girl might use to knock Savannah over the head with? Let her do her part and focus on the job, Evans."

Tawni was right. Savannah could take that scrawny musician if anything happened. He had experienced the impact of her punch and knew the musician was no match for Savannah.

Savannah's pulse strummed through her veins as she hurried up the steps for the stage. She searched the crowd, and a sense of dread filled her spirit. Each man who'd been infiltrating the room finally set their sights on her.

Once they honed in on her location and started for the stage, she hurried to the microphone and unapologetically cut in front of the next contestant, who pushed her back.

"Hey, I'm next."

"Get in line, honey," Savannah whispered. "I've got bigger people after me than you, so you don't scare me a bit. You'll get your turn, but this is my time."

The young girl glared at her before turning to the stage manager. "Can she do that?"

Tawni's manager searched over the crowd for direction. When Tawni waved in acceptance, he said, "Yeah, looks like she's tight with the owner, so I guess she can."

"Whatever! This is rigged." The young musician picked up her guitar and stomped down the steps to wait her turn.

"Here's hoping this works," Savannah said to no one in particular before stepping to the mic. *And here's hoping Anderson can take care of business while I'm up here.*

"Hi." Savannah cleared her throat as the speakers squelched with feedback.

She took a step back and waited for the buzz to stop before speaking again.

"I'd like to sing a little for you if you wouldn't mind."

"Just sing already!" Someone yelled from the crowd.

Now that everyone's attention was on her, there was no way Benny's thugs could swoop in to drag her offstage without causing a scene. They'd be forced to wait until she was done.

As she adjusted the mic, the men fanned out and strategically positioned themselves around the bar. She swallowed and let out a breath. Once her song was finished, there would be no escape.

It's okay. Savannah took a breath and closed her eyes. *Anderson has this.*

Savannah just hoped the goons were spread wide enough that they'd not only be unaware of Anderson's presence but that they wouldn't see how vulnerable they'd become.

As she searched for her protectors through the crowd, she was unable to see either Anderson or Tawni.

If I can't see them, maybe Benny's guys won't either.

She prayed for divine intervention.

"What is she doing?" Anderson grumbled.

Tawni retrieved a stun gun from under the bar and slid it to Anderson.

"She's giving you time," she said, searching the crowd to signal one of her bouncers over.

"Yeah, boss." A man from the side entrance jogged toward them.

"I need you to help us to get these five guys out of here quietly." She looked at a few that had scattered through the room.

"Got it." He stuck his hand out to Anderson with a smile. "Kevin."

Anderson introduced himself, thinking Kevin looked to be able to power-lift an army. He reminded him of John Cena, only bigger and, hopefully, more powerful.

"We only have a couple minutes. Be ready to catch 'em after I drop them with this stun gun."

Tawni slipped some zip-ties in Kevin's jacket pocket and added, "The stun gun won't knock them out completely. So, drag them to the kitchen cooler and tie them up."

Anderson's eyes twinkled when Tawni grinned a little too enthusiastically. "I think I like this side of you."

She chuckled. "I learned a thing or two from you when we were on the run. Lead the way."

While Anderson made his way through the crowd for the first of the five men, Savannah leaned toward the stage manager and whispered, "Do you have a spare guitar?"

After she was handed an acoustic, she asked, "Is it tuned and ready to go?"

He nodded as she slid onto the stool with a deep breath. It had been a long time since she'd picked up a guitar. The smooth wood in her hands was like coming home. When she placed her fingers along the fret for a G-chord, her muscle memory kicked in. The taut strings were like heaven to her fingertips.

She strummed a few chords and opened her mouth to sing, but paused when she saw a few people in the crowd with their smartphones up to video her performance.

After all of Anderson's talks of shying away from cameras – another nagging thought ran through her mind.

If someone uploads a video to social media, will that alert Odyssey to our location?

Suddenly, she decided to switch things up and hopefully keep them under the radar. She stopped playing to raise a hand in greeting to the impatient crowd.

"Hi, folks. I'm uh, I'm Monica. And I'll be singing one of my favorites. I hope you like it."

Anderson slipped behind one of the men and prepared to place the Taser at the base of his spine when Savannah's smooth voice floated through the room. It took his breath away. He stood as if in a stupor when Kevin nudged him.

"Dude. You only have a couple minutes."

Anderson shook his head and freed himself from the spell Savannah's voice cast. "Yeah, sorry. You know what to do."

Kevin nodded, slipping in front of the target as Anderson placed the Taser at the base of his spine.

Immediately, the heavy-set man dropped and almost hit his head on a table, if Kevin hadn't caught him and dragged him away.

"This guy has had one too many." Kevin winked at a bystander who happened to glance in their direction.

Anderson searched for their next target as Tawni approached.

"Which one is next?" she asked.

The gleam in Tawni's eyes mirrored his own, yet he wasn't quite sure she should be doing any of the heavier lifting. Even as sturdy as she was, she may not have been up to carting off a two-hundred-plus-pound man. Anderson scanned the room and noticed one who was more her size.

"This way." He spun with Tawni tight on his heels.

Savannah was surprised she could focus on her lyrics as Tawni and her bouncer helped Anderson in taking down Benny's guys one by one.

Just one more. Savannah paused for the third chorus of Bon Jovi's, *It's My Life,* and then sang the words as if her life depended on it.

When she finished, cheers exploded throughout the room. From the back, someone started chanting, "One more song! One more song!"

Savannah slipped from the stool and took a bow beaming with pride. Singing was her first love. If she'd had her choice of careers, music was at the top of the list. It had just never taken off for her, like it had for her friend, Ava.

As hard as she tried, record executives paid her no attention. Her sweet girl-next-door looks weren't the right package, according to Nashville's elite, which is why she eventually took a step back from her dreams and solely focused on her business.

"Thank you." She adjusted the mic.

Anderson frowned at Tawni as Savannah's song came to an end. They still had one more person to take down.

He watched the last guy with eagle eye precision as he searched the room for his compadres.

"He knows something is wrong." He swore under his breath. "Savannah needs to keep singing. It's too soon." A look of worry crossed his face.

Tawni sent Kevin a look while jutting her chin toward Anderson and stepped backward through the crowd.

Dangerous Visions

"I'll take care of Savannah. You guys take care of the last man standing."

When she disappeared into the massive crowd, the only thing that could be seen was her fist as she pumped it in the air.

"One more song! One more song!" Tawni hopped on stage, mimicking the chant that had spread through the bar. "Let's hear it for S-"

"Monica." Savannah quickly cut her off.

Tawni smirked. Whether she wanted to or not, she liked Savannah. She was a fast thinker and willing to jump into the action. No wonder Anderson was falling for her. The two suited one another.

She leaned toward the mic and beamed. "How about one more? What do you think, Monica? Do you have anything else you could sing for us?" Tawni stepped back from the mic and whispered out of the side of her mouth. "You need to stall."

Savannah stared at her feet as if they were glued to the floor. "Ummm."

"Come on! One more!" A heavy-set biker yelled from the bar.

"Um, okay. Yeah." She shrugged with surprise, amazed that anyone – especially this crowd – would want to hear more from her.

The joy that radiated through her heart deterred any fears surrounding her current circumstances. At the moment, she was just a singer making people happy.

"Yeah, I can do that." She bit her lip with wonder. "Any suggestions?"

"Stairway to Heaven!" The same biker yelled and raised a bottle of beer toward the ceiling.

"Okay, I don't know that one as well, so how about an

original?"

Tawni disappeared off stage as Savannah started strumming her guitar.

She's a good girl they say, but she's done her time. She's walked down that road and crossed that fine line...

Once more, Savannah's unexpectedly slow and smooth tone mesmerized the rowdy group, allowing Anderson to finish the job and make sure Savannah stayed safe.

11

"That's the last one," Kevin grunted as he pulled the cable tie around the fifth man's wrists and stood to face the group he'd lumped into the freezer.

Anderson stepped forward as the men groaned with pain. He nudged one with his foot.

"Who sent you?" Even though he could guess, he needed confirmation.

"Cayate!" One of the men yelled, sending them a warning to be quiet.

"Spanish? I can speak that too." Anderson squatted next to the man, who seemed to be the leader among the group. He turned his military class ring so that it was face down before whacking him on the head with it.

The man howled in pain, as Anderson was rocked with another image. This time he saw another man waiting in the parking lot of the Brass & Buckle, and he was almost twice the size of Kevin and more ominous than half the men he'd been up against.

In his heart, he knew it was Benny lying in wait to

capture Savannah personally once his men exited the bar with her.

"Are you okay, man?" Kevin reached under his arms to help Anderson to stand.

Anderson shook his head and then kicked the man nearest to him and yelled, "How many are outside with Benny?!"

All five blinked with awe, yet said nothing. When it was clear the men weren't budging, he spun to face Kevin.

"Whatever you do – don't touch me until I say so. Okay?"

A look of confusion crossed Kevin's features, but he nodded in agreement.

Anderson dragged a breath in anticipation as he was about to attempt the unthinkable. He flexed his fingers and blinked, unsure if purposely laying his hands on someone was wise considering how much it took out of him. It may not have been the smartest thing he could do, but it was necessary.

Cautiously, he kneeled near the leader of the group and braced for impact. Anderson gently pressed his fingers against the gang member's neck and waited.

"Hey, get your hands off me." The leader thrashed and rolled away from Anderson's touch, but not before Anderson caught a glimpse of the man spying on a family from behind a bush.

At that moment, Anderson observed a little boy running to another man and calling him 'Daddy.' In his vision, Anderson had a sense of envy...longing. When the second man's face came into focus, Anderson recognized him as one of the other gang members being held captive in the room.

"Don't touch me, dude!" The leader jerked his head from Anderson's palm just as Anderson blinked and shook his head from the fog that dissipated from his mind.

"So, you can speak English?" Anderson's eyes glinted with anticipation. "From what I can tell, you slept with your friend's wife." He pointed to one of the other men who was tied up nearby.

"What?" The man's face froze with horror.

"Manny, I knew it," the second man yelled. "I'm going to kill you!"

Anderson looked to the other man in the group who was propped up against a sack of potatoes. "Do you know that your son isn't yours?"

"Shut up, Kenny!" Manny yelled and kicked the back of Anderson's leg with his feet.

Anderson stumbled forward and grabbed a produce rack to stabilize himself as Kevin yanked Manny's legs and rolled him face down.

Anderson turned with a gleam in his eye and placed a foot in the small of Manny's back.

"What? You didn't tell Kenny that his son was really yours?"

Just then, Kenny screamed something in Spanish before he launched his body toward them. He didn't get far as both his feet and hands were bound. Instead, he lay on the concrete, looking like a flailing fish as he struggled to get closer.

Anderson shoved him toward the corner and pointed a finger in his face. "Stay, Kenny. You can kill your friend later."

He then turned and nodded toward Manny. "Kevin, can you hold him in place?"

"Sure thing." As Kevin approached the man, Manny's eyes bulged as if he were about to endure some sort of torture. He tried to scoot on his belly away from Kevin's grasp, but it was to no avail.

As soon as Kevin had him pinned, Anderson put both hands on his head to keep it firmly in place and squeezed his eyes shut to concentrate on any images that came.

"Man! What kind of voodoo are you doing to me?" Manny yelled. "Get him off me! I'll tell you whatever you want. Just get that freak away from me."

All Anderson could derive was a few bits of Benny and the group as they drove to the Brass & Buckle earlier in the day. He shook his head and stood.

Kevin took his place next to Anderson in awe. "How did you know about the kid?"

Anderson shrugged it off and whispered, "Lucky guess."

Benny checked his phone once more. What was taking them so long? He sent in five of his enforcers to search for one tiny girl. It should have been an easy feat. They had already texted him once inside the bar to let him know it wasn't a trap. That was the whole reason they went in first. The last thing he needed was to get caught by the police after skipping bail.

Benny drummed his fingers on the steering wheel and shut off the engine, wondering what the delay was. As soon as he entered the dimly lit bar, he scanned the room and cursed. Not one of his men were in sight.

He narrowed his eyes. Surely, they wouldn't have double-crossed him. No, they wouldn't...not when their lives were on the line.

Benny reached for his phone to text Manny.

Where are you?

He waited. When there was no reply, he slunk behind a couple in the crowd, thinking it could be a trap. Had the feds uncovered their line of communication and texted him to draw him out?

Finally, he slid up the to the bar and ordered a beer, watching the room for government types, but he saw nothing out of the ordinary. At the thought of the authorities, he grimaced.

After his arrest, he became a threat to his organization. Once he made bail, his superiors were ready to wash their hands of him. Simply put, Benny knew too much. His arrest led to more arrests within their organization, yet it didn't put a dent into the widespread structure in place.

Although there was a sense of anonymity outside each cell in the organization – more information could eventually be discovered if he were convicted and the feds connected the dots.

That's why he had to find both Savannah and his former dancer, Jade. His commander had tasked him personally to execute both of them. To save face and stay above ground, he would stop at nothing to make that happen.

Jade was in government protection, so his first priority was finding Savannah, who was alone and on the run.

How hard could it be to find Savannah and send him a signal? He checked his phone once more. There was still no message from Manny.

"Care for something?" A sturdy but voluptuous woman with long black hair and sultry eyes slid behind the bar to serve him.

Benny pulled out his wallet. "Tequila."

When Tawni stepped behind the bar and saw her

newest customer – the hair on the back of her neck stood at alert. The tattoo wrapped around his elbow was identical to those of the guys in her cooler.

Her first instinct was to hide Savannah, but Tawni couldn't alert the girl to run for cover with enemy number one waiting for her to serve him. Instead, Tawni turned her back and searched the room for Savannah as she grabbed a top-shelf brand.

As soon as she laid eyes on Savannah, she breathed a sigh of relief. Although Savannah had a pained look on her face from her new-found notoriety, she was safely cornered by a handful of new fans. Tawni released the tension in her shoulders, knowing Savannah was out of harm's way. But, for how long?

Tawni eyed Benny and slid up to the edge of the bar. She put her most flirtatious foot forward and slid his shot glass forth with a wink and a suggestive smile. Even though the sight of him made her insides crawl, there was no sense in throwing up any red flags, especially if it would take the focus off of Savannah.

As he pulled a twenty-dollar bill from his wallet, she laid a hand on his arm and said, "On the house."

Benny raised his eyebrows in appreciation. His day was looking up. Not only did he receive a free premium shot of tequila, but he might get something more than he bargained for at the end of this.

Benny knocked back the shot. The liquor burned his throat, and he closed his eyes, savoring every inch as it pooled at the bottom of his stomach. Just as he was about to ask her name, she placed the bottle of tequila on a well-lit shelf, leaving him to admire her backside.

Tawni hurried from her position and did a lap around the bar before weaving toward Savannah's location. If Benny was watching her, which she was sure he was, she didn't need to lead him straight to her.

She glanced over her shoulder to make sure she was in the clear and slid up to Savannah's side in efforts to relieve her from one of the corporate types that regularly frequented her bar.

She tapped him on the shoulder and grinned.

"Mind if I steal Monica from you?"

He blinked and shook his head, but before he let her go, he turned to Savannah and said, "Here's my card. I'm serious about that offer. Call me."

Savannah slipped his card in her jeans and spun, thankful to see Tawni at her side. The relief must have shown on her face because Tawni stared her down and said, "Hold off on that grateful spirit for a second, sister. We've got trouble."

Tawni's grip on her wrist tightened as she pulled her around the corner, toward the bathrooms.

"What do you mean?" Savannah's hushed voice could barely be heard over the next singer that took the stage.

"I mean, peek your head out carefully and tell me if you recognize that guy at the bar." Her words tumbled from her mouth faster than expected.

Savannah looked into Tawni's dilated eyes and groaned, "Oh gosh. Don't tell me."

"Well, hopefully, it's nothing. Whoever that is—" Tawni pointed to her arm. "Has the same tattoo as one of the guys Kevin zip-tied in the cooler."

Savannah peeked around the corner. When she turned to face Tawni once more, she was frowning.

"I don't see anyone."

"What? Wait." Tawni glanced around Savannah's shoulder once more. Bile rose in her throat. The bar stool where Benny had been seated was empty. "Oh, crap. I don't have eyes on him."

"Are you sure it was even Benny? Was he dark-skinned with dark hair and about yea big?" Savannah stretched her hand as high as she could reach. "With oversized muscles like he worked out a lot?"

Tawni swallowed, eyes wide. "Uh-huh."

BENNY SEARCHED for the bartender through the crowd, but she'd disappeared. When another waitress sauntered toward him with a cocktail napkin and a wink, he stood to focus on his primary mission and searched the room for Savannah and his men.

As he wove through a few tables and approached the dance floor, a photo on someone's phone caught his eye. It was a selfie, but the girl in the background was of particular interest. She'd changed her hair, but after the amount of time he'd spent studying Savannah's photos, he'd recognize that face anywhere.

"Do you mind?" He approached and motioned to the phone in the woman's hand. "I think I know that girl."

"You know, Monica?" The woman gushed. "She's going to be famous one day. I just know it."

She showed him her phone and continued, "Were you here for her songs?"

"She was here singing on stage?" He cocked his head.

"Oh, yeah. You just missed her. She was great. Much

better than some of these local wannabes." The woman waved her hand to the stage where another hopeful sang for the crowd.

"Did you see where she went?"

"Well, she was talking to a bunch of us after she came down from the stage, but the last I saw her – she was over there talking to Randall." She pointed across the room.

"Randall would be?" Benny waited for her to finish.

"See that guy by the tall, skinny blonde in the blue shirt?"

Benny made his way across the dance floor, but before he approached Randall, he caught a glimpse of his bartender talking to a brunette who had her back to him. As the girl raised her arm, the buxom bartender's eyes made contact with his and widened with awe.

When panic ran deep within them, he grinned. She recognized him from more than serving him a shot of tequila.

Tawni listened to Savannah's description of Benny, just as he came into view. When he made eye contact, her eyes widened with shock.

"Savannah," she hissed. "He's coming our way. We have to move."

Savannah spun as Benny took long, hurried strides in their direction. She didn't know what was scarier - the determination on his face or whatever he was reaching for in his jacket.

"Oh, God, help us," she stammered and took a step back.

"We're pinned in here." Tawni pulled Savannah behind her and took a protective stance. "Your only way out is through the men's bathroom window. Get going, and I'll hold him off for as long as I can."

"Come with me. I don't want you to get hurt." She tugged at Tawni's shirt from behind.

"Don't worry about me. I'll get the attention of one of my guys. Kevin and Anderson won't be long. Just get out the window and start running for the stream behind the bar. Find someplace to hide out by the water. There are caves. Go! Now!"

Benny approached just as Savannah's petite frame disappeared into the men's bathroom. The only thing standing between them was the bartender, whom he should have no trouble taking care of. He wasn't about to let a woman stand in the way.

"And I had such high hopes for you and me." He sneered and took out a knife.

"Oh, sweetheart. Don't you know that I go for the blonde boy-next-door look? Besides, you couldn't handle me." Her eyes gleamed with determination.

Even though she stood about six-foot-tall, she still wouldn't be able to delay him for long.

"What are you gonna do? Hit me? Not when I have this?" He rolled a pocket knife from one hand to the other, taking a few steps forward. "I'll carve up that pretty face of yours."

"In a public place? I don't think so." She took a step back. "I'll yell for help."

"With all this music - no one will hear you." He chuckled. "If we were alone..."

"Help!" she yelled.

Unfortunately, Benny was right. The country singer's voice was far too loud and raw to allow room for any other noise from the back of the bar. And, since the narrow hallway sat at least fifty yards from the rest of the crowd, not only would no one hear her – no one would be coming to her rescue unless she was lucky enough that one of them had to relieve themselves.

Tawni slipped a thick towel from her back pocket and twisted it – holding both ends tightly. As Benny lunged forward with the knife, she expertly looped the towel around his wrist and flung it to the side, causing him to lose his grip on his blade.

Once the knife scattered down the hall, Benny lunged forward, placed his large hands around her neck, and began to choke her. Thankfully, Tawni wasn't a stranger to battling someone twice her size. Without a second thought, she placed her hands in a praying position and shot her arms through Benny's, hoping to break his hold, but Benny's grasp was too firm. As her air was slowly being cut off, Tawni did the only thing that came naturally. She kneed him in the groin.

They briefly broke apart as he doubled over in pain, but the reprieve didn't last long. Within seconds he angled his shoulder toward her chest and rammed her into the wall.

The last thing she remembered was heavy footsteps as Benny pursued Savannah into the men's bathroom. She just hoped she gave her enough of a lead to find a safe place to hide.

12

"Tawni!" Anderson patted her cheeks as he waved smelling salts in her face.

A burning sensation wafted up her nose, waking her from her seated position on the floor, where Kevin, Anderson, and a couple of employees were hovering over her.

Her first thought was for Savannah's safety.

"Where is she?" Tawni tried to scramble to her feet, but dizziness kept her rooted in place.

Anderson's brow furrowed. "I thought she was with you."

"How long have I been out?"

Kevin pointed to another employee. "Jasmine rounded the corner just as you went down, and someone ran to the bathroom. She waved us over. It's been maybe two or three minutes."

"Outside the bathroom – through a window – down by the stream. Benny." Her words tumbled out.

Anderson didn't wait for any further explanations. He started for the door and noticed the wood was splintered as if kicked open.

Once inside, a few droplets of blood made a path to an open window. Anderson's heart seized with dread. He prayed it wasn't Savannah's. Immediately, he yelled for Kevin down the hall.

"Go outside and head for the stream! I'm going through the window."

"Got it!" Kevin yelled from afar.

When Kevin caught up with Anderson, he was kneeling at a dirt path, studying the footprints. Anderson lifted from his position and pointed.

"They went this way. What's over that hill?"

"A canyon, a stream...a few caves." Kevin squinted over the horizon.

"Hiding spots." Anderson let out a breath and pushed off for the hill.

It was then that a gunshot rang out, and any hopes that Savannah had found someplace safe were gone. The sound echoed through the canyon, followed by Savannah's scream.

"Over there!" Kevin pointed.

Anderson whipped around in time to see Benny jumping over a small boulder beneath a tree. Benny stood with his back to them as he looked up into the branches with his gun trained above.

"Do you have a weapon?" Anderson asked as he retrieved his handgun from his holster.

Kevin shook his head. "Everything happened so fast. I left it behind the bar."

"Go get it and meet me down there as soon as possible." Anderson glanced the grove where Benny stood.

As Kevin retreated, Anderson swiftly ran in stealth mode in Savannah's direction.

Savannah's legs burned as if seared by a thousand fire ants, but she couldn't stop now. Tawni wouldn't be able to hold Benny off for long. Although she looked to be able to hold her own in a boxing ring – Tawni wasn't a match for the likes of Benny.

As soon as Savannah approached the stream, she paused to catch her breath and survey the area. There were plenty of places to hide throughout the cavernous topography, but that would be hiding somewhere obvious. She needed to think bigger.

Bigger. Bigger than Benny...

To her left was a cluster of oaks that provided shade over the crook of the stream. She wrapped her arms and legs around the thick trunk to climb to the first branch. From there, she continued to move up as high as the branches would allow. The cuts and scrapes against her skin were well worth it if the thick layers of leaves would provide her the cover she needed.

Please don't let him see me up here. Please protect me.

Benny followed fresh tracks toward the stream and came to a stop once the dirt path ended. He swore under his breath. There was no way to determine which way Savannah escaped.

As he surveyed his surroundings, his hand began to throb. He glanced at it to discover fresh blood. He sucked some of it away before wiping the rest of the blood on his jeans. He winced. The knife must have sliced his hand when it flew from his grasp.

Benny glanced downstream. The area was littered with foliage and caverns, which made for convenient cover if someone wanted to hide. Who knew there'd be so many caves near San Antonio? He knew Savannah didn't have much lead time. She had to be close by.

With that thought, he cupped his hands and yelled. "I know you're out here! I can smell your fear, chica!"

Savannah bit her lips to keep from crying out and held on to the tree for dear life. Benny's voice sounded close – too close. She closed her eyes and breathed in through her nose, hoping to calm her erratic heart rate.

You're okay. Savannah peered through her eyelashes at the branches around her. Unless something or someone was directly below her, she could stay hidden.

Benny took a step forward past a cluster of trees that sat just outside a cave. Just as he was about to search inside the dark cavern - he heard a sneeze as if someone was directly behind him.

He spun around, wondering if his ears were playing tricks on him. The girl was nowhere to be seen. He shook his head and turned back for the cave, thinking it to be an echo from inside.

Savannah slapped a hand over her mouth, praying that would be the end of her allergies. It was then that she noticed the welts on her arms and legs.

Benny swiped the flashlight option open on his smart-phone and scanned the shallow cave. Without evidence of Savannah's presence inside, he spun back toward the entrance. The second he stepped into the sun, he shielded his view the sun wondering how long she could hide in this heat.

He looked up as a single leaf fell from a group of trees. That's when he heard another sneeze. With a look of triumph, he trailed it with his eyes as it made its way to the ground.

He ran to the base of a few oaks and peered through the foliage, finding a very scared and scraped up girl, clinging to one of them as if it were a lifeline.

"I've always enjoyed a good hunt." A lazy smile claimed his features as he feigned charm. "One thing that I always bring with me is enough ammunition to wait out my prey."

Benny withdrew a gun from his jacket and waved it in the air, taunting her. His grin widened when he noticed tears streaming down her face.

"Aw, I hate to see a pretty lady cry." He laid a hand over his heart. "I'd give you a tissue, but you'd have to come down. I'll make you a deal..."

He sat down in the grass below her tree. "If you come down, I promise I won't hurt you. It looks like you might need a bandage or two."

At the mention of a bandage, Savannah stared the blood smeared on his jeans and shivered. She hoped that Tawni was okay.

"What do you say? Come on down, and we can be friends?" He laid his gun in the grass next to him.

She shook her head.

Benny shrugged and retrieved his pistol before standing and taking aim at her head.

"Have it your way. I warned you." He sneered. "This is going to be fun."

As he pulled the trigger, Savannah secured her legs around the tree and jerked her head behind it for protection. The bullet blasted the side of the bark, lodging a few splinters into her neck. The shot barely missed her, but at least she was alive.

"You're gonna make me work for it, aren't you?"

The sound of Benny's eerie laughter made her skin crawl. When silence finally greeted her, she peered around the tree to find the spot empty where he once stood.

"Dear God, please help me," she whispered.

Just as she was about to lower her legs onto a branch, another shot came from behind. She yelped and clung tighter to the tree. From the corner of her eye, She could see him as he stood with his gun in the air.

"Turn around, you bitch. I want to watch your face when I shoot you dead."

Savannah glanced over her shoulder to find Benny standing on a rock on the other side of the tree. This time, his gun was pointed at her back.

Her legs, which had suffered from the long run and the climb, now shook as she placed them back on a branch to face her death. She took a deep breath, accepting that she was about to meet her maker and reunite with her parents.

At that thought, her heavy heart calmed. She pulled her lips inward and clamped down with her teeth, dragging a breath in through her nose. She was ready.

Savannah hugged the base of the tree and squeezed her eyes shut. As she waited for Benny to take his shot, she fervently prayed and mouthed the words only her Creator could hear.

"The Lord is my Shepherd. I shall not want..."

The sound of Benny's slow chuckle crept through the tree, enveloping her like a snake would its prey. Savannah sobbed, knowing this would be the last thing she would experience when a gun blasted from a distance followed by the sound of Benny's moan.

Startled, Savannah opened her eyes as Benny fell to his side, blood pouring from his neck. She almost lost her balance and fell from the tree. She gasped and gripped a branch to steady herself as both relief and terror swept through her spirit.

Benny's empty gaze peered toward the sky. It was clear he was no longer in this world. With his focus solely on Savannah, he never saw Anderson approaching with his gun trained at Benny's back.

Instantly, Savannah tucked her head behind a large branch to shield her view of his lifeless eyes. Her breath hitched in waves as chills penetrated every inch of her body. It was as if Benny's glacial spirit passed through her.

"Savannah!" Anderson called from below.

When she didn't respond, Anderson kicked Benny's gun to the side and searched for her face among the leaves. He finally saw her, clinging to the center of the tree. Her head was tucked in the crook of her arm against the bark.

"Savannah!" he yelled once more through the branches. "It's me, sweetheart. Look at me."

When she sat unresponsive to his call, he took a quick inventory of her injuries. The blood pouring from her temple and down her neck looked to be from a superficial wound. Other than some welts and scratches along her arms and legs, she looked unharmed. He said a silent prayer of thanks that Benny's aim was off.

"Hey." He tried once more. "I'm here."

Savannah was unable to move. At the sound of his voice, she let out a shaky breath, yet kept her head tucked in the crook of her arm.

"Okay." He slipped his gun into his holster and eyed her for any other telling signs of trauma. "Just tell me if you're okay – other than the obvious."

When she didn't answer, he said, "Just nod your head if you're okay."

When she nodded, eyes closed, he let out a slow breath and opened his arms.

"Okay. I'm right below you. All you have to do is fall backward, and I'll catch you. I promise."

Her small voice finally sounded. "Is he still down there?"

"Yes, but he can't hurt you anymore."

Savannah sniffled but didn't move.

Anderson bit his lip. When the sound of sirens in the distance closed in, he glanced up the hill as Kevin's bulky frame appeared along with two officers on his heels.

Anderson groaned. It made sense that someone would call the cops, but it was an unwanted complication. A news story or police report would be like waving a red flag for Odyssey.

Kevin pointed a few police officers in Anderson's direction as the group jogged toward the tree.

"Is she okay?" Kevin asked.

"I think so, but she won't come down." Anderson frowned at the officers as they approached.

The first of two glanced up at Savannah before turning to Anderson. "Officer Harrison." He sent Anderson a look. "Mind telling me what happened here?"

As Anderson was about to tell him, the second of the two officers interrupted.

"Do you know who this is?" The officer pointed at the body. "It's Benny Hernandez."

"You took out Benny Hernandez?" Officer Harrison turned back toward Anderson with raised brows. When Anderson nodded, the officer cocked his head. "The rest of the world thanks you, son."

As Anderson filled him in, the valley where they stood was soon swarming with officers and firefighters, who immediately went to work.

Two firefighters positioned a ladder against the trunk. Just as one started to climb to retrieve Savannah, Anderson excused himself from the officer. He laid a hand on the firefighter's shoulder and flipped out his government badge with authority.

"Do you mind?" he asked. "She's under my protection, and I'd like to be the one who brings her down."

"Sorry, sir. With all due respect, this is our scene now. You'll need to step back and wait like everyone else here."

Anderson's jaw clenched. He glanced once more toward Savannah and then sent the firefighter a look of contention.

"Sir, step back. I promise I'll take care of her."

Kevin stepped forward. "Let them do their job, dude."

Anderson relented. Kevin was right, but that didn't make the pit in his stomach go away. He watched the firefighter climb into the mass of the tree, ready to step forward the second he could.

"Miss?" Savannah heard from below. "My name is Calvin. I'm going to bring you to safety. Okay? Everything is going to be alright."

Savannah peered from beneath her lids as the firefighter approached.

"Is he gone?" she asked him.

"Your friend?"

"No." She shook her head. "Benny."

A look of compassion crossed Calvin's face. He glanced

beneath them, where an investigator was taking photos of the crime scene. Once he saw the medical examiner pull the thermometer from the deceased body, he knew he was close to wrapping things up.

"I can assure you they're about done. He's almost gone."

"Then, I'm not going anywhere. Not until they take him away."

"Okay. Is it alright if I stay up here with you?"

Savannah nodded, relaxing some of the tension in her shoulders and arms.

Calvin looked her over from head to toe.

"Are you hurt anywhere else that I may not see?" he asked.

"The bullets missed..." Her eyes watered.

"Okay. That's good." He sent her a reassuring smile before glancing below them.

Once Benny's lifeless body was loaded into a bag and rolled from the premises, he made eye contact and extended his hand to Savannah.

"He's gone. Are you ready?"

Savannah breathed a sigh of relief. "Is Anderson still here?"

"The guy with the official-looking badge?" His eyes twinkled with mischief, causing Savannah to giggle. "See for yourself."

Savannah peeked over Calvin's shoulder, where Anderson and Kevin anxiously waited. When she noticed the policemen standing arms crossed, her eyes widened.

"Am I in trouble?" she asked.

"No, ma'am. You just have a lot of people who care about you." He motioned to her. "Why don't you turn your body a little to the right and place your feet on the ladder? Here." He pointed to a spot in front of him. "And then, face the tree.

That way, I can shield you with my body, keeping you safely pinned in. Okay?"

Savannah loosened her grip on the tree, wondering if her limbs would withstand any more pressure.

"I can try."

"Easy does it. I've got you."

The moment she rolled to place her foot on the ladder, a cramp shot from the base of her hamstring to her thigh. Savannah yelped and reached for Calvin's arm as she slipped from the branch.

Fast on his feet, he wrapped his arm around her waist and pulled her close.

"I got ya," he whispered in her ear. "Set your feet on the rung in front of you."

Savannah's mouth went dry. She clamored for the ladder, allowing one foot to rest just above Calvin's while the other still seized in pain.

"That's it." He gently coaxed her. "Just lean back into my chest, and we'll take it one step at a time whenever you're ready."

Anderson held his breath as he watched everything transpire. Procedure or not, no one was going to keep him from taking Savannah into his arms once she was safely on the ground.

It seemed like forever until she was in reach. Once she stepped foot on the grass, and the firefighter released his hold, Anderson rushed to embrace her.

Savannah fell apart the second she was in Anderson's arms.

"It's okay, Sav," he whispered as her body shook against his chest.

Anderson stroked her hair and eyed the crowd that had accumulated around them.

"Sir, we're going to need to take a look at her." an EMT with an expectant stare appeared at their side.

"Give us a minute. Please?" His eyes beckoned over the top of Savannah's head.

"Let us take a look at her, please. The blood." The young woman motioned to Savannah's face and neck.

"Okay. Hold on." He laid a soft kiss on Savannah's forehead as her sobs slowly subsided. "Hey, slugger – you think you can go with this nice lady to get checked out?"

The warmth Anderson's body provided was like salve to her broken spirit. When he pulled back, even as slight as it was, she shivered.

"She's in shock." The EMT quickly stepped in to wrap a blanket around her shoulders.

"I'm okay." Savannah sighed. "Anderson?" She grasped his arms for support. "My leg - I need you. Help me to the ambulance?"

"I'm not leaving your side." He swept her in his arms to carry her up the hill as Kevin brought up the rear.

Once they reached the ambulance, another EMT checked Savannah for any other wounds, other than the superficial ones. When they found nothing serious, the EMT laid Savannah on the stretcher to pull some splinters from her neck and bandaged it before tending to the cuts and welts that covered her arms and legs.

"Tawni?" Savannah squeezed Anderson's arm.

"She's gonna be fine." Anderson sent her a look of reassurance.

"Did he hurt her?" Her worried eyes searched his.

"He knocked her out, but it could have been worse."

"Speaking of," the EMT interrupted. "We need to take you–"

"I don't want to go to the hospital." Savannah shook her head.

"Miss. We need to make sure you're okay. You've had quite an ordeal."

Savannah shook her head. "All I need is Benadryl, some cortisone, and rest. There's nothing you can do for me there that Anderson can't do for me here."

"Are you refusing our care?" The EMT – although perturbed – relented with a sigh.

When Savannah nodded, the woman pulled off her latex gloves and pushed an electronic tablet in her direction.

"You need to sign here." She pointed to the line at the bottom of the screen. "Then, I need to call my supervisor, so I can release you."

Savannah signed as if on autopilot. *Did any of the last hour really happen?*

Once the ambulance and fire trucks rolled from the scene, Savannah sagged against Anderson's chest. At that moment, her only desire was to be wrapped in his arms and go to sleep.

Anderson spun her to search her face, gently running the pads of his thumbs over the bandages on her arms.

"Are you going to be okay?"

"As long as I'm with you." She put a hand on his chest and leaned up to kiss his cheek. "Have I thanked you yet?"

He placed an arm around her as she limped alongside him back to the parking lot of the Brass & Buckle.

"You don't need to thank me, Savannah." The warmth from her warm lips on his cheek sent flutters through his chest. "It's my job."

Those three words were like a dagger through Savannah's heart.

"Of course, it is." Her voice took on a bitter edge.

Anderson wanted to explain himself but was interrupted by Officer Harrison.

"I still need to finish taking your statement." The officer stepped alongside them.

As they walked toward the front of the bar, the first thing they noticed was a large crowd gathered along with a few news crews. Anderson groaned as he observed the cameras. This was the last thing they needed.

In hopes of disguising his appearance, he snagged the cap from Kevin's head and said, "I need to borrow this."

Just as he pulled it to cover his eyes, a newscaster pointed a camera toward them. Anderson whispered to Savannah, "Keep your head down and away from the camera."

He took a card from his wallet and handed it to the officer. "You have my statement. Anything else can be given to you via my direct supervisor at the CIA. This girl is in protective custody and can't be caught on camera."

"Well, I'd say it's a little too late for that." Kevin stepped forward to block the camera crew from capturing Savannah from across the lot. "Her performance has hit social media with a bang. Tawni told me her cell phone is already ringing off the hook. People are asking how to reach Monica or her manager."

"Great." Anderson groaned. "Officers, we need to get her back into custody – stat."

Officer Harrison shook his head. "I just can't release you without authorization, Mr. Evans."

"That's Agent Evans." Anderson's eyebrow arched.

"Agent Evans, all the same...I need clearance before you leave without a complete statement."

"Kevin, can you sneak her in the back door, so she can

rest upstairs in Tawni's apartment while I take five minutes with Officer Harrison?"

"Ten minutes." Officer Harrison corrected him.

Anderson gave Kevin a look. "Okay. Ten minutes? And guard her with your life."

"Got it. Tawni is also upstairs resting. She refused to go to the hospital."

"Why am I not surprised?" Anderson rolled his eyes and helped Savannah into Kevin's arms.

"I can walk," Savannah grumbled, uncomfortable being in anyone else's arms other than Anderson's. The thought sent her reeling. Since when had she become so attached that she couldn't fathom being in another man's arms?

Then it hit her. She was falling in love with Anderson Evans – correction Agent Evans – a man who was just doing his job.

Her heart sagged as limply as her body did when Kevin took her from Anderson's arms, and they made their way to the back door.

"Monica!" The closer to the building she came, the louder the yells grew, but Savannah ignored them as Kevin escorted her inside.

"You already have a few fans, Monica," Kevin said with a look of admiration.

"It seems I do." She sent him a half-smile. She sighed, thinking she'd trade them all for the love of one man, who seemed to think of her as his duty above all else.

Kevin searched her face, noticing the dimples she showcased in return. She may have been tough enough to fool most, but he saw through her façade. Her grin couldn't replace the emptiness that settled behind her eyes.

13

Once upstairs, Kevin perched Savannah against the wall as he unlocked Tawni's door.

"Come on. I'll help you to the couch." He offered her an arm before shutting the door behind them.

"I leave you alone for five minutes, and you're all over the news!" Tawni's sarcastic voice sounded from down the hall.

Savannah glanced at Kevin, who pointed to Tawni's door. "She's in her room."

"Can I go in?"

Kevin chuckled. "She wouldn't have been yelling out to us if she didn't want the company. Can you make it okay?"

Savannah limped towards Tawni's room.

"I'll be okay," she said over her shoulder.

"I'll bring you some muscle rub, aspirin, and a cold compress." He left for the kitchen.

Savannah blinked. Kevin seemed to know his way around Tawni's place well enough.

As she approached the partially open door, she knocked before peeking her head in. There she found Tawni tucked in a king-sized bed that was made with black satin sheets. Tawni was wrapped in a soft grey robe and surrounded by overstuffed pillows. She reminded Savannah of a vixen princess.

"Come." Tawni extended her arm.

"How are you?" Savannah hopped on one leg to sit next to her.

Tawni scoffed. "I'll make it. What about you? Maybe you should have called yourself Grace instead of Monica."

Savannah tilted her head and raised an eyebrow. "Maybe."

Tawni reached for her hand. "I'm glad you're okay, but with Anderson as your protector, I wouldn't expect anything less."

"Well, that *is* his job." Savannah's eyes hardened.

Tawni chuckled. "You know it's more than that, don't you?"

"When I thanked him just now - that's what he said. That it was his job." Her mouth flattened.

Tawni shook her head. "Well, as a girl with experience, trust me, I've been in your shoes - I was in awe of him too."

"Oh, I'm not -"

Tawni held up her hand. "You can lie to yourself, but not to me. I see the way the two of you look at each other."

"He's maddening!" Savannah threw up her hands. "There's no way."

Tawni placed a hand on her arm and sent her a warm look. "He's crazy about you. Just give him time."

Savannah made a face and blinked, unsure of what to think. Not two hours ago she was at odds with this woman yet now, here she was giving her advice on her love life?

"How do you know, and why do you care?" She sent her a look. "I mean no offense."

Tawni shrugged her shoulders. "None taken. Listen, I will always love Anderson. He rescued me from a pretty bad situation. Trust me when I tell you that I've been in your shoes. But I'm a tough girl, and I'm not afraid to speak my mind. If I see something I like – I go for it. Trust me, I tried."

Savannah's gut burned with envy. "You love him?"

"I used to be madly in love with him. I would say I was even up to the moment he stepped back into my bar today, but then I saw the way he was with you." Her eyes temporarily clouded before she smiled. The reluctant joy that shone through the moist tears she held at bay pulled at Savannah's heartstrings.

"He belongs with you," Tawni said with finality. It was as if she was speaking to herself as much as she was Savannah.

Kevin cleared his throat from the doorway. "Did someone call for meds and cold packs?"

When Kevin sought Tawni's eyes, Savannah dropped her gaze. The tender acceptance in his face and the love that shown behind his eyes was apparent. Savannah wondered how long Kevin had been waiting in the wings for Tawni to realize it.

Savannah's first thought was that Kevin would no longer be the one waiting in the wings if Tawni had released her claim on Anderson.

"How much did you hear?" Tawni held out her hand for the baggie full of ice.

"Enough." He crossed the floor and kissed the top of Tawni's head. "I'll be out here on the couch if you girls need me." He laid the other bag on the bed next to Savannah before setting an antihistamine on the nightstand and tossing some muscle rub in her lap.

"You should take an allergy pill now." He eyed Savannah's skin. "And, Tawni can help you put some cream on your hamstring. I vowed never to touch another woman again after I met Tawni." He winked in Tawni's direction and left the room.

"Thanks," Tawni called at his back.

Savannah watched him disappear through the door before whispering, "You two?"

"Sort of." She shrugged. "But I have had too many walls and too many ghosts to let him in."

"Anderson?"

"Yeah, but he's not my future while..." Tawni paused. "Kevin's been here all along. He's patient. I'll give him that."

Savannah smacked Tawni's arm. "He's more than that. He's hot!"

"He is. Isn't he?" Tawni brought a pillow to her face to cover her smile.

Savannah chuckled, but her smile fell flat once she glanced at the television. When Benny's mugshot flashed on-screen, Savannah shuddered and buried her head in a pillow.

Tawni sighed and ran her fingers through Savannah's short, spiky locks.

"He can't hurt you anymore." Her tender voice was just above a whisper.

When Savannah didn't move, Tawni continued, "And those five guys were carted off before you were found. They're probably being booked right now."

Just then, Tawni's phone vibrated on the nightstand. She nudged Savannah's shoulder.

"That's probably another talent agent calling my phone asking how to reach the elusive and rising star, Monica – with no last name."

That was enough to bring Savannah up to rest on her

elbows. The sadness in her eyes softened as a look of wonder crossed her face.

"Someone really wants to talk to me about my music?"

Tawni tossed her hands in the air and threw her head back. "Not just someone! Everyone!"

"No." Surely Tawni was pacifying her.

"Honey!" She reached for her cell. "Look at how many voicemails I've received. They're all about you!"

Savannah took her phone and stared at the number of messages. There were over twenty. Her jaw dropped.

"You know," Savannah smirked. "The first time I saw what was on your cell phone, I wanted to kick your butt." She snickered. "Now, I just want to kiss you."

"Hey!" Anderson bellowed from the door. "There will be no more talk like that. I leave her here with you for ten minutes, and you're corrupting her?"

Tawni laughed. "Shut up! If you'd have taken me up on it – I wouldn't have to make a move on your girlfriend." She threw a pillow at Anderson and then groaned in pain. "I'm hurt, and you're making it worse."

Anderson ignored the remark about his girlfriend and stepped next to the girls to offer a hand to Savannah.

"It's time to go. Your singing is all over the web. They'll find us if we stay."

"They?" Tawni rose to a seated position. "Who is after you? More of Benny's guys?"

"No." Anderson shook his head. "And if I told you who, it would just put you in danger."

Kevin helped Tawni settle into her pillow. "You need to rest." He then turned to Anderson with a scowl. "Seems when you come around, danger isn't far behind. Is anyone else going to give us trouble?"

Anderson cocked his head. "Only if you act like you're

expecting it. Just nod when they show you pictures and answer all of their questions. They'll want to know if we were here, and it's obvious that we were."

Anderson pointed to the television. "Even though I believe we avoided getting caught on camera - when they show you photos of Savannah and me, play nice. It will keep them from being suspicious. Point them toward the highway and feed them a crumb. Tell them you heard we were heading to Arkansas."

"Are you going to Arkansas?" Kevin blinked.

Anderson shrugged. "Sure."

The less Kevin knew, the better. The men shook hands as Savannah knelt over Tawni to pull her into a soft embrace.

"Take care," Savannah whispered.

Tawni's face softened. She lowered her voice. "Take care of Anderson and be patient with him. He'll open up on his own time."

Savannah hobbled toward the door but spun back when inspiration struck. She leaned against the door frame and said, "You know before all this, I was a wedding planner and a professional maid of honor. If you ever need one." She looked over her shoulder down the hall, where both men were waiting out of earshot. "I'd be happy to help with yours."

Tawni smirked. Of course, she would. She could picture Savannah in the mix of someone's wedding chaos handling it with a dose of sarcasm while still putting people at ease.

She tossed the bottle of allergy medicine in Savannah's direction. "Never gonna happen. Go! And, take those pills before you swell up like an elephant."

Savannah grinned and tossed a carefree wave over her

shoulder as she limped toward Anderson, whose look of concern about took her breath away.

"You need help to get to the car?" He extended an arm.

It's just his job. The words rang in her head and pierced her heart.

She narrowed her eyes. "No, I can take care of myself."

Kevin sent Anderson a curious look.

"Don't ask." Anderson shook his head and turned to follow her down the steps, but paused with a concerned look.

"Remember, you only saw us. You don't know us, and if I were you, I wouldn't even speak our names. You never know who could be listening." He raised a brow and pointed toward Kevin's phone.

Kevin eyed his cell phone with concern before nodding. "Good luck."

They shook hands once more before Anderson started after Savannah, who was still descending one careful step at a time.

When he closed the gap to guide her onto the bottom step, she tugged her arm free from his tender grasp.

"I got it." Her voice was barely audible.

Anderson blinked in awe. He shook his head and started for the door to hold it open for her.

"Well, I'm helping you in your seat whether you like it or not." He grumbled, pulling out the Slim Jim to unlock the truck.

Once outside, a vast sky shone down as incandescent stars beckoned above. Savannah took a deep breath and reminded herself to count her blessings.

Even amidst her swirling emotions, God's canvas loomed overhead, telling her how small she indeed was. Her gaze swept from the twinkling lights above to Anderson's dark stare. She may have been just a job to Anderson, but she meant much, much more to her heavenly Father.

She breathed in and told herself to be grateful for Anderson's protection and friendship. She didn't need anything more. And, just when she'd convinced herself - her heart cautioned her. *You may not need anything more, but what do you want?*

She bit her lip to hold back the urge to cry. She knew the answer but wasn't willing to dwell on it.

"Ready? We've got a long trip ahead of us." Anderson broke her thoughts as he waited by the open passenger door.

She winced at the pain that throbbed with each step. Between her cuts and bruises, it promised to be an uncomfortable ride.

As Anderson scrutinized her every move, Savannah dragged her gaze to meet his. The distress that she read within his baby blues made her heart constrict. At that moment, she knew a long car ride was the least of her concerns. It was clear that he was a man driven to the brink.

"I guess I'm as ready as I'll ever be." She finally allowed him to support her weight and shift her inside.

When he buckled her in, his arms brushed her waist.

"I'm not an invalid," she mumbled and shooed his hand away.

His stormy eyes narrowed as he pulled back and firmly shut her door. As he rounded the front of the truck, Savannah stole a glance through the windshield as he waved an arm in the air and said something to himself. Savannah hid a grin at his open frustration. She may have been just a job to him, but it would be one he'd never forget.

Then her heart whispered, *Neither will you.*

14

Franks lived for the thrill of a chase, but in the last twelve hours, his targets seemed to have fallen off the map. An hour after Danny and Anderson's trails went cold, Franks was still confident they'd pick up a crumb to lead them to their destination. Now, as the light of day was pushing against the horizon, he was desperate for any sign of them. Franks glanced at the clock on the wall. He was due to report to Brennan soon.

He wiped the sweat from his brow and glanced at the empty energy drinks and nicotine gum wrappers, knowing their efforts wouldn't be in vain. It couldn't be. He had to be getting closer, because, if not, he'd be left with nothing more than a six-foot hole in which to retire. The Director would make sure of that.

Franks stared at the photos of both Evans and Stone on his monitor and sneered. He'd never been the sentimental type. The fact that both former operatives used to be on his team meant nothing. The desire to see them dead burned within his gut as if someone had stoked the fire with gasoline.

Just then, a couple of cheers came from the pit. With a sigh of relief, Franks pushed from his desk as his second wind spurred him. Yells were good. It meant victory.

As he joined the crew at the center of the room, a local news report from a small town in Texas flashed on-screen. A beautiful reporter with a microphone in hand stood in front of a rundown bar at the outskirts of a small town in Texas. He motioned for a team member to turn up the volume.

"I'm here outside the Brass and Buckle, reporting live. Tonight a crazed fan stalked, attacked, and ultimately lost his life when he tried to kill a woman who performed here at a local singing competition."

Franks frowned and reached for the remote.

"Why are we watching this?" he asked.

Just as he was about to turn it off, an analyst laid a hand on his arm.

"Sir. Wait," she said.

"Unless you have something for me – this is a waste of time." His dark eyes bore down on the junior analyst.

Quick to defend herself, she nodded with urgency. "I do, sir. Give me the remote." She held open her hand.

Franks glanced at her badge and narrowed his eyes. "How long have you been with us, Ms. Joiner?"

"Long enough to know what I'm doing, sir." She sneered in return. "And, that's Agent Joiner."

She snagged the remote she and hit rewind, pausing the image on-screen. Next, she reached to touch the monitor with her thumb and forefinger, spreading them wide to zoom in on someone standing in the background.

Joiner tapped the screen with a gleam in her eye. She applied just enough pressure on the face of her subject that digital red lines framed the partial profile.

Franks squinted to see the man on-screen. Whomever it was had hidden fairly well beneath a ball cap.

Joiner tapped the monitor within the red frame a second time.

"We're running a digital scan, sir." She looked at the secondary monitor that had a thousand profile pictures scrolling on it at light speed. "Even with a partial face, profile, or even an ear – our program can identify someone with ninety-nine percent accuracy."

Within a few seconds, Anderson's agency profile photo popped up on-screen next to the partial face of the man in the crowd.

"And that..." Agent Joiner raised a brow with a look of triumph. "Is Anderson Evans."

"How'd you stumble across this story?"

"I didn't stumble, sir. We have a specific program that looks for anything in this region." Agent Joiner drew a circle on the map, and continued, "Where we thought either Stone or Evans could be in this targeted area. We give our program enough data so that the computer will search for any breaking news in the area, which includes things like certain body language - like those trying to avoid the camera. We also ask our computers to keep facial recognition in mind when scanning the networks."

Franks sent her a look of appreciation and asked, "Do we know how he's connected to this singer?"

"We don't think there's a connection," another eager team member butted in.

"Either way, run a search for anything related to the bar."

"I got something!" another analyst yelled from behind his work station. "I'm putting it on-screen now."

As the primary monitor filled with social media images, Franks' face lit up when he recognized Miss Miles.

"That's her." He turned to the analyst who'd found a key piece of evidence. "Good work!"

"It still doesn't tell us why they were there." Agent Joiner frowned, feeling upstaged.

"Doesn't matter." Franks raised a brow.

He stepped forward and tapped a secondary screen that displayed a map of the nation. He searched the icons that represented any number of their operatives that had been positioned in various states.

"Do we have anyone in that area in close proximity?"

A third member of the team handed a list of targets to Franks. "No, sir. When the trail went cold on both Evans and Stone, we had other priorities that needed attention. We were told to pull them from Texas until further notice."

"By whom?" He frowned.

Four of the five analysts glanced at one another with unease.

The fifth, Joiner, cocked her head and sent him a look.

"By me. You were in with the Director, so I..." Her voice fell when Franks' jaw twitched as a shade of purple rose from beneath his collar.

Franks was on the verge of yelling. It took everything in him to keep from wringing her neck on the spot. The entire team must have sensed it as some took a step back to distance themselves. At that moment, any allies she may have had quickly cut their ties.

Franks snapped Joiner's badge from her shirt.

"You don't have the authority to make that call, Ms. Joiner. Grab your things. You're no longer needed." He nodded to the rest of the group. "And that goes for the rest of you if you do anything outside your job descriptions. Do you understand?"

Franks tapped the badge of the young man next to Joiner and said, "Agent Thompson, contact Underwood and Blaire. Send them the coordinates and tell them they're on the first flight out."

Thompson picked up a cell phone, saying, "On it."

Franks pointed at Joiner. "I'm off to let the Director know of the latest development. It's up to her as to what she decides to do with you. She may be generous since you were behind the discovery – or she may not."

Joiner swallowed, unable to move from the spot. As the rest of her former team scurried around her as if their lives depended on it – she wondered how she would get out of this with hers intact.

15

As minutes turned into hours, the musical lull of the tires against the pavement lured Savannah into a deep sleep. Anderson glanced in her direction as her eyes moved beneath her lids in a rapid pattern.

He slowly shook his head. For the last two hours, they'd driven in complete silence. Her usual fiery spirit had transformed into a distant somber one. Her run-in with Benny had clearly taken its toll, but something more had her giving him the cold shoulder.

A few short sounds of distress escaped through her lips as Savannah's head jerked to her left.

Anderson tried to fight the urge to comfort her, but he couldn't help it. She had him worried. Nightmares could very well haunt her for some time if she didn't come to terms with what happened today.

He stopped just short of touching her knee. Would her emotions plague him to the point that he could have another blinding vision?

Anderson checked the rearview mirror. When it was clear that no one was behind them, he pulled to the side of the road and put the car in park. He held his breath and hesitated just short of touching her arm.

Although these visions were becoming somewhat bearable, he still needed to prepare for the unknown as it could be any number of things that could flash before his eyes. Finally, he reached out to stroke Savannah's arm just as another moan burst from her throat.

"No!" Savannah screamed as her eyes flew open.

"Hey," he said, thankful to have a clear mind so that he could solely focus on her.

"You're safe," he whispered while pushing some matted hair back from Savannah's face. "You're okay."

Anderson took her hand in his, tracing circles in the center of her palm and saying nothing as he gazed into her eyes. The silence that followed was deafening. Finally, she sunk into her seat and closed her eyes.

"It was just a dream." She sighed, pulling her hand away.

Savannah's mind drifted to Benny's lifeless gaze as he lay on the ground. She shivered and almost let out a whimper as she fought back the tears.

"It's okay to cry, you know." He was doing his best to reassure her, but it seemed all he did was make her withdraw further into her shell.

After she removed her hand, Anderson's palm cooled. He frowned and flexed his fingers, unsure if he liked the vulnerability that followed. Since when had he let a woman get this close? When had the smallest sign of rejection had him recalling what it was like as an awkward teenager with his first crush?

"I don't need to cry anymore." Her hushed voice was laced with emotion. It tore at his heart.

"Okay." He searched her tear-rimmed eyes, but true to

her word, not one single tear fell. "Whatever you need. I'm here to help."

"Because that's your job, right?" Her eyes hardened.

"Savannah." His voice fell.

Explaining himself at this point would be like throwing a bowling ball into the air and expecting it to fly. It was totally illogical and absolutely impossible, but he tried anyway.

"It is, but..."

"Just don't." She turned her head and paused. When she finally swung her gaze back to meet his, she said, "I get it. I've had a really rough day, and I don't feel like doing this right now."

Anderson clenched his lips together. He wanted to explain, yet was sure it wouldn't be received.

The two stared at one another in silence until her flat voice finally broke the silence.

"How much further?" She blinked.

Anderson's tender expression tore at her heart. Instead of lamenting about what was going through his mind, she turned to stare out her window.

"Only a few more hours, but we have to find a new vehicle soon." His soft voice beckoned.

Savannah turned to retrieve a blanket from the backseat and rolled it into a makeshift pillow.

"Whatever," she said as she turned her back on him. "Do what you need to. Just wake me up when I need to get out."

Savannah closed her eyes. Although she'd rather avoid any bad dreams that came with sleep, she didn't have the energy to deal with Anderson. He had her so confused that she didn't know which way was up.

Thankfully, Anderson had been raised by strong independent women. Since Savannah's body language basically shut him out, he let the subject drop and put the truck in drive.

Once he pulled onto the road, he turned the radio on but kept the volume low so it wouldn't bother her. As he drove toward the city of Sweet Valley, he prayed they'd be able to gain some ground – on the road and with each other.

AFTER MAKING one more stop to trade their truck for an older station wagon, Anderson drove through the night and allowed Savannah to sleep the harshness of the last twelve hours away. Although she harbored a few uncomfortable dreams, they weren't enough to wake her.

He glanced in her direction as the morning light finally settled around them. He hesitated to wake her, but it was time. They needed to dump their station wagon.

"Savannah," he whispered as he tapped her shoulder.

"What?!" Savannah shot straight up as if ready to take flight. Her wide eyes took in her surroundings.

When it dawned on her that she was in the middle of nowhere with Anderson, she sunk back into her seat with a sigh.

"Sorry." She rubbed her eyes.

"It's okay. You were sleeping hard." He reached for bottled water from the cooler behind his seat. "Here."

"Thanks." She tucked her head as she twisted off the cap.

She didn't plan to fall asleep. The thought of snoring or

drooling in front of Anderson was mortifying, but her fatigue took over whether she liked it or not.

Anderson mistook her chagrin for dissatisfaction and said, "You probably need caffeine. Sorry. I took back roads to get here. There really wasn't any place to stop that would have had any decent coffee. Speaking of, I bet you need to go to the bathroom?"

At that exact moment, Savannah's bladder screamed in agony as if punishing her for ignoring it for so long. She nodded with wide eyes.

"I thought so. I would have woken you earlier, but you were sleeping so soundly." He grabbed a roll of toilet paper. "Sorry for the rough accommodations, but we need to stay off the radar. Take this and step behind those trees."

He jutted his chin toward a mass of cedars at the side of the road. "No one will be driving by here at this time of the morning, and if they did – they wouldn't notice you."

Savannah raised her eyebrows. "What about you?"

It was bad enough that he watched her sleep. How could she let nature take over with the thought of him nearby?

"Scouts' honor." He raised his hand, holding up three fingers.

"You were a scout?"

He sent her a grin and winked.

"Not like you couldn't see that one from a mile away," she grumbled and took the paper from him as she jogged toward the thick tree line at the edge of the road.

When she returned, what she saw had her stopping in her tracks. Anderson was unloading their beat-up station wagon with another man who looked to be in his sixties.

Anderson glanced up and waved her over.

"Savannah." He jogged to meet her. "Come meet my dad."

As the pair approached, Hank Evans watched his son place a protective arm around the woman's waist. Although unhappy to be in this position, where they were all hiding from whatever Anderson had gotten in the middle of – Hank's heart warmed at the sight.

Hank strode forth and stuck out his hand for an introduction at the same time, Savannah raised the roll of toilet paper with a grimace.

"Oh, yeah," Hank stammered. "Here." He reached for some hand sanitizer he'd just taken from the glove box of the old station wagon.

Savannah took the container and blushed. When she sent him a grateful smile, it transformed her serious look into something that begged to be admired.

Hank glanced from Savannah to Anderson and hid a grin at the look of wonder that spread across his son's face. For a trained operative, Anderson seemed to have forgotten his poker face.

"Thank you." She wiped her hands clean and handed it back.

"This is my dad, Hank." Anderson stepped away from Savannah's side to toss an arm around his father's shoulders. "And, Dad, this is Savannah. She's Danny's cousin."

When a look of confusion played across his dad's face, Anderson explained.

"I was in the process of protecting her from a situation – at Danny's request when everything broke loose."

"I'd say so." Hank eyed the scrapes across Savannah's arms and legs and the bandages on her neck. "Are you okay?"

Savannah touched her neck and nodded without uttering a word.

Hank frowned. "What have you gotten us all into, Son?"

"Later, Dad." Anderson opened the back of the station wagon. "Right now, we have to store all of this in your SUV."

As Anderson lifted a blanket off the top of the weapons and gear in the back of the car, Hank's jaw dropped.

"That's quite an arsenal you've got yourself there." Hank rocked back on the heels of his boots and cocked his head. "Alright. Let's get going."

Anderson placed a hand on Savannah's elbow to usher her to the backseat of his dad's vehicle.

"Your blanket's already in the back along with your water and a bottle of Motrin. Just wait for us until we're done here. Okay?"

The sentiment was enough to soften the walls she'd thrown up last night, but she firmly clung to them, holding them in place. She nodded in thanks and sent him a half-smile that almost reached her eyes.

Anderson sensed the chink in her armor and was grateful for anything he could get.

Once she was safely settled inside, he and his dad finished loading the back of the SUV. As Hank slipped inside the driver's side, he peered at Anderson, who was wiping the station wagon and from top to bottom.

"What's he doing?" Hank whispered to himself as if he'd forgotten that Savannah was lying in the back seat.

"Getting rid of any trace of fingerprints. He also has a portable handheld vacuum that he'll use if I'm not mistaken."

Savannah rose up enough to peek over the dash just as Anderson rolled up the floor mats and vacuumed the seats.

"Sounds like you've done this a time or two." Hank's eyes darted in her direction.

Savannah shrugged. "A few."

Anderson jogged over with the floor mats rolled and

tucked under his arm. He rapped on his dad's window and waited for him to lower it.

"We'll need to take these with us. Wait here while I dump the car in a more secluded spot."

Hank blinked in awe, yet said nothing. He closed the window as his son hotwired the station wagon, drove it from the road, and through some trees until it was out of sight.

"This simple farm boy is at a loss," Hank said, shaking his head.

"You get used to it." Savannah's voice went flat.

Hank twisted in his seat. "Should you have to? I don't know why he chose this sort of life – always expecting the unexpected. Always flitting from one place to the next, unaware of what's going to happen."

Savannah shrugged. It's not that she didn't agree with Hank. She missed her day to day life, in which all she had to worry about was what tantrum her bride might throw next. Those were the kind of curveballs she was prepared for, but Anderson was wired differently. And, he was good at what he did. She couldn't fathom him doing anything different with his life other than saving others or the world – one person at a time.

It was then that it hit her. Once they were safe from this present danger, Anderson would move on to the next emergency. Once she was safe, he would leave her.

"It's what he does." Her rough whisper sounded a million miles away. She shifted in her seat and shut her eyelids.

It didn't take long before footsteps approached, and Anderson flung the passenger side door open. He sat down in the seat with an immense sigh of relief, peeling the gloves from his hands.

"Did you scratch off the VIN number?" Savannah's emotionless voice sounded from the backseat.

Anderson grinned with appreciation and turned expecting to meet her gaze, but she was cuddled in a blanket and had her back to him as she lay across the seat.

"Yeah." He nodded at her back.

He glanced at his father, who had an incredulous look on his face. He fought back the urge to laugh at his dad's expense and sent him the most strict look he could muster.

"What?" he asked his dad.

Hank just shook his head. "Let's go. Your mother is impatiently waiting, and we still have a couple of hours or so to get to the house."

16

The rest of their journey was a blur. They drove for a few more hours until they turned onto a two-lane road toward a sleepy town. The area was a mixture of renovated buildings from the turn of the century yet had modern conveniences. It looked as if they'd stepped back into the pages of history as the cobbled streets and stone laid buildings adorned the main drag.

Savannah could almost picture nineteenth-century Americans wandering the city until Anderson's father would drive around a corner, where she'd discover a modern building overlooking a lake that spanned as far as the eye could see. She loved how well the old harmonized with the new.

"What is this place?" She sat up in awe.

"Welcome to Sweet Valley Cove." Hank grinned from ear to ear. "If our son is shuffling us away from our home, at least he is providing a charming place to hide away."

"This is our stop?" She eyed the main strip where the county courthouse proudly stood with a multitude of Texas state flags that rippled in the wind as if waving to her.

"Not quite yet." Anderson's voice shone with amusement.

When Anderson twisted to gaze into her eyes, it was as if time stopped. Or was it her heart? Savannah cut her eyes to continue taking in the sights and avoid any emotions that Anderson evoked.

The exchange wasn't lost on Hank as he watched Savannah with interest from the rearview mirror. He chuckled in his seat as they turned from the heart of the town toward the docks of Sweet Valley.

"This is last the leg of our trip." Anderson frowned at her indifference.

"All aboard." Hank slowed to drive down an embankment toward a loading dock at the lake. He stopped at the end and waited.

"Want me to do the honors?" Anderson asked.

When Hank shrugged, Anderson popped open the glove box to reveal a remote and pushed a button.

Savannah watched in awe as a submerged platform broke the surface of the water and motored toward the end of the dock. Once the ferry secured itself to the dock, three panels rose, giving the ferry barriers at the front and sides. After Hank parked onboard and killed the engine, the rear panel slid into place, securing their passage so the ferry could traverse across the water. To where — Savannah had no idea.

Her luminous eyes widened as she gazed at the lake. It seemed to span for miles, twisting and turning out of sight. There were portions of it that narrowed while others looked to continue as far as the eye could see.

She searched the horizon for the other side of the coast and squinted. It was far enough away, she'd need binoculars to see it.

She swung her attention to the front, where she caught Anderson's eye. His face was plastered with an adorable grin. While she wanted to smile back, she didn't. His attention was the last thing she needed. She turned her back and continued to take in the sites.

Once the ferry rounded the bend – the landscape drastically changed. The lake widened, and a small island that looked to be uninhabited appeared.

"What is that?" she asked.

"Your new home until all this gets sorted out," Anderson said.

Anderson wondered how long they would have to stay hidden away and if they'd been careful enough not to alert any unwanted attention.

To an outsider, their small ferry looked innocent enough. The locals knew that the owners of the island were an elusive group. He had heard the multiple rumors around town. Locals speculated that it had to be someone famous or infamous, but without any proof, the legend of the inhabitants of their home soon died down.

Once they docked at the island, Anderson activated the front panel of the ferry with his remote. Once he was able, Hank drove the SUV onto an embankment mixed with gravel and sand.

As the SUV took a narrow, gravel road along an incline, it wound through what looked to be a dense forest until a small clearing came into view. Although there was still enough greenery to camouflage their existence, it was apparent how much work had been done to clear the path toward their destination.

Within minutes, they approached a massive concrete wall that was covered in moss. It reminded Savannah of a bunker, yet the moss appeared to be growing from the concrete.

When Hank glanced in the rearview mirror at Savannah's expression, he cleared his throat and said, "It's a lot to take in."

As she studied the perimeter wall, he continued, "Anderson had the contractor mix the concrete with some kind of moss or something...for a faster way to camouflage the area."

She blinked in response and craned her neck to see how tall it was. The only thing overhead were the treetops that was scattered with bits of blue sky. She assumed from above - it would be harder to spot as it blended in with the surrounding foliage. After driving the length of it for quite some time, Hank finally slowed to a stop outside a steel gate.

"I never would have imagined this was here. From the water, it only seems like a bunch of trees."

"That's the point," Anderson said with pride. "Danny and I bought this island about five years ago for that exact reason. Then, we hired a trustworthy contractor to build this property. It's as private and secure as it gets."

Hank punched a code into a remote as the massive gate doors opened to reveal a large two-story home that was surrounded by the most beautiful gardens she'd ever seen in her life. It was something straight out of the pages of *Anne of Green Gables* - only it was under a partial canopy of foliage.

"How? Can't they trace you here?" Her mouth fell as they pulled further onto the property.

Anderson shook his head. "It's under the name of a shell corporation. We prepared for the worst in case our families ever needed protection. And, Danny and I knew we could do that better together than apart."

"What about food? This is out by itself."

"Food and supplies get dropped to the island when needed, all in the name of our shell company."

"How do they get dropped?" She blinked, imagining a helicopter lowering a huge box overhead.

"By drone, of course." Anderson gave her a look.

"Of course," she whispered.

"And your company is what exactly?" Savannah turned to stare over her shoulder as the gates closed behind them. It was nothing short of miraculous. She never knew something like this could exist in real life.

"Sanctuary Services. Officially, this is a home away from home for struggling artists who are needing a bit of inspiration."

Savannah's gasp could be heard from the front seat.

"What's the price tag on something like that?" she asked.

"Two hundred and fifty thousand dollars a pop."

"And do you actually board people here, or is it all a façade?"

"We've been known to let a few select pop stars or actors take refuge here. We've got to pay for property taxes somehow." He grinned.

Just then, the front door of the home flew open as a group of people shot down the porch steps toward the car. Savannah looked from one person to the next, thinking the family resemblance was astounding.

"I hope you're ready," Hank murmured before stepping from the car.

Anderson's mother yanked his door open and pulled him into an embrace only to shove him in the chest and swat his arm.

"That is for scaring the daylights out of all of us," Amelia said with a frown.

Savannah stepped from the car with trepidation as now

all eyes were on her. She swallowed, not knowing what to say when she felt a small hand slip into hers.

Savannah turned her attention to her side to find the sweetest angelic face upturned with a perfect set of dimples, much like Anderson's.

Anderson kneeled next to his niece and cupped her chin, before kissing her cheek. "Lani, meet Savannah. Savannah, this is my niece – the one I told you about."

Savannah's eyes lit up with acknowledgment. So, this was the young girl who could communicate with her dearly departed grandmother.

Savannah gently squeezed Lani's hand. When she leaned down to say hi, the little girl wound her arms around Savannah's neck. A warmth flooded Savannah's heart like nothing she'd ever experienced.

Lani's spiritual gift may have allowed her to talk to the deceased, but another of her gifts was putting people at ease. And, right now more than anything, Savannah needed it.

"So, are you going to introduce the rest of us?" Anderson's mom blurted.

Hank rounded the car to tug on his wife's arm.

"Give the girl a minute, Amelia. Savannah's had a harrowing ordeal."

Amelia eyed the dark-haired girl. Even with her many cuts and bruises, she was alluring, yet when she looked closer, it wasn't hard to miss the strain around her eyes or the tension she still held in her shoulders. Both spoke volumes.

"Of course. Don't mind me." Amelia turned toward her daughter and granddaughter. "Girls, take Savannah in and help her get set up in the room upstairs by the bathroom.

Show her where the towels and the linens are while Anderson and the rest of us get caught up."

"First, can I ask? Is Danny here?" Savannah eyed the group hoping for some good news.

"He is, but he took a boat into town for a few things. He thought you might need some clothes."

"Thank God." Savannah placed a hand over her heart, only to hear Amelia say, "Every day."

"Go on." Amelia nudged Lani from behind, motioning for the girls to lead Savannah up the porch.

As Lani, Alexis, and Savannah ascended the stairs to enter the home, Amelia turned her steely eyes toward her son and pointed a finger in his direction.

"Now, about you. You have some explaining to do."

There was nothing like a steaming hot shower to wash away the stress of the day. Once Savannah dried off with an ultra-soft towel, it was almost as if the last twenty-four hours never happened. She finally let go of the tension coiled at the pit of her stomach, thinking she'd seen the last of it until she touched the towel to her neck and winced in pain. Her wound was a quick reminder of the trauma she'd endured.

The memory of Benny's pursuit and final demise came tumbling back with a vengeance. The sound of his gun ricocheted through the edges of her mind. Savannah stumbled and reached for the side of the tub to sit as her breath hitched and came in waves. Tears that she thought she left behind came streaming down her face once more.

She shook her head in defiance.

"Get a hold of yourself," she whispered.

Savannah inhaled through her nose and filled her lungs with air. Slowly, she released it and wiped away the last tear that she would shed for her ordeal.

She stood to wipe the fog from the mirror, stared herself down, and said, "If you cry, you let him win. You survived. You're okay."

Suddenly, a soft knock sounded on the door.

"Vannah." Lani's soft voice called from the other side.

Savannah's heart warmed at the sound of it. "Yes, sweetheart. I'm almost done. Do you need to use the bathroom?"

She heard Lani shuffling from foot to foot outside her door and reached for a robe that Alexis had left for her. Once Savannah wrapped herself inside the thick goodness of it, she immediately thought of her mother's bathrobe, which had provided much comfort after her passing. Savannah tightened it around her frame and reveled in the soft fabric before opening the door.

"I'm sorry." Lani's little voice trembled. "Mom told me to wait, but Uncle Anderson is in the shower downstairs. Gramps is in the other one, and he takes a long time. I need to go really bad."

"Sure." Savannah sidestepped into the hall as Lani rushed inside and slammed the door shut.

Within seconds, running water sounded as the toilet flushed. Lani cracked the door open and sent her an inviting grin as she washed her little hands in the sink.

"You wanna come in?" Her dimples peeked at the corners of her mouth.

Savannah shrugged and found herself back at the side of

the tub as she sat and waited for Lani to speak. Savannah cocked her head and studied Lani as she dried her hands. When the little cherub turned in her direction, she had the most curious look on her face.

"What?" Savannah gave her a sideways look, unsure if she wanted to know.

"I heard you talking. Were you talking to yourself or...?"

Savannah grinned, finally understanding her meaning.

"Myself." She nodded with assurance.

"Okay." Lani shrugged her shoulders.

"Why?" She smirked.

Lani grinned. "Well, if you were talking to anyone other than yourself, that would be okay, ya know."

"In a room by myself?"

"Oh. We're never alone." Her wide eyes filled with wonder as she counted on her fingers. "There's Jesus, God, and don't forget the Holy Spirit. They're everywhere all the time. And then, there are people like my family. And when I say my family – I mean the ones with me here and there."

"Where's there?" Savannah asked.

She just couldn't help it. This young girl's banter reminded her of watching a Shirley Temple movie. The way Lani communicated was intoxicating, and her facial expressions captivated Savannah to no end.

"There." Lani pointed at the ceiling. "Heaven. Well, almost heaven."

"How do you almost make it to Heaven?" Savannah giggled. "I was taught it was one place or the other."

Lani's mouth formed an O as she nodded. "Oh yeah. But, while they're waiting for Jesus to come back – they're sleeping," she said in a hushed whisper like it was a secret. "Only sometimes, my grandma wakes up to come to visit. And that's when we talk."

Either this child had a very over-active imagination, or she was the wisest eight-year-old on the planet. Savannah grinned from ear to ear.

"That's pretty exciting." She put her elbows on her knees and leaned forward. "I wish I had that superpower."

Lani cocked her head. "You're gifted, too. We all are, but sadly I'm the only one that has this." She paused and let out a dramatic sigh, before adding, "It's a burden sometimes."

Savannah narrowed her eyes. "How?"

"Well, right now, I'm trying to determine how to tell you that your mom is here with you. The second you put that robe on – she slipped her arms around you and has been holding you in her arms like you were a little girl."

A lump formed in Savannah's throat as her eyes welled to the brim. A sense of contentment washed over her like the ocean as it skims the sand. At that moment, it was as if her mother's arms were around her.

"She-she." Savannah cleared her throat. "She is?"

"You're welcome." Lani stared at a space over Savannah's shoulder.

Savannah turned, hoping to have the same revelation that little Lani did but was disappointed to find nothing except a white tile tub surround and a towel rack. She squinted her eyes, thinking that if only she could imagine her mother's face – it would appear, but she had no such luck.

Sadly, she faced Lani. "I don't see her."

Surely the child was making this up, but how could she have caused the staggering sense of her mother's spirit which had washed over her? Or, had Savannah experienced that because she wanted to?

"That's okay. Your mom says she loves you and that you can count on Uncle Anderson... that everything is going to be okay." She eyed the space near Savannah's head, and added, "She said she's proud of you."

Just then, Alexis rounded the corner and caught the tail end of their conversation. The second she saw the overwhelming look of confusion that crossed Savannah's face, she ushered her daughter out, saying, "Lani, let our guest get dressed. You shouldn't be in here."

"But I had to go to the bathroom, and then I just needed to tell her about her mom. If it were me, I'd want to know."

"Honey, we've talked about this." Alexis shook her head.

"That's okay." Savannah stood and patted Lani's back as the girl shuffled out.

"Apologize to Savannah." Alexis laid her hands on her daughter's shoulders and turned Lani to face their guest.

Savannah bent to her knees and opened her arms.

"Come here." She enveloped Lani into a soft hug. When she released her, Savannah said, "Thank you for sharing your gift with me. It blessed me more than you know. I miss my mom terribly, and knowing she's here – well, you have no idea how much that means to me."

Savannah sniffed and sent Lani a look of thanks.

"Now, you know you're never alone." Lani leaned in to kiss her new friend's cheek before spinning on her heel to run down the hall.

"Grams! I'm hungry!" Lani's voice rang throughout the house.

Savannah looked at Alexis and let out a breath.

"Wow." She blinked. "I mean when Anderson told me that she talked to her grandmother – I just thought it was the product of highly creative child with an overactive imagination."

"I'm sorry." Alexis grimaced. "She means well, but it's

hard for her to understand how mind-boggling it can be for others."

"Is she always so forward?"

"I'm afraid so." Alexis chuckled and then reached for the door. "Oh, before I forget."

Alexis stepped into the hall to retrieve a plastic bag.

"Danny got you a few things." She set the bag inside the doorway. "He's downstairs waiting."

The thought of Danny being a few feet away made her face light up with joy.

"Great!"

"I'll let you finish in here." Alexis started to pull the door shut, but paused. "Again, I'm sorry about Lani."

Savannah put her hand on the door to stop Alexis and opened it slightly so that the two stood eye to eye.

"Really. Don't apologize. Lani is a joy to be around. After what I've been through – I need a bit of that right now. If anything, consider her my therapy after an ordeal."

Alexis' look of compassion could have easily been interpreted as pity, but Savannah waved it off. "I'm fine. Your brother saved me."

Alexis almost snorted. "He has a habit of doing that."

"Yeah, I know," she whispered to herself as she shut the door. She placed her back against it and slide down until she came to a sitting position on the floor. She gathered the robe around her and leaned into it as if she were being cradled.

When minutes turned into moments, she finally dug through the bag that Alexis had delivered. Her mom, whether here in spirit or not, was not making any appearances while her cousin was downstairs waiting.

17

Hank slapped his knee with glee as the group around the table hung on his every word.

"And, then she popped her head up and casually said, 'Did you scratch off the VIN number?'" Hank wiped away a tear that fell from laughing so hard. "Just like that! As if she was double-checking something as simple as turning off the oven."

It was apparent that Hank's amusement was shared by the whole group, as Savannah sailed through the door to hear them collectively howling with delight at her expense.

"Someone has to keep him in line." Savannah raised an eyebrow at Anderson before crossing her arms and leaning against the kitchen island.

Amelia watched her son's face light up at the sight of Savannah and kicked her daughter, Alexis, from under the table. The two exchanged a secret look as Hank sent them a frown.

Anderson was oblivious to it all. His focus was on Savannah. As he searched her eyes, he noticed they were much brighter than the day before. Maybe some downtime with his family was just what she needed.

"Where's Danny?" She searched the room.

"He's doing a perimeter check. He should be back in a few." Anderson nodded behind her toward the bay window that overlooked the cove.

"Why didn't you go?" Savannah tried to keep the irritation from her voice, especially since Anderson's family was watching. "You know I'd want to see him first thing."

"Knock it off, Smiles." The sound of Danny's loud voice boomed from behind.

Savannah spun and fell into his arms for the tightest embrace she'd had in years. Once Danny released her, he took her by the shoulders and skimmed her from head to toe.

"You okay?" The lines around his eyes deepened.

Her mouth curved into a slow grin. "I will be."

"Heard you had quite a scare."

"Nothing I can't handle."

Danny's warm eyes lit up as a smile transformed his broad features.

"Okay, then. I hate to cut our reunion short, but my partner and I have some catching up to do." When his cousin's face fell, Danny added, "It won't take long, Smiles."

Savannah sent him a glare as she punched him on the shoulder for effect.

Just as Danny feigned a shoulder injury, Anderson pushed his chair back and stood to join them. "Her right hook is no joke. I felt the full effects of it for two weeks."

Danny looked at his partner with awe while Savannah ducked her head in shame.

"I thought he was one of the bad guys and ended up

giving him a black eye." She winced, hoping Anderson's family wouldn't think she was a total loon.

As she glanced at the group sitting around the table, it seemed they did as every single person's eyes were wide. Amelia's jaw looked as if it would hit the tabletop.

It was Hank who broke the ice.

"Now that's my kind of girl." Hank winked at his son, beaming with amusement.

"Yeah." She shrugged. "I didn't mean to."

"You're ruining my reputation as a tough guy."

When Anderson whispered in her ear, his warm breath sent chills along her spine. When Savannah shivered, Anderson sent her a look of concern and gave her a once over. Although her welts had subsided, the multitude of cuts and bruises along her body would take more time. It was then that he wondered how long it would take the scars on the inside to heal.

If Savannah hadn't experienced the unusual sensation from her mother's visit upstairs, the way Anderson skimmed her with his eyes would have been enough to unnerve her.

"What?" She turned to him with a frown.

He immediately held up his hands. "Nothing. Just making sure you're okay."

"I'm great. I'd be better if you'd stop staring at me." This time, she didn't even try to hide the irritation in her voice.

Amelia covered her mouth as a chuckle escaped. It seemed her son had his hands full. It was then that she extended a free hand to Savannah.

"Come sit with me outside on the back porch." Amelia sent Savannah a look of amusement and continued, "You'll love spending time among all those glorious flowers we have outside. It will do your soul wonders. It always does mine. And, before we know it... those two will be done colluding behind closed doors."

Amelia put her arm around Savannah's shoulders and ushered her through a door that led from the kitchen to a lush garden. As soon as Savannah stepped outside, her eyes rounded with awe. If she thought the entrance to this home was grand, it was nothing compared to the back gardens.

"This is amazing." She descended a few steps to find a hammock and some Adirondack chairs nearby.

"Well, if we have to hide away somewhere—" Amelia shrugged and lowered herself to a chair, motioning for Savannah to do the same.

Savannah closed her eyes and exhaled, wondering when the last time was that she was able to truly let go since this ordeal started.

"Between my shower and this, I'm almost human again," she said.

"Anderson didn't tell us much, but I heard you had a close call."

Savannah forced her eyes open. She nodded, unsure of how to respond or if she wanted to.

Amelia noticed the tense look on her face and pat her arm.

"Why don't I give you some time to unwind?" She stood from her chair. "I'll send Alexis out with something warm to drink?"

Savannah's lips upturned in thanks.

Amelia reached for a soft blanket that was folded nearby.

"Here." She held out a hand to pull Savannah from the chair and ushered her to the hammock. "This is the most comfortable spot on the property."

As Savannah sank into the oversized hammock, Amelia

fluffed a small pillow under her head before tucking the soft blanket around her.

"There." Amelia stepped back. "That's nice, right?"

As a cool breeze skimmed around her body, Savannah snuggled into the blanket with a sigh.

"Thank you." Her soft voice barely escaped. Savannah blinked in efforts to stay awake, yet had a hard time doing anything except drift off to sleep.

Amelia's soft voice replied, "Just rest."

Once Amelia took the steps to the house, she paused and looked once more over her shoulder to find Savannah burrowing deeper into the fleece blanket and letting out a soft sigh of satisfaction.

"Sleep well," she whispered before slipping inside.

The second she stepped into the kitchen, Lani came barreling toward the door. Amelia threw her arms around the child's waist and caught her in mid-air.

"Whoa there, Lani. You're not going anywhere."

"But, I want to be with Vannah," Lani pouted.

"She's asleep, sweetheart. You need to let her rest."

Lani pleaded with her eyes and whispered, "Can I sit next to her and wait?"

"No." Amelia shook her head and raised her brow.

Lani tucked her chin and spun toward the living room.

"Fine. I'll wait, but I don't like it." Her bottom lip protruded.

"Well, I don't think she'd like it if you woke her up." Alexis approached with a steaming mug of hot chocolate. "I made this for her. I take it she's not to be disturbed?"

Amelia gave her a short nod. "You can leave it by the hammock. Just be quiet."

Just as Alexis was about to exit for the garden, Anderson stepped in next to her. "I'll take that."

When he slipped the mug from her hands, Alexis did a double-take.

"I thought you and Danny were talking." Alexis put a hand on his arm. "I can take it."

"We were. Now, we're not," Anderson said with a shrug. "This is mine, Sis. You take care of Lani – but Savannah is my responsibility."

"I think she's Danny's responsibility now." Alexis cut her eyes at him. "Your job was to deliver her safely... and you did."

Anderson narrowed his eyes but said nothing. He wouldn't fall for his sister's baiting. Instead, he spun on his heel and slipped out the door.

Both women scurried to the window to watch his approach.

"Are you thinking what I'm thinking?" Amelia's eyes sparkled with mischief.

"I think he's in deep."

Just as Anderson placed the mug on a table by the hammock, Lani snuck up to the window. "What's so interesting out there?"

When she noticed her uncle settling into a chair next to Savannah, she let out a dramatic sigh.

"Aw, I wanted to be the one that went outside to watch her."

Alexis uncrossed her arms to pull her daughter into her side and shook her head. "I don't think your uncle would appreciate that very much. We're not to interrupt them, okay?"

"Okay." Lani sighed. "I'm bored."

"Go upstairs. Grab some of your books, and we'll read. I'll be up in a second."

Lani cocked her head and narrowed her eyes in her

uncle's direction. "Just how long is he going to stay out there?"

"As long as it takes. Now scurry off, little one."

Alexis pursed her lips and pointed toward the stairwell with a look that every child understands, sending Lani running upstairs two at a time.

Amelia chuckled and shook her head. "She's only asking the million-dollar question. Do you see what I do?"

Both women eyed Anderson through the window with curiosity.

Alexis sent her mother a knowing look. "There's definitely something there."

Just as her mother was about to respond, Danny stepped in behind them and peered through the glass. Once he noticed the strain on Anderson's face as his partner gazed at Savannah, he cleared his throat, announcing himself. Both Amelia and Alexis turned around eyes wide.

"Do they train you guys to do that?" Alexis' hand flew to her chest.

Danny's crooked smile revealed a perfect set of teeth.

"Something like that." He stared out the window. "He knows the assignment of keeping her safe is over, right? The guy who was after her is dead. I can take care of her now."

"Well, there's still the matter of whatever the two of you were discussing behind closed doors." Amelia's right eyebrow arched for effect. "Are you going to let us know what or who we are supposedly hiding from?"

"That's a need-to-know topic, Amelia." Danny crossed his arms.

"Mom, look!" Alexis tugged on her mom's arm to alert their attention back outside.

Anderson rested his elbows on his knees, leaning forward to study Savannah's frown. She was wrestling with something deep within her sleep. Just when he was about to lay a hand on her arm for reassurance, she bolted to a sitting position nearly falling to the ground.

"Whoa!" Anderson lurched to steady the hammock. When he was sure she was secured in place, he searched her eyes, which were filled with anguish.

Savannah laid back down and clung to the blanket as if it would magically protect her from the dangers of her dreams.

"You're safe." He lowered himself next to her and took her into his arms.

Savannah let out a puff of air before biting her bottom lip. She would not lament over demons that could not harm her. It was then that it struck her that she had not prayed – at all.

Anderson lifted her chin, so they were almost nose to nose. When he saw a sense of realization pass through her eyes, he cocked his head with a frown.

"What is it?" He ran his fingers through her short locks and internally groaned. He hadn't planned on being this close or intimate, but it seemed anytime she showed distress, his first instinct was to comfort her.

"It's nothing." She held her breath, eyes wide. The thought of kissing him was forefront.

"Tell me." *Please tell me.* He needed any distraction

possible to keep him from closing the gap and sampling her lips.

Savannah relented with a sigh. "These dreams. Benny's eyes after he...died. The chase...the gunfire."

"He can't hurt you anymore." He pushed a few strands of hair back from her face.

She sighed. "I know, but these dreams are so real. And then it dawned on me that I've been so caught up in reacting that I haven't given any of it up in prayer."

Anderson's lips were claimed by a slow upturn. He thought it was sweet how tender her heart was and how her faith was forefront in all she did. Even the fact that she admitted she forgot to pray, meant that she had a strong enough relationship with God that he reminded her to.

Just as he was about to comment on it, she blurted, "Do you have to do that?" She let out a huff.

"Now what?" He grinned, absolutely unaware of how he affected her.

Savannah threw her legs over the side of the hammock and stood, taking a few steps. She needed the space to give her some clarity. It seemed every single time she was at her most vulnerable, he was there.

Anderson stood from the hammock as she spun to face him. While it was clear she was upset, he was clueless as to what he did.

He sent her a frown and crossed his arms to wait it out. If there was one thing he knew about Savannah, it was that she would give him a piece of her mind when she was ready. Since her scare at Tawni's place, she'd been harboring a chip on her shoulder. He figured at some point, it would blow. It seemed that time had come.

"Let me have it," he said.

"Look!" Savannah took a step backward, needing more

space. "I know this is just a job for you, but your job is over. Danny is here now, and Benny's not a threat anymore. You don't need to be so nice. You don't need to act like you care!"

His lips flattened to a hard line. His crystal blue eyes smoldered and changed to a shade that Savannah could only compare to a stormy sky.

"You think I don't care about you?!" he blurted.

Savannah threw up a hand. "You feel responsible for me!"

"I do, but it's more than that." Anderson took a step closer.

When Savannah let out a sound of exasperation, Anderson fought hard not to laugh. Even when she was fired up, she was adorable.

"You send me mixed signals. Tawni said you've broken so many hearts that she was surprised they didn't erect a statue in your honor for Valentine's Day."

"She did not." He shook his head in disbelief.

Savannah tilted her head and looked away. "She might as well have." She waved a hand in the air and stared off into the distance. "She told me enough. Enough to know that you leave broken hearts wherever you go."

"Are you afraid of a broken heart?" Anderson's soft voice was barely a whisper as he closed the gap and placed his hands on Savannah's hips.

Savannah caught her breath, unable to speak.

When she looked at him from the corner of her eye, Anderson's heart lurched.

She doesn't trust me. Anderson cupped her chin and brought it toward him.

"Don't," Savannah whispered. "Unless you really mean it."

Anderson gave her a look that spoke volumes before

leaning in. When he tasted her full lips for the second time – it was as if it were the first. This time there wasn't a car barreling past them as an excuse. This time, it was just the two of them, and it was because they both wanted it.

When Anderson's lips parted hers, Savannah's entire body sparked to life. Every part of her wanted this moment to last forever, but she knew a man in his line of duty wouldn't be around much longer. There would always be another mission.

With that thought, she pulled away, unable to meet his eyes. She laid her head on his shoulder, reveling at his touch as he tightened his arms around her.

When their kiss ended, disappointment permeated his spirit. The idea of losing her killed him, but until she fully trusted him with her heart – he didn't really have her.

"Am I going too fast?" Anderson rested his chin on the top of her head.

When she didn't answer, he lifted his head and noticed something out of the corner of his eye. He glanced at the kitchen window, where the curtains promptly closed. He chuckled, wondering how much his mother and sister had seen.

When Savannah's questioning eyes met his, he said, "I think we had some spectators."

"Ugh." She took a step back.

"They weren't spying. When I kissed you, it was unexpected. They were giving us privacy."

"Unexpected?" She sent him an icy stare.

"No, you misunderstood. I've only been thinking about it since the day I met you. Well, maybe not the day I met you – because you punched me out that first day." When he realized he was making things worse, he shook his head out of sheer frustration. "This isn't coming out right."

"You can say that again." She started for the house.

"Savannah. Wait!" He took her by the arm and spun her back into his.

"Just wait," he whispered.

"Anderson, this isn't a game. Believe it or not, I've got a heart under here." She tapped her chest.

"It's no game to me," he growled before closing the gap.

Their kiss was filled with passion and promise, leaving Savannah unable to do anything other than to get lost in the moment.

18

Tawni sensed them enter before she saw them. As she wiped her bar top clean, a foreboding swept over her as the front door of her bar opened. When she glanced up, immediately she knew the two men approaching were the ones that Anderson had warned them about.

Kevin stepped in behind her and placed a hand on the small of her back to whisper a warning.

"Just act natural. Tell them what they want to hear."

Tawni swallowed and nodded in response as one of the two men tried to catch her eye. She made him wait for it like she would any other bar patron on a Friday evening.

As Kevin slipped away at the opposite end of the bar, he sent Anderson a quick text that said, 'Your brother stopped by.'

He then looked over his shoulder and glanced at Tawni, who was filling an order for another customer as the two men in sunglasses patiently waited. He sensed their scowls beneath their pitch-black shades and stood nearby on high alert in case he was needed.

Let them wait. Tawni retrieved a couple of Coronas from her ice bin to hand across the bar to a waitress. Once her employee left, Tawni angled her chin in the direction of both men.

"What can I get you?" She threw a towel over her shoulder.

"I'm with the CIA." The man flashed a badge, only to slip it back into his jacket. "We're looking for someone."

"Honey, aren't we all?" She raised a brow. "Mind if I take a closer look at your badge?"

He shrugged, knowing she wouldn't know what to look for or if it was a fake. They didn't run around, showing Odyssey badges. They couldn't, especially since no one technically knew about it.

"Sure." He retrieved it from his jacket once more and pushed it toward her.

Tawni squinted at the tiny print. It listed the agent's credentials along with an official-looking government seal. It seemed authentic, but either way, these two were bad news.

"Agent Underwood?" she asked, reading his name on the card.

"Yes, and this is my partner, Agent Blaire."

The only movements Blaire offered since taking a position behind his partner were a short nod and a closed mouth smirk, which disappeared the second he delivered it. He then returned to his stoic stance as if a statue. He then returned to his stoic stance as if a statue.

"How may I be of service, gentlemen?" Tawni put a hand on her hip and sent them both her most flirtatious smile. The more she softened her approach – the more they'd trust her answers.

Underwood slipped his phone from his pocket to reveal two photos, one of Anderson and the other of Savannah.

"Do you recognize either of these people?" Underwood slipped off his glasses to reveal eyes of steel. He stared straight through her soul, sending waves of shivers down her back as if he could read her thoughts.

Tawni shook it off and continued to play the game. She studied the photos and enthusiastically replied, "Oh, yeah. I remember them! You missed quite the drama this week."

Although the pair knew the details, they let her continue.

"That's Monica." She jabbed Savannah's image on the agent's phone. "It was open mic night. She lit up our stage and won the whole crowd over."

Tawni softened her face at the memory, much like a fangirl would with starry eyes.

"And him?" Underwood swiped the screen to reveal another photo of Anderson.

Tawni stared at it and said, "I think that's her manager or bodyguard or something. His name was Randy or Andy."

Tawni tapped her temple. "The only reason I remember is that a crazy fan stalked Monica, and that guy had to save her. The cops showed up and everything."

"Do you have any of the surveillance videos?" Underwood raised an eyebrow, looking for cameras, but didn't notice any.

"Nope. Folks around here know that if they mess with me or my bar, we have ways of taking care of them. Just call it Southern justice." Her expression reflected that of the agent's as she sent her own silent message of intimidation. "After all, it is a small town."

Underwood clenched. He got the message loud and clear.

"Do you know which way they were headed?"

Tawni wobbled her head side-to-side and took a minute to think.

"You know. I think they said something about Arkansas or was it Kansas?" Tawni scratched her temple. "Nope. It was Arkansas. I'm sure of it."

"Mind if we take a look around?" Underwood slipped his phone inside his jacket.

"Mind if I take a look at your warrant?" She blinked a few times and flattened her lips as a look adorned her face, which said, 'not in your lifetime.'

Underwood slipped his sunglasses on before sending her a curt nod. "You've been a huge help. Thank you, Tawni."

Tawni's mouth parted as the two spun on their heel to exit.

"You're going to catch flies." Kevin approached and gently pushed her jaw closed with the tip of his finger.

"He knew my name." She shook her shoulders to rid herself of the creepy crawling feeling that spiraled through every cell in her body.

"Big brother knows everyone, babe. He did his homework. That's all." Kevin sent her a reassuring gaze.

"Why didn't you come over to back me up?" Her eyes blazed.

"I had my eye on you the whole time. If I'd rushed to your side – they'd have known we were trying to cover something up. Best to let them think we didn't have anything to hide."

Tawni grunted with displeasure and reached for a beer.

"Think we pulled it off?" She took a large swig hoping the coolness of it would settle her nerves.

"Let's hope so. From the way you were handling them, it could go either way."

"What?! I was nice!" Her voice hitched.

"Yeah, until you weren't." He chuckled. "But lucky for us, anyone could attest to your prickly demeanor."

Tawni snapped him in the side with a towel, sending his arms in the air.

"I give. I give." He drew her into an embrace and placed a soft kiss on her lips.

ONCE OUTSIDE, both men loaded into their standard-issue black SUV without a word. Finally, Blaire broke the silence. "She's lying."

"You better believe it," Underwood growled as he retrieved a small round case from the glove box.

He firmly snapped it in place inside the cup holder until it clicked. When a blue light glowed along the outer edges of the case, he slid the top open.

Underwood drew in a slow breath and blinked a few times before removing a clear contact from his left eye.

His partner, Blaire, winced and looked away. "I'm glad you're the one who gets to wear that thing."

Underwood raised an eyebrow in his direction. Having a partner with weakness was a liability.

"Pu-"

"Do you kiss your momma with that mouth?" Blaire cut him off. His eyes were blazing as if on fire.

Underwood chuckled as he placed the contact lens into the container and closed the lid. Once it was sealed, the blue light transformed into dark green.

"Play," Underwood spoke into the speaker that was mounted near the visor.

Instantaneously, the windshield went dark, and the events from inside replayed before them. Both men scanned the footage, looking for anything they may have missed while talking to Tawni.

"Wait." Blaire touched the windshield to pause the recording of their entrance. "See that guy? The one that stepped in behind Tawni. He looks our way for a brief second and says something before walking away."

Underwood tapped on the man's face and zoomed in. Since their windshield and the electronic dash was equivalent to a computer, they could tap into their central database and determine who the suspect was with basic facial recognition. He touched the screen and circled Kevin's image, before double-tapping again.

A red box popped up next to the suspect's face. Inside it, a multitude of photos began filtering for comparison. In a matter of seconds, they found what they were looking for.

Underwood glanced between the distrustful gaze that Kevin's image was sending their way to the mugshot the computer matched him to.

"Kevin Hanks. Full-time bouncer, former military, and he has a criminal record."

"They know something." Blaire reached for the door handle. "Let's go back and make them talk."

Underwood locked the doors and shook his head.

"No. I need to call it in first."

"Let me work them over." Blaire salivated with the prospect of the pain he was about to inflict.

At the gleam in his partner's eyes, Underwood immediately killed the engine. Just as the pair were about to exit the SUV, the Director's eerie voice drifted through the surround sound.

"I got your upload."

The pair stilled in their seats and stared at one another, unsure of how to respond. Navigating a relationship with this new Director was like walking through a minefield.

When neither operative answered, Director Brennen, cleared her throat, and said, "You think she knows more than she's letting on?"

Blaire blinked in Underwood's direction and whispered in what he thought was a hushed tone.

"How does she know?" He looked around him for any sign of a listening device.

"Because it's my job to know, Agent Blaire," her voice boomed.

Just then, their SUV remotely started. The pair could only assume that the Director had done it from her office.

The two stared at one another with their eyes wide.

When their boss' face popped up on the windshield, both men blinked in awe. They assumed they were never alone, yet had no idea their car could video conference with their new technology.

"Yes, ma'am." Agency Blaire swallowed.

"Did you get close enough to her to clone her phone?" She raised a bushy eyebrow in Underwood's direction.

Underwood nodded. "I did."

"Double check that it's a viable link."

When the Director leaned toward the camera, her face enlarged on their windshield. Underwood blinked and averted his gaze.

Underwood shivered in response. From the Director's

sharp nose to her stringent stare, a glimpse of her face that close was something that couldn't be unseen.

As instructed, he reached into his jacket for the phone they used to clone Tawni's. He checked the display to find it the cloning was successful.

"It's complete, ma'am," Underwood said.

"Excellent." Her voice hummed with satisfaction. "Now, we wait. Head back to the field office, sign in your vehicle, and get on the next flight back here."

"We were just about to go back inside and ask a few more questions," Blaire interrupted, anxious to dig deeper into what was really going on.

"Her phone will do the work for us, Agent Blaire."

"You heard her." Underwood pushed a button to clear the windshield reverting it back to clear glass.

As he put his car in reverse and all images of the bar or traces of Director Brennen vanished, Blaire blew a sigh of relief.

"Man, she creeps me out. I don't know what's worse… creepy clowns in horror movies or her."

Suddenly, her voice filled the car system once more. "I heard that, Blaire. Once your flight arrives, report back immediately, and come to my office."

Both men swallowed, saying nothing in return. In fact, they said nothing for the entire drive.

19

It had been three days since their kiss. Both Savannah and Anderson danced around the subject, unsure of how to behave or if they should bring it up. He wanted to kiss her again, but they'd not had a moment to themselves since. Between family dinners and closed-door sessions with Danny, there wasn't much free time for the two of them.

While Danny bantered about approaching their handler at the CIA, all Anderson could think about was how long it had been since he'd been alone with Savannah. It was then that his partner snapped his fingers in front of his face.

"Earth to Anderson." Danny's eyes narrowed. "Are you even listening, man? I was just asking you if we should send our team leader at the agency a message or if you thought Odyssey's reach went further than their organization."

"Sorry." Anderson shook his head. "You know my answer to that already."

Danny stared into the flames that blazed in the firepit in front of them. He rubbed his hands together and said, "My gut tells me we can trust him."

"I don't know." Anderson reached for a bag of marshmallows and tore it open, pushing one to a stick and holding it over the flames.

"Odyssey was supposed to be a decentralized unit with its own powers, and yet, somehow, we got Sanger killed by asking him a few simple questions. This – whatever it is – is deeper than Odyssey." Anderson sighed. "Until we know we can trust Grant, we can't approach our former team at the agency. How do we know the CIA doesn't have a mole?"

Anderson stared at his phone, thinking about Kevin's text message from earlier.

"When I called Kevin after his text, he said it was the CIA who came looking for us at Tawni's."

Danny tapped his finger on the arm of his chair. "Yeah, but we know Grant. We've been to his house for family get-togethers. His wife has even tried to fix you up…a few times. They're like family."

"Better than anyone, you should know you can't trust others in this business." Anderson's eyes clouded.

Danny rubbed his temples. "Okay. We'll wait, but what is or next step? If we can't go back in, then we're out in the cold."

Anderson shrugged and stared at their surroundings. "This doesn't seem so bad."

"We can't stay out here forever, Anderson. That's not fair to your family…or us. I'm going stir crazy." Danny fidgeted with a stick. "And, eventually, they'll catch up to us."

"I know." Anderson leaned back with an exhale to stare at the lake, knowing they had to make a move. The question was which one.

Just as Anderson glanced back to his partner, Savannah and his mom approached from the back of the house. His breath caught at the sight of Savannah in a red sundress. A white shawl slipped from her shoulders to rest at her lower back. Anderson looked where it lay on her arms and wished he could use the ends of it to pull her close.

When Danny observed his partner's reaction to Savannah, his stomach clenched. The last thing he needed was to have his partner's judgment clouded or his cousin's heart broken. In their line of work, they always had to move on. There wasn't much time for a relationship unless that person was fully aware of the loneliness this job caused.

Most operatives who married usually ended up in divorce. The lucky few with a good marriage was due to either a very understanding or apathetic spouse. Chances of the latter were higher.

Danny wanted more than that for Savannah. When he was about to say so, Anderson stood with an expectant stare, taking a step in her direction. Danny watched the silent communication between the two and frowned. It could already be too late.

When Anderson approached Savannah, he prayed what he felt wasn't written across his face for all to see. He'd never seen her look more beautiful and wanted to tell her, but not with an audience.

Savannah fidgeted with her shawl and inwardly bit her lips as Anderson looked her over. His lingering gaze had the effect of a branding iron, leaving her skin as though it had been singed from head to toe. The exchange wasn't lost on Amelia, who trailed behind Savannah.

Amelia broke the silence. "We thought it would be nice if we could have dinner out by the cove. Get cleaned up, boys. We're all dressing up tonight."

Danny looked from his cousin's curious expression to Anderson's look of desire and nudged his partner in the ribs.

"Dude, that's my family," Danny mumbled under his breath.

Anderson blinked as if snapping out of a trance and looked at Danny with a frown, before leaning forward to kiss his mother's cheek. He gave his mother a once over, noticing she'd also taken care to give her appearance a lift.

"So, what's the occasion?" he asked.

"Tyler's arriving tonight, and we have some news," Alexis said as she stepped into the garden.

Tyler, Alexis' husband, had yet to make his way to their safe haven. Tyler was the news director at a small television station near Dallas. With Alexis' ratings as the evening anchor, they'd won an award. Tyler traveled to New York to accept it on Alexis' behalf.

Although Alexis would have liked to be there to accept in person, she understood the gravity of Anderson's back-up plan in case her brother's job put them in danger.

Tyler, on the other hand, did not. He refused to let a junior department head accept the award and insisted on bringing it to Alexis after he accepted it in person.

"You realize he could put us all in jeopardy?" Anderson frowned. Even though he'd grown up with Tyler and held him in high regard, that didn't mean he agreed with his decisions – especially if they were the wrong ones.

Danny squeezed the bridge of his nose and groaned. "Smiles, want to take a walk?"

Savannah thread her arm through Danny's as he led her from a family conversation that probably should stay private.

"Excuse us." He shot a grin at both women before leading his cousin toward the docks.

Savannah let out a deep sigh. "I'm so not used to that."

"To what?"

"Family drama."

Danny chuckled and ushered her past the banquet table down the hill to the cove. They sat on a bench that gave them a view. The line between the water and sky was scattered with sparse twinkling lights from a few homes across the lake.

"They're not squabbling. That's just a normal family...communicating."

Savannah shrugged her shoulders, trying to remember what that was like.

"When it was just Mom, Dad, and me – it wasn't so..." She paused to put her finger on the right description but failed. She shook her head at the remembrance of their peaceful co-existing unit and looked up at the sky with a heavy heart. "They always gave me comfort, but I have to remember that they died before I really grew up."

Danny threw an arm over her shoulders and pulled her in so that her head rested on his shoulder.

"Savannah," Danny paused with a sigh. How could he tell her what might have been if her parents had survived? He tread lightly. "Do you know the difference between a flower and a weed?"

Savannah's brow knitted.

He smirked at the frustration that clouded her features. "It's perception."

"Since when did you get so philosophical? Are we really talking about weeds?" She chuckled.

"Flowers." Danny's lips curled into a mischievous grin. "It's all in how you look at it."

"Did you learn that in the CIA?" she teased.

"Actually, I saw it on the label of a teabag." He laughed. "But it stuck with me."

"A tea bag?" She giggled.

He raised a hand and continued. "Look, Smiles. The older you get, the more phases your family goes through. Just because the three of you didn't squabble at that time in your life, doesn't mean you wouldn't have had your fair share of issues later. What seemed rosy and easy at one point in your life could have changed...given time. And, they may seem like they're squabbling to you, but that, there..." He pointed toward Anderson and his sister and nodded. "Is love. If they didn't care, they wouldn't bother."

Danny glanced up the hill at Amelia, who stood shaking her head at her two kids. Neither looked ready to back down from the argument that ensued.

He chuckled and continued, "I remember my family when it was time for me to go to college. It was bittersweet. I know my parents loved me, but I was headstrong and ready to be on my own. And, I'm sure something in them was ready to let me." His soft chuckle reverberated through his broad chest. "It's nature's way of kicking us out of the nest."

"Well, I wasn't ready to be kicked out of the nest." Savannah pulled away from Danny's shoulder and stared at the calm water surrounding them. The rocks on either side of the cove secluded them from any unwanted visitors. It was then that she noticed the security cameras on either side and reminded herself to ask Danny about it later.

"I know you weren't." His soft voice fell to a whisper. "You were a baby when your folks passed."

"I was almost fifteen."

"That's a baby in my book."

"Maybe." A subtle look crossed her face. "I don't know what I would have done if your parents hadn't taken me in." Savannah bit her upper lip in efforts to keep the memories at bay. "The military packed up our belongings and moved me out of the only home I had at the time."

She shook her head and let out a breath. "I'll never forget sitting inside as sounds reverberated off the concrete walls and echoed through the house when the movers loaded that last few things in a truck. I know it was only base housing, but it was my home. And that concrete bunker which once held my mom's laughter bouncing through it became as empty as a tomb."

"Was that on Okinawa?" he asked. Her family moved so often it was hard to keep track.

She nodded and continued. "After they packed me up, I was escorted to a tarmac, where I boarded a C-141 and sat in a sling seat for over thirteen hours."

Savannah straightened her back at the remembrance of how it ached in those seats during her flight.

"Thankfully, because of Dad's rank – I was able to sit in front near the bathroom." She snickered. "If you want to call it that. The conditions were the bare minimum."

Savannah's smile was a slow one, but it was one just the same, and Danny took relief in it as she continued, "The only highlight on that flight home was the cute guys in their camos making their way to use the head. My seat was against the wall of the plane, which put everyone knee to knee. You couldn't see across the rows in the middle to notice who sat in the sling seats backed against the other side of the plane, but I imagine there wasn't any room to make their way down an aisle on that side either. We were all a little too close if you ask me."

Danny smirked. "Like sardines. I've been on one."

Savannah cocked her head. "That's right. So, you know. Anyway, those adorable boys in their combat boots and fatigues had to walk along the rails at the tops of the sling seats in the middle – practically swinging from the posts to reach the front. As each one approached my seat, they stared at me with curious wonder, probably trying to figure out why a young girl was being escorted stateside."

"They probably thought you were with your sponsor."

"No. He was a young Lieutenant – and too young to be my dad." Savannah raised an eyebrow. "You know. I know they were trying to do right by me."

"They?" Danny wondered if she were talking about her parents.

"The military. I was accompanied home by someone from Dad's squadron. I couldn't tell you his name now. Knowing he worked for my dad and the fact that he did his best to help me in a time of need should have been comforting. Only, it made me feel more alone than you could ever imagine. If my parents weren't with me – what did it matter? After all, I was on my own. As nice as this young Lieutenant was, I was by myself."

"You had us." Danny's voice dipped.

She shook her head. "I know, but by the time I came to live with your parents, you had already left for college."

"They adored you." He stressed with a look of concern. She'd never shared this much before. Whatever had happened over the last few weeks had obviously taken its toll.

"I know." She sighed.

Her tender demeanor vanished as a mischievous glint flashed through her eyes.

"Thank goodness for those young guys swinging from the rafters on that flight, though. They kept me sane for the longest ride of my life. I always did have a thing for a man in the service." Savannah briefly looked up the hill at Anderson. "I guess that's a hard habit to break." She pursed her lips.

Danny was about to warn her about her growing attraction when Anderson cradled his head and fell to his knees.

Neither Savannah or Danny hesitated. Like parents racing to save their child, both darted up the hill to join Alexis and Amelia, who were trying to help Anderson up without much luck.

"Let me through!" Savannah yelled.

Alexis and Amelia's grave expressions mirrored what Savannah had experienced prior to understanding Anderson's visions, yet neither woman moved out of the way.

As Anderson moaned in agony, Savannah laid a hand on his mother's arm.

"Please!" she pleaded. "I can help."

Amelia searched Savannah's face and finally stepped aside.

Savannah lowered to her knees and gently cupped Anderson's face. "I'm here."

The second she spoke, her words shattered the whirlwind that bombarded his senses. No longer was he drowning in the images surrounding him. Savannah anchored him to the present and gave him the ability to fight the vision that threatened to keep him prisoner.

20

Flashes of his sister in the future or past, Anderson wasn't sure which, reigned upon him the second he'd touched his sister's arm during their argument. And what he experienced sent his mind reeling.

Not only was Anderson unsure of what he was encountering, but he was also thoroughly confused by what the vision meant. If it were a premonition of what was to come, it meant this was a dire warning for his sister because, at that moment, she was in heaven with his grandmother. If it were a glimpse of the past...well, he couldn't wrap his mind around that.

The instant he realized he was beyond an earthly realm, Anderson acknowledged how bold and beautiful the colors were. They were unlike anything he'd seen on earth. In fact, he couldn't even place them on a color scale.

Then, he heard a distinct hum from every direction. It soon amplified into music that played on a scale that he couldn't pinpoint. The notes or half-notes harmonized in a way that left his soul tingling as if the music glided around him with energy.

Every detail begged for his attention, and he stood in awe at each fraction of light...every whisper of reconciliation...and every emotion that blanketed his soul. It was as if he could sense the knowledge of everyone who existed in this place. While content to observe his surroundings, he was unable to move as if secured in place and forced to eavesdrop on conversations he shouldn't have been privy to.

It was then that he tried to depart from this keen sense of awareness...to get distance from a concept that had him spinning, but he was unable. It was as if this place had a magnetic hold on his soul.

That's when he heard Savannah's voice. Her concern broke through the dome that seemed to push him further into this other world and covered him with a sense of peace. The second he sensed her hands on his skin, her presence pulled him back to reality. Finally, Anderson blinked and came to.

Savannah scanned his face, noticing the sweat that gathered around his hairline. Whatever had taken place – wherever his mind went – had affected him on a deeper level than what she'd experienced before. She stroked his face with the back of her hand.

His damp skin was concerning, but she said nothing as his mother and sister stood over them with an anxious look. The last thing she wanted to do was worry them more than they already were.

Savannah let out a quiet sigh of relief when she found Anderson's eyes dilated, but clear.

"You with me?" she whispered.

When he gave her a slight nod, she stroked his temples with her thumbs as if massaging the tension from his head.

Danny, Alexis, and Amelia blinked at the bond between the two. It was clear Savannah was more than capable of handling whatever was going on. This event surely wasn't the first time.

"Anderson?" Amelia's hand shook as she placed it on his shoulder, hoping for an explanation. "Are you sick?"

His low voice was rough but clear. "No, Mom. I'm fine."

Since her son's back was to her, Amelia glanced at Savannah for reassurance. Savannah dragged her eyes from Anderson's to send his mother a look of reassurance before averting her attention back to the man that had her heart beating in double-time.

"You scared me." She took his hands in hers and urged him to look at her.

"I'm okay." He searched her face, and what he saw filled him with a peace that was reminiscent of what he'd experienced in this most recent vision.

Anderson's lips upturned, showcasing the dimples that sent Savannah's stomach into fits. She glanced at the ground and counted to ten as he leaned in to kiss her forehead.

Although he wished it was just the two of them, his family was waiting for an explanation. He sent Savannah a look of chagrin, knowing it was time to face the music.

She blinked when it dawned on her.

"You haven't told them?" she whispered in awe.

"No," he whispered.

"Not even Danny?" A small crease appeared between her brows.

When he shook his head, Savannah blinked with wonder that she was the only one who knew his secret.

Anderson leaned in and whispered in her ear. "It's not like I've spent time with them since all this happened."

Savannah raised an eyebrow and cocked her head. "You've seen Danny since the accident, though."

"True, but I wasn't ready to share at that point. You just

caught me unaware, Smiles. You gave me no choice but to trust you."

Her mouth flattened as she shot him an evil eye.

Anderson bit his lips to hide a grin. Although his teasing nature seemed to always ruffle her feathers, she took it in stride.

The point he was trying to make – the reason he'd confided in her - was his way of telling her that she was special, but that sailed over her head at the sound of her nickname.

Both Alexis and Amelia glanced at Savannah, wondering how much heartbreak Anderson was in for. The more push than pull between the two – the more both women worried that Anderson was in over his head.

Although it was clear Savannah had the situation under control, the urge to know what had happened finally had Amelia looking to Danny for help.

"Up you go," Danny mumbled as both he and Amelia slipped an arm around Anderson.

Once Anderson stood, they took a step back. Anderson pursed his lips, thinking they looked like expectant parents waiting for their child to take its first step.

He reached for Savannah's hand. Just because he had recovered, didn't mean he was ready to let go of the bond they'd discovered. He frowned, wondering what that meant for him or their future. He'd never considered one before that was anything other than what the next job was.

"What was that?" His mother interrupted his thoughts.

"You didn't have to play the victim to win our argument, you know." Alexis huffed and crossed her arms.

His slow smile pulled at his sister's heartstrings. The two were as loving as siblings could be until they were on opposite corners of a subject. Then, they were like two boxers in a ring.

He glanced at his watch, wondering how long he was out and looked at Alexis in haste.

"My story will have to wait. It's time for us to bring Tyler in. I assume he knows the protocol?"

He waited for Alexis to answer. When she didn't, he added, "Does he know where to meet us?"

Alexis threw her hand in the air. "Yes. He's a big boy. He's been prepped. He knows the rules and how to stay low. He had a friend drop him off and should be waiting for you – on time. But you're right, you'll be late if you don't go."

Amelia shook her head at her son and pointed toward a chair in the garden. "You'll stay put where I can keep an eye on you. Your dad can go in your place."

"Mom," Anderson started, but his mother wouldn't hear any of it.

"Go! Sit down." She pointed toward the back of the house before yelling over her shoulder. "Hank! Get the keys. You're leaving with Danny."

Amelia gave Danny an expectant stare to which he raised his hands in defeat.

"You're the boss, Mrs. Evans." Danny conceded but whispered to Anderson as he passed. "She doesn't mess around."

"That she doesn't." Anderson grinned and took a seat under his mother's supervision. Since he still had Savannah's hand in his, he pulled her into his lap.

"Well, I feel like a third wheel." Alexis followed her mother and Danny toward the house.

"Sis, wait," Anderson called after her.

Alexis turned with a perplexed face and approached.

"Have a seat." He motioned to the chair next to him.

Savannah slipped from Anderson's lap and stood. "I'll let you two handle this from here."

"No. Stay." He squeezed her hand.

Although she wanted to - this was a family matter...and she wasn't family. The reality of it hit her like a splash of cold water. She didn't have a claim to Anderson. She wasn't his fiancé or even his girlfriend. He'd not declared what his intentions were – just that he liked her company.

"Catch me later," she said.

She squeezed his hand in return and dropped it, but not before Anderson saw a glimpse of sadness that crossed her face. She quickly covered it with the cool façade that she put on for almost everyone in her life. He may not have even noticed the depths of her emotions when they first met because of the barriers she had built around her heart, but he now knew her well enough to know something had transpired to give her concern.

As he watched her leave, his heart swirled with a mixture of emotions. He battled the urge to pursue her yet forced himself to stay. At the moment, his top priority was his sister's expectant stare. It bore into the side of his skull like a drill. It was only when his sister whistled that he finally dragged his gaze from Savannah.

"You've never been like this before." Alexis pointed her finger at him.

"I know. About earlier," Anderson started.

"No. I don't mean when you passed out. I'll get to that. I mean with her." Alexis glanced toward the house just as Savannah's willowy frame vanished through the door.

"You're different with her." Alexis studied his face. "It's like you're connected on a level that I never knew existed. You love her."

"I don't...love her?" Anderson's voice rose a half octave as he questioned himself. It was then that the realization hit him like a three-hundred-pound gorilla.

How did I not know?

As the reality of his emotions came to light, Anderson rubbed his fingers along his jaw. It was as if someone had sucker-punched him. The air in his lungs constricted and left him faint. He sat up a bit more straight in his chair to drag in a breath the best he could.

Alexis' laughter rang through the air. Her amusement should have been infectious, but it wasn't -because it was at his expense. All he wanted to do was tear after Savannah to take her in his arms.

"Stop," Alexis said between hitched breaths dabbing her eyes. "You're killing me. You didn't know?"

Anderson cocked his head.

"How could you not?!" She wiped her face dry. "You have me in tears right now. That's the funniest thing ever! You moon over her, and you didn't recognize what was right in front of your face?"

"I don't moon over her." He flashed a frown in her direction. "I'm a tough guy. Tough guys don't moon over women. They usually fall at my feet."

"Well, I got news for you, brother. This one likes you. That's clear, but she's definitely not falling at your feet. In fact, I think the jury is still out on what she feels for you at all."

Anderson sent his sister a look of steel. He didn't need to be reminded. Savannah's walls were probably higher than the one that surrounded most of their property.

"Changing the subject." He let out a huff. How could he tell his sister what he experienced without her thinking he should be committed? Anderson took a deep breath.

"Where do I start?" He shook his head.

"From the beginning is best." Alexis reached for her brother's hand and stroked his arm. "Go slow. Whatever it is, you can tell me."

"I saw you and Grandma...in heaven. I saw it clear as day."

He winced, hoping she wouldn't think he was deranged. When Alexis went pale, he reached for her arm and kicked himself for upsetting her.

"I'm sorry, Lexi. I shouldn't have said anything."

She shook her head and let out a sob while covering her face. When she finally withdrew her hands, she ran them through her hair before wiping her cheeks dry. Through her tears, Alexis met his concerned gaze with a look of assurance.

"What you saw was real," she finally choked out.

It was Anderson's turn to be shocked. Before Alexis married Tyler, she'd been in a hostage situation in which she'd been shot. It had been touch and go, but she had pulled through surgery and recovered.

"Did your heart stop during surgery? Was it some sort of near-death experience?" He scooted closer to the edge of his seat.

"I don't know what happened. I - I didn't even remember it until a few weeks later. I thought they were dreams, not memories. The more these dreams replayed in my sleep, the more real they became."

"I also saw a child among you," Anderson said, afraid to bring up the name of the child that was there with him in the vision. "He looked like he could be Lani's twin."

Alexis' eyes misted at his description. Not that she doubted her brother's intuition, but if there ever had been a glimmer of disbelief - that one sentence would have blown it away.

She covered her mouth and nodded. When she finally responded, she whispered, "I miscarried a few years before Lani. He is mine. His name is Milo."

Anderson let out a whistle, unable to believe how vividly he could recall the child's face.

"I know." She responded at the look of wonder that crossed her brother's features.

She wiped a tear away from her cheek, this time from the bittersweet emotions that pulled at her heart.

"It was the hardest thing I ever did...leaving him, but it wasn't my time. And, Grandma urged me to go back."

She shook her head and stared at the clouds as she recalled her experience.

"I often wonder what would have happened if I'd stayed, but I'm happy. Tyler and I got married. And, Lani... she will always miss her dad, but Tyler is a great stepfather. I was going to wait to tell you along with everyone else at dinner, but...we're expecting a baby."

Anderson's mouth fell open. "What?!"

"Shhh." She looked over her shoulder. Thankfully, no one was within view.

"Lexi." Anderson's voice was thick with emotion as he drew her into a soft hug. "I'm so happy for both of you."

As she sniffled, he pulled back and sent her a knowing grin. "No wonder you've been so riled up lately. You're pregnant."

He shook his head. "I remember when you were pregnant with Lani. You were a bear back then."

Anderson chuckled, thinking of how much his brother-in-law had in store for him.

"Poor Tyler." He was in stitches until Alexis smacked his knee. She tried to frown but soon joined him with a soft chuckle.

"I know." She rolled her eyes. "My emotions are all over the map. Mom thinks I'm stressed because we're here, and I am. But..."

"I know. It won't be long. I promise. Danny and I have a plan." Anderson stretched the truth. They almost had a plan.

"Who or what are we hiding from, Anderson?" Her face etched with worry.

"The less you know – the better." He stood and offered her a hand. "Can you get up?"

"I'm not an invalid. I'm pregnant, dummy." She shot him an evil eye and stood of her own accord. "And don't say anything. We wanted to wait to tell everyone until we knew it was safe. Tyler and I want to announce it together."

Anderson placed his finger over his heart and made an imaginary cross. It was then that he remembered her revelation about the miscarriage.

"Are you healthy? And the baby?"

She nodded. "Everything's fine. If anything, I should ask if you're okay. What exactly are these visions? How and when did they start? What's causing them?" She reached for his arms and searched his face. "And, what are you going to do about Savannah when this job is over?"

"Let's take a walk." He offered his arm toward the lake.

21

Once Savannah returned inside, she wound her way through the spacious home to find Hank and Danny exiting to the garage. She approached unnoticed and peered over Danny's shoulder as he punched a code into a panel just outside the doorway. She memorized the sequence of numbers for no other reason than to soothe her curious nature.

It was then that lights illuminated the five-car garage, and the men entered the short stairwell.

"Can I come?" She finally descended a few steps.

Danny looked up with surprise and said, "No, kiddo. I'm sorry. It's just a precaution."

Before Hank slipped into the passenger seat, he pointed at the door. "Amelia is probably finishing up the last touches for dinner. I bet she could use some help with Lani."

As Savannah watched their vehicle back out into the large circular drive, she watched her cousin push a button on the dash that slid the garage door in place. The sides, top, and bottom closed from the edges, much like an aperture of a camera.

Once she made her way inside, she heard Amelia singing in the kitchen and smiled. Savannah turned the corner and stepped through - instantly recognizing a traditional gospel song from her youth.

"That was always one of my favorite songs growing up," Savannah commented, as she remembered the times she'd sung the same lyrics in church with her parents.

Amelia's face softened. "It is Well with My Soul?"

"Mmm-hmm." Savannah nodded before staring into the distance with remembrance.

"Is that so?" Amelia watched her with curiosity.

She didn't want to pry but wanted to know more about the woman who had stolen her son's heart.

Savannah nodded as a bittersweet pang resonated through her chest. No matter where she and her parents lived or how many times they moved throughout all her dad's duty stations, the one constant in life was attending church and her faith. It was the mainstay of an ever-changing life. After her parents passed, her faith was almost the only thing that helped her through the grief.

Savannah cocked her head. "No matter what else life threw at me or how hard things got, that song always reminded me of how blessed I was...am."

Amelia put the finishing touches on her salad and scrunched her nose. "I knew I liked you. From the second I saw you, scratches, bandages and all, there was something about you." Amelia pointed a finger in her direction. "My son senses it too. You've knocked him for a loop. I can tell."

"Oh, boy." Savannah shook her head. "If the way I looked when I arrived isn't a metaphor for my life, I don't know what is. Although a survivor, I'm broken and bruised, yet surrounded by people who care."

Amelia squinted and pursed her lips. "Wise. That's what you are."

"No." Savannah made a face. "I've just lived a lot and learned that life is too short to be bitter when bad things happen. Bad things happen all the time, but so do good things. We just have to open our eyes and count our blessings through the chaos around us."

"Ain't that the truth?" Amelia set the salad bowl to the side and placed a hand on her hip. "I notice you've not commented on what I said about Anderson." She raised an eyebrow.

"You're nosy." Savannah narrowed her eyes. The woman didn't pull any punches.

"You're direct." Amelia waited.

Savannah nodded in agreement.

Amelia gave her a look and said, "Then why are you avoiding the subject of my son?"

Savannah groaned. "Mrs. Evans..."

Amelia laid a hand on her arm. "Amelia."

Savannah shot her a look that spoke volumes, but instead of explaining, she said, "It's complicated."

"Life usually is, yet when it's something worth fighting for, you muddle through and make it work."

"His job – his life. It's fluid and crazy. While my life...let's just say that once this is all over, I'll go back to my ordinary day-to-day shuffle and run my bridal business."

Amelia wagged a finger in the air. "I don't notice anything ordinary about you. From what Anderson's told me, you may have a budding singing career in the wings."

Savannah scoffed. "That's just a fluke. I've been down that road. I'm not the right package, or so I've been told."

"Now, I don't know you very well, but you don't seem like

the kind of girl who would put stock into what someone else thinks about you."

Savannah shrugged. "Anyway - I came in here to see if I could help with dinner."

Sensing that Savannah was done talking about her life, Amelia stared out the window toward the yard.

"You can track down Lani for me. Alexis is upstairs touching up her makeup, and Lani went out to the garden to play. Keeping that child busy is all the help I need."

"She's a handful." Savannah's heart lit up.

"Oh yeah." Amelia chuckled. "We wouldn't have it any other way. She lights up our lives. One day you'll have one of your own and see for yourself."

Savannah's face twisted with a look of dismay before she let out a laugh.

"Um, yeah – it's probably not in the cards for me." She raised her hand and said, "Always the bridal planner – never the bride."

"Never say never," Amelia sang. "Head on out. I'll call you all when it's time to set the table."

AFTER SHE SEARCHED and found the gardens empty, Savannah headed for the cove. She let out a sigh of relief when she noticed Lani exploring the shoreline, her dark curls blowing in the breeze.

"What 'cha doing?" Savannah joined Lani, who was intently studying the sand at her feet.

"I'm looking for hearts."

When Savannah blinked with a curious look, Lani giggled and said, "You know – heart-shaped things, like this."

Lani held up a tiny shell that had worn down from the tides over time. What once was a full shell was now just a fragment, and it was, indeed, shaped like a tiny heart.

Savannah touched the delicate pink shell as something sparked inside her. This child lit something within her that she'd assumed was long gone - the desire for family.

"It's pretty."

"It's how I know Daddy is with me." Lani raised her soulful eyes to meet Savannah's. "We used to search together for heart-shaped items when I was little. Every time we'd find a rock or a stone, he'd put it in a glass jar in my room."

"That's really nice." Savannah pushed a lock of hair from Lani's eyes and curled it behind her ear. She searched the little girl's face wondering how she handled such a loss at such a young age. If anyone could understand, Savannah could, but at least she had her dad until she was a teen. Lani lost hers way too soon.

"I had to leave my jar behind when we came." Lani's eyes clouded. "So, I thought I'd start a new one."

"Sounds like a good idea to me. You know, I lost my dad when I was younger too."

"I know." Her tiny voice was full of sadness. "Does it get easier...with time?"

Savannah breathed in and pursed her lips, contemplating her answer.

"You know that saying - 'time heals all wounds?'"

Lani bobbed her head up and down, waiting for more.

"Well, I used to really hate that saying. I got tired of people telling me how much better I'd feel soon...in time."

"I know." Her bottom lip protruded.

"But you know what? I'll never stop missing him or my mom, but it does get easier."

"You know what I do?" Lani asked.

"You talk to your dad?" Savannah gave her a sideways look.

Lani sighed. "No, not since I was little."

Savannah bit her lip to cover a grin. "I see."

"He only came around right after..."

It was then that Lani's expression filled with excitement. "Look! I found another heart!"

She retrieved a small stone from the shore and lifted it with a grin. It was rounded at the top with the slightest indent.

"You can have it," Lani whispered. "That way, when you're missing your dad...or your mom, you can carry their love with you at all times. At least that's what Daddy used to tell me. Whenever I look at the jar back in my room at home, I know how much he loves me."

As Savannah took the stone from Lani's tiny hand, her chest warmed with appreciation.

"Thank you."

"And if that doesn't work, you can carry your parents in the pocket of your heart," Lani whispered and tapped just below Savannah's collarbone. "Right here."

Savannah's eyes watered. This child had more insight than any adult she'd ever known.

Lani shrugged. "At least that's what I do. I carry my dad around like that. Daddy rests in the pocket, but Jesus lives inside it. Daddy just comes along for the ride wherever I go. They both watch out for me – even if I can't see them."

Savannah threw an arm around Lani's shoulders and drew her into her side for a quick hug.

"You're something else, kid." Savannah's dimples deepened. "You know that?"

"I know." When she nodded, her dark curls bounced in the breeze.

And that's how Anderson found them, linked at the side and staring out toward the water in thought. His heart surged at the sight, wishing it could last forever.

22

Ava Masters pulled into the parking lot of the Brass & Buckle and eyed the exterior with dismay. What had Savannah been doing here? And why had she disappeared only to resurface as an elusive singer named Monica? Something didn't add up. Since the owner of the bar wouldn't return her calls, she had no choice except to come in person.

"This place looks like a dump." Her bodyguard and friend, Markus, sent Ava a sideways glance. "I'm glad I convinced you to bring me along. You shouldn't be traveling like this on your own."

"I'm a big girl, Markus." Ava grimaced and turned off the engine.

She glanced through her windshield as a few people adorned in tattoos loitered outside the door. As one pulled a lighter from his pocket, he glanced in her direction with a sneer. Ava blinked in awe and quickly sent Markus a look of thanks.

"Yeah, you're welcome," Markus said with a smirk.

Once inside, they wove through the crowd with a

hopeful eye of finding the owner of the property. The faster Ava could get in touch, the quicker they could circle back for the airport, return their rental, and get home.

As the pair made their way through the crowd, Kevin blinked with recognition. Ava's music played on every country station in the nation. As she passed by with her bodyguard, Kevin reached for his two-way radio.

"Tawni, we've got some VIP's heading your way. They must be lost if they're walking into our bar."

When Kevin's voice sounded in her earpiece, Tawni searched the room to make eye contact and nodded with acknowledgment. She clipped her handheld radio to her apron and left the bar for the dance floor where a mass of people had gathered.

"Make way!" She pushed through some of her regulars who had crowded around a petite blond and her security.

Although Kevin recognized the pair, Tawni struggled to place the so-called VIP's while she nudged past the last patron that blocked her path. She raised a brow, thinking the young woman's flashy top and cowboy boots paired with a short denim skirt made her look overdressed and out of place. She looked as though she belonged on a big stage under a bright light – instead of on the dance floor of a hole-in-the-wall bar that reeked of stale beer and late nights. Nevertheless, it was her job to protect her patrons – especially those who could give her bar a bit of notoriety.

Ava Masters signed yet another autograph, thinking how thankful she was that Markus was with her as she inspected the crowd that pinned her in place. Relatively new to the music scene, she was unaware of the amount of attention she garnered. Now that she had a few hit songs on the radio, it was clear she had no right to go anywhere alone.

"Welcome to the Brass & Buckle. Would you like to go

somewhere a bit more private?" Tawni gave a few of her regulars a look to suggest they back away. Though a few grumbled, most went back to what they had been doing before Ava entered.

"Thanks," Ava muttered.

Tawni waved a hand and said, "This way."

Markus ushered Ava through the few lingering fans and followed Tawni toward a stairway that led to a loft. Once upstairs, they sat at the edge of a round lounger that overlooked the dance floor.

"Better?" Tawni asked.

"You could say that." Ava peeked over the wooden railing at her fans below, who were still looking expectantly toward the loft. A few had their cell phones turned toward them, taking photos.

"I'm Tawni. I own the place." She extended her hand.

Once Markus and Ava introduced themselves and explained who they were, Tawni's lips twisted.

"Are you the same Ava Masters that's been leaving messages on my voicemail?"

Ava nodded, eyes wide. "I came to find my friend."

Tawni crossed her arms. Although she wasn't always up to speed with the current up-and-comers in Nashville, like Ava, she was up to speed with Anderson's situation. No matter how famous or almost famous this woman was – she was still the same person who'd been leaving her weekly messages, asking how to reach 'Monica.'

"I can't help you." Tawni shook her head from side to side. "About the only thing I can offer you is a drink or some food...on the house...before you hit the road."

She offered a menu to Markus. "Once you're ready, push that button on the table, and I'll be up to take your order."

Tawni spun to descend the stairs, but before she could

take the first step – Ava leaped forward and touched her arm.

Ava took Tawni in from head to toe, hoping to appeal to her softer side. Although Tawni looked like she belonged in a WWF ring, Ava was willing to bet she could appeal to her feminine side. They both, after all, were the same species, even if they looked like they originated on different planets. Tawni appeared to be half-Amazon warrior princess half modern-day wrestler, while Ava was more like a pixie fairy in comparison.

"Look." Ava let out a breath. "Monica, or should I say, Savannah, is my best friend in the whole wide world. We all should be so lucky to have one just like her."

Tawni cocked her head but gave no inkling of recognition at the fact that Ava used Savannah's real name. Not only was Ava a stranger, but she could also be a liar. Tawni wasn't about to divulge anything that could put Anderson in hot water.

Nothing in Tawni's expression or demeanor gave Ava hope of building a bridge between them, but she continued.

"Savannah went missing one night – just vanished about a month ago with only a text saying she had to leave. 'Leave? Where to?'- I thought. I had no idea it would be the last thing I'd hear from her. She didn't even take her dog with her!" Ava threw up her hands in exasperation. "She loves that spoiled hound, and she left him with her neighbor!"

Tawni pursed her lips, yet said nothing. Although Ava seemed sincere, Tawni owed her life to Anderson and wouldn't budge for the world if it meant putting him in danger. For all she knew, this could be another attempt to gain his location.

"I'm sorry to hear that." Tawni sent her a look of sympathy. For a second, Ava thought she almost looked sincere.

"You don't know anything?" Ava sighed.

"She just showed up one night and sang on my stage. I only know her as Monica. I've never heard anyone call her by the name, Savannah." Tawni popped a hand on her hip. "Now, how about that drink?"

Defeated, Ava sat down, dropped her chin to her chest, and wiped away a tear.

Markus laid a hand on her leg. "We'll find her."

When Ava looked up, her expression implored Tawni for more.

"Are you sure you can't tell me anything? Like where she went afterward? If she was with anyone? The news said that a crazed fan made an attempt on her life. I just want to make sure she's okay and bring her home."

Instantly, Benny's dull stare and dark demeanor flashed through Tawni's mind. The memory of his attack made her shudder, but she still stood firm without divulging any of it.

Ava squinted. There was something Tawni wasn't telling her, but for the life of her, Ava couldn't understand why she was so secretive. What would it take for her to open up?

"What I don't get," Ava continued. "Is how a crazed fan could have been a fan at all since no one knew who she was until that night. Why would someone attack her when she wasn't on anyone's radar?"

Tawni pursed her lips with a roll of her eyes. *She's on everyone's radar.*

"You know how fans are." Markus reminded Ava. "You just released your first record, and if I hadn't been here today, that small crowd down there might have eaten you alive." He gave her a look. "I told you - you'd need me."

Ava rested a hand on her knee and closed her eyes.

"You're right." She was at a loss.

Tawni, ready to be as far away as possible from this

conversation, asked, "Can I get you something from the bar?"

"What aren't you telling me?" Ava's piercing eyes stared Tawni down with enough force that Tawni could swear this little pixie could read her mind.

"There is nothing to tell." Tawni spun for the stairwell.

The pair quickly followed her downstairs, where Ava dug a card from her purse. Markus laid a hand on her arm and shook his head. "I'll give her mine."

He slipped a card from his wallet and said, "If she reaches out, please call. Ava and her band go on tour next week."

Ava's face fell. "I was really hoping to find her before I left town. I can't imagine being on the road in a different city each night when she's out there somewhere. Please. If she reaches out..."

"I promise I'll let her know you were here...if she happens to call. Not that she will. I can't imagine why she would." Tawni slipped Markus' card into her back pocket.

"I know you know something." Ava stared her down. "But I can't force it out of you. If you're not telling me anything, it must be for her own good," she paused. "I think that's what scares me the most."

Tawni turned her back on the pair and nodded to Kevin, who ushered them to the door.

"Thanks for stopping in, Ms. Masters," Kevin said before offering a hand to Markus. "We hope to see you again."

"You'll call us?" Ava looked over her shoulder to Tawni, who had disappeared into the crowd.

Kevin nodded and opened the door so they could exit.

Once she felt it was safe, Tawni slipped her phone from her pocket and started to text Anderson. Kevin slid behind her and spun her to face him. "Don't."

"Savannah would want to know. Anderson..."

Kevin shook his head. "Just trust me."

Tawni cocked her head. "Okay, but something's not right. I feel it."

Tawni slipped her phone back into the front of her jeans, clueless that they'd just given Odyssey precisely what they needed.

THREE-HUNDRED MILES AWAY, in the tactical command center, Underwood clicked a link and sent a recording of Tawni and Ava's conversation to his boss.

Within the hour, Director Brenner's image appeared on-screen on a large monitor at the heart of the room.

"Yes, ma'am." Underwood waved his partner over.

Agent Blaire, who was just getting ready to pack it up for the night, slipped off his jacket and came around the desk to sit on the corner for their conversation.

"I got your transmission." She sat, typing at her desk.

"Yes, ma'am." He cleared his throat. "I told you they knew something."

"I'm sure they do, but Anderson is too smart to have given them anything that would have put them in danger. They may know he's in hiding, but they don't know from who or where he is now. I guarantee it. It goes against every bit of training in the book, and he's a rule follower."

"Do you want us to go back and question them again? Just to make sure?" Underwood gleamed with anticipation.

Director Brennen shook her head. "No. Listen...I just put a task force together." She typed her last stroke on her keyboard and turned to face the monitor with a look of determination. "Here's what you're going to do."

As Blaire and Underwood brought their heads together for their next mission, both listened with mixed emotions. Their objective could put innocent people in harm's way, but it was a means to an end. In the end – if it meant taking Anderson and his partner into custody and they were able to finish what they started - it was a job well done.

23

The sounds of gravel crunching behind them had both girls turning in time to notice Anderson approaching.

"Unc!" Lani jumped into his arms for a hug.

The sight of him cuddling with his niece did things to Savannah's heart that it shouldn't. He may have been the one with the visions, but at that moment, Savannah got a glimpse of what kind of father he would be. She frowned and turned from the pair to stare out into the evening sky as the sun hovered above the water's edge.

Anderson noticed the shift in Savannah's mood and set Lani on her feet. He tapped his niece on her nose and said, "Your mom said to go inside and get washed up. Tyler should be here any minute, and dinner will be ready soon."

"Okay!" Lani's face lit up. The prospect of greeting her step-dad immediately had her spinning on her heel and running uphill.

As Lani ran toward the house, Anderson reached for Savannah's hand. Just the touch of her soft skin had his heart pounding in double-time. Finally, he had some time alone with the woman he loved more than he knew was possible.

Although he wanted to share his realization with her, he understood she wasn't in a place where it would be well received. His heart ached for a smoother time when they could just be an average couple on a date. As it stood, their timing and circumstances were so far from ideal that it might be unfair to burden her with his emotions. The jury was still out on that one. He wouldn't rush her, though, that was for sure.

When he laced his fingers through hers, he expected her to turn toward him. When she didn't, he cleared his throat. Although she was willing to hold his hand, she wasn't ready to return his gaze. She stood and stared at the long stretch of water.

"See something of interest?" He stepped in to block her view. When Anderson forced her to look at him, her brow furrowed.

"It's like we're out in the middle of nowhere." She released his hand. "Alone. Except there's a town nearby."

"It's on the other side of this island. The cove faces east toward the river that feeds into the next state. It's why we chose this place. It's secluded – almost."

Anderson nodded toward the cameras. "And if someone is heading toward us – those alert us. Mostly it's regulars just living the lake life, but you never know. It's better to be safe than sorry."

Savannah cocked her head. "In your line of work, that's true, but doesn't it get old having your guard up all the time?"

"It does." He sighed. "But we get breaks. As soon as this wraps up, and Danny and I figure out how to get us out of this mess, I'm thinking of taking a long one."

Finally, Savannah met his gaze.

"What do you mean by that?" Her heart skipped a beat. "Is it your health?"

He searched her eyes. "It's more along the lines of my future."

Savannah played along. "Your future, huh? See something in your future that needs to change?" Savannah's lips curved. Her teasing nature, no matter how somber her mood, couldn't be denied.

He looked at her from under his eyelashes and sent her a sexy grin.

"You..." He stroked the side of her face. "You have no idea what I want to see in my future, do you?"

She temporarily closed her eyes, his touch sending tingles across her skin. She took a step back. "I'm sure it would be nice to see yourself free from this manhunt."

Just when he was about to tell her he wanted more of her in his future, she smacked him on the arm in jest.

Immediately, a fog rolled throughout the cove, and images spiraled around him, replacing reality with the progressive vision. Anderson eased himself into the premonition, hoping to stay one step ahead of Odyssey.

This time, the image of Savannah kicking his leg in efforts to get his attention was secondary. His attention diverted to the blurred sounds and impressions from his previous visions, except this time, he watching from above.

As he hovered near the ceiling, he watched Savannah struggled to awaken his future self, only to vanish from the room and search the area. There, he found their captors taking a smoke break at the back of the building.

Anderson wandered from room to room just as he would if he were there in person surveilling every detail. He memorized every corner, every door, every inch of the property, and made a note of anything that could help them escape.

Although he could view things in real-time, he knew these were images of what was to come. When a clock sounded, he noted the time and observed when the guards made their rotations, changed positions, and, most importantly, when they focused their attention elsewhere.

This otherworldly reconnaissance showed him a small window of time in which someone might escape. The only problem was - the more he visited this place, the stronger his understanding. Anderson would be bound and drugged, which meant Savannah would be on her own.

Anderson focused his attention from inside the property so he could surveil the surrounding area. If his future-self were indeed incapacitated – he'd use this time to learn where she could run and the tools needed to make that happen. Once he was satisfied with the results, he discovered he had the cognitive power to settle into his current reality – where Savannah was waiting for him on the cove.

As Savannah hugged him to her body in the sand, she was kicking herself for sending Anderson mixed signals. She had practically ignored him to protect herself, then flipped the switch and started flirting. The second she hit him in the arm, he slumped forward.

As if second nature, she lurched to catch him before he fell. These episodes were progressing way too frequently. She sat, rocking him like a child for at least ten minutes before he finally sat on his own accord.

When Anderson's spine finally stiffened, she sagged against his back and breathed a sigh of relief.

"I'm okay." His soft voice tore from his chest.

When he twisted to face her, he noticed how soiled her beautiful new dress had become and pulled her into his lap.

"I'm sorry," he whispered in her hair as he ran his fingers through her short locks.

"You can't keep doing that to me." Her voice shook with emotion. "I know I said that your visions were a gift, but right now, they seem like a curse...a reoccurring one."

"Hey." He pulled back and cupped her face. "I need to tell you... you were right. These...visions or dreams or whatever they are have given me the insight to keep you safe." He stroked her hair and raised her chin so that they were eye to eye. "You need to know what I just saw."

Her lips trembled. "We don't need to do this now." "Yes, we do." He helped her stand.

He waited as she shook the moist sand from the hem of her dress.

"May I?" he asked. When she nodded, he gently brushed her backside. Then, he pulled her in and ran his hand up her back.

Savannah's heart lodged in her throat at the thoughtful gesture.

"We need to go..." She couldn't find her voice. "Dinner." She tried to take a step back, but he locked his arms around her waist.

"That can wait a couple more minutes."

"I told your mom I'd help set the table." She shook her head.

"She was wrapping that up when I came down here. I told her not to wait for us." Anderson noticed the wariness behind her eyes and wondered why.

Savannah inwardly bit her lips. The developing familiarity between them was too close for comfort.

"You're going to give her the wrong idea."

"Am I?" His eyes twinkled.

"Anderson." The look of worry that creased her brow about broke his heart.

"I won't hurt you." His face softened.

A flash of sadness made an appearance behind her eyes. "You can't promise that."

"No," he whispered. "But I will promise that I'll try not to."

As he leaned in, she instinctively closed her eyes. When his soft lips claimed hers, she breathed him in. Even though instinct told her to take a step back, she wrapped her arms around his neck. Although a short kiss, it held promise.

"I want you in my life, Savannah." He rested his forehead against hers. "I don't know what that means or how that works. After this is all said and done, I can't imagine life without you."

"I can't either, but..."

He put a finger to her lips. "I'm not ready to think about losing you."

His words were like a salve to her broken spirit. She sighed. "I don't know what to say."

His heart ached with the thought that she may not return the sentiment, but he wasn't a man to back away from a challenge. He had yet to meet a woman who captivated him like Savannah did. Anderson wouldn't give up without laying everything on the line.

"Tell me you want a life with me, too."

"I want to." Her voice trembled. "I just don't know that it's possible. Our lives are so different."

"Our hearts are not, and I know one thing for sure. My life would be miserable without you. I need you, Savannah." When her only response was to drop her gaze, he continued, "Let's take it one day at a time. We'll find a way to work it out. When something is worth it – you fight for it."

She sniffled, this time, making eye contact. "You sound like your mom." When he looked puzzled, she rolled her eyes. "She said something similar earlier."

"You were talking to my mom about us?" He stood a little taller.

When Savannah smiled, it was as if everything was right in the world. He'd give anything to see her face light up like that for the rest of his life.

"Shut up." Savannah pushed at his chest and took a step back. "She mentioned that when something was worth it, then it was worth working it out."

"Smart lady." Anderson raised an eyebrow and flashed a crooked grin at her. "You should listen to her."

Savannah let out a shaky breath and said, "One day at a time, huh?"

"Yeah." He extended his hand.

Savannah slipped hers inside. "Okay."

"Before we go back, I need to tell you something."

"Your vision?"

He nodded and looked up at the sky with a thankful heart. He now knew Savannah had been right. He initially thought the visions were a curse when they were indeed a gift. At that moment, it dawned on him that he needed to pay closer attention to the One who had been blessing him with them.

24

There was natural ease with Anderson's family. Although she and Danny were outsiders, they were treated like family. It was the closest thing she'd experienced to being a part of something since her parents were alive.

Instantly, the thought plagued her with regret, and she glanced at Danny, who was staring out at the lake, completely ignoring the topic of dinner conversation. She studied Danny's tense frame but shook off the concern. He was probably focusing on something work-related.

Danny's parents tried to make her feel a part of their family, but at that time in her life, no one could have filled the void that tore through her. And, yet, with the Evans family – it came easy. So much so, that it seemed as if they were on a vacation rather than hiding from an unknown danger.

After Tyler's arrival, conversations didn't stray too far from the excitement over Alexis' pregnancy. Once Alexis announced her condition, with Tyler standing proudly by her side, the Evans clan contemplated over names, delivery dates, and what the future would hold with another addition to the family.

As Savannah took a sip of her coffee, she met Danny's tense gaze over the rim of her mug. When she scoured his face, he relaxed some and winked in her direction as the others conversed about plans for the future. It was then that her heart ached with envy.

What she wouldn't give to have the luxury of spending her time with a big family like the Evans. The reality of life back home – one of solitude - washed over her like cold water from a fall. She shouldn't get used to this – it wasn't hers to envision a future with or enjoy.

"Excuse me." Her lips wavered, nearly forming a smile, yet her heart wasn't in it.

Anderson stood with a curious look, but she waved him off with a shake of her head. When it looked as if he was going to follow her - Danny sent him a look from across the table.

"Sit down, partner. She's my family. I got this."

As Savannah rounded the lush greenery for the gardens by the back patio, she could practically imagine their curious stares as she disappeared into the shadows.

"I don't need you checking up on me." Savannah's voice cut through the dark as Danny approached.

"I know," he whispered and eased himself into a chair on the patio as Savannah swung in the hammock.

She stared up at the starry night, amazed at how many lights shone above them. She looked past them further into the dark night, wondering how far it stretched toward the heavens.

"Then, why did you follow me?" She dragged her attention from the sky and frowned in his direction.

"Are you kidding me? Who is to say you're not saving me

from all that talk about babies." Danny drew his shoulders in and made a face.

She grunted with a half-laugh. "Whatever. I think it's sweet."

He grunted. "I think it's sickening."

"When you find the right woman – you won't."

Savannah looked at him from the corner of her eye but soon studied him entirely. Her cousin's face held an expression she couldn't read. He was brimming with what she could only describe as disillusion.

"Want to talk about it?" She noticed the tautness that overcame his features, wondering what lay beneath.

"No." Danny was staring at the ground as if he could bore a hole through it with laser-like focus.

"Okay." She pursed her lips and scanned the cove further down the hill, past where the Evans were still seated at the banquet table.

"Then, how about this?" She finally spoke up. "How do you guys know if anyone is approaching? I saw some cameras down by the shore. Is this whole place being monitored?"

Thankful to discuss anything other than his personal life, Danny answered, "We have a security room in the house, behind the safe room we showed you when you arrived."

She tilted her head. Nothing surprised her anymore.

Danny slipped his phone from his pocket and flashed his home screen at her.

"It's connected to our phones. If anyone steps foot on the island or if anything unusual happens – Anderson and I are alerted."

"What if you don't have your phones on you?"

"We always do. They're always within reach even when we sleep."

"Since when do you sleep?" She chuckled.

"Yeah, well, normally we take turns, but out here…" He scanned the horizon. "We've settled into somewhat of a comfortable routine."

"It's almost too comfortable."

"Yeah." Danny sighed. "Like the calm before the storm. I'm just waiting for the palms of my hands to itch… as if something is getting ready to happen."

Savannah squinted in his direction. "Is that really a thing?"

Danny chuckled. "Absolutely. It's a sense I get before anything hits the fan – and it's saved my hide a time or two."

"I guess you and your partner both have a gift."

"Or a trick up our sleeves. Not sure which." Danny sent her a sideways look. "I still can't believe out of the two of us sitting here – that Anderson told you first."

"About what?"

"You know what I'm talking about. Anderson's dreams or whatever they are." He scoffed. "I guess he's like a prophet now?"

"Not everyone who prophesies is a prophet, Danny. He's not driven to motivate others with his dreams like the prophets did."

Danny raised an eyebrow and rubbed a hand over his five o'clock shadow in response.

Savannah tread lightly. Danny and his parents were good people but did not share her faith, which was another reason why she felt so lost after her parents died. There was no one to go to church with. Sitting alone on a pew in a new church about killed her, but she knew it was where she should have been even if Danny's family didn't.

"I do believe his gift is God-given though, because of these dreams or whatever you want to call them... they've helped us stay one step ahead of the danger that has been on our heels this whole time."

"Okay, so he's psychic."

"Danny." Savannah gave him a bland look.

He threw up his hands. "Okay, okay. I'll take your word for it."

"And, that's the reason..." She pointed in his direction. "That chip on your shoulder is why he probably didn't divulge his newly acquired awareness when it happened."

He stared off into the distance. "Maybe. This whole mess has me sideways."

"Can you tell me anything? Like when it's safe to go home?"

"No."

She nodded with understanding. If anything, the last few weeks with Anderson had taught her that there were some things they just couldn't explain. Savannah rose from the hammock and reached for his hand.

"Come on." She glanced over her shoulder to meet Anderson's gaze, which was still solely trained on her. "He's going to drag us back to the table if we don't return soon."

Danny stood and took her hands in his. "He's got a job to do, and when this is all over..." He let the rest sink in.

She nodded, fully aware that Anderson's intentions were honorable, yet the reality of his job would still take precedence.

"Duty calls. I get it." She blinked. "I think they're about to serve dessert. Let's go."

Once Savannah and Danny finally made their way back to the dinner table, the knot in Anderson's stomach dissipated.

"Everything okay?" he whispered in her direction as she took her seat next to him.

Savannah flashed him a bland look and nodded.

Anderson sighed, letting his eyes linger on her a bit longer than necessary before narrowing his eyes at this partner. Whatever had transpired between her and Danny had pushed Savannah back to square one. As Anderson mentally squared off with his partner, he sent him a look that told him they'd have words later.

Danny cleared his throat, thinking he'd never seen his partner so territorial before and wondered if he was wrong to set Savannah straight. Even so, she was his family, and it was his job to watch over her.

Everyone seated around them watched the non-verbal communication as if it were a tennis match and glanced from Anderson to Danny and back, waiting for what would happen next. Unable to bear another moment of tension, Alexis promptly stood and raised her glass of water.

"It's time to reflect on what we're grateful for." She beamed at her husband, who stood to take his place next to her.

She waited for each one to raise their glass.

"Life with this family is never boring."

A few around her chuckled. She glanced at her brother, whose eyes were sparkling with mischief.

"To everyone here who has made this unusual time bearable. I am grateful for each one of you."

"Amen to that." Hank raised his glass.

Tyler leaned in to brush a quick kiss across his wife's lips. He raised his glass once more. "And to the newest member on the way. May he or she be healthy, happy, and be blessed with Alexis' looks and charm because both will take it far."

It was then that Lani scrambled to stand in her chair and hoisted her sweet tea as high as she could, shouting, "I'll drink to that."

Lani's contagious enthusiasm was enough to keep whatever grudges may have been building at bay. Both Anderson and Danny nodded in resignation toward one another. Whatever conversation needed to take place wouldn't disrupt their family time. Instead, they raised their glasses, both willing to let bygones sit by the wayside.

25

Once inside the safety of the surveillance room, Anderson and Danny monitored the camera feed that spanned the perimeter of the island. The unspoken challenge served at dinner still sat between them like Fort Knox – impenetrable.

Anderson took a seat next to the door and folded his hands together, searching for the right words. Although Danny's back was turned, he knew his partner sensed the holes he was boring into it.

"I know she's your family." Anderson exhaled. "It's understandable to be protective after all she's been through."

Danny spun, pointing his finger. "You don't get it!"

"I do! I have a sister." Anderson's hands flew up.

"And would you let her fall for someone who was only going to break her heart?"

"No." He adamantly shook his head.

Danny tilted his head and raised a brow. "Then why do you think it's any different with my cousin? She's had enough heartbreak in her life. She needs safe and steady –

not here today, gone the next." He shot Anderson a look and continued, "You know as well as me that you'll be assigned a new mission once we get out of this mess. Do you think it's fair to play with her emotions like that?"

Anderson crossed the floor to lay a hand on his friend's shoulder and said, "No, but I don't plan to break her heart. Danny, I'm in love with her."

Danny's lips parted. Although the realization that his partner was in for the long haul was like a smack to the back of the head, it wasn't enough of a dose of reality to deter him.

"Being in love is great, man, but that only gets you so far. What happens when you're gone in the middle of the night for the next job, and you can't say goodbye? Or when you don't come back because someone finally caught up to you? You know that can happen to the best of us." He paused and let out a breath. "You can love her all you want, but it doesn't mean you won't end up hurting her."

Anderson shook his head and rubbed a hand over the back of his neck. He stepped back and met Danny's stern gaze. "You're right. And, I don't have it entirely figured out - yet."

Danny jabbed a finger in Anderson's chest. "That's the problem right there. You are playing with fire when it's my family who will get burned."

"No. No one is getting burned. I'm going to work this out, but you need to give me some credit, Danny. I've never been up against something like this." Anderson dropped back to his chair with a dazed look. "She's like nothing I've ever…"

"I know, dude. How the mighty fall when they encounter the scent of an intoxicating woman. I know firsthand how crazy it makes you."

Anderson met Danny's gaze with a lopsided grin. "You have someone in your life that I don't know about?"

Danny's jaw hardened. "Not anymore."

He took the seat across from Anderson, and said, "And I want more than that for both of you. You're my family too, and if you weren't in the field, I'd be thrilled for the two of you. I know you'd take great care of my girl out there." He pointed to the door. "But, we both know how this ends."

Anderson studied his feet. Danny believed what he was saying. If it were any other girl, his partner might have been on target, but this was Savannah they were talking about. He would just have to figure out a way to make it work and show Danny he was wrong.

When Anderson finally raised his head, there was a familiar gleam in his eye that made Danny's stomach churn.

"We'll see about that," Anderson said.

Just as Danny started to rebut, there was a soft knock on the door.

"It's me – Tyler."

Danny pointed at his partner. "We're not done."

Anderson opened the door to find his anxious brother in law with his phone in hand.

"I just got a text with some breaking news." He rushed in. "Alexis said you had internet access in here?"

"Maybe." Anderson frowned. "But we try to limit our activity."

"Can't you bounce your signal from country to country or something like they show in the movies?"

"Yeah, but..."

"It's important. I understand why you feel the need to shelter us here, but I still have a job to do. And I don't want to lose mine, because your job put us in danger."

Anderson and Danny glanced at one another with a look of disdain.

"How did you receive a text on the burner phone with specific rules I arranged for you? No contact with anyone and no giving out your number." Anderson glared at his brother-in-law.

"I called my assistant from a payphone before I left town and gave her the number for emergency use only."

"You did what?" Danny's gruff voice turned to stone. "You know if they're tracking any of you – they'll monitor the people you're closest to and watch for any lines of communication."

"Relax. She and I have a code. I didn't just give her the number outright, and I called her landline from a payphone."

"That doesn't matter. Landlines can be tapped, and your code can be broken. What were you thinking, Tyler?!" Anderson yelled.

"Guys, I can't change what's already done. Back to why I need you. I told her to text me with any breaking news of certain importance." He swallowed. "There's been an accident."

"What kind?" Danny asked.

"A bus crashed off a major highway in Oklahoma City. It broke through the railing and careened into a deep ditch. It's pretty bad."

Both men waited for him to elaborate.

"The people inside were severely injured. A few died. One of the survivors is an up-and-coming country music star, Ava Masters."

At the sound of her name, Anderson's heart fell. He turned to Danny and said, "That's Savannah's friend - her best friend."

Danny's eyes widened with recognition. He glanced from Anderson to Tyler and asked, "Why do you need the internet? You're already in the loop. You got your text."

"Well, it's not like the phones you gave us are smartphones." Tyler grimaced. "And before you say anything, no, I don't need to read any news or updates on the crash. I want to cover the crash from here."

"The answer is no." Danny rubbed a couple of fingers against his palm. Although his ability to sense trouble hadn't kicked in, he didn't like the way this was heading.

"Look. You just said you could bounce your signal around the globe so we could be untraceable, right?"

"Yeah, but-"

Tyler interrupted. "I brought some gear with me, including a camera and a green screen. With a green screen, we can cover the news here and insert a photo of the city without anyone being the wiser." Even though both men were staring daggers at him, Tyler continued, "I couldn't bring a mobile upload unit from the department since I didn't know how long I'd be gone. We only have so many of those. With budgets and such, I couldn't take one with me. The problem is that my camera must have been damaged while traveling here. I just checked, and it's not working."

"Okay. No camera - no broadcast." Anderson crossed his arms, still upset that Tyler broke the cardinal rule and contacted anyone from work or his social circle.

"That's why I need to borrow one of yours." Tyler motioned toward the monitors. When he realized both men were about to object, he held up his hands. "It's not like you don't have a million on the property. It would be quick. I'll superimpose a photo in the background to match the news story since we obviously can't be there live – which means I'll need internet access to upload the footage."

"Can't one of your news team handle this in person?" Anderson asked.

"Yeah, but Alexis really wants to cover this story." Tyler grimaced before looking over his shoulder and lowering his voice. "With her mood swings since the pregnancy, I just thought it'd be nice to give her a distraction."

"You mean - you feel like you have to cave to your wife," Danny muttered under his breath and spun on his heel. He scanned the monitors and said, "No way. These cameras are vital to keeping us safe, so we know what to expect."

Alexis popped her head into the doorway and gave her brother a look.

"We don't have much time," she said. "This story just broke, and that means our network needs to have a presence – now."

"Let one of your staff handle it from the field. You don't need to be the one to do this, Lexi." Anderson sat on the countertop behind him and crossed his arms.

"No?" She raised her eyebrows.

Anderson shook his head. He knew that look. She had decided to handle this, whether he let her or not.

"No. This isn't up for a debate." Anderson raised a brow. "This isn't some family squabble you're in the middle of here, sis. Keeping us safe takes precedence over your career."

Alexis blinked and sent him a smile. As she opened her mouth to speak, Anderson cut her off.

"Lexi, every camera is designated. We can't spare any of them, or we'd have a blind spot, and it could put us in danger."

"You mean one of these…" She pointed to the monitors behind him. "I know you could pan out to capture an entire area with at least one camera. Couldn't you just work it out so that we could utilize another camera for like ten minutes?"

"No." Anderson frowned at his sister. "Every camera in the house covers a specific area like a door or a hallway. Every outdoor camera covers a zone. So, sorry. It's not an option."

Tyler scrutinized the monitors and stopped when he discovered two of them were dedicated to the cove.

"Those two." Tyler pointed. "Can you pan out to a wide shot with one of the cameras in the cove, so we can set up a green screen on the dock with the other?"

Danny turned his back and rolled his eyes. These two never gave up. He sent Anderson a look of warning and sat in a chair in the back of the room, leaving it in Anderson's hands.

Anderson paused as if mulling it over. Finally, he said, "Well, yeah, technically, but–"

"Great. Thanks!" Alexis kissed Anderson on the cheek and spun to face her husband with a glowing look of satisfaction before dashing from the room.

"Now, wait a minute." Anderson stepped forward.

Tyler gave him a look. "You heard the woman. We won't take but ten minutes. We'll go set up on the dock. Let me know when we can start filming."

"Tyler." Anderson blocked his path.

"Don't give me that look. She's your sister. You know she gets what she wants."

Tyler followed Alexis, leaving both men in a state of flux.

"We're not doing this," Danny said.

"If we have a camera that would cover the entire cove..." Anderson shrugged.

Danny sneezed and reached for a tissue. "Fine, but I'm going on record saying that it's not a good idea."

"You okay?"

"Yeah, it's just allergies."

Anderson looked him over. His partner's face looked a bit puffy as if he were suffering from sinus congestion.

"Are you sure?"

"I'm fine. What isn't fine is this mess your family is getting us into. I thought you would handle it." He frowned at the monitors before them.

"Things with my sister are always a bit tricky." Anderson paused. "It'll be okay. I'll keep an eye on everything."

Anderson reached for a lever on the panel and pulled one of the cameras back to a wide shot.

"Here." Anderson retrieved a small device that wasn't any bigger than a button from a drawer. "Take them a microphone. If their camera isn't working, they'll need audio."

Danny snatched the small mic from his partner's hand with a look of chagrin and spun for the door.

The second he was alone, Anderson's first thought was of Savannah. He searched the monitors, but there wasn't a trace of her. The only place cameras couldn't track them was in their private quarters, like bathrooms or bedrooms.

She must be in her room.

Since Anderson couldn't leave the control room unattended, he reached for his phone to call her. When she didn't answer, he poked his head out of the door to find Lani skipping by with a doll in her hand.

"Are you going upstairs?" he asked and glanced behind him to check the progress on the monitors.

"In a minute." She peeked her head inside. "What'cha doing?"

"Secret agent stuff." He grinned and poked her in the ribs.

When her giggles subsided, he asked, "Think you can

ask Savannah to find me as soon as you find her? She didn't answer her phone."

"Sure!"

"Tell her it's important. I've got to tell her something that she'll want to know." He put his hands on her shoulders and gave her a look. "You won't forget?"

"I'm on my way, Unc!" Lani scampered away, happy for any reason to look for her new friend.

AFTER SAVANNAH APPLIED antibacterial ointment and fresh bandages on her neck, she inspected the few cuts and scrapes along her legs and arms, thankful the wounds were healing. If she were lucky, the pain that had been inflicted internally would fade over time as well.

Her mind wandered to her last bride and client, Jade. Although she assumed Jade was safe since there was no longer a target on her back, she couldn't be sure. She longed for information on anyone or anything from home. She hoped Jade had a fresh start in life.

As she inspected herself in the mirror, she fingered a few stray locks along her forehead and thought it was time for a decent cut. Blunt scissors and dollar store hair color hadn't done much for her girl-next-door look. As it was, she felt more like an 80s rockstar at first glance now.

"I wonder what Ava would say if she saw me now." Savannah chuckled to herself.

The twinkle in her eyes soon disappeared at the thought

of her friend. Ava must be sick with worry, and Savannah wanted nothing more than to let her know she was okay.

As Savannah exited the bathroom, she caught a glimpse outside where Alexis and Tyler were slipping green fabric onto some stands. She watched with intrigue, wondering what they were doing when Lani tore around the corner and jumped into her arms.

"Hey, slow down." Savannah stumbled and steadied the two of them as Lani wound her arms around Savannah's neck.

"Sorry," Lani replied through her giggles.

Savannah gave her a quick peck on the cheek as Lani wiggled from her grasp. Once the pair separated, Savannah glanced out the window once more.

"What's going on down there?" She pointed.

Lani tiptoed to peek over the edge and look through the tall window.

"Oh. Not sure. Me and Miss Molly..." Lani showed Savannah her doll. "We were down by the shore, looking for more treasure when Mommy and Tyler came outside. See?" She held out her other hand to show Savannah a few rocks she'd taken from the sand near the cove.

"You found some good ones." Savannah's eyes gleamed.

"I know. Then, Mr. Danny came out and told them to be quick about it. My mom told me to go inside. All I know is Mr. Danny did not look happy." Lani widened her eyes and shook her head.

Savannah chuckled and put Lani down. "Thanks. Where are you headed?"

"Well, first, I was coming up here to put more rocks in my jar, but then, Uncle told me to find you. He said it was very important and that he had something to tell you." Her face lit up with excitement as she glanced down the hall toward her room. "Want to put these treasures in my room with me?"

"Actually, I think I'm going to check out what the fuss is all about down there." She eyed the activity below.

"What about Uncle Anderson?" Lani frowned.

"I won't be long. I'll see him right after I step outside."

"Promise?" Lani turned her head and stared at her from the corner of her eye. When Savannah crossed her heart and nodded, Lani shrugged.

"Suit yourself." Lani skipped down the hall for her room.

By the time Savannah walked outside, she realized something was amiss. Her cousin paced the area as if ready to pounce while Alexis and Tyler struggled to set up.

"I didn't think we'd have an issue keeping this green screen up." Tyler attempted to hold the backdrop upright against the stiff wind that blew in from the lake.

"The best-laid plans..." Alexis shrugged.

"I thought you said you'd be in and out in ten minutes." Danny eyed the green screen. It didn't look like it would withstand the winds that were sweeping in.

Savannah cleared her throat as she drew near.

"I can hold one side steady if Danny can help with the other."

Tyler spun in her direction with a look of relief.

"That would be nice." He waved her over. "Stand behind it, hold your pole steady, and try not to bump into the fabric."

Savannah looked at her cousin, but his back was turned as he searched the horizon.

"Danny."

As soon as he spun to face her, a look crossed his face that was either confusion or constipation. She couldn't tell which.

"You shouldn't be out here, Sav. Why don't you head inside and find Anderson for me?"

"And just why shouldn't I be out here?" Savannah tightened her grip as the wind swept in from the cove and pulled the fabric like a sail. "Besides...it seems you could use the help." She smirked.

Alexis laid a hand on Savannah's arm and sent her a look of reassurance.

"We'd welcome the help." Alexis glanced at Danny and continued, "Besides with two of you to keep these stands stable, the wind won't knock them down. If you pull it tight – chances are it won't ripple from the wind."

Alexis glanced at the camera mounted on the tree across from them with a curious look.

"How will we get sound?" Her brows furrowed. "I'm pretty sure as fancy as that camera is, it doesn't have audio."

Danny offered her the microphone. "Here."

Alexis turned the small gadget over in her hand, wondering how it worked.

As if reading her mind, he said, "Just pin it near your collar. It's designed to pick up your voice and mute any background sounds, like the wind."

The group looked at him with wonder. He winked. "You can't hang out with spies without expecting fun toys, now, can you?"

Alexis chuckled while attempting to affix the mic to her shirt, but she fumbled, and it fell the ground.

"I got it. Here..." Danny retrieved it. As he attached it to Alexis' top, he glanced over his shoulder, saying, "Savannah, I've got this under control. Why don't you go back to the house?"

"What's your deal, Danny?" Savannah asked.

The muscles in his jaw twitched when he realized his stubborn cousin wasn't budging from her spot. He started for the backdrop just as another gust of wind almost toppled it over.

"Watch it!" Tyler yelled.

Danny leaped to help Savannah hold it steady as Tyler studied the surveillance camera at the cove. Once the lens widened and came to rest in an open position, Tyler texted Anderson for confirmation.

Ready to record?

When Anderson sent his reply, Tyler nodded to his wife. Immediately, Alexis straightened her hair and cleared her throat as if getting into character.

"In five, four, three..." Tyler counted the other two down with his fingers in silence.

Alexis beamed at the security camera and prayed it was a good enough shot to work.

"Good evening. I'm Alexis James reporting live in Oklahoma City. A fatal bus crash has claimed the lives of some of the crew members for Ava Masters, an up-and-coming Nashville recording artist. Ava is listed in critical condition and was sent by med-flight to a local hospital in the heart of the city."

Savannah gasped. The initial thrill of being a part of something so intriguing as a clandestine broadcast came to a crashing halt the second she heard Ava's name. She let go of the screen and stumbled back when she realized just how close she was to losing her friend. Danger or not – she had to find a way to be by Ava's side.

Savannah blinked as if on autopilot and stared at the ground until another stiff breeze swept across the cove. Savannah steadied her side of the screen and tuned out the rest of the broadcast, biding her time until she could find out how her friend could be in the hospital without her knowledge.

She glared at Danny.

"Are you okay?" he mouthed.

She shook her head in return and turned from his worried gaze.

Once Alexis wrapped up her report, Savannah spun on her heel and ran toward the house.

"Savannah!" Danny sprinted to catch up and spun her by the arm.

"Were you even going to tell me?" She yanked her arm free, her eyes blazing with fury.

"Yes!"

"When?" She jutted her chin forward.

"I don't know. I just found out when Tyler barged into the security room twenty minutes ago."

"Does Anderson know too?"

"Yeah. What's the big deal? We were going to tell you."

"So, everybody knew…except me." Tears of frustration rolled down her cheeks.

Danny chewed on the inside of his lip. "Well, when you say it like that. It's not how it sounds."

"Could have fooled me." Her accusing glare left him without a comeback. "I don't have time to deal with you right now. I have to get to Oklahoma City."

"Oh, no. You won't."

"Just try and stop me."

After Savannah stormed inside, Danny texted his partner.

Incoming.

He just hoped Anderson could talk some sense into her.

26

Anderson sagged in his chair after watching the exchange between Danny and Savannah on the monitor. He didn't need to read the text to know why Danny contacted him.

Once Alexis and Tyler waved him off from the docks, he returned the cameras back to their regular positions, spun his chair to face the door of the control room, and waited for Savannah to approach. He heard her coming long before she threw open the door.

"How could you not tell me?" She stormed across the room and placed her hands on the armrests of his chair, bringing them nose-to-nose.

Anderson inhaled and folded his hands in his lap. Through her rage, her eyes shone like diamonds. The effect had him transfixed. The urge to claim her lips was stronger as ever, yet he kept his desire in check. He needed to explain himself first.

"For starters, I didn't know where you were."

"It's not that big of a house, Anderson." She pushed off of his chair and took a step back before pacing the floor. "I never expected to get blindsided like that! You say you care for me, yet you didn't take any steps to let me know. Ava is one of the most important people in my life. I need to know how she is."

"I know." He stood and ran his hands down her arms to bring her to a stop. "Listen, I had to stay here to monitor things to make sure everything was okay. That came first. Your safety came first, but when Lani came inside, I yelled for her and asked her to find you. I guess she didn't?"

His concerned gaze had a calming effect – taking her to a place where only the two of them frequented. All she had to do was look into his mesmerizing, turquoise eyes to find her center.

Once the tension drained from her arms as she slid into his, he sighed with relief.

"Lani found me upstairs, but we were talking about other things..." She recalled their conversation. "She mentioned you, but I didn't think it was any big deal."

"Well, it was." He kissed her forehead. "I knew you'd want to know... I tried calling you."

She pulled back to check her jeans pocket. "I must have left it in my room." Savannah paused as a look of concern crossed her features. "How is Ava?"

"Let's check." He ushered her to one of the chairs that sat in front of the monitors. As his fingers flew over the surface of a digital keyboard – images of the bus crash populated a large screen on the wall.

"Oh my gosh." She covered her mouth and held her breath. "How did this happen?"

"No one knows yet." He swiped the bus photo off-screen and searched the hospital database for Ava's medical record. When he found it, he scanned through a few documents for more information.

"Isn't this illegal?" she asked.

He winced and made a hand gesture, spreading his fingers and wobbling his hand from side to side.

"Will you get in trouble?"

"Nah." His grin lifted her spirits until she returned her focus to the screen.

Savannah wrapped her arms around her midsection in disbelief at what Anderson uncovered. Although relieved to find that Ava was listed as stable, her friend was still in critical condition.

"Thank you," she whispered and dropped her gaze.

Anderson shut down the server and cleared his search. "Danny wouldn't be too happy that I was accessing any records like this."

"What Danny doesn't know won't hurt him." Savannah finally met his gaze.

Anderson took her hands in his and searched her face. It was then that he had a flash of her in a car driving somewhere, but he couldn't place where or when.

He frowned, unsure of what it meant and how it tied into everything he'd been envisioning - if at all. Maybe it was a flash of a calmer future after everything here was said and done. However, he couldn't shake the feeling that something was off.

"Are we okay?" he asked.

"Yeah."

"And you?" He traced circles in the palm of her hand with his thumb.

"I'll be fine." She almost said, 'once I get to Oklahoma City,' but she bit her tongue. The less he knew, the better.

Just then, Tyler tapped on the door. "Am I interrupting?"

Anderson cleared his throat but didn't take his focus

from Savannah. There was something she wasn't telling him, but he wasn't sure what it was.

Finally, he turned and said, "No."

"Great, because I need your help to get this broadcast uploaded to my assistant in the next five minutes. I wouldn't know where to start with your equipment."

Tyler placed the microphone that Danny had given them on the counter and sat in the only other chair, which was on the other side of Anderson.

Savannah stood and squeezed Anderson's shoulder, saying, "Go. Do your thing and help Tyler. I need to get my Bible and pray for Ava."

Anderson's questioning eyes trailed her to the door. Savannah paused in the doorway and spun with a feigned air of confidence, hoping her lighthearted tone was enough to kill his suspicions.

"I'm good. Thank you for all your help. I'll catch you later. Okay?" She smiled.

Anderson nodded, unsure of what to trust – his gut or her. He didn't have much time to decide. Once she left the room, his focus was on helping his brother-in-law.

"So, Alexis tells me you can see things?" Tyler interrupted his thoughts.

Anderson shrugged. "Sometimes. Not sure what good it does me when there's so much guess-work when it comes to certain things." He glanced over his shoulder as Savannah disappeared from view.

Although his visions had been about saving Savannah from future events, it did nothing to clarify their romantic future. What he wouldn't give to understand what was running through that beautiful mind of hers.

Tyler chuckled and slapped a hand on Anderson's

shoulder. "Dude, if you figure that out – let me know. Most of us would pay big time if you could give us insight."

"I know, right?" Anderson smirked.

After Savannah slipped into her bedroom, she prayed for Ava – exactly like she'd told Anderson she would. Only God could protect Ava now, and she needed to express how thankful she was that He spared her life.

Afterward, she devised a plan to slip away without alerting the others of her departure. It didn't matter that she could put herself in danger. She could never live with herself if Ava passed and she didn't at least try to see her.

27

It was nearly midnight when Savannah entered his room. To her surprise, Anderson sat up from his bed as she tiptoed through the dark.

Anderson peered through the dim room, knowing he should be flattered that she was sneaking into his bedroom, yet her body language was that of someone trying to sneak in without getting caught.

His gut screamed something was off, yet without concrete evidence, he had no reason to believe Savannah was there for anything other than a visit. He propped up on an elbow and cleared his throat.

When Savannah realized he was awake, she bit her tongue to keep from yelping with surprise.

"I thought you'd be asleep," she whispered and sat on the edge of the bed, trying to act as natural as possible. As the heat rose to her cheeks, she hoped Anderson couldn't sense her frustration.

"You know we sleep light," he said, referring to himself and Danny. He reached for her hand in the dark. "Everything okay?"

When she didn't answer, he stretched to turn on the lamp on his bedside table, but she was quick to lay a hand on his arm. "It'll be too bright."

"Okay." He placed another pillow behind his back to close the gap between them.

"What's wrong?" His eyes had adjusted just enough that he could make out her face. She looked tense.

As the moonlight filtered through the window, it revealed the curves of Anderson's bare chest. Savannah swallowed and averted her gaze. Between the real reason she entered his room and the fact that he had never looked more alluring, she choked on every word.

"I... can't sleep."

She clutched her hands together, fighting the urge to touch every muscle along his torso. When he opened his arms to her for comfort, her pulse quickened.

Remember why you're here.

Savannah hesitated before folding herself into his embrace. She adjusted her robe so that the phone in her pocket wouldn't be discovered.

As he spooned her from behind, the warmth of his body enveloped her. Savannah sighed with regret as he tucked his chin over her shoulder. Anderson was none the wiser. To him, it sounded as if she were relaxing into his arms.

"Bad dreams?" His warm breath on her neck sent shivers down her spine.

"Something like that." She squeezed her eyes shut, thinking of anything other than how much she'd like to press her body against his.

"This is dangerous." He kissed her just beneath her ear and stroked the side of her face.

"Anderson." she moaned. "We can't."

When Savannah pulled away to sit on the edge of the bed, Anderson's entire body mourned the loss.

"I would never pressure you for anything. You know that." He sat up and rested his chin on her shoulder from behind.

"I know." She turned to face him and sighed. "I just don't know where this is going, and I don't want to regret–"

"I know. It's okay." He stroked the side of her face before trailing the edge of the small bandage at her neck. "How is everything?"

Savannah's breath hitched. She bit her lip, thankful for the partial cover of night.

"The cuts have about healed." She reached for his hand and drew it into her lap, lacing her fingers through his.

"And what about the bad dreams?"

Anderson stroked the inside of her palm, sending chills up the length of her arm. Savannah fought the moan that was at the back of her throat.

"Um, better. Thanks." She cleared her throat. "Except tonight's dream, they seem to be fewer and far between."

She hated lying to him. Her decision to come to his room wasn't for comfort, and she'd not been dreaming. At the moment, her mind spun with options of how to escape the island without getting caught.

Just then, a buzzing noise vibrated from the nightstand drawer. Anderson dragged his gaze from Savannah to retrieve his phone and check the screen.

Savannah glanced at his phone. She shook her head, reminding herself to focus on her plan and not how every nerve-ending sizzled when she came within feet of the man with whom she had fallen in love.

When the phone illuminated and highlighted his chiseled features, Savannah averted her gaze. She couldn't lose her focus.

"Any news on Ava?" she asked, eyes closed.

He shook his head. "It was just an alert. The camera picked up a small boat on the water a few hundred miles from the cove, but it sailed by without approaching."

"How do you get any sleep when you're alerted about every single movement outside?"

Anderson chuckled. "It's programmed not to respond to things like trees, with movement from the wind, or a small animal that may be roaming the area. The program understands those types of things and can filter them out. It's only when people approach or leave in vehicles or by foot that either mine or Danny's phone goes off. If anything is amiss, the algorithms do their thing and let me know what's going on."

Savannah's heart raced. Alexis had given her a few details about how the system worked earlier in the day, but not the whole picture. She knew if she were to approach Danny or Anderson with too many questions, it might have raised suspicion, but with Alexis – it was just small talk. Now, she just needed to fill in the blanks and hope it seemed inconsequential to Anderson too.

"Would Danny's be going off right now too?"

Anderson shook his head. "No. He wasn't feeling well. He took some medicine and is probably out cold right now."

"What if the phones don't work?" Her gut twisted with worry.

"If anyone tried to get into the house – the alarm would be loud enough to wake up the dead." He brushed a lock of hair from her face. "Don't worry. We're safe."

Savannah let go of the nerves that were bundled

between her shoulder blades and allowed herself to rest easy for the first time since entering Anderson's room.

Anderson assumed he was easing her mind, not offering vital information that would allow her to sneak away in the middle of the night. Although she hated the deception, it was necessary to find her way. She stared at him through the dark.

"Shouldn't you be in the control room?"

He chuckled. "A man can't live without sleep. It's not like we're on high alert here. Especially since I have programs to keep me in the loop."

When he slid his phone on the nightstand, Savannah found it hard not to let out a sigh of relief that he didn't put it back in the drawer. She focused on Anderson's chest as she contemplated the timing of what was to come next. As she gazed into his eyes, she slipped her phone from her robe in the cover of darkness.

Savannah licked her lips and ran her free hand up the smooth skin on his chest – all the while despising herself for her trickery. Although Anderson would recognize the phone wasn't his in the morning, she'd be long gone before he would know the difference. Her heart ached at the betrayal she knew he'd experience, but she couldn't risk letting anyone know that she was leaving, and any alerts from Anderson's phone would keep her landlocked.

Savannah shifted to block Anderson's view of the nightstand, knowing she had to distract him if this was to work. She lowered her lips to his and slid her phone to the nightstand to make the switch. With expertise, she didn't even know she had, she slipped Anderson's phone into her robe before wrapping both arms around his neck.

Savannah's heart twisted with guilt. Anderson was so focused on the chemistry between them - he never even saw the switch. When they parted, he let out a soft breath. "Savannah, I..."

He wanted to tell her how he felt, but before he could, she cut him off.

"Shh." She placed a finger on his lips. "It's okay. Really, Anderson. I wish things were different too."

"No, that's not it." He tried again.

Savannah shook her head. "I - I should go to bed, but I just needed to see you. Thanks..." She double-checked her pocket to make sure the phone was in place. "For making me feel better. I think I can get some rest now."

Anderson's voice was laced with disappointment. "Goodnight, Savannah."

"Night." She bit her lips to hold back the tears. The fact that she'd lied to him was tearing her apart. She just hoped he wouldn't despise her after he awoke to find her gone.

After she exited his room and closed the door, she pulled his phone from her robe, leaned against the wall, and whispered, "I'm sorry."

SAVANNAH DISCARDED HER ROBE. Underneath it, she wore some yoga pants and a tank that could have easily been mistaken for pajamas. Once she donned a thick hoodie and her running shoes, she snuck to Lani's room to leave her a small token of her appreciation. She was in and out without incident but paused at the door.

Her heart pulled for the child, knowing how hurt she'd

be once she awakened. The two of them had grown very close over these last few weeks. She sent her an apologetic smile through the dark before closing Lani's door. Then, Savannah tiptoed down the stairs with her bag in hand to make sure Danny was truly sound asleep. Although he had taken cold medicine, a girl couldn't be too careful.

She set her bag outside of his room and cracked the door, hoping the sound it made wouldn't wake him. When Danny's soft snores cut through the darkness, she let out the breath she'd been holding and stepped inside.

The full moon shone through a hallway window just bright enough to illuminate Danny's room. In a rush, she scanned the area to find her cousin's phone sitting on the side table by his bed. She crossed the floor and powered it off before setting it back in place.

The second she spun on her heel to exit, he groaned. She laid a hand on his forehead, finding him warm to the touch. Upon her caress, Danny wrestled in his sleep and turned to face the wall, leaving his back to Savannah.

Knowing he couldn't hear her, she whispered through the dark, "Sleep well, Danny." She then added a phrase they'd said since they were kids. "I'll see you when I see you."

Savannah rushed to the kitchen and took the hallway that led to the garage. She thanked God she'd seen Danny punch in the code for the alarm when they first arrived, knowing it was her saving grace at this moment.

Once she disarmed the alarm and the light was green, she armed it in silent mode, closed the door behind her, and turned the lights on in the garage.

"Now what?" she asked herself as she faced the five-car garage.

Each bay had an intricate door that opened like an aperture of a camera. How in the world would she open it to drive one of these monstrous vehicles out?

She dug for the key fob she took earlier in the day. However, when she swiped it from the kitchen counter, there wasn't any indication of which SUV it belonged to.

Savannah pressed the unlock icon on the black fob just as a set of headlights blinked. With a sigh of relief, she scurried down the steps, slid inside the SUV, and tossed her bag in the back seat. She scanned the interior, looking for anything that would be a clue as to how she could exit the garage.

What did Danny do when they left the garage to get Tyler?

She searched the visor, but there was no opener attached.

"Ugh!" She rolled her eyes. "How did Danny open this thing?"

She glanced through the windshield to study the door she came from. She hoped to see a garage panel with an opener, but there was only the light switch. There had to be a button somewhere, but she didn't have time to search the vast garage. Even if she found it, she couldn't be sure which button worked her door. Randomly pushing buttons to find the right one would cause too much commotion and wake the family.

She squeezed her eyes shut, struggling to recall how Danny had navigated from the garage last time he left the property. The image of her cousin pushing something near the dash flooded her memory.

Savannah reached for a couple of buttons on the dash but paused. Her hand shook. What if she hit the wrong one?

"You'll never know unless you try," she whispered.

Finally, she pushed a button. When nothing happened, she dropped her hands to the steering wheel as the cuff of her jacket got caught on a small lever near the base of the steering wheel.

As the lever pulled forward, a panel opened above her head, exposing something similar to what she'd expect in the cockpit of a small plane.

"Of course." She groaned. "Why would they have a simple garage door opener?"

Her eyes widened only to fall flat when she realized there were too many buttons, and she had no idea if pushing anything could trigger something inside the home.

"God, please let this work." She clasped her hands together. "I know it's not the smartest move to leave, but I have to go. Ava's been my lifeline, and I can't leave her alone in the hospital. I just can't. Please help me."

It was then that she pushed the button closest to her and held her breath. When that one didn't work, her stomach churned. Knowing her luck, she may have just set off an alarm that could send Anderson flying into the night with guns blazing. When no one came running from the house in a panic, she released the breath she'd been holding.

When she pressed the second button, the garage light shut off. She pushed it again as the light powered back on.

"Okay, so it's not button number two. Let's just hope the first button didn't do anything to get me in all kinds of trouble."

She bit her lip and shrunk into her seat with a wince. Finally, when none of the buttons helped with the garage, she rested her head on the steering wheel with a sense of utter failure.

"I just need the garage door to open," she said.

It was then that the dashboard lit up like a computer screen, and a woman's voice echoed through the sound system. "Command accepted. Garage door opening."

As the panels slid open to reveal the night sky, Savannah let out a soft cry of joy and pumped a fist in the air. She dropped her head back and said a silent prayer of thanks.

"Okay. Here goes." She sighed with relief, choosing to ignore the churning that continued to swirl in her gut.

Savannah knew she could be putting herself in harm's way once she left the property, but she would never forgive herself if anything happened to Ava, and she wasn't by her bedside.

Ava had been her best friend since she moved overseas in the seventh grade. Both new to the far east, they discovered their new world together and experienced many things that most people would never understand, let alone, believe.

Ava and all of their classmates were family. There were no classes, races, or lines drawn within their school. They were all shoved into the same test tube, expected to live together in a foreign world. Each stepped up to the plate, eagerly forming bonds with every classmate – as they were all 'in this together.'

While she had a lot of people she considered her family around the globe, Ava was the one person she was closest to. Though she finished her last three years of high school with Danny's family due to her parent's death, the pair stayed in contact. Later, they attended the same music university in Nashville.

Through the years, each girl had been what the other needed in times of good and bad. After losing her parents, Savannah realized the importance of being present for your loved ones. She couldn't lose Ava too.

Once the engine rumbled to life, Savannah put the SUV in reverse and backed onto the driveway.

"Close the garage door."

She watched the angular panels slide into place before

driving onto the gravel road that led from the property. Once the SUV made it through the canopy of trees, she looked up and scrunched her nose.

"God, help me. Here I go."

She drove down the hill just as a clap of thunder unfolded from above. It was followed by a flash of light that illuminated a sequence of clouds on the horizon. She glanced through the windshield with a look of dismay as drops began to pelt her car.

"Great," she whispered. "Just great."

She flipped the wipers on and glanced over her shoulder at the house one last time. She prayed no one would wake before she could successfully escape.

When it was apparent that all was quiet, a bittersweet pang seized her heart. Anderson slept while she snuck away in the middle of the night. Would he forgive her? More importantly, was she putting them in danger by leaving the island?

It was then that Anderson's warning came back to her. During their last conversation by the shoreline, he gave her step-by-step instructions for escape if she were ever captured by Odyssey. She shook the chills that deluged her from head to toe, knowing that her disappearance from the island might be how they would catch up to her. She let out a slow breath and decided to put her faith in God and what she learned from Anderson to keep from being detected.

She had to try. If she could fly under the radar long enough to make it to Ava's bedside, her friend's bodyguard would protect her. She was sure of it. However, if she were wrong, Anderson's premonition and vital instructions would be paramount.

Savannah chewed the inside of her lip and pumped the brakes to come to a stop.

"Guide me," she prayed while she gazed at the stormy sky with determination.

Savannah nodded and pushed the gas to navigate through the trees toward the compound gate. She would tackle one problem at a time. And, right now, she had to figure out how to maneuver through the main entrance, load onto the ferry, and safely cross to the other side.

28

The morning started like any other. The smell of bacon greeted Anderson as he stretched and reached for a shirt and a pair of jeans. The sense of Savannah's lips still lingered as he breathed in. He hoped they would get the chance to revisit their conversation before she abruptly left his room. Without a glance, he slipped his phone in his pocket and left for the kitchen.

"Morning, sleepyhead." Amelia tiptoed to give her son a kiss on the cheek as he slipped past her.

"Morning, Mom," he mumbled in reply. He snuck a few pieces of bacon only to drop them with haste.

"Ow." He frowned and blew on the tips of his fingers.

"Just pulled them from the oven. They've not cooled down yet." Her eyebrows shot up as she took in her son. There were dark circles under his eyes. "Are you feeling okay?"

He shook his head. "I'm fine. I was up a few times last night. That's all."

When a look of concern crossed her features, he waved her off.

"Just routine stuff. Nothing to worry about. Then, Savannah woke me up."

"Anderson." Amelia's voice dipped with a warning.

"Nothing like that." He reassured her. "She's a good girl. She just had a bad dream."

Amelia's face filled with concern. As she was about to comment, a few more stragglers made their way into the kitchen.

"I need coffee," Danny mumbled before tumbling into a chair next to Anderson.

Alexis pulled a few mugs from the cabinet and asked, "You want some, Anderson?"

When her brother nodded, she began the task of working with her mother in tandem in the kitchen.

"Where's Tyler?" Amelia asked her daughter.

"He's outside with Dad. He heard some strange noises last night, so they're checking the perimeter."

Both Tyler and Danny stood on alert.

"Where outside?" Danny's palms began to itch. As he rubbed one of them, he gave his partner a look that both knew too well. He might not have visions like Anderson, but he was all too familiar with the way his gut had a sense of danger.

"Why didn't you come and get us?"

"Calm down." Amelia laid a hand on her son's arm. "We know your systems can detect the worst. You would have known first if there was any danger. Hank just wanted to make sure with the storm last night that the trees or the house didn't take any damage."

"Still." Danny set down his mug.

The palms of his hands tingled as if crawling with ants. He rubbed them together and stood.

"Relax." Amelia's soothing voice beckoned, but neither

of them was trained to do anything of the sort. "Besides, Danny, you're going to run yourself into the ground."

"My fever broke last night. I'm fine." He frowned in her direction. "Thanks, though. Are they out front or in the back?"

Amelia waved a hand in the air. "I have no idea, but feel free to go find them. I assure you it was nothing." She looked at her son.

Anderson reached for his phone to check the history. Surely, he wouldn't have slept through any notifications.

"What the-" Dread swept through his chest.

"What?" Danny looked at him with interest.

"This isn't my phone. There's no security app on it. It must be Savannah's." He pushed the burner phone toward him.

All eyes were on Anderson, but before he could put the pieces in place and comment, Lani rushed through the door, holding a small heart-shaped rock.

"Mommy, Unc! I went to Savannah's room to say thank you for the present she left me, but she wasn't there!"

Ice coursed through his veins. He took the rock from his niece to find Savannah's name scrawled across the surface. He immediately knew the significance.

"She left me a piece of her heart." Lani pouted.

Anderson's steely eyes turned on his partner. "Check your phone, Danny."

When Danny pulled it from his pocket, it had been turned off. He raised his eyes to meet Anderson's with a sense of apprehension.

"I know I left it on when I went to bed. I must have been out of it from the medicine..." His voice trailed. "I had a dream that Savannah was talking to me last night."

"She turned it off." Anderson's jaw flinched.

"Why would she do that?" Danny asked before his face fell with recognition. "Ava."

Lani, wise beyond her years, crossed her arms and glared at her uncle.

"What did you do to make her leave?"

"Lani." Alexis knelt in front of her daughter. "We don't know that she's gone, and it surely isn't your uncle's fault." She sent her brother a questioning stare. "There's no way she'd know how to with all the gadgets around here, right?"

Anderson didn't waste any time. He barged toward the garage to find out for himself. The group hurried after him just as he flung open the door to find that the vehicles were all accounted for...except one.

"How would she know?" Danny sputtered.

"She's smart. That's how," Anderson replied a little too quickly.

Lines pulled around Danny's dark brown eyes as he squinted and searched for a hidden button at the base of the stairwell. The house was designed to keep intruders out but also designed to keep intruders from accessing their technology, giving the family more time to escape.

"There's no way she'd figure out how to get across to the other side. I'll go check." Danny stepped down the stairwell into the garage.

Anderson powered Danny's phone back on to check the camera footage from last night.

"There." He pointed to the feed where Savannah drove off in the middle of the night.

Danny's frame sagged with despair for a split second before he trained his accusing eyes on his partner. He stepped toward him and shoved him in the chest.

"With all your visions...and you couldn't predict this?!"

The second Danny placed his hands on him, Anderson

saw a flash of Danny in a helicopter with Savannah before Danny was shot.

Anderson's heart seized. This was how it started. This was how the pair would get captured. Only, now, Danny was in the mix with who knew who else?

ONCE SAVANNAH PULLED AWAY from the house, she was relieved to find that the voice-activated system was intuitive enough to help her navigate each improbable obstacle that lay ahead. With a simple verbal request, the system opened the front gate to the property, helped steer her onto the ferry, and activated the motor to send her on her way.

Once she reached the halfway point across the lake, the light rain gathered strength and turned into a strong storm. Savannah wrung her hands in her lap as the once- looming utility vehicle seemed to shrink in an instant. The waves slapped the sides of the ferry, pushing it from side to side and sending sprays of water over her windshield.

Savannah frantically searched her surroundings, wondering what to do if her car was swept overboard or if the ferry capsized.

It was by the grace of God that it crossed the lake without succumbing to the water. Once the ferry docked, the front ledge lowered, offering a bridge to the gravel at the shore. She drove until her tires met concrete.

It was then she braked and let out a sigh, thinking about what the Apostles might have experienced in the middle of their storm. Though she hadn't been in the middle of the ocean, fierce winds and Texas flash floods were just as dangerous in her book. She closed her eyes and said a prayer of thanks.

Five hours later, she crossed the state line into Oklahoma, which meant it would only be a couple more hours until she reached the hospital.

As the sun ascended, she glanced at her watch with dismay. If Anderson hadn't already started his day, he would soon.

Savannah groaned. He'd be coming after her as soon as he put all of the pieces together. She just prayed when he found her, they wouldn't also be in Odyssey's crosshairs.

29

As Anderson reached for his gun, Danny stood firm in the hallway. With one look, Anderson understood he wouldn't get past him without a fight.

"Don't think you're leaving without me." Danny crossed his arms, but his challenging stare had little to no effect on Anderson.

"That's exactly what I'm doing. Besides, you need to stay here and protect the rest of them."

Anderson reached for his belt. He double-checked the slit hidden on the inside of the belt at the back of the waist, still housed a small, hidden blade.

"Over my dead body. Savannah is my cousin. You should be the one to stay." Danny grabbed Anderson's arm and spun him to face him just as Anderson's eyes flashed with anguish.

When a burst of light seared Anderson's consciousness, he massaged his temples and focused on the sounds of Danny's voice. He made a focused effort to push past the images. When they disappeared, he shook his head.

How had he avoided the vision that hovered on the

edges of his mind? Maybe he could control his premonitions after all.

After a few deep breaths – when he was sure his mind was free from the clutter of whatever Danny's touch evoked – he jerked his arm free from his partner's grasp and asked, "Do you trust me?"

"Normally, yeah. But, lately..." Danny wavered. "It doesn't matter. She's my family."

Anderson sighed. "Odyssey will be waiting for me at the hospital. Somehow, they're going to capture both me and Savannah. Trust me when I say this is a trap I'm walking into."

"How do you know these visions of yours are real?" Danny ran a hand through his hair and sighed. "Never mind." He shook his head. "We don't have time for this."

Anderson slipped his bag over his shoulder and placed a hand on Danny's arm.

"I'm going to get her. It's time for you to call our handler."

"I thought you said you weren't sure he could be trusted."

Anderson cocked his head.

"If the image of you in a helicopter rescuing Savannah from a ledge near some water says anything about that – I'd say it's a safe bet."

"I'm still going with you. I can call Craig on the way." Danny's face hardened.

Anderson was smart enough to know when he was fighting a losing battle.

"Okay." He finally relented. "But you're not coming into the hospital. You need to wait for Craig in the parking lot. Maybe you guys can secure the team from Odyssey before they take custody of us."

"Maybe, but if not..." Danny looked at Anderson from the corner of his eye.

Anderson winced. He had seen that look before.

"Hear me out." Danny led the way to the garage and continued, "I've got an idea."

As the two loaded their gear into the garage, Alexis and Amelia descended the steps.

"Be safe." Amelia hugged her son. She pointed a finger at Danny. "If anything happens to him, I know how to find you."

"No, you don't," Danny teased.

"I'd think twice about challenging her, Danny. Where do you think we got our tenacity from?" Alexis raised a brow and smirked in his direction.

"You don't have to tell me." Danny cocked his head and slipped into the driver's seat.

It was then that Alexis hugged her brother and whispered something only he could hear. "Come back safe and sound, and bring Savannah home."

Anderson pulled from their tender embrace and gave her a solemn nod. No words were exchanged, but he didn't have to say anything for her to recognize he had a heavy heart. When they parted, he gave his father and Tyler a look before he exhaled.

"You know how the safe room works?" When they both nodded, he added, "And where the weapons are if you need them?"

Hank clasped his son on the shoulder. "Go. We'll be okay."

Anderson paused, hoping his father's touch would provide a vision proving him right. When nothing registered, he said, "Odyssey is after us. If my predictions are right, we're walking into the thick of it. Just in case...be smart and stay alert."

His father nodded and motioned him toward the SUV.

As he was about to open the passenger door, Lani burst from the house, flew down the steps, and into Anderson's arms. Anderson scooped her up and placed a kiss on her forehead before returning her to stand next to Alexis.

"I'll be back soon." He tapped Lani's nose before looking toward the door where both Tyler and Hank stood.

"See you guys soon." Anderson took one last look, praying they'd all stay safe when Danny murmured through the open window, "Time's a ticking."

After Anderson slipped into his seat, Danny backed the SUV out into the early morning light. As the family watched the vehicle disappear into the trees, Lani's knowing eyes filled with concern and her bottom lip quivered.

"I don't want him to go," she whispered before looking up at her mom. "What if something happens to him, Mommy?"

Alexis fell to her knees and stroked Lani's cheek with her knuckles. She'd do anything to ease the concern in her daughter's eyes, but the One whom they could trust to protect Anderson and his partner would do it through divine intervention.

"We will cover them in prayer." She glanced toward the door.

Lani nodded and squeezed her mom's hand.

As the girls took the steps two-by-two, the rest of the family faced the horizon and said a prayer of their own.

Savannah eased her car into a parking spot that faced the hospital entrance and surveilled the area.

If I can just get to the front door. Her mind swirled with scenarios that could take place before she reached the automatic doors.

An overactive imagination had her envisioning agents repelling from a helicopter above to scoop her up and whisk her away. She looked at the sky with worry and rolled her eyes.

"Now, you're just being silly." She berated herself before reaching for her bag and stepping from the car.

She locked the vehicle and leaned against the door, unable to move forward. She tightened her purse on her shoulder and scanned the parking lot once more, looking for any sign that she was being watched. Nothing seemed out of the ordinary, yet the hair that stood on the back of her neck told her otherwise.

"Here goes." Savannah let out a deep breath.

With a firm hold on a can of mace that she'd found at the bottom of her bag, she sprinted through six rows of vehicles and finally slowed to a walk.

A deep growl had her spinning on her heel as a frenzied dog barked from the car next to her. Eyes wide, she made a beeline for the hospital entrance, stopping only to let an elderly couple pass before she reached the automatic doors.

Once inside, she caught her breath and approached the visitors' desk, where a petite elderly lady wearing scrubs looked at her with an expectant stare.

The knot in Savannah's stomach finally unfurled when she saw the woman's friendly face.

"Can I help you?" The woman asked.

"What floor is the ICU?" Savannah asked.

"Here, honey." The older woman's voice shook as she struggled to reach a stack of papers by the phone. "Let me give you a map."

Savannah clenched her fist, reminding herself to be patient as the woman seemed to move in slow motion. When the woman finally pushed a pamphlet toward her and pointed to the wing where Ava was supposed to be, Savannah sighed.

"Thank you," Savannah said, hoping she could navigate to the intensive care unit. With her luck, she'd get turned around.

"Take those elevators." The volunteer extended her shaky finger and pointed toward a long corridor. "It's on the sixth floor, but it's across the breezeway in the wing across from this one."

Savannah mentally recounted her instructions, committing them to memory. She nodded in thanks before starting for the elevators when once again, a strange sensation overcame her. She glanced over her shoulder, but the only other person in the lobby was a young mother who was solely focused on her stroller.

Savannah whisked around the corner, unaware that the woman with the stroller lifted a hand to talk into her comms, alerting Odyssey of her arrival.

30

It was clear which room was Ava's the second she pushed through the doors and entered the intensive care unit. Ava's was the only door with a bodyguard positioned outside.

Savannah's face lit up when she recognized Markus, a longtime friend, who stood watch outside Ava's bay. She tried to wave at him to get his attention, but a nurse stepped forward intent on flagging Savannah down.

Savannah sidestepped her and continued to push through a couple of scrub-clad nurses to make her way to Markus. She hadn't come this far to bother with anyone else. She rounded the circular desk toward Ava's door when the nurse finally caught her by the elbow.

"I'm Andrea - Miss Smith's nurse for the afternoon. How are the two of you related?"

"Miss Smith?" Savannah's brow furrowed. "I don't know anyone by that name. I'm here to visit Ava."

"I'm sorry we don't have anyone by that name." The nurse tried to turn her by the elbow to escort her out.

Savannah yanked her arm free and searched for Markus

over nurse Andrea's head. With the commotion, Markus finally noticed her, did a double-take, and started in her direction.

"Savannah?" His voice almost shook.

He placed his free arm around her shoulder and pulled her into his side. Savannah sank into him, but with some difficulty as his other arm was set in a cast. Before she could ask how he was, he took a step back to look her over.

"We've been worried sick about you," he whispered. "Where have you been?"

Savannah bit her lip. She couldn't tell him anything yet. Before she could spin an answer, nurse Andrea politely interrupted and saved Savannah from lying.

"Excuse me."

Savannah and Markus broke eye contact.

"How are you related?" she asked Savannah.

Before Savannah could answer, Markus spoke up and said, "She's Ava's sister."

Savannah sent him a smile of thanks for the white lie and stuck her hand out to shake for the introduction.

"I'm Savannah."

Andrea gave a short nod. "Nice to meet you. Do you have any questions about Ms. Smith's...your sister's condition?"

"Why are you calling her Ms. Smith?" Savannah sent Markus a look of confusion.

"For security. So, fans can't figure out where she is."

Savannah nodded with understanding and turned to Andrea to ask, "How is she?"

"She's pretty banged up." Markus stared off in the distance with a look of regret.

Andrea explained, "She has some broken bones, including a rib that punctured her lung. She had some internal bleeding. It took surgery to find the cause and stop it. Currently, she's sedated, but could wake up at any time."

"Can I see her?" Savannah's voice wavered as she wiped away a tear.

"Yes, but only two people at a time," nurse Andrea said just before laying a hand on Savannah's wrist. "Don't be surprised at her appearance. She has a chest tube to drain her lung."

"Okay." Savannah's eyes filled with uncertainty.

Andrea gave her a look of reassurance. "Make sure to speak to her. Let her know you're here, but don't overdo it. She needs her rest."

Savannah nodded and followed Markus through an open sliding glass door. As he pushed through the curtain, Savannah's breath hitched.

Her friend's tiny frame lay battered and bruised. Ava looked like she was near the end of a losing battle. Savannah bit her lips to imprison a cry that was desperate to flee.

She wasted no time crossing the cramped space, yet stood as if frozen in place once near her friend. Finally, she reached out and tenderly caressed the bruise that spanned the width of Ava's arm.

"Oh my gosh." Savannah's eyes mirrored Markus' whose were filled with pain. "You weren't kidding. She's..." Her voice faltered.

"Yeah." His raw voice was but a whisper.

It was then she remembered his cast. "How are you? And the rest of the band?"

Markus glanced at his sling and hung his head.

"I walked away with a few minor bruises and a broken arm. The guys have a few injuries, but they'll make it." His voice was laced with guilt. "But..."

Markus leaned against the wall and stared at the ceiling. A look of guilt flashed across his face before he said, "We lost a few of our roadies and the driver."

"Markus." Savannah rushed to his side and placed a hand on his cast. "I'm so sorry."

"I'm the one who should be sorry." He looked out the window with a blank stare.

"This wasn't your fault."

"That's just the thing, Savannah." When he dragged his attention back to her, his eyes were filled with anguish. "It's my job to keep everyone safe. They said the brakes went out...which is impossible because it was a brand-new bus. I had it serviced as a precaution before going out on the road. There is no earthly reason why those brakes should have gone out."

Chills skimmed Savannah's skin as if someone were trailing a feather down her neck. Instantly, she shrugged, shaking off the sense that something sinister was underway.

"This was just the start of our concert tour. There were no indications of a mechanical problem, none since we'd been on the road. How could the brakes go out on a new bus?" Markus frowned with worry.

"I don't know." Savannah shook off the sense that it could have been more than an accident. She searched his face and noticed the circles under his eyes. "But, you need to get some rest."

"I can't leave her." His voice filled with misery.

"You're not doing her any good by standing guard outside or moping around...wracked with guilt that you shouldn't even carry." Savannah looked through a gap in the curtains where Andrea was staring at them. "I'm surprised her nurse hasn't kicked you out on your butt by now. When was the last time you slept?" Savannah tried to nudge him toward the door.

"I got a couple hours." He widened his stance.

"In a bed?" She gave him a knowing look.

"In that." He pointed toward a chair in a cramped corner near Ava's bed. It didn't look conducive for anything more than sitting. With Markus' size, even that would have been difficult.

She gave him a look. "They've got a hotel in the hospital. I saw it on the way up. You should get a room."

"I have one already, but I can't leave."

She laid a hand on his good arm. "I'm here now. I'll stand guard. You take the next watch." When he gave her a wary look, she added, "Besides, I'm not the one with a broken arm. If any crazed fan catches wind of 'Ms. Smith's' room, I'm sure between the nurse and me – we can handle it."

Savannah let out a sound that was a cross between a chuckle and a sigh of exasperation.

"Go." She nudged him.

"Okay, but let me text someone who I've put on standby. He's my back up." Markus saw the look on Savannah's face and held up his hand to cut her off the second she opened her mouth to argue. "I'll agree to rest, only if you allow someone else up here to stand watch."

Savannah shrugged. Extra protection wasn't a bad idea since there was a target on her back. She looked over her shoulder toward the desk, knowing that Andrea had a watchful eye, but the threat of Odyssey was only a step behind her. And, if Anderson's vision came true – they were probably close.

"Yeah, fine. I'd like that."

Before he left, Markus toyed with a lock of her hair.

"What did you do to your hair? And where have you been?"

"Later, Markus." She sighed.

He promptly ignored her and asked, "Why the 'Monica' persona? It was a genius move - if you ask me. You're quite the buzz on social media. The public is wondering who you are and where you went."

"Really?" She wrinkled her nose, her face lighting up with surprise.

"Yeah. Whatever the reason behind your disappearance, it's only increased your following. Someone set up a twitter page in your honor, and you have quite the fan base."

The mention of a following made her think of Odyssey, and her heart fell. Her mouth flattened into a line.

"Well, I don't have time to think about that right now."

Markus noticed the shift in her mood and could tell she was hiding something.

"Seriously? Where have you been, Sav? More importantly - are you okay? Are you in any trouble?"

Markus' concern was touching. She cocked her head and forced a smile. She prayed it was enough to put his questions off for a while longer because she wasn't sure how to explain any of it when she wasn't yet sure what the outcome was going to be.

"I'm okay." When Markus angled his chin and cut his eyes at her, she added, "I'll answer all your questions once you've had at least six hours of sleep."

"Four." He looked down his nose at her while reaching for his phone and sending a text. "Someone should be up here within a half-hour."

"Okay. Okay." She pushed him out and added, "I'll see you soon."

Once she was alone with Ava, she sunk into the chair

next to the bed, leaned her head onto the mattress, and rested. The only sounds permeating the room were Ava's ragged breaths as she slept.

Savannah closed her eyes and folded her hands. "Lord, please take care of Ava. Thank you for bringing her through this so far. Please...please help her recover. Let her be okay."

After her prayer, Savannah took a few cleansing breaths and rested her head in her hands. Anguish tore at her heart for what her friend must have endured during her ordeal. Between Savannah's brushes with death and now her friend's accident – Savannah's head began to throb.

She rubbed her temples and lifted her head to find Ava's lopsided grin.

"You're awake." Seeing Ava alert was enough to push her heartache at bay.

As Ava searched her face, her friend's features filled with relief. Savannah took one of Ava's hands and found herself mirroring those same emotions, pushing the fear aside.

With her free hand, Savannah covered her mouth as her eyes welled with tears.

Ava's groggy voice broke the silence. "I guess...it takes a... near-death experience to get your...attention?"

Watching Ava struggle to breathe had Savannah took a deep one of her own. Just as she was about to apologize, Ava smirked and said, "You've had a makeover...I see?"

"Yeah, well. There's a reason for that." Savannah glanced over her shoulder. "Should I get your nurse?"

"Shh." Ava grimaced. "It's hard to talk...breathe. Wait."

Savannah hated to see her friend in pain and would have done anything to switch places with her.

"I've been so worried about you." Savannah stroked her friend's arm.

"Same here." Ava sucked in a short breath and groaned, before asking, "Where have...you been?"

Just as she was about to answer, a man in a suit stepped in.

"Excuse me. Ms. Miles, can I speak to you outside?"

Savannah frowned over her shoulder. How did he know her name?

Ava must have thought the same thing because she gave him a look of distrust and struggled to ask, "Who...are you?"

"Markus sent me." He smiled at Ava. "I'm here to watch over you."

"I don't...know you." Ava reached for the button to call the nurse.

"There's no need for that." He stepped forward and laid a gentle hand on Ava's arm. "You can call him if you like. He asked me to help out since – the accident and all."

Savannah stood and shrugged. "He did say he had someone coming to watch over us. Markus needed to get some rest."

Savannah cut her eyes and looked over the man from head to toe.

"Although, he said he'd have someone here within a half hour – not minutes."

The man cleared his throat and flashed a perfect set of teeth.

"Yeah, well. I was already on my way when he called. Do you mind?" He pulled the curtain back to usher Savannah outside.

Something didn't sit right with her, yet the last thing Ava needed was stress. She turned to her friend and gave her hand a squeeze.

"I'll be right back."

"Promise?" Ava's huge eyes beckoned.

"Promise."

Savannah stepped from the bay and slid the glass door in place behind her.

"Walk with me." The man started for the exit.

"I'd rather not." She crossed her arms and stood firm. "Why do you need to talk to me?"

It was then he spun on his heel with military precision and turned his steel-grey eyes on her. Something about the way he looked at her had her taking a step back and searching the area for a quick exit.

"Okay. We can do this here. See that nurse over there? The one with her hair in a bun?"

Savannah glanced toward the nurse's station where Andrea and a couple of others were seated. Behind them was a woman who not only matched the description but was staring at Savannah as if she'd committed a cardinal sin.

When Savannah recognized her, her heart skipped a beat. It was the woman who had been attending to her baby in a stroller...or, so she thought.

"W-what about her?" Savannah swallowed, thinking it would be easier to ingest broken glass.

"She's with me." His cold eyes gleamed with pleasure. "If you don't do what I say, she'll see that your friend's medical condition takes a turn for the worse."

Savannah's stomach dropped as if the ground beneath her feet fell. She should have been more careful. She was so focused on finding Ava, she didn't pay enough attention to her surroundings and put Ava and herself in jeopardy.

"No. You wouldn't." Savannah's mouth went dry. "Markus has someone coming up here to stand guard. He should be back soon. I can call him."

"He's going to be asleep for a long time, Savannah." He sneered.

"What did you do to him?" Her heart plunged with fear.

"We just gave him a sedative. He'll be out for at least twelve hours."

"Who are you?" She lifted a hand to her neck. "How did you get a nurse to..." Savannah searched for the woman who had been standing over Andrea and the other nurses, but she had disappeared.

"All you need to know is that there's not a soul coming to help. And, although, she's not a nurse, she knows how to administer a needle if needed. You'll do as we say if you want Ava to make it through the afternoon."

"We?" Savannah blinked and looked around the room, unsure of who to trust. "What do you want?"

"Hand me your cell phone." When she didn't comply, he raised an eyebrow and nodded for her to hand it to him. "You'll stay safe - for now, and you'll get to be with Ava once we come to an understanding."

She dug through her purse to retrieve her phone. The second he had it, he passed it to Nurse Evil who Savannah swore appeared from nowhere.

"Why do you need my phone?" The words barely escaped her lips.

"To ensure you won't warn off your boyfriend."

The man sneered at her from the tip of his nose.

Even though she knew whom he was referring to, she made a face and said, "I don't know who you're talking about."

Nurse Andrea chose that moment to glance in their direction and send a disapproving frown.

The agent waved at Andrea and sent her a natural smile before turning back to Savannah.

"Play nice, or you'll have to worry about innocent bystanders as well as your friend," he said through his teeth.

He tucked a lock of hair behind Savannah's ear to which she batted his hand away.

"Don't touch me again." Savannah's amber eyes flashed with something that could only be compared to combustion.

"Or what?" He chuckled.

"You don't want to know." She smirked.

"Well. It's no matter. Once Anderson makes his appearance – you'll both be in too much hot water to bother with anything else." He leaned forward and inhaled through his nose, taking in her scent.

When Savannah leaned back with a look of disgust, he chuckled and said, "Now, go back inside and keep Ava company. Make sure to tell her how much you love her. She's going to need some good memories to recall once you're gone."

He started to walk away but paused.

"By the way. Don't think about using any of the hospital phones. The one in your room has been disabled, and I've got the entire wing under surveillance." He smirked in her direction. "Play nice, Savannah. Be a good girl."

Although she was a Christian, it wouldn't have been a stretch to say that she had murderous thoughts as he exited through the double doors. Once he was out of sight, she sagged against the wall with a sigh.

Just by coming to visit Ava, she had unintentionally lured Anderson into a trap. Savannah dropped her head.

The fact that they expected her meant they'd either been watching for an opportunity such as this, or... Savannah shuddered. Or, they'd created one to force her hand, and she'd played directly into theirs. When Savannah looked up, she found Nurse Evil sending her another death stare from across the room.

She checked her watch, wondering how much time she had and if there was a way out of this, when Andrea approached, none the wiser.

"Time to change her fluids." Andrea motioned to the fresh bag of saline in her hand. "Give me a few minutes to check her vitals, and then you can go back in. Okay?"

Savannah nodded as if in a trance and glanced at Ava through the glass door, knowing these last few hours with her were vital. She might have served Anderson on a silver platter to a group that wanted them both dead, but at least she had time with her best friend. Now, if only there were a way she could warn him.

31

Their SUV crunched over the gravel as Danny and Anderson approached an entrance of a remote park. Anderson's jaw clenched, thinking they should be speeding down a highway, not crawling through a gate toward an empty parking lot. They didn't have time for this detour, but Danny had insisted on a quick meeting with their handler.

As they rolled to a stop, both men stepped from the SUV and scanned their surroundings. With the exception of a mom in yoga pants, attending to her toddler on a slide, the park was empty.

"There." Danny noticed a chalk mark on a wooden post near a path. "This way."

Anderson glanced at his watch.

"We're losing time," he grumbled and followed his partner.

The dirt path curved through a wooded area that served as a bike trail. Anderson could see why their handler, Craig, chose it. It was secluded and covered with trees, and it gave them complete privacy.

After a couple of minutes, they rounded a bend and saw Craig waiting with a female operative. Craig waved them over and extended a hand to Danny with a look of relief.

"I'm glad you're both alive and well. We've been looking non-stop since we got word that you were off the grid."

"Thanks, Craig." Danny nodded with a look of solace. "I'm glad we are too."

"You know that you're walking into a trap?" Craig asked before glancing at an operative next to him.

As the woman slid her hand into her jacket, Anderson reached for his gun. He still wasn't sure who the players were and whom he could trust – visions or no visions.

"Relax." Craig chuckled. "It's just your wire."

Anderson cracked a reluctant smile.

"Sorry," Anderson said with a shake of his head. "We have been out there for a bit."

"I had to convince him to let me call you." Danny slapped Craig on the shoulder.

"You thought I was..." Craig's voice trailed before he burst out laughing. "Guys, come on."

"Excuse me. Agent Evans." The petite woman stepped up to his side. "I need you to take off your shirt."

"It wouldn't be the first time." Danny clamped his lips to hide a grin as Anderson sent him a look. "Sorry, man. You walked right into that one."

"Real funny, Danny." Anderson grimaced and unbuttoned his shirt.

"Sorry about the gun, Craig. Anderson was convinced there was someone on the inside."

"You thought I was a mole." Craig looked from Danny to Anderson, eyes wide.

"We couldn't trust anyone, especially after they killed Director Sanger." Anderson tossed his shirt to the woman next to him and crossed his arms over his bare chest. "And, now, they may have Savannah."

"My cousin. She's..."

When Danny's voice fell, Anderson interrupted. "She's in danger."

A look of understanding crossed Craig's face.

"And you're going to be the white knight." Craig raised a brow in Anderson's direction.

Anderson sent his handler a look before addressing the woman who was promptly searching the side seams of his shirt as if looking for a flaw.

"Excuse me." Anderson watched the agent with interest. She was threading a needle and pushing it into the seam of his shirt.

"Tally," she said. "You can call me Agent Tally."

"Can I have my shirt back yet?"

"Yup. Done." Tally handed it back without a glance.

"What did you put in here?" Anderson slipped his arms inside and buttoned it back up before feeling the side seam where she'd been fashioning something. He just wasn't sure what.

"Newest technology," Tally said. "It's a tiny and undetectable wire with the same consistency as a thread. We'll be able to hear everything."

"That's fine for a pat-down." Anderson frowned. "But, what if they scan me for it? Will the frequency be discovered?"

Craig shook his head. "Nah. Tally, here, is our newest in the tech department. She designed this to be completely undetectable and untraceable."

"That's impossible." Danny frowned.

"Until now." Craig raised his brow with a look of confidence.

Danny sent Agent Tally a look of respect and extended his hand to shake hers.

"Nice work." He smiled.

"Can we go now?" Anderson frowned.

"Not yet." Craig pulled a small round chip from Tally's duffle bag. "Make sure this gets placed somewhere in the vehicle. It won't do us any good to record what's happening if we don't know where to extract you from."

"I thought you guys were going to be on-site to intercede." Anderson looked at his partner with concern. He could handle whatever was coming, but could Savannah?

Even though he shared his vision with her, it wasn't proof of future events. His gift was still new enough that he wasn't sure what the reality of it could be and how that may have changed now that Craig was involved.

Danny nodded to Craig, who said, "That's the plan, but if we're unable to get her out, it's best to have a backup."

Anderson's gut churned, knowing that the backup plan was 'the' plan.

"You want us to get nabbed?" Anderson's jaw twitched.

Craig shrugged. "If it gives you any reassurance, Director Sanger is alive and well."

"What?" Anderson stared at Craig in disbelief.

"But..." Danny frowned.

Craig raised a hand to explain. "He came to us the night before you two went dark. He'd found some evidence and thought the sub-group within Odyssey could be after him."

"So Odyssey..." Anderson started.

"We think an international group influenced a handful of them from within. Once you two were on the inside and Danny approached Sanger with questions, Sanger's suspicions grew. He already speculated some of his team had some sinister dealings on the side, but couldn't piece it together to make a case against them." Craig drew a breath. "He tasked his assistant to dig into a few of the operatives' finances and found some offshore accounts."

Anderson met Danny's grave eyes while Craig continued, "The money trail led to a handful of Odyssey officers, but there were no ties that could identify where it was coming from. We think there was a trigger placed on their accounts to alert them if anyone came looking."

"What happened?" Danny asked.

"Sanger's assistant had a car accident that very night and died at the scene. His brakes had been cut." Craig shrugged. "Once the Director found out, he came to us and told us what he suspected. We staged Sanger's death, thinking whoever was controlling things from the outside would put one of their own in his place."

"Director Brennen." Anderson's skin crawled at the sound of her name.

"We think - but we need proof. A string of Odyssey operatives has died. We can't be sure of *the why* behind their killings, but can only assume they were agents, like yourselves, who don't fit the new Odyssey regime. You're both wanted men."

Craig pushed the tracking device into Anderson's hand.

"Once they have you, we don't think they'll harm you right away. Odyssey will expect Danny to rescue you. I can't have him anywhere near the hospital. You have to go in alone."

"That was always the plan." Anderson glanced at Danny.

"No. I couldn't have let you do it your way, man," Danny said as he gave him a look. "It left you without help. This way, we've got your back."

"And I appreciate that." Anderson glanced at his watch.

Craig tapped Anderson's hand. "Place the tracker somewhere in whatever they transport you in."

"Yeah, I got it." Anderson slipped the device in the pocket of his jeans.

"Let's roll." Craig waved his hand, motioning for Danny to follow.

"Hey, Craig." Anderson paused and waited for him to turn toward him before adding, "Thanks."

Craig winked in reply as Danny tossed Anderson the keys to the SUV and gave him a fist bump.

"I got you," Danny said.

The moment their hands made contact, a flash nearly took Anderson to his knees. Anderson stumbled and leaned against a tree as a white-hot light seared his vision, sending a burst of pain through his body.

Danny lunged to catch Anderson before he fell and guided him to the ground.

"Another vision?" he whispered.

Anderson bent, putting his head on the ground, unable to answer. It was then that he saw the image of a bullet searing through Danny's leg, entering the front and exiting the back while he and Savannah escaped in a helicopter from a cliff.

Craig took a knee next to Anderson and laid a hand on his arm.

"No, don't touch him." Danny shoved Craig's hand away.

"What the hell?" Craig jerked his chin toward Danny before placing his hands on the ground and peering at Anderson. He was covered in sweat, and his face twisted in pain.

"Are you okay?" Craig asked.

Anderson dragged in a breath and knitted his brows together. While some of his visions were a short flash of something just beyond his grasp, others, like this one, were so palpable they encompassed every cell of his body.

Anderson counted backward from one hundred as he focused on his breathing. It was a technique he'd come to rely on in the last few weeks.

Finally, he lifted his head to face his partner. "Your left leg. Protect it once you're in the copter."

"A helicopter?" Craig frowned, glancing at the pair. Something had transpired between them that he couldn't understand. "Agent Evans, what are you talking about?" He then stared at Danny and added, "Has he gone mad?"

"Never mind. Just give me some room, guys." Anderson rolled to his side and pushed to stand.

"Did you hear me?" Anderson sent Danny a look. "Protect your left leg."

"I got it." Danny narrowed his eyes, concern pouring from them. "Are *you* going to be able to do this?"

"I'm fine." Anderson took a step backward toward the entrance of the path. "Once she's in the helicopter, get out of the line of fire as quickly as possible."

"Okay." Danny grimaced, knowing whatever Anderson saw didn't look good for him.

Craig let out a slow breath, still dumbfounded by whatever had exchanged between the two of them. He turned to his partner and said, "Agent Tally, let's do a quick soundcheck before we part ways."

"Already done. Everything's fine." She slipped her tablet into her duffle bag and started down the path away from the group.

"Okay." Craig sighed. "It's up to you, my friend."

"Be safe, Anderson," Danny murmured as Anderson disappeared around the bend.

THE SUN WAS MAKING its descent when Anderson finally pulled off the expressway onto the frontage road for the hospital. While the campus had multiple buildings, he had already familiarized himself with the floor plans of the hospital and knew where the ICU was housed.

Anderson slowed to a stop at the far corner of one of the parking lots and reached for a small tablet that had tracking software installed. Once he opened it, it pinpointed Savannah's stolen car.

He pulled a ball cap tighter over his eyes and tilted his head to avoid any cameras as he drove through the parking lot. He navigated through the maze of small roads within the large campus to a parking lot near the main building.

Anderson slowed when he approached her SUV and sighed with relief. There were no signs of a grab – no loose items on the concrete nor any signs of a struggle. Chances were good that Savannah was safely inside with Ava.

Once he found the emergency room sign, he circled until he secured a parking spot on the row nearest the entrance. He shut off the engine and slipped on an EMT jacket he pulled from a duffle bag in the back seat.

He glanced outside. It wouldn't be long until the sun would set, leaving him in the cover of darkness. While he waited, he did a last-minute check on the situation at hand.

Anderson slid a panel in the dash aside to reveal a hidden keypad. When he entered a sequence of numbers, the windshields and windows darkened, making it impossible to peer inside. Next, he slid a keyboard from the console of his car and began typing.

From inside his vehicle, the windshield now served as a monitor. Once he tapped into the hospital's security feed, he scrolled through it until he saw Savannah pull into the parking lot.

Just as he thought, she made her way inside the building unscathed. She looked nervous, yet it was clear nothing was going to keep his Savannah from her friend. When he was about to exit out the surveillance feed, he noticed someone who gave him pause.

Delilah. He shook his head. This complicated things.

Delilah, a member of Odyssey, was dressed like a new mother, complete with a diaper bag and stroller. When she trailed Savannah through the front doors, Anderson pinched the bridge of his nose and exhaled.

An ambulance sounded nearby. Anderson glanced over his shoulder to find the emergency vehicle tearing around a corner for the ER. He returned his focus to the monitor imbedded in his windshield and hit escape on the keyboard before shutting down the system.

"Gear up, Evans." He stared in the rearview mirror for a brief moment before flexing his hands and taking a deep breath.

When the ambulance pulled to a stop and EMTs scrambled from the vehicle yelling instructions to approaching residents, Anderson slipped in unnoticed and moved with the group inside the building. From there, he headed for the elevator, hoping to save Savannah from the danger that loomed ahead.

32

Once she made her way through the cafeteria, Savannah selected a table next to a handful of women who were on their lunch break. She set her soda and soup down as her mind spun with possibilities. She eyed a cell phone at the corner of their table.

When one of them glanced in her direction with a quizzical expression, she smiled.

Act natural. Savannah reached for a spoon and took a sip. Outwardly she focused on her soup while inwardly, she played out different scenarios, of which half would draw too much attention to her.

Savannah sighed and slid her tray forward. Ava insisted she get something to eat, but she wasn't the slightest bit hungry.

Savannah glanced at her watch and wondered how much time she had before Anderson arrived. While she didn't leave a note or tell anyone where she was going, she expected Anderson to piece it together and follow her.

After a few minutes, she stole another glance at the phone only inches from her grasp. How could she take it in her possession without being caught? If she was successful, how would she contact Anderson? She had no idea what number he'd be using since she'd stolen his phone.

She chewed the inside of her cheek and shook her head. The only way to keep him safe was to warn him. The thought of his safety had her recalling Anderson's strict instructions for if or when they'd become captive.

Savannah glanced up in time to notice Nurse Evil pass by with a sneer that sent shivers down her spine. No, she needed to secure the cell phone to make contact. But who could she call?

Savannah's eyes lit up. If she could call Tyler's news station, she could get word to them. She scanned the area. When there was no sight of Nurse Evil, she crossed her fingers and closed her eyes.

Here's hoping this works. And if not, here's to remembering how to get out of this mess.

Anderson had instructed her on what to expect if they were captured, but it was hard to put stock in something that she hadn't experienced firsthand. While his visions were real to him, were they legit?

She bit her lip, praying she could remember the sequence of future events and sighed. Staying in the present was the only thing she could control. She glanced at the cell phone on the corner of the table next to her. Savannah loosened the lid from on her cup. As she gathered her things, she placed her jacket over her arm to shield what came next and stood, stumbling forward as soda spilled in the lap of the woman next to her.

The lady stood with a shriek, wiping her lap dry. While the group at the table was focused on the mess – Savannah swiped the cell phone and wrapped it in her jacket with no one was the wiser.

"Oh, my goodness! I'm sorry." Savannah grabbed a napkin from a counter behind her.

She patted the woman dry until she found herself on the receiving end of a look that told her she should do otherwise. Instead, she offered the group a stack of napkins.

"I'm so…so sorry," she said again and took a step back.

"It's – it's okay," the woman replied with a wince. She lifted her hand to put some distance between her and Savannah. "I think we've got it."

Savannah turned, shoved her jacket into her bag, and clutched the straps, thankful the phone was secured inside without detection. She looked over her shoulder and exited the cafeteria.

"Breathe," Savannah told herself.

Just as she started for the elevator, she saw a familiar and unwanted face.

Nurse Evil. Savannah cursed under her breath and turned the corner to search for an alternate route upstairs.

Savannah sensed her on her heels as if the woman's malevolent nature preceded her, touching everything in its wake.

"That was smooth, but hand it over." Nurse Evil grabbed her by the arm and extended a palm.

"I don't know what you're talking about."

"Hand me the phone, Savannah."

"I already gave my phone to your sidekick upstairs."

"And, I'm asking for the one you just stole from the cafeteria." The woman's flat eyes bore into hers.

Savannah rolled her eyes, withdrew her jacket from her bag, and unrolled it to reveal the cell phone.

"You sure you didn't go to the academy?" Nurse Evil asked.

"I'm sure you've done a background check on me. You

should know." She raised a brow in her direction before spinning on her heel to find another elevator.

As she left the woman behind, she turned the corner and flattened her back against the wall, taking in a deep breath. She stared at the ceiling, hoping that there was a way out of this. As of now, it seemed as if she was on the losing end.

God, help me, she prayed. *I know you've been with me this whole time. You've kept me...Anderson...Danny – all of us safe. Help me get us out of this.*

It was then that she sensed – not so much heard – but sensed the words, *I'm here.*

Savannah blinked as an indescribable peace washed over her.

"I know you are," she whispered.

ONCE UPSTAIRS, it didn't take Anderson long to find the wing where Ava was staying. As he rounded the corner and headed for double doors of the ICU, unaware of his presence, Savannah barreled through them and almost knocked him down.

"Watch it, buddy." Her eyes blazed with fury. "I'm tired of you goons harassing me." She wrestled from his grasp.

"It's me," Anderson whispered.

She peeked under the brim of his hat as a look of relief crossed her face, but it was quickly replaced with worry.

"They're looking for you," she whispered over her shoulder and ushered him down the hall.

Anderson looked over his shoulder.

"I know." He tried to open a janitor's closet door, but it was locked. "This way."

He pulled her toward the elevators just as one of his former associates stepped forward with a look of anticipation.

Anderson pushed her behind him and said, "Run, Savannah. They want me - not you."

"No." Savannah shook her head. "I'd never forgive myself."

She eyed the agent from behind Anderson. The man stood still as a statue - waiting for Anderson to make a move.

"When I give the signal – head as fast as you can for the stairwell. I'll be right behind you," Anderson whispered out of the corner of his mouth. He eyed the man and pushed Savannah back, trying to formulate a plan. If he could get them to the main floor - they had a fighting chance.

Savannah braced for whatever would come next.

"You're not going to win this one, Evans. Don't try to be a hero." The agent widened his stance and waited for Anderson's attack.

"Champ," Anderson called him by his nickname as if the two still were companions. "I'd be more concerned about yourself if I were you."

"Oh, yeah?" Champ licked his lips. "Bring it on."

Champ pulled out the comms from his ear and slipped it into his pocket.

"Why'd you sell out?" Anderson glared.

"You always were a saint." Champ lunged toward Anderson.

Savannah shrieked and jumped out of the way as the

pair tousled. She searched the hallway for anyone who she could call for help, but it was as desolate as a ghost town.

"Where's a security guard when you need one?" she mumbled and reached for a heavy vase that sat on an end table near the elevator.

Just as Champ twisted Anderson on his back, Savannah slammed the crystal vase over his head, sending shards in all directions. It wasn't enough to knock him out, but it was enough to catch him off guard.

Champ released his grip on Anderson's throat enough to give Anderson the split second he needed to flip Champ onto his back. Once Champ landed, Anderson popped up and kicked him in the head hard enough to knock him unconscious.

"Thanks." Anderson's chest heaved. He sent her a look of gratitude before he searched Champ's jacket.

Once he found what he was looking for, he gave Savannah a curious grin and slipped Champ's earpiece into place.

"Now, I can hear every word they utter." He reached for her hand and pulled her toward the stairwell. "They'll be looking for him if he doesn't check-in. We need to hurry."

"I need to say goodbye to Ava!" She pulled back.

It was then that Anderson spun on his heel, eyes wide.

"You've got to be kidding me! Your trip here to be with Ava is what got us into this mess. We can't risk it."

Savannah chewed on the inside of her cheek as she glanced down the hall toward the ICU ward. Before she could make up her mind, Nurse Evil stormed through the doors.

"It's her," she said frantically. "Let's go."

She pushed Anderson, and the pair fled down the stairs.

"Do you think she saw us?" Savannah puffed as they took two stairs at a time.

"Even if she didn't, they know I'm here." Anderson tapped the earpiece and listened to the chatter.

A team of men burst through a door a few flights above them. Anderson paused and looked up through the stairwell as a few operatives spotted them below.

"We're out of time," he said over his shoulder as the pair continued down the stairwell.

His mind spun with options. It wouldn't take long before the group of agents caught up to them. He had to think of something fast.

"Come on. This way." Anderson stopped short of taking the last few flights for the main floor and flung open the door of the fourth floor. The pair scurried down the hall toward a breezeway.

"I studied the floor plans. If we can get to the other wing, we should be okay," he said.

"What's over there?"

"Enough individual doctor's and administration offices, so that maybe we can slip in somewhere unnoticed until I can think of some way to get us out of here."

"Anderson, I'm not sure there is a way out of here. They've tapped into the hospital's security system. They'll know how to find us wherever we go."

The pair reached another janitor's closet just as shouts filtered down the hallway behind them. Anderson took Savannah by the hand, thankful to find the door unlocked. He pulled her in behind him and locked the door.

"Start from the beginning," he whispered, but then laid a finger on her lips. Heavy footsteps trod past their door and continued down the hall.

Once he felt they were safe, he said, "Who approached you?"

"Just some guy outside Ava's room. He took my phone... your phone."

Anderson's gut twisted. If they had his phone, they could search the GPS and track where he'd been. He slipped a new burner from his jacket and sent Danny a text.

Contact my family. Tell them to leave the house immediately. They've been compromised.

Savannah read the message on Anderson's phone and shook her head.

"It's my fault." Her eyes welled up. "If anything happens to them..."

"They'll be okay. These guys have me right where they want me now. They probably don't care about my family anymore." Anderson stashed the phone in a bucket of water, covering it with a mop just to be sure.

Savannah's shoulders slumped as she hung her head in shame.

"This is still all my..."

Anderson slipped a finger under her chin and laid his soft lips on hers. His tender touch transported her from a dark closet to a private island where only the two existed. There was no looming danger – no family drama – and nothing to separate them.

When she opened her eyes, she knew her fantasy couldn't save her from the reality they were facing. There was some solace in that they would face it together.

"You remember what I told you?" he whispered through the dark. "When we get captured, there will be a few things to look and listen for. You'll need to be the one to take the lead. I'm not sure why, but I think I'm going to be incapacitated to some degree."

"You're going to be okay? Right?" The concern in her voice tugged at his heart.

"I'm going to be fine. I'm a tough guy, remember?"

She snorted and then covered her mouth. "A tough guy who needed saving by a girl a few minutes ago?"

Though the closet light was off, it wasn't so dim that he couldn't see the mischief that emanated from her amber eyes. Even amidst their circumstances, his heart filled with joy.

"I love you, Savannah Miles. I have from the first moment I saw you. You're...unexpected and familiar all at the same time."

Savannah breathed in and held in a sob. She never expected to hear those words from him, especially in such a moment of turmoil.

"I...I don't know what to say." She wanted to express her love but was too scared.

"It's okay. I just needed you to know." He stroked the side of her face. "We're getting ready to walk out of here and into...I don't know what. Be ready when it's time. Listen for the clock to strike twelve. Okay?"

She nodded and wiped the tear that tumbled down her cheek away.

"You're acting like this is goodbye." She sobbed.

Anderson exhaled but said nothing more. Although the pair had successfully hidden away, he understood it was for a limited time. As they exchanged words, chatter picked up in the earpiece he'd stolen from Champ. Their location was compromised. It was only a matter of minutes before they'd be discovered.

"Take this." Anderson pulled a tiny chip from his jeans pocket. "It's a tracking device. Hide it in whatever vehicle they put us in."

"Anderson." Her brow furrowed.

"Take it." He searched for her hands through the dark. When she tucked it inside the waistline of her pants, he breathed a sigh of relief. "Good."

Suddenly, scratching noises sounded outside the door. Anderson could only assume Odyssey was picking the lock. In a matter of seconds, the closet door flung open.

Savannah jumped behind Anderson and stared, awaiting the grim reality that awaited. Anderson gave her a look of reassurance and reached for her hand. They were left with only one choice. As she followed Anderson from the closet, she did so with blind faith that his recurring vision would help guide her along the way.

As a small team surrounded them, Nurse Evil strode up behind the pair with a wheelchair and said, "Goodnight, Anderson."

Agent Blaire stepped forward with a hypodermic needle.

"Blaire." Anderson lifted a brow, sending him a look of steel.

Blaire shrugged. "This is nothing personal, Evans. I always liked you, but I have a job to do."

"Then do it." Anderson stared him down. "But know when this is over, I'll be left standing, and you'll be the one who is sorry. Nothing personal or anything, but I never liked you."

"We'll see about that," Blaire said with a glint in his eye.

Another member of Odyssey put Anderson in a chokehold while Blaire sunk the needle into his neck. Anderson tried to fight back, but whatever drug was injected had Anderson falling to his knees in a matter of seconds.

"No!" Savannah yelled.

As Savannah lunged for Anderson in a panic, a pair of

hands pinned her arms behind her back. She winced in pain.

"He'll be fine as long as you behave."

As the agent's noxious breath rolled down her neck, Savannah twisted to find the man who approached her in the ICU. Her eyes widened with horror at the gleam of desire that flashed through his eyes.

"Stay away from me." Her voice shook.

The second the agent loosed his grasp, Savannah yanked her arms free and elbowed him in the stomach.

"Follow the rules, or your boyfriend won't wake up." He grabbed her arm and twisted it so hard that Savannah was sure his fingers would leave a bruise.

"You're just going to kill us anyway. Why go to all the trouble?" She glared, refusing to give in to the pain that shot up her arm.

"Your cousin is out there somewhere. We can't kill you before we bring Danny in, can we?" He reached for a lock of her hair, but she swatted his hand away.

"I said-" Savannah glared.

"Underwood. Enough foreplay." Delilah cut her off.

When Agent Underwood dropped Savannah's arm, she spun to find Anderson slumped over in the wheelchair. She took a step toward him only to be blocked by another agent. Savannah never felt so helpless in her entire life.

"Sit him up, Delilah," Underwood said. "We've gotta get out of here." He spun on his heel and headed for the elevators.

"Don't just stand there!" Delilah barked at the two remaining members of her team. "Get him upright and strap him into position."

Both agents adjusted Anderson's body and put a blanket over his chest to hide the straps that held him upright.

"Move it." Delilah urged Savannah forward. "And don't do anything else stupid like trying to escape."

As the team escorted Savannah toward the elevator, she checked her watch. It was only six p.m., which meant another six hours until midnight. Anderson mentioned a clock striking twelve but also had alluded that her escape would be during the day. How could she be sure without asking him?

When she checked her watch once more, Delilah sent her a smirk and said, "Are we keeping you from something, sweetheart?"

Savannah rolled her eyes and said nothing in return. The sooner they got to the car, the sooner she could hide the device Anderson gave her. If she took this one step at a time, maybe she could wrap her mind around what was to come... whatever it was.

33

"Hey!" Savannah yelled from inside the door. "I need to use the ladies' room!" She scooted her chair across the floor and kicked the door.

After a five-hour drive to wherever they were taking them, and only one stop to use facilities, Savannah's bladder was about to burst. She looked over her shoulder at Anderson, who was still out cold on the bed and handcuffed to a headboard.

"At least you got to sleep through all of it," she murmured with a sigh.

Savannah recalled the previous night's events. Once they were escorted from the hospital, she and Anderson were loaded into a black van where Savannah had the entire backseat to herself. She studied her surroundings, wondering how to plant the tracker that Anderson gave her without drawing unwanted attention.

As if Delilah read her mind, she spun to face Savannah with a knowing look and said, "Underwood, did anyone search them?"

Underwood nodded. "I did Anderson. He's clean."

"What about her?" Delilah sneered over her shoulder.

"What about – her?" Underwood shrugged his shoulders. "She's a civilian."

"A crafty civilian. Check her." Delilah reached over the seat and grabbed Savannah's wrists, which were zip-tied in her lap.

"Although we want Danny to find them, we don't need the entire cavalry breathing down our neck."

Savannah gritted her teeth at the memory. Because of Delilah's uncanny sixth sense – they found the tracker, which meant no one could find them.

Savannah kicked the door again.

"Can anyone hear me?!" she yelled.

"What do you want?" A gruff voice sounded from the other side.

"I need to use the restroom," she pleaded.

Silence greeted her.

"Ugh." Savannah dropped her head just as she heard someone unlocking the door from the other side. Delilah stepped through the door with a knife and worked the zip-ties free that bound Savannah to the chair.

"Don't try anything, or I'll use this on you next." Delilah waved a butterfly knife in front of Savannah.

Savannah gulped and nodded, eyes wide. When Delilah was satisfied that Savannah would behave, she walked her across the hall to the bathroom.

Now that the sun illuminated the hallway, Savannah could get a feel for her surroundings. It had been dark when they arrived last night.

"Don't get any ideas," Delilah muttered. "We have got someone stationed at the end near the stairwell. There's no way out that ends well for you." Delilah shoved her into the tiny bathroom, and added, "The window is nailed shut, and all the drawers and cabinets are empty. The only thing you can do in here involves that toilet. And, I'd get to it because if you don't open this door in one minute, I'm coming in after you."

Savannah sent her a look and shut the door in her face.

"You have sixty seconds," Delilah shouted through the door.

True to her word, the door flew open as Savannah was buttoning her jeans.

"Can I at least wash my hands?" she asked with exasperation.

"Hygiene shouldn't be your top priority now, sweetheart." Delilah pulled her into the hall and shoved her back into the room.

After Delilah zip-tied Savannah's wrists to the chair, she smacked Savannah on the back of her head and said, "If it were up to me, you would be dead by now."

Delilah, who still stood behind Savannah, swirled a lock of Savannah's hair around her finger before tugging on it.

"Once Danny comes to your rescue. I've got plans for you." Delilah chuckled from behind.

Savannah squeezed her eyes tight and bit her lips to keep any sounds from escaping.

I won't give her the satisfaction of reacting. Savannah fought the dread that quivered inside, threatening to extinguish the faith that they'd make it through this ordeal.

With her back to the door, all Savannah could hear were the sounds of Delilah's combat boots thudding across the floor before she exited. When Delilah finally slammed the door behind her, Savannah flinched.

"Breathe. Just breathe." She closed her eyes, inhaled, and held it in her lungs before exhaling with a moan.

Savannah counted to ten and then opened her eyes to stare at the ceiling.

"God." She paused. "I know you're with me. I know Anderson thinks I can handle what's to come, but I'm scared."

Delilah chuckled from behind the locked door. "Calling on your god won't help you now."

Instead of dignifying her with a response, she scooted her chair toward the bed and laid her head on Anderson's chest.

The sound of his heart calmed her mind and gave her a sense of belonging. She breathed in his scent, thankful that she had him in her life. As she listened to the breath flow into his lungs, it was a reminder of her Creator.

She stared through the window as the clock sounded from down the hall. Her stomach churned. At every turn, anxiety had been one step away from swallowing her whole, but fear was the opposite of faith. How could she call herself a woman of faith if she didn't follow through on it?

"I'm going to trust you, Lord." She closed her eyes.

Anderson mentioned her escaping when the clock struck twelve times, but when Odyssey shuffled his body into their room at midnight, instinct told her it wasn't the right hour. Midnight had come and gone, and now the clock resounded eleven times.

She studied Anderson's chiseled features and whispered, "One more hour."

She wished she could run her hands along his jawline or touch his face. Instead, she pushed to her feet while the chair rested on her back. She brushed her lips across his five o'clock shadow before resting her cheek against his.

Anderson murmured in response as if sensing her presence. She drew back and searched his face, yet he gave no indication of waking up.

Savannah lunged in place, setting the chair on all four legs. She gave the mattress a hard shove with her feet. When he groaned in response, she repeated it over and over, trying to awake him.

"Wake up!" she yelled, but it was to no avail.

Savannah dropped her head in defeat, knowing that what came next would happen without guidance. Even though it was a stretch, she hoped he'd miraculously awaken.

Before she knew it, the clock chimed once with a solo bell. Thirty minutes had passed, which meant she only had thirty more to awaken him.

"Anderson," she groaned. "Wake up!"

She scooted the chair closer to the mattress and kicked his thigh so hard she almost knocked her chair over.

"Can you hear me?! Anderson?!" she yelled.

Her words were like a concerto as if heard from underwater. Anderson turned his head, but it was of no use. He was submerged under the effects of the drug they'd injected him with, unable to open his eyes or speak. When he tried, all he achieved was a moan.

While he wanted to scream, 'I hear you. I'm here,' nothing pushed past the haze that bound him.

As the minutes quickly dwindled, Savannah glanced at her watch. She'd been trying to alert Anderson for nearly half an hour. Just when she had given up hope, he turned and opened his eyes as if for the first time.

Anderson struggled but finally lifted his heavy eyelids. He swallowed, thinking that if only he could speak. When he tried, nothing came out. It was then that twelve bells resounded down the hall. His eyes went wide.

This was it. Anderson had to try again. It took everything in him to mumble, "Now."

"Now?" Savannah asked incredulously. "Are you okay? Are you sure I'm supposed to do this?"

Although she trusted him, a part of her wasn't clear how or if his visions worked. Were they accurate? Relying on him was one thing, but taking stock in his premonitions was another.

When her eyes filled with insecurity, Anderson understood. How could she trust what she didn't see? Yet, he already had. Most of the team would be taking a break in the kitchen, and the rest would be outside at the opposite end of the house.

He nodded with conviction, aware of the path she had to take. He only wished he could reassure her, but there wasn't time for him to recover, nor was there time for a conversation.

"Now." His voice faltered.

"Are you okay?" A few tears streamed down her face.

"Go. You. Have. To." His eyes penetrated her with such conviction that Savannah stood and took a deep breath for what came next.

She mentally prepared for a few seconds before she fell to her back, smashing the chair to pieces. When her hands sprung free from the chair, she started for the door and put her ear to it.

Sure enough, no feet were pounding down the hall. Wherever the agents were, they were unaware.

Zip ties still lay like bracelets around her wrists. Without the wood wedged between them and her skin – she was able to slip her hands from the binds. Anderson looked toward his waist to remind her of what came next. Savannah recalled his plan and nodded with understanding. She inspected his belt buckle, trying to detect whatever he'd hidden and breathed a sigh of relief when she found it.

Just on the inside edge of the frame, she found a tiny flaw in the metal. She ran her finger over it and pushed as if it were a button, yet nothing happened.

"Pull." He pointed his chin at the ceiling.

Savannah blinked, unsure. She dragged her fingernail along the edge and tried scraping it down. Once she applied pressure, the flaw finally gave way and transitioned along the inside of the buckle. A pick sprung from the prong. She withdrew it with a look of relief.

"For my cuffs," he said, glancing at the handcuffs that bound his wrists to the metal bars in the headboard.

"Am I supposed to pick them?" She stared at the handcuffs, unsure if she was up to the task.

He shook his head and struggled to move his arms closer together. Once he maneuvered the handcuffs up the metal bars – they were close enough that he could use the pick himself.

"Hand it to me." His voice sounded almost normal as if the effect of the drugs was wearing off.

"Can you come with me?"

"There's no time. It's going to take me too long to get these cuffs from my wrists." He paused. "Before you go - hand me my blade?"

She slid her fingers beneath the leather belt to find a miniature blade inserted inside. It was a miracle Odyssey didn't search him more thoroughly. Since he had been knocked out, they likely assumed he didn't pose much of a threat. Savannah slid the blade into his back pocket.

"Are you going to be okay?" she asked.

He nodded and jutted his chin toward the window, signaling her to leave. She cut her eyes to look outside where a line of trees lay a few feet away, just as Anderson had previously described.

"I can do this," she told herself as she opened the old window. Once again, she cocked her ear to listen. No sounds were apparent except the wind that rustled through the trees.

"No one is watching this side of the house," he said with confidence. "Trust me. It's now or never."

"Trust me." She mimicked, eyeing the drop from the window.

Just below the window sat an extended rooftop from the porch. From there, all Savannah had to do was drop one-story to the grass below.

Savannah's stomach churned at the thought. Although the roof beneath the window kept it from being a two-story drop, it was still quite the jump. It reminded her of the first time she jumped from a high dive.

"You can do it. I've seen it. Drop and roll once you hit the ground." His speech seemed to be improving by the minute.

The clarity in his eyes gave her the confidence she needed to push past the last of her reservations. She bit her lips, ready to take the plunge, but not before kissing Anderson one last time.

"I love you," she said, searching his face. "I will see you soon. Pray and be careful."

"I promise."

After exiting the window, Savannah took one last look over her shoulder as Anderson watched her disappear from view.

SHE HAD no idea how much time had passed, but with every step she ran, she hoped she'd remember what came next. She recounted Anderson's directions, praying they were steps toward freedom when she tripped and came crashing down on her side.

When she fell, the wind was knocked from her, and she struggled to catch her breath. Once she could drag enough oxygen into her lungs, excruciating pain emanating from her arm finally registered. It was then that she knew she'd broken it.

"God! No!" she cried, rolling to her other side and cradling her arm. "I don't have time for this!"

She bit her lip, staving off the pain as she stared at the sky above. A few birds shrieked overhead as she closed her eyes and said, "Mind over matter. Mind over matter."

Savannah rolled from her fetal position to shrug her jacket from her good arm before carefully removing it from her injured arm. Then, she fashioned a knot, tying both the sleeves with her free hand and her teeth to create a makeshift sling. She slipped it over her head and rested her broken arm within, hoping it would be enough to help her push forward.

When Savannah heard shouts through the wind, she stood and scanned the area but saw no movement. Her heart raced. Odyssey had discovered she was missing.

You've got to move.

Savannah's feet pounded the dirt trail in cadence with the throbbing in her arm. She grit her teeth. She would not let her injury slow her down. After all, Anderson's life was in her hands.

She sprinted along the course until she saw a clearing

through the trees. She knew a road would follow. Although she didn't know what it would look like, she knew to look for an old gas station around a bend.

Savannah ran until she found a narrow, two-lane road that seemed to span as far as the eye could see to her left with a curve to her right. His words came back to her as she looked to her right, thinking it was just as he described.

"Take a right and follow the bend in the road," he said.

Savannah made a face. Anderson understood her enough to know that using words like 'east' or 'west' were lost on her. She wouldn't know what direction it was if it hit her in the butt.

Like a shot, she took off around the corner where she hoped to find help. When a gas station came into view, a sense of dread overcame her. It was deserted.

She jogged up to the dilapidated building and glanced through a dirty window, pushing her emotions aside. Fear would only hinder her progress. Besides, even if there were someone inside – could she trust them? At this point, she trusted no one.

She shook her head with a look of determination. It didn't matter because she still had a mission to complete. Anderson told her to find a payphone. When she spotted the phone booth, she sighed with relief.

"No time to relax now." She still had a job to do.

Savannah retrieved the phone from the cradle and recalled the code Anderson had drilled into her memory. According to him, as cell phones became more popular, it made payphones a thing of the past.

What modern culture saw as a dying breed, the government seized as an opportunity - as a means of untraceable communication.

When specific codes were punched into the keypad, the

need for coins was bypassed. The sequence always started with the pound key, and then whatever number followed, determined which organization answered.

"Please let this be right." Her fingers shook as she struggled to remember the sequence. "Pound. Three. Pound. Four - four seven."

Screeching soon replaced the dial tone. Savannah swallowed, pressing three more digits followed by the pound sign.

"Station?" When a woman's voice came through the line, Savannah cried with relief.

"Bluebird has fallen." Savannah's voice shook.

A couple of clicks sounded followed by a pause. It seemed an eternity before Savannah finally heard the words that gave her hope that she and Anderson may be saved after all.

"We've got animal rescue on the way."

"Don't you need to know where I'm at?" She looked over her shoulder.

"We've got you, Miss Miles. Thanks for reaching out."

Once the line went dead, she slid down the length of the booth out of sight. Her stomach knotted with uncertainty when she realized that this was the last instruction that Anderson had given her. There would be no more guidance. Whatever happened next, she was on her own.

Savannah adjusted from a sitting position to a squat. She peeked from the booth to search the road for any sign of Odyssey. Now that they were in pursuit, it was only a matter of time to determine who found her first. The good guys or... Savannah swallowed with a shake of her head. She refused to think about any other outcome.

She noticed a glimmer through the trees as someone approached the road. If she stayed put, she might as well sign her death warrant. She fumbled to push open the door of the booth and bolted for the back of the gas station, hoping to find a hiding place.

When she rounded the corner, a bullet whizzed by taking a chunk of brick with it as it barely missed her shoulder. She screamed and bolted toward the back door only to find it locked.

Frantic, she shook the door handle. The building was her only cover. Without access, the only two options were running for the tree line, putting her on a path toward Odyssey, or descending a drop off behind the garage.

The cliff it is. She jogged toward the cliff to stop at the edge and peer down to the water.

The descent was steep, but there were a few nooks and crannies to support her if she could reach them. She wondered if she could slide down on her backside, but then remembered her broken arm. Who was she kidding? It would be difficult with two good arms. With one, it would be next to impossible.

Savannah searched the clouds, wishing she had some heavenly help. If only she knew her guardian angels were standing by her side. It was then that the Word that had always been in her heart sang through her soul. *"Nothing is impossible with me."*

Peace infiltrated her spirit and provided her the courage she needed to face whatever circumstance came her way. Savannah looked to the sky with a grateful heart just as a bullet zinged by sending dirt flying near her feet.

Savannah lost her footing and careened down the dirt slope on her back. Instinct took over as she dug in her heels, hoping to slow her fall. With her good arm, she grasped at anything could find.

Save me.

It was then that an exposed tree root lodged under her injured arm, sending shooting pains through her chest. Out of sheer will, she held on for dear life. It gave her enough support so that she could burrow her heels into the drop-off and stabilize her position.

Savannah sobbed with relief only to hear a cackle from above. She twisted and looked toward the landing above where Delilah stood with a smug grin.

"Oh. I'm going to enjoy this." Delilah raised her tactical rifle and sneered. "Goodbye."

Just as Delilah was about to pull the trigger, a shot sounded from somewhere in the distance. Delilah's eyes widened seconds before she pitched forward and fell over the edge. Savannah tucked her chin into her shoulder and squeezed her eyes shut, unable to watch Delilah fall to her death.

More shots, accompanied by the sounds of a helicopter, ensued from the distance. Although every muscle in Savannah's body shook from fatigue, she clung firm, knowing it was her only lifeline until help arrived. She just prayed whoever was coming to her rescue could find Anderson and her in time.

34

After Savannah disappeared from view, Anderson attempted to free his wrists from the cuffs. Once he finally was able to lower his arms, he sat up and tried to stand, but the room spun in all directions. He dropped back to sit on the edge of the bed and closed his eyes to get his bearings.

Once his vertigo subsided, he scanned the room for anything he could use to fight his way out. He had the small knife hidden in his back pocket, but that meant getting in close for hand-to-hand combat. In his condition – he'd be on the losing side of that battle.

He searched the room and came up empty. The only tools he could use were some scattered pieces of wood from Savannah's broken chair. He frowned. He needed something stronger. Unfortunately, the room was cleared of anything he could fashion into a weapon.

He half-laughed. Who was he kidding? His legs and arms were so heavy it was as if they had weights attached. It would be a miracle if he could walk across the room, let alone defend himself or take someone down.

He struggled to stand only to find that his body had other plans. When he attempted to take a step, his legs collapsed, and he fell back to the bed.

He blinked, wondering how much time he had. While he'd been able to find his voice to communicate with Savannah, the rest of him hadn't caught up just yet. He dropped his head in defeat and wondered how much longer he'd be incapacitated.

When the clock chimed once down the hall, he struggled to remember how much time had passed. Was it the half-hour chime making it twelve-thirty, or was it one o'clock?

Anderson breathed a silent prayer, knowing someone would be coming soon and discover Savannah missing. He willed himself to stand, but his knee buckled beneath him. He grabbed the headboard for support.

"You can do this," he breathed, willing himself forward.

He stared through the window to the horizon. Savannah was probably halfway to the road by now.

"Be with her." His raw voice sounded foreign, even to him. "Be with us."

As if on cue, he heard a key slide into the lock from the other side of the door. Whether he was ready for a fight or not, Anderson knelt and retrieved a piece of the broken chair.

Adrenaline tumbled through his veins like the tides during a storm giving him the boost he needed to take action. With seconds to spare, he slipped behind the door as Blaire cursed under his breath.

"What the-" Blaire stormed into the room just as Anderson knocked him over the back of the head in hopes it would give him the lead time to escape.

When Blaire spun - his eyes fumed with something unspeakable.

"All you did was piss me off." Blaire lunged toward Anderson and tackled him to the floor.

As the pair tousled, Anderson thrust his elbow into Blaire's nose, sending the man staggering back.

Anderson, finally free from Blaire's hold, bent to rest his hands on his legs and heaved as if he'd finished a race.

"I'm impressed. That stuff we injected you with should have sucked you dry for another hour." Blaire wiped the blood from his nose. "But, you're spent, dude."

"That's what you think." It took everything he had, but Anderson stood tall.

"Nice try." Blaire grimaced. "But that's all you've got."

The last thing Anderson remembered was a laugh from behind before someone hit him over the head. Anderson crumpled to the ground as everything went black.

WHEN VOICES SOUNDED, Anderson wondered if they were coming from somewhere deep within a tunnel. His eyes fluttered open, and he realized the echo he heard was within his head.

Anderson moaned and tried to cradle his head, but he was lying on the floor with his arms tied behind his back. His first thought was of the small knife hidden in his back pocket. He felt for the blade, relieved to find it was still in his possession.

"He's coming to." Director Brennen's sharp tone washed over him like a rising tide.

Two sets of strong arms sat him against the wall just near the open window.

"Snap out of it!" The Director barked before kicking Anderson's feet. "I know you're awake."

Finally, Anderson lifted his chin to face the woman who'd placed the target on his back.

"Hey, boss." He raised an eyebrow with a smirk. Even though it was clear the two would never work together, he might as well have a little fun at her expense.

"Where is she?" Brennen's cold eyes narrowed.

Anderson inhaled, thinking her stare could penetrate the pit of his soul yet said nothing. When it was evident he wasn't going to answer, Brennen nodded to Blaire, who leaned in with a sneer.

Anderson braced, knowing that whatever pain Blaire would inflict would merely be a warm-up. When Blaire kneeled and punched him in the gut, Anderson pitched forward and moaned in pain.

"The girl," Brennen tried again. "Where is she?"

"She left." Anderson gasped through the pain.

"Where to?" Blaire grabbed him by the collar.

"How am I supposed to know where she is? What am I, psychic?"

Anderson chuckled at his joke until Blaire served him a left uppercut that snapped his head back. As the taste of metal filled his mouth, Anderson ran his tongue across his teeth, relieved to find them intact. He spat blood to the floor before sending Blaire a look that spoke volumes.

"It's no matter." Brennen smoothed down her jacket with her black gloves. "We have a team out looking for her.

Delilah offered to lead the charge. She has a taste for violence, that one."

The anticipation that flashed through the Director's eyes set Anderson's heart on edge. His mind swirled with questions. Had his visions failed him? Would Savannah make it? Then, a single gunshot sounded in the distance.

"That can only mean one thing." Director Brennen looked through the open window with a smirk.

Anderson cocked his ear toward the window and hoped Savannah was still alive. He focused on his faith rather than letting fear win the battle that was waging inside his soul.

Brennen kicked Anderson's foot once more to get his attention.

"One target. And my people don't miss." An evil grin spread across her stern face.

Anderson took a shallow breath, helpless to keep Savannah safe. Instead of submitting to the panic that assaulted his spirit, he nodded his head to pray for her safety.

To a bystander, he painted a picture of a man who had been defeated, but the strength that filled Anderson revealed a different narrative. A surreal sense of peace washed over his soul, giving him the much-needed assurance that she was safe.

When he opened his eyes, he thought of the wire threaded into the seam of his shirt. He smirked as a sense of mischief re-emerged. Once he trusted that it wasn't a sniper but God that had Savannah in his sights, he did the only thing he could...he helped build a case against Odyssey.

"Just who are your people?" he asked.

When she said nothing in reply, he sighed and continued, "Odyssey used to save people and only take someone out if they were a threat to humanity."

"Well, where's the fun in that?" She blinked.

"You're..." He stopped short.

"In a position of power." She pointed at Anderson. "Which you're not."

"Obviously."

Anderson worked to loosen the ties at his wrists behind his back. He couldn't reach for the knife in his pocket without rolling to his hip and angling for the blade. For now, he worked on loosening the binds by pushing against the best he could without giving himself away. "I was going to wait until your partner tracked you two down before killing you. First..." Brennen raised a finger. "I was going to give you a show by torturing Miss Miles - just for fun."

Anderson's heart seized at the thought.

"Then, I was going to let Blaire and the rest of my team beat you to a pulp until you begged for mercy." She paced the floor and stared out the window, before turning back to Anderson. "It seems Miss Miles stole that pleasure from me."

She glanced at Agent Blaire and gave him a clipped nod. "Work him over." She paused. "Then, kill him."

Blaire's face lit up with satisfaction as he kicked Anderson in the head, knocking him to his side. Anderson saw shooting stars as the pain shot through his skull, but he focused on the fact that Blaire had given him the opening he needed to slip the small blade from his pocket without being noticed.

When Blaire lifted his arm and pointed a .44 magnum revolver at Anderson's temple, an array of shots sounded from outside the window. When the group simultaneously diverted their attention to the commotion outside, Anderson palmed the blade and hit it behind his back.

Once he freed his wrists, he still had to cut through the ties around his ankles.

Another round of gunshots sounded from deep in the woods, followed by a few yells. Brennen laid a hand on Blaire's arm.

"Go find out what's going on and report back to me immediately." She glanced around the room to all her agents. "All of you."

During the commotion, Anderson raised to a sitting position in the corner where he could finally slice through ties that bound his wrists.

In efforts to keep Brennen's focus on anything except him, he said, "Sounds like more than one target may be out there."

Once her team exited the room, Brennen slipped a .22 caliber pistol from her jacket. Without a word, she sat across the room. A deadly silence stretched between them like a rubber band ready to snap.

Anderson had been trained never to speak first in a battle of silent wills, yet the CIA needed conclusive evidence to prosecute Director Brennen and her team. Not to mention the fact that he needed more time to work through the ties at his wrist.

"Why didn't you ask me to join your team instead of trying to take me out?"

"Trying to delay the inevitable?" Her eyes sparkled with interest.

"You're going to kill me." He shrugged. "At least that's your plan. So, if I'm a dead man, indulge me with the truth."

Even with his blood-laced grin, Brennen couldn't resist his charm. She raised an eyebrow and cocked her head before twisting her mouth to the side in thought.

"You and your partner are practically saints. You don't fit

the mold. I needed cold-blooded killers, and anything less was unacceptable."

A flash of concern crossed his features at the thought of the others who found their death at her team's hands. As if she could read his thoughts, she added, "Don't worry. There was just a handful that wasn't on my draft list."

"Why not fire us? Or transfer us? Why death?"

"Because you've all seen too much of the inner workings of our department. If you were to transfer out – there would be too many of you with a conscience... like former Director Sanger who could put the pieces together."

Although he knew Sanger was still alive, he played along.

"What pieces?"

"Someone dies, a stock price goes up, and bank accounts are lined. Someone else dies, an office opens up, and allegiance is owed. Plus, there's a signature to each job that would look too familiar."

Anderson swallowed as the taste of bile hit the back of his tongue. He closed his eyes, thinking every word this woman uttered made him sick.

"See?" She gleamed. "You can't stomach the work, and I can't have people out there putting the pieces together. Our mission is too important to risk tumbling down over a few good men."

Anderson prayed that his wire was transmitting.

"You're going down, Brennen," he said, jaw clenched.

She cackled. "Aren't you sweet?" She stood and crossed the floor. "You think I'm going down?"

"You just admitted everything." He looked at her from under his eyelids, too tired from his beating to face her. He had to reserve what strength he had left.

"Honey, I'm not pulling the strings. And there's no one here except you and me."

She waved her gun in the air.

"And once I kill you – no one will be the wiser."

"Danny's still out there." He seethed.

"Not for long." She grinned. "I have your phone, so I know where you've been. I have a few people on the way to find him now."

"You won't find him." Anderson's stomach churned. Had his family escaped the island before anyone breached their safe house?

"I found you, didn't I?" She chuckled. "I'll draw him out just like I did with you. Although with his cousin missing, I'll have to try a different angle." She placed a finger to her lips.

"It's not going to happen." Anderson shook his head just as he freed his wrists from the ties behind his back.

The Director pointed her gun between his eyes. "Goodbye, Anderson. Let's hope your good deeds serve you well in the afterlife."

As the sounds of chopper blades approached, Savannah searched the skyline above the cliff. Within a few minutes, two ropes uncoiled and descended the ledge.

"You okay down there?"

Savannah's heart swelled with relief at the sight of Danny's smiling face. She closed her eyes – too exhausted to fight the noise and the winds that whipped around them.

He waved his hand toward someone out of sight as he and another agent rappelled with a vertical basket. Once the pair navigated the terrain to meet her, he eyed her makeshift sling.

"You hurt?"

Upon hearing his sympathetic voice, she teared up. With a nod, she said, "I'm pretty sure it's broken."

Danny turned to the other field operative who had found secure footing and said, "Brandon, let's get her inside."

As Danny maneuvered the basket next to Savannah, he sent her a look of reassurance.

"I'm going to put you inside while Brandon secures you. Think you can hold on to my neck?"

She nodded through the tears that she finally allowed passage down her flushed face. The pain in her shoulder and arm sieged her.

As the pair expertly worked in tandem, Savannah found herself strapped in and secured, as the basket dragged up the slope.

Danny cupped his hands and yelled out, "Be careful bringing her up. She's got a broken arm."

After she was pulled to the top and freed from the basket, Savannah sagged into Danny's side with relief. When she finally stood on her own two feet, she blurted, "Anderson! We have to get Anderson. He's–"

"There's a farmhouse not too far from here – due east. Is that where he is?" Danny asked.

"It's the one - that way!" Savannah frowned and pointed toward the direction she came from.

Danny chuckled. "Exactly. East."

"How many other cabins are there around here?" Her concerned eyes scanned the area.

"A few, but none that have any heat signatures. We're positive we've found him. It's okay, Savannah. We have a team heading there now." Danny searched her eyes before he ushered her toward the helicopter.

"They drugged him."

"We know. We heard everything."

Savannah sent him a look of confusion.

"He's wired."

As she was about to ask how, the pilot yelled, "We've got incoming!"

Danny looked over his shoulder as three men with handguns rounded the corner of the gas station.

"Get her to the chopper!" Danny pushed Savannah toward Brandon as he drew his weapon. He was able to squeeze off a shot and take out one of Odyssey's team before running for the helicopter.

Once Savannah was safely out of harm's way, Brandon turned an assault rifle on the remaining Odyssey agents. As the group exchanged fire, Danny leaped into the helicopter and fell into a Kevlar-lined seat as the chopper lifted from the ground.

Danny panted as a burning sensation seared through his leg. It was then that Anderson's warning came to him, and he knew he'd been shot.

As he stared down the barrel of a gun, Anderson knew he had seconds to spare. His mind swirling, he considered his options. There weren't many that didn't have a grim ending.

Suddenly, the sounds of chopper blades hovered over the roof. Brennen looked up with surprise as the helicopter flew by at top speed. She shielded her view as a gust of wind tore at the curtains hanging from the window.

Anderson saw his window of opportunity and sliced through the ties at his ankles to free his legs. Fully mobile, he placed his weight on his hands and used his left leg to side-sweep Brennen while trapping her on the ground with his right leg.

When Brennen's feet flew from underneath her, Anderson straddled her, thinking he'd have to fight her for the gun. Instead, she landed on her head, stunning her into submission. With one smooth motion, Anderson stripped her of the weapon and slipped it into his waistband.

Brennen howled and cradled her head as warm blood trickled down her neck.

"You haven't won!" She struggled to sit once Anderson loosened his grasp.

Blaire burst into the room, gun drawn, giving Anderson only one choice. Anderson spun and pulled Director Brennen toward him to shield his body, barely avoiding the bullet that tore into Brennen's shoulder.

A micro-expression - barely a wince crossed Blaire's face as he glanced at his boss before he advanced toward the pair. With his gun trained on Anderson, he said, "Let her go."

Anderson chuckled. "I told you I'd be the one left standing, and you'd be one who was sorry."

Blaire raised a brow. "I'm the one with the gun."

"And I always make good on my promises."

Anderson's eyes gleamed. Before Blaire could respond, Anderson slipped a gun from behind Brennen and pulled the trigger.

When Blaire crumpled to the floor, Anderson looked away. He didn't need to check the man's pulse to know he was dead, and he didn't want his expressionless face to haunt him tonight.

"And that's why you're more suited for extractions," Brennen whispered. "You're not a killer."

"I may not be a murderer." Anderson tightened his grip on her arms. "But I can defend myself when I need to, so don't get any ideas."

He kicked Blaire's gun away before pushing the Director toward a chair.

"Sit," he ordered.

With his gaze trained on her, he took a step back. Although injured, she could easily escape if or when the opportunity presented itself. Without missing a beat, he retrieved a pillowcase from one of the pillows on the bed and tore the fabric into strips.

"Stand up and turn around with your hands behind your back." He aimed his gun at her.

As Brennen struggled to stand, she staggered toward the bed seeing double the whole way.

"You think you won!" She groaned through the pain as the sounds of heavy steps approached. "You only took out the pawn."

Anderson spun toward what sounded like an army advancing down the hall and braced, unsure of who was flying toward him – enemy or calvary. In a split-second decision, he put a gun to Brennen's neck and used her body as a shield once more.

"Using a lady to protect yourself?" Brennen struggled to

stay upright. If it hadn't been for Anderson's hold, she'd have crumpled to the ground.

"You're no lady," he said.

Loud commands came down the hall as a few men in tactical gear carrying automatic weapons stormed through the door. Anderson breathed a sigh of relief when he noticed Craig bringing up the rear, his gun trained on Brennen.

Anderson sent him a look of gratitude.

"You okay?" Craig asked. "You look like you've seen better days."

"Never better." Anderson cocked his head. "Can someone take this from me?" He released Brennen, who fell to her knees.

"Yes, sir." One of Craig's team members stepped forward and relieved Anderson before cuffing the Director and ushering her away.

"You didn't win!" she yelled from the hall.

"I'd say it looks like we did," Craig responded with a wink.

Once she disappeared from the doorway, Craig eyed the fabric Anderson still had clutched in his hands. "What's that?"

"I was just about to tie her up when you all busted in." He tossed the ties to the bed. "Where's Savannah?"

"Safe."

"And Danny?"

"Both have been rushed to the hospital, but they'll be okay." Craig inspected Anderson's injuries and continued, "It looks like you could use a little TLC yourself."

"I'm fine." Anderson waved him off and started for the door, but before he could, Craig laid a firm hand on his shoulder.

"How did you know Danny would be shot in the leg?" Craig widened his stance, standing between Anderson and the exit.

"He got shot in the leg?" Anderson blinked, sending him an innocent look.

"Yeah." Craig stood firm and crossed his arms, unwilling to move out of Anderson's way.

"Wow. Because... I thought he'd be shot in the back." Anderson shook his head with wonder and chuckled. He saw the intrigue in Craig's expression, but his friend finally nodded, letting the subject drop.

"Let's get you to the hospital." Craig stepped aside and nudged him forward.

"It's not necessary."

"It's mandatory. Move it, Evans."

As the pair made their way downstairs, Anderson breathed a sigh of relief. Before he entered Craig's SUV, he turned toward the house that had haunted him for weeks.

"If I never see this place again, I'll be thankful," he murmured and slipped into the back seat.

Craig sent him a curious look. "Why would you?"

Anderson shook his head. "I won't."

35

Three months later.

After wading in the cold water, Savannah stepped to the sand, in awe how so much had transpired in such a short time. In some ways, the journey she and Anderson had been on seemed like an eternity, yet in others, it was like yesterday when she was a wedding planner without an inkling of how adventurous life could be.

As if he could sense she was contemplating her life, Anderson stepped down the sandy walkway of the cove and slipped his hand within hers. The familiar sensation of his rough hands sliding onto her skin filled her heart with hope.

When she turned - her heart said a prayer of thanks as his peaceful demeanor washed over her. After their rescue, she wondered if she'd ever see him again. He certainly could have spirited away to his next mission never to be heard from again, and she would have understood. That was his life, but what she'd yet to comprehend was that she'd changed him. And, his life was not worth having without her by his side.

Once Savannah was released from the hospital, she exited with a singular focus – to go back to Oklahoma City and see Ava. Only...she found Anderson waiting outside with a car.

The second she saw him, she ran into his arms, cast and all, and clung to him for dear life.

"I thought you left," she whispered through her kiss.

Anderson rested his forehead on hers. "You can't tell a man you love him and expect him to ride off into the sunset alone."

She sighed as a few tears ran down her face.

"Is that what we're doing?" Her heart warmed when she noticed a sky-blue backpack in the back of his car. She sent him a look of thanks for remembering to replace the one he ruined.

He shrugged. "I don't think I can take another trip without you next to me – badgering me, threatening to beat me up–"

"You like the abuse. Admit it."

"I love having you in my life." He stroked the side of her face.

"What about your job?"

Anderson's dimples deepened as his eyes shone down on her.

"That's the thing. I took that job because I wanted to change the world."

"I know..." she started.

"Will you let me finish, woman?" He chuckled. "I wanted to take on the world, but what I now know is that I can't take anything on without you. You make me feel like I can do anything, yet nothing without you."

"What are you saying?"

"I filed my retirement paperwork this morning."

"Are you crazy? I can't let you do that."

"You aren't letting me do anything," he reminded her.

"Don't you guys have to stick around for certain benefits or something?"

"Or something." He shrugged. "But I have skills, and I don't have to save them for the agency. I can do anything." He dropped his arms. "As long as I have you."

Anderson pulled a small box from his leather jacket.

"Marry me," he whispered.

Savannah's eyes filled with surprise as her mouth fell open.

"You heard me," Anderson said before taking a knee.

Finally, Savannah's sensibilities kicked in, and her father's voice filled her head.

"I heard you tell me. I didn't hear you ask me." She crossed her arms with a smirk.

On bended knee, he chuckled. "Will you marry me, Smiles?"

She let out an exasperated sigh and shook her head at him.

"Shut up and kiss me," she said.

As he raised from his knee, he asked, "Is that a yes?"

She nodded as tears streamed down her cheeks.

Anderson let out a yell, picked her up, and spun her around.

The first stop they made was in Oklahoma City, where they spent time at Ava's bedside until she was released. After they drove her home, the pair traveled on route 66 like tourists. They saw the sights and experienced everything *Main Street USA* offered.

One night, they stopped along their route for another

small, hole-in-the-wall bar that had a monthly karaoke contest. Anderson, anxious to hear her sultry voice fill the room once more, asked her to sing for him to which she happily obliged. They had no way of knowing the bar live-streamed every performance.

Savannah's time behind at the mic reignited the allure of her mysterious 'Monica' personality. Overnight, the news networks picked up and ran her story. Of course, Tyler and Alexis had the rights to an exclusive interview, but before either knew it, the pair couldn't go anywhere without being recognized. They'd been at the lake house ever since.

Savannah basked in the memories and stepped from the cove. As she dried her feet on the grass, Anderson approached to stand at her side.

She raised on her toes and kissed him on the cheek.

"When does everyone arrive?" she asked.

"In about a half-hour." He pushed a lock of her hair from her face. She'd grown it back out over the last three months. It was finally long enough to run his hands through. "Lani is chomping at the bit."

"Tell me about it." She pulled her cell phone from her linen pants with a chuckle. "She's been calling me non-stop."

Anderson grinned until he noticed her far off look.

"What's wrong?"

"It's just... for so long, we had to hide. No cell phone... laying low. Now, to have a line of constant communication." She shook her head. "It's just a bit overwhelming."

"That's why I thought a long road trip was what you needed after that whole Odyssey mess. I thought it would ease you back into normal life."

"I should feel safe." She winced and glanced off into the distance.

"You are." He stroked her cheek with the back of his hand.

He'd been reassuring Savannah for weeks that the threat of Odyssey was over. As far as a more substantial network Brennen eluded to, there was no evidence of it at this time. And if the CIA discovered anything else, it was Danny's job to cut down that monster... not his.

At the thought of his former partner, he asked his fiancé, "Is Danny coming for the wedding?"

"He promised he would, but I don't know." She shook her head.

After Danny was released from the hospital, he left on a mission to parts unknown.

"Don't." He caressed the worry lines that appeared between her eyebrows. "This weekend, I get to marry the love of my life, and no one is allowed to be sad."

"It's not just Danny. It's my parents, too. I always dreamed my dad would walk me down the aisle, and my mom would here."

Savannah grinned down at her dog, who'd slipped underneath her hand and leaned into her leg.

"At least I have you. Huh, boy?" She ran her fingers through Brody's thick fur thankful Anderson had him flown in once things settled.

Anderson patted the dog on its head before pulling Savannah into a tender embrace. "And, if Lani were here, she'd tell you your parents are here and they are with you."

Savannah chuckled. "That's so true. She would."

Anderson lifted her chin for a short but sweet kiss.

When she pulled back, she sighed, saying, "At least Ava is coming." She clapped and drew in her shoulders. "We're getting married."

"We are." His eyes twinkled.

Just as he was about to sample her lips again, a horn honked in the distance.

"They're early!" Her face lit up with excitement.

Anderson tugged her by the hand to run up the hill and greet their guests. When the pair rounded the home for the driveway, Savannah arrived in time to see Danny climb from the minivan, followed by Anderson's family.

"Ahh!" she shrieked and threw her arms around Danny's neck.

Danny lifted and spun her in the air, coming full circle until he set her down with a grin.

"I couldn't let my favorite girl walk down the aisle without someone giving her away. Now, could I?"

Savannah's heart warmed, and she whispered, "Thank you."

"I know he'd want to be here," he whispered in return.

"But, you're the next best thing." Savannah wrapped her arms around his burly shoulders.

"Savannah Miles, get your butt over here!" Ava yelled from the van as she stepped out with Markus.

As the girls greeted one another, Alexis pulled Anderson to the side and asked, "Are you sure Savannah doesn't want something a bit fancier than a small garden wedding?"

"Lexi, Savannah is a wedding planner. She could have had anything that she wanted." Danny took her by the hand.

Alexis nodded in agreement.

"All we care about is having everyone we love here with us." As the thought of Savannah's parents, Anderson lifted his hands with a shrug. "Well, almost everyone. Besides, we don't need anything extravagant. We just need each other."

Two hours later, Savannah touched her bare foot onto the steps that led to the garden. She wore gardenias in her hair and a simple white slip dress. The backyard was decorated with twinkle lights, and a humble floral arch stood near the pond.

As Anderson's tender look beckoned to her from across the garden, everything around her faded. It seemed as if she'd been transported into an English countryside where magic filled the air, and it was only the two of them. If it weren't for Lani, who tugged at her dress with an expectant stare, she might have been oblivious to anyone around them.

"Can I call you Aunt Vannah now?" Lani's toothless grin widened.

"It's Sa-vannah, sweetheart." Amelia corrected her.

"Of course, you can, Lani. I'd be honored." Savannah leaned down to tap the child's nose.

When Lani's face lit up with joy, Savannah's heart filled with love for the child who had captivated her from the moment they met.

"Remember, slow and steady with the petals." Alexis brushed by the group and temporarily placed a hand on her daughter's head as she and Tyler made their way to their seats.

"I'll do a good job." Lani's face filled with determination.

"We know you will." Amelia beamed at Lani, before turning toward to her husband. "I'll be there in a minute, Hank. Mind getting our seats and waiting for me?" Hank knowingly looked from his wife to his now daughter in law and nodded before taking the steps toward the garden.

"Danny?" Amelia sent him a look. "Give us a second?"

"Sure. Lani and I can hang out here for a minute while you do whatever is..."

Danny didn't even have time to finish his sentence as Amelia spirited Savannah around the corner.

"Is everything okay?" Savannah's concern was evident.

When she nodded, Savannah noticed the mist that clouded her eyes.

"Oh, Mrs. Evans! Why are you crying?" Savannah reached for the hanky that she'd wrapped around her bouquet to dab the moisture away.

Amelia wanted to wave her off, but couldn't. The simple gesture of compassion pushed Amelia's tender heart too far, and the tears that had been at bay were now streaming down her face.

"Oh," Amelia cried. "I'm sorry."

Savannah's heart filled with awe. "Don't be sorry. We've all been through so much. It's normal to get emotional."

Amelia dabbed the handkerchief to dry her eyes before cupping Savannah's face in her hands.

"I want to tell you how proud I am of you and how proud I know your mother would be, too."

Without skipping a beat, Amelia dabbed Savannah's eyes just as they filled with the tears she knew would come.

"From the second, I saw how you challenged my son, pushed him and how protective he was of you – I knew." Amelia took a deep breath. "I knew you were his... and ours."

"Ours?" Savannah's voice was barely a whisper.

"I hope your mother doesn't mind, but I wanted to ask if it's okay that I call you - daughter."

A myriad of emotions tore through Savannah. Although she said nothing, the look on her face spoke volumes. When a tear cascaded down Savannah's cheek, Amelia wiped it away and blew on her face.

"Dry eyes. Okay?" Amelia chuckled. "Leave the crying to Alexis. With all her hormones, I expect you'll be tossing this hanky to her mid-ceremony."

Savannah was quick to laugh. "You're probably right."

"Okay, then – my daughter. Let's get you married."

As Amelia took her by the hand to escort her back so the ceremony could begin, Savannah paused and dropped her hand.

"Everything okay?" Amelia tilted her head, hoping Savannah wasn't getting cold feet.

"I just need a moment. I'll be there - I promise." Amelia nodded and disappeared around the corner, leaving Savannah to shake her nerves. She dropped her head back to gaze at the clouds that had scattered through the afternoon sky and did a double-take.

Just above, billowy clouds cupped the blue sky like a frame. One cloud, in particular, caught Savannah's eye. In it, she saw a woman smiling down at her.

A sense of peace washed over her, similar to when Lani declared that Savannah's mother was present in the bathroom on the first day she arrived on the island. Savannah did something next that only she would understand. She blew a kiss toward the cloud with the belief that her mother was there to catch it.

Danny approached with his hands in his pockets, strolling as if he had all the time in the world. He cocked his head and looked between her and the sky with a chuckle.

"Smiles, have you gone crazy?"

Savannah sighed, wishing she had more time to reflect on the cloud, but she had a groom waiting on her. She dragged her focus from above and said, "No. I'm just reminiscing."

She looked at her cousin from beneath her lashes with a smirk. "Are you ready?"

"I think the question is – are you ready?" He offered his arm, to which she gladly accepted.

As Danny accompanied her for the short walk to the floral arch, he could have sworn Savannah was glowing. Maybe it was the dimly-lit moon that had just begun its ascent or the twinkle lights that were strung along the path. Whatever the reason - the energy that surrounded them was evident. Savannah and Anderson had found their happily ever after, and the love they shared gave Danny hope.

After he offered Savannah's hand to Anderson, Danny took his place as best man, wondering if he'd be lucky enough a second time to find a love worth risking everything for. The first time he'd found it, he'd lost it, and it was something he carried with him like a rock chained to his heart.

"Mr. and Mrs. Anderson Evans." Ava waved her arms to introduce the newlyweds as they approached the banquet table.

The group stood and clapped as the pair made their way across the lawn.

"Did we just do that?" Savannah asked in awe.

The pastor seated at the end of the table nodded with certainty and said, "By the power vested in me, I'd say you did."

"You can't back out now." Anderson's eyes sparkled.

Once everyone was seated, Ava leaned forward and raised her glass.

"A toast."

As the group raised their glasses, Ava stood and beamed at her best friend.

"My partner in crime." She wiped a tear away. "We've had many escapades throughout our lives..."

Savannah looked at her friend, her heart filling with warmth.

"Meeting you was one of the best things that happened to me on that small island in the Pacific."

"You're going to make me cry." Savannah sniffed.

Ava sent her an impish grin before addressing the rest of the group.

"You all have only had the honor of knowing Savannah for a short time, but we've been friends since we were teens. She and I met when our fathers were stationed in Okinawa. We were instantly thick as thieves, experiencing things only a military brat or the daughter of a Marine could understand."

Ava sighed. "Like the time we snuck out of the house for the beach in the middle of the night. Your dad..." Ava kissed her fingers before lifting them toward the sky. "He woke up, locked the both of us out, and called my dad to pick me up." A collective chuckle sounded around the table. "Needless to say, we were both grounded." Savannah lifted a hand to her mouth to hide her grin. If it weren't for the tears welling behind her eyes, she might have laughed.

"Let's just say a typical grounding for most teens back then would have been a month without a social life our phone privileges." Ava shook her head. "But no. With our fathers, it was that and then much more. We got to clean the cars - and mow the lawns and..."

Savannah chimed in. "And we were woken up at zero dark thirty on the weekends for whatever random reason he could think of."

Ava's eyes watered. "Your dad was the best, though. And..." She raised her glass toward Anderson. "He would have approved of you, Anderson."

Savannah retrieved the handkerchief Amelia had given her and dabbed her face dry before Alexis blew her nose so loudly that everyone at the table turned toward her. "Oh!" Alexis wailed. "You're killing me."

Savannah met Amelia's eyes from across the table and bit her lip to hold back a laugh. Her mother-in-law was right. Alexis' hormones were on high alert.

"Seriously, though." Ava inhaled. "Anderson, you're exactly who Sav needed, but never knew - until your paths collided."

Anderson touched his face where there used to be a bruise and wobbled his head as if unsure. As the group knowingly laughed, Ava finished her speech.

"Thank you for making my best friend happy. Take good care of my Sav or Monica, or whatever she calls herself now."

Savannah's heart tugged as the memories of their adventures in various parts of the world came flooding back. She mouthed the words, 'Thank you,' before winking and taking a sip of her champagne.

Ava continued, "And now that she'll be opening for me on tour, we'll have even more moments of mischief together." She winked in return.

"And, Anderson will have a whole new world ahead of him." Ava pointed at Anderson. "You'll have to keep a careful eye on her."

"I'll give new meaning to the term, bodyguard." He gave Savannah a sideways glance with words that were meant for her ears only.

Savannah flushed at the concept and took a sip to hide

her blush behind her champagne flute.

Just as Danny was about to give a toast, Anderson laid a hand on his arm.

"Do you mind?" Anderson asked.

Danny shook his head and took a seat as Anderson stood, raising his glass in the air. When he turned toward Savannah, he paused, unable to believe any of it was real. How did he get so lucky?

"My beautiful wife." Anderson took a deep breath and sniffed, fighting back his emotions. "What a journey it has been. I was blessed with visions of you before I knew who or what you would be to me. And, I'm eternally grateful for all that we have in front of us."

Anderson's eyes darted around the table.

"And no, before any of you ask, I haven't seen anything in quite some time now."

Savannah sent him a look of empathy. Whatever drug Odyssey had injected him with had curbed his visions. Just when he was getting used to having a road map – it was stripped from him.

Anderson's tender look was directed at her once more.

"To whatever life has in store for us, and to trusting God with the unknown."

"Cheers." Savannah touched her glass to his.

Anderson leaned forward to brush his lips across hers, before glancing at Danny, who pulled his phone from his vest and frowned.

"Hate to be a downer, but..." Danny sent the newlyweds a look of apology.

Anderson's heart raced as the familiar sense of pre-mission jitters and adrenaline coursed through his veins.

"Duty calls?"

"Yup. I'll reach out when I can." He stood and grabbed Anderson for a tight hug.

Suddenly, a flash of Danny and an attractive woman on the beach displayed before Anderson. He shook off the image and cut his eyes at Savannah, who pursed her lips and raised a knowing brow in his direction.

Before she could comment on what she assumed had happened to her husband, Danny pulled Savannah into his side and kissed her cheek.

"Love you, cuz," Danny whispered. "Take care of him."

She nodded as Danny tapped Tyler on the shoulder.

"Do you think you or Hank could take me across the lake to land?"

As Tyler stood, the pastor joined them and said, "Great! My bags are still packed."

The pastor sent a wide grin toward the group and turned toward his hosts.

"Anderson, Savannah...although I appreciate the offer to stay for the weekend, it looks like my services are needed elsewhere."

Danny looked surprised. "Did you get a secret alert that we're all unaware of?"

"My alerts come from above, and I've learned not to ignore them. If you're running into danger, Danny boy, I'll pray you into town."

Danny rolled his eyes and reached for his jacket as he mumbled under his breath.

Savannah covered her mouth to hide the chuckle that escaped as Danny strode through the dark with the pastor on his heels.

"Think he'll convert him?" Savannah's eyes twinkled.

Anderson watched as Tyler started for the pair and said, "It would take something drastic for him to find his way." He watched his partner disappear over the hill as a glimpse of what could be Danny's future flashed through his mind.

He glanced at his glowing bride with a knowing look and said, "But if there's anything I've learned...is that with God, nothing is impossible."

A TEASER FOR DANNY'S STORY

Turn the page for read more about Danny Stone and Samantha Dennet's journey.

BLIND INSTINCTS

A tropical storm ripped across the Gulf as Danny navigated the winding road that led through the heart of the small town of Fair Point. He wiped the fog from his window and peered outside as the trees gnashed in the wind.

On either side of the road lay a variety of beach cottages that ranged from those of humble beginnings to multi-million dollar homes. The mixture of old and new had always appealed to Danny, even amid a vicious storm.

Danny was tempted to pull over, but with his luck, someone would slide off the road and smack into his rental car. He was too close to his final destination to stop now. Although not a category five, a bad tropical storm along the gulf was nothing to disregard. Rainwater filled gullies alongside the narrow road and threatened to turn the pavement into a small river.

He shook his head, peered through his rain-washed windshield, and breathed a sigh of relief when he saw the bright orange mailbox in the distance. It was the one thing that signaled that he was almost home as it sat a few feet away from his great aunt's street. He slowed to take the turn and pulled down the narrow road, which might as well have been named Memory Lane.

As lighting traveled through the sky, an image of Samantha Dennet's smiling face haunted him. He took a deep breath and turned up the radio, pushing any more thoughts of her from his mind.

A small row of colorful beach cottages finally came into view. He may not have been able to see their details through the driving rain, but he didn't have to. Danny remembered this stretch of the drive as if it were yesterday. Their colorful exteriors still called to him, bringing with them the memories of a young couple walking hand-in-hand past these same houses many summers ago. He stared at the rows of baby blue, coral, and sea green siding and wondered if any part of himself, that young kid from so long ago, still existed.

Finally, the beach cottage he'd spent most vacations appeared around the next corner just as a grim realization hit that although this was once his summer home, he was now a stranger to it. He dropped his head and wondered what to do now that it had been passed on to him.

Could he sell it without feeling like he betrayed his great Aunt whose dying wish was for him to spend some time at the cottage to return to his roots?

Danny killed the engine, thinking about her will. It stated that he had to live at the family beach cottage for eight weeks. If not, then his home and the rest of Cottage Row would sell to a local developer.

He stared out his window through the rain, wondering how his Aunt had come to own so many of the homes along the street. It was then that he realized how much of her life he had missed.

Guilt besieged him, much like the rain that tormented his vehicle. He touched the door handle, contemplating making a run for the front porch but hesitated as movement from above caught his eye.

He used his sleeve to wipe the fog from his window to discover that someone was kneeling on the incline of his roof, trying to secure a tarp as the corners flapped in vain.

"He's going to get himself killed," Danny muttered before stepping into the deluge.

Who in their right mind would be up on a roof in ninety-five per hour winds? Not to mention hammering on a rooftop with the threat of lighting. It was a death wish.

Danny slammed his car door shut and cupped his hands.

"Hey!" He yelled through the wind.

Just then, an ominous clap of thunder rolled through the sky like an approaching stampede. Danny searched the grey clouds as the hair on the back of his neck stood at attention, and his palms tingled. Lightning wouldn't be far behind.

"Hey! You need to come down!" He tried again, but it was of no use.

He wiped the water from his face and approached, squinting through the rain when a gust of wind tore the ladder from his home, taking with it a gutter that was attached. While the ties used to secure it were strong, they were no match for mother nature.

Danny dove to the ground as the ladder whizzed by, barely missing his head. It tumbled across the lawn, taking with it the mailbox. Once he jumped to his feet, he swung his attention back to the roof when the palms of his hands began to burn with more intensity. He flexed his fingers, praying the tell-tale sign of danger was wrong, or the ladder wouldn't be the only dire straits ahead.

After all his years with the agency, he'd learned to trust

his senses. When his insides hummed as if someone started an engine, whatever came next would get dicey. If the ladder whizzing by and barely decapitating him wasn't enough to put him on high alert – a bolt of lightning flashing before him, splitting a nearby pine tree in two, would have done the trick. The loud crack had him bracing for whatever came next.

The rest of the sequence happened as if he were on auto-pilot. He glanced above as a flying branch sent the handyman tumbling through the air with arms flailing. With precision-like moves, Danny widened his stance and prepared to catch the man, thinking him lightweight enough. However, with the wet conditions - who knew if the handyman would slip from Danny's grasp.

Samantha Dennet didn't feel a thing as the electricity rippled around her like waves from the ocean. One minute she was blindly attaching a tarp to the roof, wiping a torrent of water from her eyes. The next, she found herself knocked from her feet by a branch that sliced through the air.

In an instant, her life flashed before her eyes. And although it was filled with a mixture of regret and mistakes, she also remembered steps taken to become the woman she was today - someone who fought to make a life for her and her boys regardless of how hard it was. Thankfully, she knew her Maker and was prepared for death, if indeed that was her fate.

What she wasn't prepared for was to land in the arms of a stranger below.

Danny buckled to his knees after catching the stranger that pummeled him from above. When the handyman's ball cap flew off, revealing a handful of matted black curls, his heart lodged in his throat.

When the realization hit that he was holding a woman - he searched for her face as they tumbled to the ground. Before all went black, recognition unfurled throughout every sense, as the familiarity of her curves against his chest and the weight of her body sparked something he'd long forgotten.

Thunder clashed above as Samantha untangled herself from the man who saved her. Just as she was about to thank him, she realized he wasn't moving. She wiped the rain from her eyes and felt for a pulse with a sigh of relief, thankful she hadn't killed him. She angled his chin toward her so she could see who her anonymous hero was. It was then that she saw his face.

"Danny!" She sucked in a breath as her heart seized with panic. "No. No. No. No."

She covered her mouth in horror and looked around, hoping this wasn't real. She closed her eyes as if a toddler, thinking her lids would provide adequate cover.

She hoped when she opened them that Danny would have been a figment of her imagination or a bad dream. Only when she finally did, he was still lying next to her, getting more drenched by the second.

Samantha sighed and dropped her head. She knew her choices would come back to bite her in the butt one day – but never planned for how to handle it.

She dashed for the covered porch and retrieved her cell

phone to call her sister before stealing another glance at Danny, who still lay as still as a stone on the lawn.

"Come on. Answer." Her heart pounded in overtime.

When her sister's voicemail sounded, Samantha hung up and sent Jenny a text, all the while praying Danny wouldn't come to before help arrived.

FROM ANDERSON & SAVANNAH'S WEDDING

My inspiration for Savannah's wedding day

I took this photo five years ago while on a walk with my best friend after her cancer diagnosis. At that point in her journey, it was a comfort.

If you look closely – you can see a cloud in the middle looks like a smiling woman peeking below. We both thought it looked like a guardian angel peeking at us.

Email me at **kimberlymckayauthor@gmail.com** if you see it!

This book is the seventh book I've released in just over ten years. My first book, Finding Kylie, was released with a traditional publisher; however, it wasn't an ideal partnership.

That experience spurred me to become an Indie Author. Indie Authors rely on readers to spread the word and leave reviews so that others discover our books.

If you were touched by Anderson and Savannah's story, please leave a review at Amazon, Goodreads, or any other online retailer. Also, tell a friend and ask your library to carry my book(s).

From Anderson & Savannah's Wedding

Thank you so much for all your support! I truly appreciate every one of you. Also – send me a photo of you with a copy of Dangerous Visions. I love seeing readers with my books, and your photo may make my website!

Made in the USA
Middletown, DE
30 April 2020